TAKE ME APART

MCD | Farrar, Straus and Giroux | New York

TAKE ME APART

■

SARA SLIGAR

MCD

Farrar, Straus and Giroux

120 Broadway, New York 10271

Grateful acknowledgment is made for permission to reprint an
excerpt from "In Plato's Cave," from *On Photography*, by Susan Sontag. Copyright ©
1977 by Susan Sontag. Reprinted by permission of Farrar, Straus and Giroux.

Library of Congress Cataloging-in-Publication Data
Names: Sligar, Sara, 1989– author.
Title: Take me apart / Sara Sligar.
Description: First edition. | New York : MCD / Farrar, Straus and Giroux, 2020.
Identifiers: LCCN 2019049274 | ISBN 9780374272616 (hardcover)
Subjects: LCSH: Psychological fiction.
Classification: LCC PS3619.L56 T35 2020 | DDC 813/.6—dc23
LC record available at https://lccn.loc.gov/2019049274

Canadian / International Edition ISBN: 9780374539009

Designed by Gretchen Achilles

Our books may be purchased in bulk for promotional, educational, or business use.
Please contact your local bookseller or the Macmillan Corporate and Premium Sales
Department at 1-800-221-7945, extension 5442, or by e-mail at
MacmillanSpecialMarkets@macmillan.com.

www.mcdbooks.com • www.fsgbooks.com
Follow us on Twitter, Facebook, and Instagram at @mcdbooks

1   3   5   7   9   10   8   6   4   2

For my parents

TAKE ME APART

Photography is violent. When we capture a subject in a photo, we steal that person out of time and flatten them. We reduce them so we can preserve them forever. You have to acknowledge that violence. Rejoice in it. I think that's why I do so many self-portraits. All my life, the person I felt most comfortable harming was myself.

—MIRANDA BRAND (1956 1993)

1.

KATE

California revealed itself to Kate as a series of spots, like a scratch-off lottery ticket, the forested hills emerging in patches as the plane lowered through the clouds. The landscape had been split into pieces: the purple mountains, the long oval of the bay. Just as the last wisp of cloud disappeared, the plane bounced on a gust, lurching everyone against their seat belts, so when Kate first saw the whole view laid out beneath her, her throat was clogged with fear. The plane righted itself, and she was annoyed at the turbulence for tricking her, for ruining her first impression. The man beside her crossed himself.

"I hate landings," he said as he popped a Ritz cracker into his mouth "Seems like no one knows how to fly a plane these days."

Kate realized she was clutching the armrest. Only the left one: the man had commandeered their shared armrest somewhere over Colorado. She forced herself to relax her grip. Her eyelashes were matted together and her mouth tasted like dishwater. The morning—the bleary, hungover wait for the delayed plane; the ill-advised airport pretzel during her first layover— already seemed distant, sopped up into the grimy sponge of cross-country travel.

"Did it used to be better?" she asked the man, not because she especially wanted to talk to him, but because it was in her nature to ask questions. In elementary school, her parents had stopped taking her to the supermarket because she would interrogate them mercilessly about how the grocery cart was manufactured or how the vegetable mister worked. In college, she had been told she had a talent for the Socratic method.

"Oh, yeah," Ritz-cracker guy said. "I've been flying for business for thirty-three years. I only just started getting sick maybe, I don't know, the last decade. You'd think new technology would have smoothed out the ride, but it's all about the training." He selected a new cracker. "Are you from San Francisco?"

"New York. I'm out here to start a new job."

"Oh, yeah? What do you do?"

"I'm an archivist." The word felt unfamiliar in her mouth; she rolled it around, like a marble. At her seatmate's blank look, she added, "I work with old documents."

"That's a real job?"

"Yep."

"You always done that?"

"No. I used to work for a newspaper."

His expression cooled. "You're a journalist?"

"A copy editor."

"Like with the semicolons?"

"Yes. And I checked facts, things like that." The past tense was a dull hurt.

"Didn't know anyone *checked* facts these days," he said. "I get all my news from people I trust—my wife, my friends. I like to have a direct line. Straight from the source."

Kate pressed her lips together. She already regretted encouraging the conversation, but she didn't know how to end it politely. There were rules. Be accommodating. Pretend interest. Give them what they want. You started it. He smiled at her and drummed his fingers against the armrest, scattering crumbs.

"Anyway," he said, "it sounds to me like you made a good choice, switching careers."

This guy. He reminded her of Leonard Webb, although Leonard would have hated to hear that. He would have hated this guy's rounded gut and checkered button-down and Midwestern twang. And Kate hated the guy for reminding her of Leonard at all.

The plane bounced again. Someone screamed behind them. The seat belt light blinked off overhead, which couldn't be right. Out the window, the unfamiliar skyline tipped sideways in its oval frame, and Kate's stomach swayed.

The guy was waiting for a follow-up, so she asked, unwillingly, "What do you do?"

"Insurance. For farmers. I make sure they're not undervaluing their land. A lot of site visits."

"So you're kind of a fact-checker, too."

He looked at her like she was crazy. "No."

The plane dipped. They were coming in over the water now, so low and close Kate felt sure they would topple in. She imagined the water closing over her head. Would she be relieved? Before she had figured out the answer, the ground materialized beneath them, an asphalt miracle, and the wheels touched down.

Baggage claim. Kate waited with the rest of the tired passengers while the suitcases circled like alligators. The belt went on and on, the crowd thinned as others were reunited with their luggage, and still Kate's bag did not appear. The back of her neck grew sweaty. Three months was a long time, and she had brought only the one suitcase. If her clothes vanished now, she would be truly alone. Not even an outlet-store sweater to keep her company.

When it was just her and one nervous college student left standing at the carousel, her fraying red bag tumbled down the ramp. Relief made her light-headed, like helium filling her skull.

Outside, she scanned the congested arrivals area for her aunt. The lanes were a mess of honking cars, panicked drivers bent double over their steering wheels as they searched the sidewalk for their loved ones. She finally spotted Louise waving from behind the windshield of a recently waxed Volvo. Louise parked the car in the middle lane and leaped out to hug Kate, which earned her a few sharp tweets on the traffic marshal's whistle. Louise ignored him. She took Kate's shoulders in her hands, even though Kate was a good six inches taller than her, and held her away to scrutinize her.

Kate did her own inventory. She hadn't seen her aunt in three years, but Louise looked exactly the same. Only more tan. Like a deck that had been re-stained to a fresh but unrealistic brown. She was petite—she had a metabolism that could process pig lard into sinewy muscle—with a head of tight, tiny curls that always looked just a little wet. Louise was a harder, shinier version of Kate's mother, a version that had been dipped in enamel and set out to dry. Kate remembered Louise as nosy and annoying, but she hoped that her aunt had changed, or that she herself had grown more patient, or that she had simply misremembered.

At last Louise dropped her hands and declared, "You look exhausted."

Kate managed a smile. "It's been a long day."

"I bet! Three connections! You should have booked a direct flight." Louise grabbed the suitcase and, over Kate's protests, started wrestling it into the trunk. "I have an under-eye cream you can use. It'll take away the circles. And did you eat? We have plenty of food waiting at home. Oh— I should call Frank, remind him to defrost the steak."

If Louise was a renovated deck, Kate was a plaster wall under demolition. Pieces of herself were falling off in the balmy California air. "I can text him from the road if you want."

"Oh, yes." Louise nodded, as if Kate were reminding her about a city she had visited a long time ago. "Texting."

Louise chattered all the way through San Francisco's endless loops of overpasses and underpasses, gushing words like a sprung fire hydrant. She told Kate how they had prepared the guest room, how excited they were to have her, how she had planned out all kinds of activities. They crossed the Golden Gate Bridge into Marin, the turnoff to Sausalito, a sign for Tiburon, and still Louise talked.

Kate tried to listen, but the words floated over her without touching down. She rested her head against the window and watched the surroundings through half-closed eyes. Up here, the light was rich and liquid, more golden than down near the airport; it pooled on the huge houses in the hills, the boats in the marina. People must pay a lot of money to live in that light.

"By the way," Louise said as they took a steep exit, "I saved last week's *Atlantic* for you. There's an article I thought you should read."

"Yeah?"

"It's all about how your generation is feeling very lost. Something to do with the brain chemicals released when you look at television screens. Also, the economy. But by the end, the guy they profiled was feeling much better. He had realized he needed to go to law school. It helps a lot when you discover the right thing, you know?"

Kate's eyes slid over to her aunt. "Yep," she said.

She knew the article Louise meant. It had been everywhere. For a couple days, the internet had been full of memes and think pieces about the trite quotes and obviously staged photos. Her college friends had pilloried it by group text. Or at least the people in the group with good jobs had pilloried it. The others, the ones like Kate, stayed silent.

"Your job just wasn't the right fit," Louise continued. "It wasn't your *passion*. Otherwise you wouldn't have . . . well. My point is, your feelings are perfectly normal."

"Thanks," Kate said.

"And law school is always an option."

"Okay."

"I mean, you would have to take the LSAT. I think Faye's son took it, if you want to borrow his books while you're here."

She means well, Kate told herself. That was her family's private saying about Louise. *She means well.* They had used it that time when Louise lectured a recovering alcoholic cousin about the importance of "letting loose once in a while," and that time when Louise was babysitting seven-year-old Kate and took her to the emergency room for what she thought was a fatal rash and turned out to be a sunburn. They used it every year when Louise sent offensively large checks for birthdays and Christmas, not realizing that her proud New Englander siblings saw the money as an insult. Louise was brash, oblivious, and eager to intervene, but she did have good intentions.

Desperate to change the conversation, Kate said, "Have you met Theo Brand yet? He said he was coming in last week to open up the house."

"Roberta saw him at the general store. Apparently, he was—" Louise broke off.

"He was what?"

"Nothing."

"Tell me." Now Kate sat up straight. "I'm going to meet him tomorrow anyway."

"Well, Roberta just said he wasn't very . . . nice." Louise twisted the steering wheel; they had come onto a series of browned switchbacks. The ocean lay ahead of them like a blue tarp pulled snug across the furry line of the earth. "He wouldn't talk to her."

"Maybe he was tired. He has two little kids." Their voices had been in the background at the end of their phone interview, high and plaintive.

Louise sniffed. "Lots of people have kids and still manage to say hello."

"Okay."

"Anyway, it was more than that. She said it was like he looked right through her." The car pitched to one side as Louise shivered. "I don't know about you being all alone in that big house with him. You'll tell me if anything kooky goes on in there, right?"

"No," Kate said. "I can't. I signed a nondisclosure agreement."

"You what?" The car lurched sideways again. Kate grabbed the handle above her door.

"It's not that unusual."

"It sounds *very* unusual."

"Well, it's not." Kate was almost laughing. So much for misremembering what Louise was like. "I thought you thought this job was a good idea. You're the one who got it for me."

"I am not. All I did was pass your résumé to his cleaning girl."

"You know what I mean."

Louise's fingers tightened on the steering wheel.

"I didn't vouch for him," she muttered.

Kate sighed. This was just like her family. Urge you to do something, and then when you did it, imply you were stupid for doing it.

They were right along the ocean now. Beyond the flimsy guardrail, the water silvered and coruscated beneath a white evening sky. Gulls stretched their wings and dove toward dark Jurassic cliffs. Pulled up at the last moment, then dove again. Looking for the thrill of wind in their feathers—or for the kill.

Twenty hours earlier, Kate had been in New York, or more specifically in Bushwick, at the birthday party of someone she didn't know. Her best friend, Natasha, had dragged her along. Kate had once loved parties. She had been charming, adept at shunting her excess energy into clever conversation. It was harder these days. She got nervous and shaky. She missed cues for witty lines. She didn't want people recognizing her, staring at her, wondering if she was still crazy, what meds she was on, if she had gotten a settlement from the newspaper. Worse, she didn't want them thinking she was boring.

But Natasha had leverage: Kate was crashing in their old apartment the night before her early flight out of JFK, and even though her name was technically on the lease through the end of the month, the rules of hospitality were in effect. A good guest was game for anything.

Now it was past midnight—long after she should have left, given how early she would have to get up for her flight. It was getting to *that moment* in the party: the playlist had shifted from indie electronic to nostalgia pop, the alcohol from microbrews to PBR, and an array of medical-grade joints were being discreetly passed around. Kate was standing by an open window, studying the skyline. She had drunk just enough to take the edge off. Not enough to dull her anxiety entirely: if she pushed against it, she would still bleed.

Wet metal tapped her shoulder. Natasha, with a new beer. Thank God. Kate took it and used the windowsill to pop off the cap.

"How you doing?" Natasha asked. Her voice too kind.

"Fine."

"No one you know, right? I promised."

"Right. Yeah, it's cool. I'm glad I came."

If Natasha knew Kate was lying, she didn't comment. "I wish you weren't leaving," she said instead, dragging her braids forward over her shoulder. "What am I going to do? Who am I going to hang out with?"

"You'll be fine," Kate said. "What am *I* going to do, out in California, with my crazy aunt and uncle and a bunch of weird old shit?"

"You love weird old shit. You're going to get super tan. And you can find all kinds of secrets about Miranda Brand and write a book. You can get a million dollars and buy one of those pink Victorian mansions. Go on all the TV shows. You'll never come back to New York."

That didn't sound so bad. New York was contaminated now. Whenever Kate stood on her usual subway platform or passed a familiar bar, she remembered what it had been like to see those places before her life had tipped upside down. And she couldn't get a job here, anyway, not at the *Times* or the *Post* or any place where Leonard Webb had friends, which was everywhere on the East Coast. California was an empty sheet on a clothesline, a place bleached clean of knowledge.

"I'll mention you in my Pulitzer speech," Kate said.

"Hell no, bitch. You're aiming for the Nobel fucking Prize."

Kate laughed and shook her head. Out the window in front of them, a sea of flat roofs stained with bird shit swelled out into the black snake of the East River. Beyond lay the tiered glow of the Williamsburg Bridge, the starry needles of Manhattan. The liquor store sign fizzing neon on the opposite corner. The smell of plantains and jerk chicken rising from the late-night Jamaican place down below. Out in the night, half a mile off, a helicopter hovered in the sky. *Thump-thump-thump.* The spotlight hunting its prey.

The sight made Kate shiver, and she said what she had been thinking for the past hour. "Those guys over there have been watching me."

"Which guys?"

Without looking, Kate tilted her head to the kitchen, where several men in identical thick-framed glasses were standing in a small group. "They know about Leonard."

Natasha glanced over. "No, they don't."

"They're journalists."

"They're lawyers," Natasha said. "I've met them before."

"Maybe they're with the firm that I talked to about suing."

"They don't recognize you," Natasha said, her tone final, and Kate felt herself recoil in surprise. Natasha must have realized how she had sounded, because she hugged Kate around the shoulders and added in a softer voice, "I'm going to miss you."

"I'll miss you, too," Kate said.

It was true and not true. She felt like she had been wearing a mask for years, and suddenly the elastic had snapped, and now she couldn't hold it in place. She would miss Natasha, infinitely. They had been friends for more than ten years, had turned twenty and then thirty together, had consoled each other through heartbreaks and deaths and many daily disappointments. But now when Kate saw Natasha, she only remembered that morning when Natasha had come into her room to tell Kate (unwashed, unmoving, watching the radiator eat a circle of frost on the window) that she had called Kate's mother to come pick her up and take her home.

She wouldn't miss that. The shame of having been seen at her worst.

And she wouldn't miss the carefulness she now heard in Natasha's voice. Or this feeling she got sometimes, that on some level Natasha would be relieved to see her go.

Two sweaty arms wrapped around Natasha from behind. Her boyfriend, Liam, reclaiming her.

"You have to dance with me," he said. "You love this song. Kate, you come, too."

"Right behind you," Kate said.

Natasha believed her, or pretended to, because within a few seconds she and Liam had vanished into the crowd. Kate turned back to the window and leaned farther out, propping her elbows on the greasy rail. She gazed down eight stories to the sidewalk below. It was cracked and dirty. A Styrofoam takeout container had been discarded on the pavement and smashed underfoot. Two floors down, someone's hand flashed in and out of view as they gestured over the rail. A minnow thumbing through the silt.

Coming tonight had been a mistake. She should have stayed on the raggedy Craigslist couch in their living room, shaking and sweating beneath her borrowed duvet, waiting for things to get better. Forest animals did it when they hibernated: they made nests for themselves out of leaves and dug tunnels through the roots of trees, they put themselves into a dark warm place and slept through winters that could kill them. Only humans thought self-protection was a sickness. When Kate had been waiting out her winter, everyone told her to get over it, work through it, talk it out. As if prepositions could protect her. As if others knew whatever lay beyond was better. In reality, all anyone knew was that it came next.

As Kate looked over the balcony, she suddenly saw her own body splayed out against the pavement, head wrenched to the side. Blood trickling from her nose and skull. The image was vivid and bright like an oversaturated photograph, the lines so sharp they were like a command. *Jump.*

She leaped back, bumping into someone. They swore. Something wet spilled across her left shoulder.

"Sorry, sorry," she mumbled, without looking at them.

She had to get out of here.

She shoved her way through the crowd to the apartment's front door and slipped out into the musty hallway, where she punched the elevator button over and over again until its doors shuddered open.

Inside, she looked at herself in the warped metal surface of the door. Her hair had gone flat. The lipstick had faded. Lately she had begun to notice tiny lines at the corners of her eyes. She used to catch sight of herself at night, traces of eyeliner, tousled blond hair, and think, *Damn, yes*, but now she didn't always recognize the person in the mirror. It wasn't age, exactly. The past year had changed her, weakened her, stretched her out.

"You just need some color," her mother had said the week before. "A little sun."

Kate wanted her to be right. She wanted to believe California could fix it all: tan her wan skin, shine her dull hair, and when that was done, reach down into the broken, taped-together mess inside her and repair that, too.

The elevator slipped past another floor. It wasn't so different than jumping. Gravity was still pulling her down. Only the elevator moved steadily, sedately, the floor catching her as she fell. Catching her here, and here, and here, until at last she was at the ground floor, as low as she could go, and the doors opened, splitting her reflection in half and then taking it away.

MIRANDA

SERIES 1, Correspondence

BOX 1, Personal correspondence

FOLDER: Eggers, Hal (incl. 39 photocopies of letters from MB, from HE private collection)

December 27 1990

Dear Hal,

Thanks so much for the invitation to write a "confessional essay." I will have to respectfully decline.

Here's why, you fucking tool.

You want something juicy, rich, spilling, like biting into a ripe fig. But confessions aren't sexy. Confessions are hernias. An organ pushing through an opening. Hacking up your body. Wet and bulging. Confessions should never be exposed to sun.

Of course the fans "want it." They're sybarites, cannibals, starving predators, they want to sink their teeth into the organ and rip it apart. They want to be in the inner circle.

But I won't cater to them. I can't.

I'm not a stock option.

I'm not publicly held.

My photos are already making you rich, aren't they? So what do you care?

These essays, press releases, lectures to donors, they're just WORDS. The photos will sell themselves. The photos will say everything I want to say.

Yours truly,
your money bank,
Miranda

1/4/1991

Miranda sweetheart,

Of COURSE I don't want you to feel that I'm USING you—I thought the confessional would be a good experience to tell your STORY!!

Also, I think you are discrediting the confessional genre. It is VERY popular. Haven't you read Sylvia Plath? I'm not saying you have to give everything away. You can create the ILLUSION of a confession. Everything these days is about performance, think Cindy, think that adorable little gent from North Carolina that I signed last year . . . you're being too LITERAL, as always!!

I did tell Romi that you would say something for the exhibit catalog. He has a VISION for your contributions that will feel very FRESH. We can stage it as an interview, WHATEVER, but we need SOMETHING. And anyway I think the "recluse" schtick is a little overplayed now. You've been doing it too long.

Meanwhile, I have a buyer interested in purchasing a complete set of Bottle Girls, but have no more prints of #4 available after the last one sold. We've only sold 7 out of a print run of 10 so I think you must have more at your place. Can you check?

Hal

January 18 1991

Hal,

I have couriered down the 3 remaining prints of BG#4. I can do another print run next month.

Let me guess what Romi wants me to write about.
Motherhood.

Marriage.

Too much fame.

Not enough fame.

My vagina. Who's gone in it, who came out of it, whether I got that extra stitch postpartum.

Whether my moment has faded.

Whether I'm overpriced.

Whether I'll be forgotten.

What happened in Nangussett.

Whether the scars in my photos are real.

Or whether I made it all up.

No? None of these?

Really?

Next time Romi is jacking you off in a bathroom stall, instead of telling him I'll do shit I'm not going to do, maybe you can remind him that I want the show to include the version of Capillaries #6 that is at MoMA, not the one at Chicago. The saturation is different. I don't care which one is cheaper to insure.

M

2.

KATE

The house where Miranda Brand had lived and died was, on the outside, unremarkable. It was perched on the crown of the hill like a dollop of mayonnaise on the bald curve of a hard-boiled egg. The color might have been beautiful once, but the wind coming off the ocean had beaten the paint to a drab gray, the same shade as the sky, so that in some places it was hard to see where the fog stopped and the building began. Two overgrown lemon trees fanned across the front, their tallest branches just brushing the windows of a third floor. It could have been any house on any hill in a coastal town, East Coast or West, and yet as soon as Kate saw it, her heart gave a strange, swift beat.

Maybe it was just exertion. In a terse, unpunctuated email a few days earlier, Theo Brand had given her directions to the house via a "walking path" from town, as well as the combination for a lock on the gate to the property. Kate had imagined an easy stroll, but instead she had found herself climbing a steep, tangled furrow through redwoods until sweat bloomed between her shoulder blades. As for the gate, the lock was so rusty that she had spent five minutes scraping it with a bobby pin just to get it open.

Despite the delay, she was fifteen minutes early. Too early to knock. She stood at the edge of the clearing, eyeing the house and huddling into herself to stay warm. It was colder here than she had expected, the morning air as wet and icy as a dead fish, and all the little hairs on her arms were standing up. Dinner last night had been weird—her aunt and uncle tossing out information on everything from area hikes, to the guest room toilet's quirks, to the local beach's rules, while Kate chewed an overcooked steak and tried not to worry about her new job.

Kate had dismissed her aunt's concerns in the car, but the truth was, she had spoken to her new boss only once before, a brisk thirty-minute phone interview during which he had shared almost nothing about himself. Afterward, through Google, she learned he had gone to Harvard, bounced between a few successful internet start-ups, and now ran some computer-related consulting business, which had gotten him featured on an important 35-under-35 list for the tech industry. His name came up in a few magazine articles—and, of course, in his father's obituary from six months ago. But the press coverage was bland and uninformative. In interviews, he declined to comment on anything unrelated to work. The only personal information Kate had found was a line item in a Bay Area gossip blog about his divorce last year from a woman named Rachel Tatum.

Not a single article where he spoke about his mother.

Kate had been on the wrong side of enough news reports over the past year to understand the desire for privacy. On the other hand, she had taken this job assuming she would learn more about him at some point. She had figured that they would talk again before she moved all the way across the country, or that he would send detailed instructions about what exactly the work would entail. She had meant to do a deeper dive into the tech blogs. Now, as she stared at the house, she realized that she had gotten so distracted by the logistics of moving that she had done the unimaginable: she had stopped researching. The critical moment was here and she had run out of time. This was it. This was all she knew.

She checked her watch. Thirteen minutes now. Across the brittle brown loop of the lawn, there was a notch in the tree line. She could at least walk over there, try to get a glimpse of the ocean. With another glance at the silent house, she hitched her tote bag up on her shoulder and started across the lawn.

In the backyard, the slope spilled down into the edge of the woods, and below that a cliff. No luck on the view, even through the break in the trees: the fog blanked out whatever lay beyond, leaving the clearing swaddled in a gray cocoon of mist.

Far down the incline was a glint of metal. Her stomach twisted. The fence she had come through must encircle the entire house. When she had closed the gate and rejammed the lock, she had trapped herself inside.

"What are you doing?" a voice said from right behind her.

Kate started, almost losing her footing. When she turned, she saw a man standing about ten feet away, between her and the house. Tall, dark-haired, olive-skinned, a lean frame. His feet were spread wide—defensive—and his hands were in his pockets.

Theo Brand.

There was an intensity to him that the images online hadn't captured. He was more vital, less coiffed. Her elbow clamped her tote bag to her side. Fear, excitement, something sharp and glowing, slicked through her veins. She shouldn't have had that second coffee.

"I'm Kate," she blurted out. "Your archivist." She didn't know why she said *your*.

"I figured. I guess you missed the front door."

She swallowed. "I wanted to see the view."

He looked at the opaque sky and raised an eyebrow. When Kate flushed, he said, "You know, I prosecute trespassers."

He couldn't be serious. And yet his voice was cool, and his eyes were steady. The laughter died in her throat. She cast her mind back to their emails. Had she gotten the start date wrong? No, she would never have messed that up. She was good with details.

"I know I'm a little early," she said haltingly. "But I think . . ." She waited for him to jump in and correct himself. He didn't. She could barely conceal her disbelief as she asked, "Are you saying I should go back around front?"

"Of course not," he said. Then, as she was beginning to relax: "You should enjoy it a little longer."

"Enjoy what?"

"The thrill." He nodded in her direction. "That's where she died. Shot herself right where you're standing."

Kate looked down at the sparse, matted grass.

"Go ahead, get down on the ground," he said pleasantly. "See what it feels like. Get the full experience."

Her heart had finally started to slow after the surprise of his arrival, but now it picked up again, indignant. But what could she say? There was no possible appropriate response.

"I'm . . ." She cleared her throat. "I'm sorry for your loss."

Theo gave no sign of hearing her. He just kept watching her, his expression growing cooler by the second, until Kate started to wonder whether she had somehow said the words in the wrong order. She remembered how he had signed his emails. *TJB.* She had figured it was an automatic setting he used at work. Now she understood that it had been a warning. Even before he met her, he was pulling her to a halt, yanking the reins until the bit stuck in her mouth.

At last he said grimly, "Come on, then," and angled his head toward the house.

He turned without waiting for her to follow. And without introducing himself.

By the time her limbs unlocked, he was halfway to the house. She scrambled up the hill after him, her feet skidding against the damp grass. Up close, the house was in worse shape than she had realized. The back porch stairs creaked, age had creased the paint on the banister, and the floorboards were peppered with little lakes of raw wood.

"Do you—" she began, then stopped.

"Do I what?" He kicked the doormat flat.

She sighed. "Never mind."

A squeal came from inside. The porch door was flung open. A little girl, maybe six or seven, hung on the door handle and beamed up at them. Her nightgown was covered in cartoon Disney princesses. Below its hem, her bare feet pattered with excitement.

"Hi hi hi," the girl said, sticking out her hand. "I'm Jemima."

Kate smiled and shook the hand. It was light and soft in her own. "Kate. I like your nightgown."

Jemima turned to hold the door open with her back so she could pick up the hem, flounce it about. "It's magic. It means I can fly."

"No flying," Theo said. "I told you. Feet on the ground. Where's your brother?"

She shrugged. "I don't know. Probably being a big baby."

"Jemima, don't start." Theo pulled the door the rest of the way open and gestured Kate inside.

The kitchen was outdated, with a plastic-coated fridge and orange tiles. At the signs of current life—dirty breakfast plates on the table, crayons scattered around them, a spill of milk on the floor—Kate relaxed. Theo had children, whom he fed and kept alive: he couldn't be so bad.

Jemima ran into the center of the room. She raised the hem of her nightgown higher, spread the fabric like wings to get Kate's attention, and turned in a wide circle. "I'm a bird!"

"You're a very beautiful bird," Kate said obediently.

"Oscar," Theo said. "Come out from under there."

Kate didn't understand who Theo was talking to until he approached the table and bent down, and she saw that there was a boy sitting underneath with his knees drawn up to his chest.

"I *told* you," Jemima said to Kate in a stage whisper.

"Jemima," Theo warned, "I mean it." He helped Oscar out from under the table. The boy was younger than Jemima, perhaps four or five, but with the same wild brown curls. His mouth bowed in nervously.

"He's a little shy," Theo explained.

"That's okay." Kate understood the desire to hold yourself apart, to see and not be seen. She would have crawled under the kitchen table too if she could have. "Hi, Oscar."

He hid behind his father's legs.

"Daddy said you're here to look at the grandma papers," Jemima said to Kate. "I *love* the papers. I'm going to look at them, too. Right! Now!"

"I don't think so." Theo collared Jemima before she could dart away. "Why don't you take Oscar back to the living room and finish your movie?"

"I'm tired of the movie."

"Then you can clean up your Legos."

"I hate cleaning up my Legos."

Theo raised his eyebrows. "Then I guess you should watch the movie."

Cornered, Jemima let out a high-pitched shriek and blazed out of the room. Oscar gave Kate one final, curious look before following his sister.

Theo rescued a plate teetering off the table and placed it in the sink, then grabbed a paper towel to wipe up the spilled milk.

"They're sweet," Kate said.

"Famous last words," Theo replied. His voice was flat; she couldn't tell if he was joking. The kids' movie came on full blast in the next room.

Kate looked around the kitchen, trying to take everything in. A few weeks ago, she hadn't thought about Miranda Brand since that Contemporary Art lecture in college, and now here she was inside the woman's house. She remembered that last party in New York two days ago, the thickness of the summer midnight, the throwback playlist and the carefully shellacked story of her move, and she felt disoriented, as if she had missed a step while going down the stairs.

Theo dropped the towel in the trash can, wiped his hands, and turned to her. "Okay. Let me show you what we've got."

In their first phone conversation, two weeks earlier, Theo had told Kate he was looking for someone to organize his mother's papers, which were "kind of a mess." Which Kate knew could mean anything. Every person organized their files differently. One of her old coworkers kept tabbed binders of research, while another placed all his hard copies in a single, wobbling pile. As for Miranda Brand—

"Holy shit," Kate said.

It looked like a dump truck had backed in through the bay window and unloaded an entire town's worth of recycling. Underneath the mess, Kate could see hints of a mahogany dining table and a truly terrible rug. Orange and blue paisley swirled with pastel pink, the kind of $10,000 atrocity that would receive prime placement in an avant-garde design magazine. Most of the floor had disappeared beneath a spill of papers and rubbish. Cardboard boxes of random sizes; stacked clear plastic boxes with negatives, unused film, discarded prints; a tall pile of notebooks that had slid sideways into a ruffled ramp of curled page edges.

"My mom was a pack rat," Theo said wearily.

Pack rat was too cute a term for this.

Disorder had always stressed Kate out. That was one thing she could say for herself: she was neat. As a child, she had always put away her own toys. When she was six, she had asked her parents for a mini vacuum for Christmas. In college and after, she was the roommate who did the dishes on time, who folded everyone else's strewn belongings into tidy squares and set them in front of their bedroom doors—at least until Natasha had told her it came across as passive-aggressive. Kate hadn't meant it like that. She cleaned for her own comfort. Clutter gave her a physical reaction: an itch up the legs, a scratch in the spine. Her own binders at work had been alphabetized and color-coded.

To hide her distress, she began picking her way around the fringes of the room, trying to marshal her thoughts.

"How many rooms are there like this?" she asked Theo.

"Just this one. I put everything in here. The kids needed room to run around."

"Right. Okay." She stopped and looked around. "So what's the system?"

"System?"

"Like, when you moved things, which rooms went where?"

"Oh." Theo looked blank. "I guess they all went . . . everywhere. I was consolidating."

"You just piled it all in here?"

"Sure," he said. "It's not like it was organized to begin with."

She tried to keep the panic out of her voice. "Maybe it didn't seem organized, but we can learn a lot about a collection based on how the original owner had it arranged. We can see when things date from, what was with what . . ."

"I'll tell you how it was arranged," he said tersely. "It was arranged like my parents threw down whatever they had wherever they happened to be."

Kate pressed her lips together. So this was who Theo Brand was. Successful, rich, handsome, kids. He had his whole life figured out, and he was used to getting what he wanted. Whereas she had staked her whole life on coming here. Whereas she was thirty years old with $180 in her bank account, $4,000 in credit card debt, and $18,000 remaining in student loans.

There was already an imbalance between them, and it made everything unsteady, like a chair in an interrogation room with one leg sawed short.

"It's yours now," he went on. "Organize it however seems logical. Mainly I need a catalog of the contents, as detailed as possible. What did you call it over the phone, a guide, a—?"

"A finding aid."

"Yeah. Something bidders will understand."

"And the bidders are museums? Libraries?"

"Both. Universities, too, hopefully. Somewhere publicly accessible."

Kate nodded. "How long has it all been here?"

"I guess since 1993." He shrugged. "I thought my dad had cleaned it out, but—obviously not. I don't know if he even ever came up here. I know I haven't."

"You haven't been here in twenty-four years?"

He gazed at her evenly. "You can leave that kind of commentary out of the aid, thanks."

Kate opened her mouth, then closed it. She didn't need to get fired on her first day.

She stepped over a box and crossed to the bay window that looked out onto the yellow lawn. One of the windows was cracked open at the bottom, and the air that blew into the room was cold and wet. She put her hands on the sill and pressed it closed.

"The damp," she explained.

When she turned around, Theo had hooked his thumbs into his pockets and was watching her. He was larger than she had realized: not so lean after all. A long, raised scar ribboned up his forearm and terminated in a small black tattoo just before the crook of his elbow. He was attractive, Kate realized, and the thought unnerved her. After what had happened with Leonard, the last thing she wanted was to be attracted to her boss. Or anyone. It was no coincidence that attraction felt the same as panic. The speeding heart, the tingle in the neck.

"I set the payment up with the bank," Theo was saying. "Thirty-five hours a week. If you go over, let me know and I'll add it on. The special boxes you had me order are supposed to arrive tomorrow. During the days I'll be working right upstairs, so I can come down, help you with any names or anything like that. As much as I can. I mean, all this"—he waved at the mess—"happened a long time ago."

"Okay."

"And as you . . . as you go through this all, please be discreet. That's the most important part. If you find anything—personal—I . . . I don't want it getting into the wrong hands."

"Of course." They had already talked about this over the phone.

"If you find anything like that, I want to know about it right away. Immediately."

"Of *course*," she said again, tamping down her irritation.

Theo looked at her for a moment. There was something precise in his gaze, like he was peeling off her outer husk. Kate fought the urge to put her hands in her pockets.

At last, he said, "Well, then. I guess I'll leave you to it."

Dinner that night was served on the screened-in porch at the back of Louise's house, on a shiny wooden table surrounded by hosta and tall rubber plants. The fog had faded by the afternoon, and now the air was warm, windless, nearly sticky. Frank, Louise's preternaturally inoffensive husband, had bought a bottle of champagne and four dozen Point Reyes oysters to celebrate Kate's first day at work. Kate had tried oysters before once or twice, but only on beds of ice and lettuce. These were different, raw and wild, so fresh they were practically squirming in their shells. They slid down her throat in a slip of salt and brine.

"So," Louise said, clapping her hands together. "Tell us about the house."

"The house? It's a house." Kate dropped an empty shell into the discard bowl. "A living room, a dining room, a kitchen."

"Katie, come on."

"I assume there are bedrooms, too. I didn't see those."

"You know what I mean."

"There's not anything to say," Kate said, reaching over to refill her aunt's glass. "It's pretty boring."

It was true, sort of. After that first uncomfortable meeting, Theo had disappeared upstairs and she had spent the rest of the day alone in the dining room, sneezing dust and pushing boxes around. In addition to the massive quantities of papers and documents, the dining room was full of random objects. Already Kate had found eighteen Lego pieces, four melted lipsticks, three staplers, two rolls of masking tape, a nail gun, and a weird china marionette with a broken arm. More than once, she had put something down only to discover that her fingers were coated in a mysterious sticky substance. Her back ached from bending over. Her eyes were red from squinting. She had spent half an hour going through a thick stack of bent notecards, only to determine that they were indeed all blank and could be safely set in the discard pile.

Yes, it was boring. Boring, repetitive, and way less fun than watching reruns of *Vanderpump Rules* on her parents' sofa.

But. *But.* Boredom was like pain. When it was gone, it no longer felt real. Six hundred notecards took up the same mental space as sixty as six as one. That half hour had already become a millisecond in Kate's memory.

The money helped smooth the rough edges. Kate's contract said that on top of her hourly rate, she would receive 0.5 percent of the proceeds from the sale of any art. Online auction records said Miranda's prints went for anywhere between $60,000 and $900,000. Before entering the Brand house, Kate had assumed she might find a couple prints, max, and get a nice little bonus of a few thousand dollars. But it was quickly becoming apparent that the dining room, crammed as it was with trash, was also full of valuable material. Shortly after setting aside those infuriating notecards, she had found a small photograph in decent condition: the ink dense and shiny, the paper unwarped. It was one of Miranda's nature photographs, a close-up of a leaf's corded vein.

That was how it was sometimes, in the archive. Big discoveries sandwiched between trash. The day-to-day touching the phenomenal.

Now she felt drunk on the knowledge that she had earned money. Real money for real work. She had felt so worthless for so long that the mere fact of employment was as sharp a relief as taking off a heavy backpack at the end of a long hike. Even if her boss was a dickwad.

"It can't all be boring," Louise said. "Everyone wants to get inside that house. Now you're there. Give us some details."

"Honey, leave her alone," Frank said. "She can't tell us anything. She signed that agreement."

"The agreement doesn't apply to *family*," Louise said.

Frank was swallowing oysters like a happy hour special was about to end. Like Louise, he had taken to retirement with gusto, spending his days tinkering with CB radios and kayaking around the lagoon. Instead of a tan, his skin had adopted a permanent pinkish sheen. Even now, in the lilac dusk, he wore his wraparound sunglasses hooked on backward, like they were shielding another set of eyes in the back of his head.

"You'll get your behind-the-scenes sooner or later," he said to his wife. "Anyway, what do you think the guy's going to do? Come right out and say he killed his mom?"

Kate spat out a mouthful of champagne.

"Frank!" Louise exclaimed, jumping up with her napkin as Kate coughed and coughed.

"What? What did I do?"

Louise glared at her husband as she pressed the napkin onto the table-cloth. "Have some *sensitivity*."

Frank looked bewildered. "You didn't tell her? I thought that was your whole thing."

"It's not *my* thing."

"Okay, your friends' thing. Katie, do you need any water?"

"I'm fine," Kate said, still coughing. "I just—I was surprised."

"Ignore Frank. He's trying to stir the pot."

"It's more a joke than anything," Frank said uncertainly. He fidgeted his sunglasses up and down the back of his head.

"It's not a *joke*," Louise said. "Poor thing. He was a little boy. If he shot her, it was obviously an accident."

"I'm sorry, back up," Kate said. "What do you mean, if he shot her? I thought Miranda committed suicide."

"She did," Louise said, just as Frank waggled his eyebrows and said, "So they say."

Kate gritted her teeth. "Everything I read says she killed herself."

Her aunt and uncle exchanged looks. Louise sighed. "The police ruled it a suicide. But only after they made a huge stink about it. They interrogated a bunch of people in town. Obviously we didn't live here at the time, but my friend Roberta said the place was swarming with cops."

"And *my* friend Victor was one of the detectives on the case," Frank said. "According to him, they treated it as a full homicide investigation. They didn't think she could have done it herself. Something about the forensic evidence. Like on *CSI*."

"There's all kinds of theories," Louise said, talking more quickly now. She had resisted this course of conversation, but now that they were on it, she was going to lead the charge. "I mean, number one, Jake. *Obviously.* It's always the husband. If you watch Lifetime, you know. Not that I watch Lifetime."

"People just say Jake because they have to," Frank said. "But everyone who knew him swears he was the nicest guy you ever met."

"That's what they always say about serial killers," Louise said,

"Oh, yeah," Frank said, remembering. "That's another idea. The Zodiac Killer. You know he was never caught."

"So basically," Kate said, deadpan, "Miranda Brand was killed by Theo, Jake, or the Zodiac Killer."

"Or someone else. Like maybe a crazed fan. I told you, there's lots of theories."

Kate shook her head. "Why would people think *Theo* did it? He was, what, ten, eleven?"

"Children do all kinds of crazy things," Louise said.

"Yeah, crazy things like eating their own snot. You're talking about shooting his mother. There must be some reason that rumor got started."

"Apparently he was a very weird kid," Frank said. "No friends at all.

Sam Loomis said his nephew's girlfriend saw Theo standing over a dead squirrel one time. Just poking at it with a long stick. Totally emotionless."

Kate tried not to roll her eyes. An uncle's friend's memory of what his nephew's girlfriend had said twenty years ago was not high on her list of reliable sources.

"And he hasn't talked to anyone since he got here," Louise put in. "He moves here for the whole summer, you'd think he'd try to get to know people a little. Especially the people who remember him from when he was younger."

Kate said, "Yes, but—"

"And Miranda wasn't all there. Did you know she was hospitalized?"

"Of course I did."

"For wanting to kill her son," Louise whispered. "Can you imagine? If Theo killed her, maybe it was self-defense."

"To recap," Kate said, "you think Miranda attacked Theo, he shot her, and then he covered it up."

"There are lots of accidents with guns," Frank said. "Just last week, in Tulsa—"

"Covered it up," Louise scoffed. "I didn't say that."

"I agree he's an asshole," Kate said. "But those are some pretty sick rumors to spread about someone."

"I'm not spreading rumors," Louise said, shocked. "I'm just repeating what other people have said."

"Right," Kate said.

"And like we said," Frank put in, maybe realizing the conversation had gone off the rails, "there are a lot of different options."

"It's not like anyone thinks he's *dangerous*," Louise said. After a pause, she added, "I did pick up a travel hair spray at Costco for you to bring to work, just in case. You can use it like pepper spray. Aim at the eyes."

"You want me to *pepper spray my boss*?"

"*Hair* spray. I only got it as a precaution." Louise patted Kate's hand. "Your mother told me to keep an eye on you."

At that last part, Kate felt a hiccup of surprise, which she concealed by sponging up a stray splash of champagne Louise had missed. She should have known. Her mother had been so overprotective the past few months. Terrified that the slightest inconvenience would send her daughter into a tailspin, Darcy lied about minuscule things: a speeding ticket, Kate's father failing his cholesterol test. Whenever Kate found out about one of these fibs, her mother would say, "I'm just trying to make things easy for you."

So of course Darcy had asked Louise to watch out for her daughter. But now Kate was thinking about how many conversations her mother and Louise must have had, prior to her coming out here. Talking behind her back about how fragile she was. How easily rattled. Now they would want evidence of her stability, and she had nothing to show. She had a job, but so what? Lots of people had jobs—and kept them. Her stability, such as it was, was fleeting. She was a spun quarter wobbling to a stop, on the brink of falling over. Look at this dinner spread. You had to be a real failure for your family to think that seven hours of work deserved a celebration.

Her earlier optimism was draining away. She wondered if coming to California had ever been fully her decision, or if it was just a plan her mother and aunt had hatched together. *Give Kate a life, but add training wheels.* And the woman charged with watching her pedal around the cul-de-sac believed both that Kate's boss might have killed his mother, and that he might be held off by a two-ounce bottle of TresEmmé Super Hold.

When Kate picked up her glass again, her fingers felt unsteady on the stem. "You should have told me what people were saying," she said, not quite meeting her aunt's eye.

Frank cleared his throat and held out an oyster. Kate took it dutifully. The shell's pearlescent sheen made her think of the fog that morning, wrapping around the house, and how Theo had emerged out of it so suddenly. *Go ahead, get down on the ground. See what it feels like.* The oyster's liquid sloshed onto her hand. She tipped the shell back into her mouth and swallowed the creature whole.

MIRANDA

Certificate of Live Birth
State Department of Health
Bureau of Vital Statistics

COUNTY: Morris
STATE: New Jersey
TOWNSHIP: Morristown
1204 S. Marmion St.

FULL NAME OF CHILD: Miranda Rose Planchart
SEX: female

FULL TERM: X
LEGITIMATE? Yes
DATE OF BIRTH: December 18, 1956

FATHER

FULL NAME: Michael Andrew Planchart

AGE AT LAST BIRTHDAY: 27

BIRTHPLACE: Manchester, N.J.

MOTHER

FULL NAME: Leanne Lessig Planchart

AGE AT LAST BIRTHDAY: 24

BIRTHPLACE: Allentown, Pa.

NUMBER OF CHILDREN OF THIS MOTHER BORN ALIVE AND NOW LIVING: two

NUMBER OF CHILDREN OF THIS MOTHER BORN ALIVE BUT NOW DEAD: none

STILLBORN: none

I hereby certify that I attended the birth of this child, who was born alive on the date above stated at 4:19 P.M.

SIGNATURE H. M. Helliwell, Physician

SERIES 2, Personal papers

BOX 5, Childhood papers, 1956–1974

FOLDER: Report Cards & Transcripts

Harry S. Truman Elementary School
Ridgetown, New Jersey

Progress Report

STUDENT: Miranda R. Planchart

TEACHER: Miss Graham

GRADE: 3

ENGLISH: Excels
READING: Excels
WRITING: Excels
MATH: Needs Improvement
SCIENCE: Excels
HISTORY: Satisfactory
ART: Satisfactory
HOME EC.: Needs Improvement
PHYS. ED.: Not Applicable

NOTES:

Miranda is a smart and capable child. She reads above her grade level and did very well in our storytelling unit (understands beginning, middle, end).

When Miranda completes her homework it is exemplary. However, she does not always complete her homework. She has told outlandish lies about her missing homework on several occasions resulting in disciplinary measures. She disobeys teachers and works on her own projects even when the rest of the class is focused on the assignment. She must learn to be more compassionate and polite.

Overall Miranda is a gifted child but needs to cultivate respect for authority. Her most recent disciplinary hearing (the Duck and Cover incident) indicates not enough progress has been made on this front. She might benefit from more discipline and structure at home.

3.

KATE

Over the next few days, Kate fell into a routine. Leave Louise and Frank's place just after nine, up to the Brand house by ten. Polite hello to Theo. Work for a few hours, a quick lunch in the kitchen with the leftovers Louise had packed her, and back to it.

She started work on the collection by establishing general categories, weeding out the miscellaneous objects (toys, pens, used batteries) that had been scattered in with the papers and prints, and setting up spreadsheets. Eventually, once she had a sense of the extent of the materials, she would start listing each document in the spreadsheets—a painstaking, messy process that involved shifting items around seven or eight times and muddling over whether a letter about an informal loan qualified as "Correspondence" or "Financial documents." For now, the categories were rough. Personal letters, photographs, miscellaneous weird junk. It required little brain power, and she was grateful for the distraction of Oscar and Jemima, who kept sneaking into the dining room to ask her questions like what was her favorite month and did she know if snails had bones. At five o'clock, she packed up her things and trekked home, where she joined Frank and Louise for dinner and their nightly two episodes of *Madam Secretary*.

For so many years in New York, she had lamented her rigid work routine and taken its security for granted. Freelancing, flexible hours, mobile workspaces—these had been the perks she and her friends sought to obtain. As members of New York's liberal-arts-educated, semi-creative class, they considered predictability boring, even pathetic. So it was with some shame that Kate now found herself taking pleasure in her rigid schedule. All that flexibility and looseness was for people who could hold themselves together. People who could be trusted to take care of themselves. Maybe predictability was what she needed now. Maybe the routine could work like an elastic band. Wrapping around her, holding her in.

S he wasn't sure what to do with Frank and Louise's information about Miranda's death—if you could call it information. After Monday's dinner conversation, Kate had discreetly buried the travel hair spray in the bathroom trash, then retreated to the guest room and spent several hours researching Miranda's death online. After watching a bootlegged copy of a *60 Minutes* documentary on the subject, Kate had fallen deep into the rabbit hole of a forum called Murder Solvers. The reigning theory among the so-called Solvers was that Miranda had fallen victim to a serial killer who had been preying on teenage girls in Sonoma in 1992 and 1993. There was also speculation that Miranda's art dealer had killed her in order to limit supply and raise her value. Jake was a popular suspect ("IT'S ALWAYS THE SPOUSE!!"). Possible motives included: a mistress, a murder-suicide pact, exhaustion from Miranda's sadomasochistic sex games. Theo's name cropped up, too: some Solvers believed he had been playing with the gun and it had gone off accidentally; others thought he was a child psychopath. In one of the more convoluted hypotheses, several well-known New York artists had hired an assassin as part of a complex revenge plot dating back to a declined party invitation in the early 1980s.

The site trafficked in paranoia. Still, compared with some of the other threads on Murder Solvers, Miranda's was pretty bare. There was a lot of chatter about the documentary, and then about specific photographs, trying to decipher possible clues in the background. But without any new leads over the years, the debate dried up. Some people thought the topic should be closed altogether.

This forum is called MURDER Solvers, one person wrote. *Why r we discussing a suicide? I watched the whole 60 Minutes & this thing is a crock of shit. Everyone knows the lady was depressed. Just google MIRANDA*

BRAND PSYCH WARD. Pls lets focus on REAL mysteries. Ones we can actually SOLVE w/ known facts.

He was right that the Solvers' theories lacked evidence. There was no sign of the inconsistencies that Frank and Louise had mentioned. Nothing from the police report was publicly available. There was nothing to prove or disprove any of the assertions, including the theories about Theo.

Don't be ridiculous, Kate told herself, clicking out of the window. *Your boss did not kill his mother.*

But. She knew the kinds of things that men could hide.

Miranda and Jake had kept so many papers. It made no sense. Multiple folders with the same useless labels, like *1991 MISCELLANEOUS* or *SOME MEDICAL*. Coupons and bills layered together. Letters always packed inside their ripped envelopes. Jake had written Miranda hundreds of notes, always starting *M—* and ending *Love, Your Jake*, as if reminding Miranda she owned him. Miranda had never thrown them away.

Then there were the receipts. Infinite receipts. Postage, groceries, gas: nothing unusual, except the quantity of the documentation. Miranda and Jake had even taken home receipts that didn't belong to them: there were two restaurant receipts signed G—(squiggle) BO—(squiggle), and a $380 purchase from a bookstore in San Francisco made by someone with the unlikely name Ranger Wittensdorf. Stuffed in a shoebox were about fifty receipts from a San Francisco parking lot chain with an annoying habit of putting their dates in the corners, which then wrinkled and tore. All the little shards that fell off everyone's life. Kate's job was to stick the Brands' shards back together again.

She had hoped the task would seem clearer as the days wore on, the way puzzles became easier once you had the edges laid out, but instead the project only grew larger and more complex. Archivists were supposed to keep to the collection's original order wherever possible, mimicking the creator's logic, but Theo's carelessness and Miranda's sloppiness made ascertaining an original order nearly impossible. There was no rhyme or reason, even within individual boxes. Almost everything was loose paper. Whenever she tried to ask Theo what he wanted, he just repeated what he had said that first day, "whatever seems logical," and left the room.

And then there was the collection's sheer *dirtiness*. The dust wedged into folds of paper, dried ink splattered on bank statements, old lozenges melted into their waxy wrappers. Mold crept over entire folders. Foxing, the red stains of age, spotted papers like chicken pox. Kate tried to approach the mess with clinical detachment, but that was easier said than done. Her legs started itching again. Nothing at the museum had ever been in such terrible condition. Several times she had to go out onto the back porch and stare out at the woods, the sun, just to get away from the room for a minute.

Out in the wild bright air, she would put her hands on the small of her back and visualize the finish line. The part where she had contained the mess. The clean room, the labeled boxes. The perfected state, when everything was fully under control and the auction house's truck would come and take it all away.

Of all the materials that had deteriorated through neglect, the photographs made Kate the saddest. Evaluating the photos was not officially in her purview—they would be sold individually, after being assessed and repaired by a team of conservationists at the auction house—but she did need to catalog them and transfer them to archival boxes for later transport. The percentage-based bonus was good motivation for doing this job well, and she followed conservation rules dutifully. Gloves on if she was handling photographs or negatives; tissue and foam layered delicately between each print. But many of the photographs were beyond saving. They were shoved in shirt boxes whose bottoms had gone black and ripe with mold. They were rotting, foxed, bleached partly pale. Dust was caked onto their satiny surfaces. Most prints from the Bottle Rocket series, which was well known and would have fetched a large amount at auction, had been housed together in a box that a mouse had nested in, and were now irretrievable.

"It's disgusting," she complained to her mother one night over the phone. She considered her parents and Natasha permanently exempted from the NDA. "Stuff is *everywhere*."

"I'm imagining an episode of *Hoarders*," Darcy said. "Oh, now I want to watch that."

"It's not quite that bad. There aren't bugs." Although actually just that day she had lifted a box and found an enormous millipede, each one of its many legs bristling and articulated. She had covered her mouth just before shrieking: she refused to give Theo the satisfaction of hearing her scream. "But think how much money they must have lost. Hundreds of thousands of dollars. Probably millions. How could they have just left it all sitting up here?"

"Not everyone is as neat as you," her mother said. "And besides. Maybe there were just too many memories."

Late on Friday afternoon, Kate was sitting cross-legged on the floor of the dining room, weeding her way through one of the boxes destroyed by mold and mice, when a small cough came from behind her. She turned and saw Oscar clutching the door frame.

"Hey, Oscar," she said, stretching her back. "What's up?"

"Want to see a mab?" he asked.

"A what?"

"A mab."

"I don't know what that is." Kate squinted at him. "You have something on your cheek."

He came forward for her to wipe it away. It was a long red streak. It looked like blood. Hiding her concern, she licked her thumb and rubbed the spot away. The skin beneath was intact, and the substance was sticky. Jam.

Oscar pushed his stomach out. "Come see."

"What?"

"The mab. Come see."

"Where is it?"

"Upstairs."

Kate glanced at the door. Theo might swoop through it at any moment. "I kind of have to stay here," she said. "Can you bring it down?"

He shook his head. "It's stuck."

"What do you mean, it's stuck?"

"Come see," he insisted. He was starting to sound agitated. His fingers knotted into his sleeves.

Jemima barreled through the door, nearly knocking her brother over.
"Don't steal it!" she told her brother. "It's *my* secret. I found it."

Oscar looked down and toed one tiny sneaker against the ugly carpet.

Jemima turned to Kate. "I found a secret," she declared.

"Where's your dad?" Kate asked.

"I dunno. Working?" Jemima jogged in place, fizzing with excitement. "Come on. Come see."

Kate considered. Theo was MIA. The kids were bored. *She* was bored, after picking through tollbooth receipts all day. And she did love secrets. Ferreting them out, dusting them off, seeing where they led. She remembered how bare the Murder Solvers thread had been, and she closed out of the finding-aid spreadsheet on her laptop and got to her feet.

Oscar and Jemima led her through the living room and up a narrow set of stairs. The rosebuds on the wallpaper puckered like a row of kisses. In the kitchen and bathroom, Kate had seen other signs of the house's age. Teal tiles, gold handles on drawers. The living room was painted mustard. Theo hadn't said anything about renovating the house before selling it, or about what he would do with all the furnishings, and Kate doubted buyers would like the house's current condition.

Oscar and Jemima led her around the second-floor landing and up the next flight of stairs. They had turned the bend in the staircase and almost reached the third floor when Oscar stopped and crouched down, so fast that Kate nearly tripped over him.

There was very little light in the narrow stairwell, and at first Kate thought there was a pattern along the molding—some kind of decorative stencil. Then her eyes adjusted to the shadows, and she saw that it was a long strip of pencil drawings, six or seven inches high, like an ancient Mesopotamian frieze.

"What . . . ?" She knelt down beside Oscar.

Some of the drawings were jagged enough that they could have been done by a child, but others were more detailed, certainly the work of an adult. Asterisks and lightning bolts, triangles and spiraling clouds. Over and over, a woman's face, roughly drawn, her eyes filled with two Xs and her hair pouring like serpents from her head. There were letters, too. MB, MB, MB, repeated again and again, over which Oscar's fingers hovered reverently.

"Mab," he pronounced.

"They're initials," Kate said automatically. "M.B."

A small, contented sigh. "Em-bee."

Jemima slithered up the stairs to sit next to Oscar. Her thin calves, covered in a fine layer of down, poked out from the hem of her sundress. She touched one of the faces, tracing her thumb over the line of the woman's neck, which terminated abruptly in a shimmering starburst of lead.

"I think she is sad," Jemima said.

Sad, yes. Frightened and frightening. *Secret*, the kids had said, and now Kate understood why. There was something private about the drawings. You could tell just by looking at them that they hadn't been made for anyone else's eyes. Her throat went tight. She was excited, she was astonished—

"What's going on?"

Theo. Kate jerked backward, hitting her head on the handrail. He was standing a few steps below them. Now that Kate heard how his voice sliced through the air, as sharp as it had been that first day out on the lawn, she realized that he had been softening toward her over the past week. It had been so gradual she hadn't noticed.

Sensitive to the undercurrent in his father's voice—treading it, without understanding where the waves had come from or why—Oscar gripped the back of her knee. Kate resisted the urge to reach down protectively. Whatever she thought of Theo, she shouldn't encourage his own kids to be afraid of him. But her own pulse was still racing.

"Who is she, Daddy?" Jemima asked. Either she didn't sense his anger or she didn't care. "Is she a ghost?"

"There's no such thing as ghosts," Theo said.

"I heard a ghost," Oscar said. "Last night. It was making weird noises. Like woo-oo-oo . . ."

Theo sighed. "That was the wind. It makes those noises when it goes through the trees."

Oscar looked unconvinced. "Never went woo before."

"Definitely a ghost," Jemima said, giggling. "Come to eat you!"

Theo was unimpressed. "Why are you up here? You know you're not supposed to be."

Jemima wiped the smile off her face and adjusted her posture to project innocence. She was clever. "You said we couldn't go *upstairs*," she said. "You never said not *up the stairs*."

Theo gave her a look. "Jemima. You knew what I meant."

"Oscar's little" was her second attempt. "He doesn't know what he's doing. And I was . . . helping him out."

The ploy was so transparent, Kate couldn't believe it would work. Theo was always telling Jemima to go easy on Oscar, and now she was reciting his own lines back at him. Her voice had even taken on a bit of his timbre. But after a moment, Theo sighed and dropped his shoulders.

"Downstairs, both of you," he ordered. "I don't want to see you up here again. You understand? It's *off-limits*."

Oscar needed no convincing. He wiggled around his father and began to bump carefully down the stairs on his butt. Jemima tagged along behind, whispering furiously into her brother's ear. Kate would have followed them, purely out of self-preservation, but she couldn't. Theo was standing right there. There was no room for her to pass.

Without saying a word, Theo came up the steps and knelt down to look at the drawings. He touched one, dragging his thumb down across the tail of a star. The graphite smudged ever so slightly. When he took his hand away, he rubbed his finger and thumb together until the pencil dust disappeared from his skin.

He was crouching in front of her; she could see his scalp glinting up from the part in his hair. The tendons in his back, the rise of a vertebra above the collar of his shirt. She averted her eyes.

He was quiet for a long time, and she hoped maybe he had forgotten she was there, but then he stood up, looming over her even though he was on a lower step.

"What are you doing up here?" he demanded. "I told the kids not to come up. There are chemicals . . . the darkroom. It's not safe."

She stilled. "Oscar and Jemima wanted to show me something. They insisted. I didn't know it was off-limits." She tried to say it evenly, but *off-limits* still came off with a sarcastic edge.

"It's private," he said. "As is the rest of the house."

"I'm not going to play around with any chemicals," Kate said, half-joking.

"It's not just the chemicals."

"Then what? You said you brought everything to the dining room." She gestured at the wall. "This counts as your mother's art, right? We could sell it with everything else."

"*I* could sell it with everything else," he said.

Kate's patience was wearing thin. The brusque tone had been annoying enough when she was skulking around the backyard and they hadn't yet met. Now she had been working in his home all week, playing the subservient employee and treating his parents' belongings like fine china. And she had only come up here because she was entertaining his children.

"You hired me to organize the collection," she said. "It makes my job harder when there are things missing. Her darkroom? Shouldn't I see that?"

He must have realized she had a point, because he didn't answer. The stairwell was so small that his breath rustled her hair. Awareness spiked through her limbs. She took that, along with his silence, as a sign she should leave.

She moved to slide past him. He put his fingers on her wrist, stopping her.

"I put everything relevant in the dining room," he said.

"You don't *know* what's relevant. That's why you hired me."

His fingers tightened around her wrist. Just a small twitch, probably instinctive. But enough to make Kate sweat.

"Don't come up here again," he murmured. "You understand?"

Like she was a child. Like she could be ordered around. The air shifted and heated. A strange itch began in her throat, like the beginning of a cough. She had a sudden desire to lean up to him and press her mouth to the small divot in his lower lip—an urge so unexpected and inappropriate that it only made her angrier.

"Yes," she said coldly. "I understand."

And with that, she wrenched her arm away and clattered down the stairs.

MIRANDA

SERIES 2, Personal papers
BOX 6, Falkman College, 1974–1978
FOLDER: Disciplinary records

Falkman College
Office for Student Affairs
Conduct and Decency Board

Internal Document
Copies furnished to named parties only, upon request:

Miranda Rose Planchart
Richard Cameron Rohber
A. F. Fitzhugh (faculty investigator)
Joseph Smith (faculty investigator)
Tina Fry (faculty investigator)

TRANSCRIPT OF MEDIATION
04/28/1977

FITZHUGH: I think it's working now. Hello, everyone. Thank you for joining us. This recording is for reference and information only. A tran-

script may be provided to you upon request. I will be leading today's inquiry along with my colleagues Professor Smith and Professor Fry. I can speak for all of us when I say that we were extremely disappointed to learn of this incident. The purpose of today's mediation is to settle upon a resolution that will enable everyone to move forward peacefully. Is that understood?

ROHBER: Yes.

FITZHUGH: Miss Planchart, please speak for the recording.

PLANCHART: Yes. I understand.

FITZHUGH: Wonderful. All right. The incident in question took place at the campus art gallery's spring opening. I have in front of me a statement by an anonymous student who says she first saw you two arguing in the main gallery. Miss Planchart, you apparently stormed out of the room and returned ten minutes later carrying a bucket of paint. You approached Professor Rohber's photograph *Lesson Repeated*, and—

ROHBER: *Lessons.*

FITZHUGH: I'm sorry?

ROHBER: *Lessons.* Plural. The photograph is entitled *Lessons Repeated.*

FITZHUGH: Okay. *Lessons Repeated.* Miss Planchart, you threw the bucket at the photograph, breaking the glass. The paint got on the photo and on several bystanders. The witness says a shard of flying glass almost hit her in the eye.

PLANCHART: That's a lie. There was no flying glass. He hadn't put any glass over the print.

FITZHUGH: If you could hold your rebuttal for a moment, I'm simply reading you the statement.

PLANCHART: And I'm saying the statement is wrong. No one got hurt. There was no glass. If there had been glass, I would have used something besides paint. Like the hatchet by the fire extinguisher. I thought about using that.

FITZHUGH: Miss Planchart . . . you're not helping your case.

FRY: Our point is, many staff and students were frightened.

ROHBER: And the print was ruined. Earlier that night, several friends of mine, very well connected in the art industry, had expressed interest in buying it. So we're also talking about a *significant* monetary loss.

FITZHUGH: Miss Planchart, would you like to explain your actions?

PLANCHART: *My* actions? What about *his* actions?

FITZHUGH: Professor Rohber didn't throw a can of paint at his photograph.

PLANCHART: It wasn't his photograph. It was mine.

SMITH: If I may interject . . . we've established that the image was Professor Rohber's. He showed us his negatives and the objects he used to stage it. We spoke with another faculty member and she has assured us that Professor Rohber took that image.

PLANCHART: Yeah, he took that particular shot. Whatever. But it wasn't his idea. It was my idea, and I was going to make it part of my senior project. I've been working on it for months.

SMITH: You had the idea to make an image of thirty-six remote controls laid out in a grid?

PLANCHART: Yes. It was one of my repeats.

SMITH: Repeats?

PLANCHART: That's what I call them. It's a series I was working on. Arranging a bunch of identical items. I did them with wooden toys, with copper pots, with dolls . . . I got all the objects from different places, and they all look the same at first, then you put them together and you can see the little differences. How they changed just by being used differently. Like on the remote controls, you can see the different buttons, how they're worn differently based on what channels people watch. But it's not just the content. The lighting, the layout, even the size and the processing technique . . . Did you look at the examples I brought over last week? You put them side by side, they're obviously the same.

FITZHUGH: Yes, yes, I saw them. Unfortunately, there's no indication that you actually began work on these before he did.

PLANCHART: I brought my notes . . .

FITZHUGH: There are no dates on the notes.

PLANCHART: So?

FITZHUGH: So we don't really have evidence to prove whether he copied you, or whether you copied him.

PLANCHART: Wait. Wait. You think *I* copied *him*?

ROHBER: If I may say something . . .

FITZHUGH: Please.

ROHBER: The word *copying* keeps coming up. And it seems to me that we are having a very interesting discussion about what an idea is, who can own an idea . . . Miranda's points about the similarities between our work resonate with the message of my photograph, which is about reproducibility, mechanical copies . . .

PLANCHART: So you're saying you *did* copy my photograph.

ROHBER: I'm saying if there are similarities, the similarities are a *statement*.

PLANCHART: Are you fucking serious?

SMITH: Professor Rohber has a point, Ms. Planchart. College is a time of mutual intellectual exchange. Even if he found inspiration in your work, and I do mean if, perhaps you should take it as an honor. Imitation is the highest form of praise.

PLANCHART: I should be *honored* he stole my idea and tried to sell it?

FITZHUGH: Let's backtrack. Miss Planchart, even if we were to grant that you created your photographs first, I'm failing to understand when you think that Professor Rohber would have stolen these ideas. He was on sabbatical last semester, when you claim you were working on this series, and he hasn't taught you since . . . [*papers shuffling*] your sophomore year spring? Is that correct?

PLANCHART: Yes.

FITZHUGH: So if you made these images last fall, as you claim, then how would he have seen them?

PLANCHART: Well, because we were fucking.

[*Commotion*]

FITZHUGH: I'm sorry—what did you say?

PLANCHART: Yeah. We fucked. A lot. We've been fucking ever since I took his class sophomore year. I used to give him blow jobs in the darkroom. He said that was the best way for me to advance my promising career.

ROHBER: Excuse me, I—

PLANCHART: You can ask Lynn. My best friend, Lynn Toby-Jarrett. She knows all about it.

FITZHUGH: Ms. Planchart, these are very inflammatory accusations.

PLANCHART: I thought the plagiarism thing was the inflammatory part.

FRY: Professor Rohber, are these claims true? I mean about the sexual intercourse.

[*Long silence*]

ROHBER: She's making it sound . . . Listen, she's manipulating you. *She se-duced me.*

PLANCHART: That's how he got my images. I gave him a folder to show to one of his contacts. He said he could try to get me into a gallery show in the city.

FITZHUGH: Let's focus on the other allegations for a moment—

PLANCHART: Some women's college this is. You care about protecting our bodies but not our minds. You take our ideas and pay us nothing. Put your name on our discoveries. You can see a man scoop a woman clean of creativity and you just shrug and change the channel. But our vaginas? Those better stay pristine.

FRY: Miss Planchart!

PLANCHART: Seeing that photograph up on the wall was one million times more painful than any time he shoved his dick inside me.

SMITH: Please. The inappropriate language needs to stop.

FITZHUGH: I agree with Professor Smith. We obviously need to investigate these allegations further, so for now we'll adjourn this meeting. We'll reconvene when we have more information. I'm turning off the tape recorder. Professor Rohber, if you could stay behind for a min—

4.

KATE

Kate had low expectations for the squat tan building with the broken plastic sign, but the name on it—Pawpaw's Drinking Hole & Entertainment—suggested it sold alcohol, which was all she really needed. Beer, and a few minutes to recalibrate. Frank and Louise would be home when she got back from work, and Louise would inevitably pepper her with questions about what she had done that day and how she was feeling. Kate would have to answer in a way that both discouraged further questions and satisfied Louise's curiosity enough that she didn't bombard Kate's mother with alarmist texts. It was a delicate balance—one that Kate, still shaken by Theo's veiled threat, wasn't yet ready to negotiate.

Inside, Pawpaw's was a charming dive, crammed with maritime decor and furnished in cracked black leather. A few frat bros sprawled across a booth beneath a string of sailing flags. At another table, an elderly woman was shredding the pith from her Blue Moon's orange slice into a frothy white pile. Kate's nose twitched against the smell of spilled beer and lemon cleaning solution. She took a seat at the bar, on a stool that wobbled when she shifted her weight, and ordered a draft beer at random. The bartender spun a paper coaster down onto the bar, then set the pint of beer on top of it.

Whatever it was tasted like heaven. Citrusy, malted. The world evened out a little. Kate set the pint down with a relieved sigh.

The bartender smiled. "Good, right?" He was compact and angular, in his mid-twenties, with a knit cap pulled down over his longish hair.

"Delicious," Kate said. "I haven't seen the brand before."

"It's local. They probably don't sell it out east."

She looked down at herself, trying to figure out what had given her away. "How do you know I'm from the East Coast?"

"You're Louise's niece, right?" He gestured to her face. "Family resemblance."

Right. The whole week, neighbors had been dropping by to meet Kate, oohing and ahhing when they saw her, like they had just completed a pilgrimage to some saint's relics. Kate was six inches taller than her aunt, with different hair and different eyes, so it hadn't occurred to her that they looked similar until everyone started commenting on it. The nose, apparently. The chin.

"Everyone knows your aunt," he said, almost apologetically.

Kate sighed. "She keeps introducing me to her friends. I think I've met more people in a week here than I met my whole time living in New York."

"Louise runs this town," he admitted. "But she's a kind and generous overlord. I'm Nikhil, by the way."

"Kate," she said. She reached across the bar to shake his hand. "Do you own this place?"

"Pawpaw's? No way. I'm just the bartender. Slash manager, slash toilet unclogger. The owners live in Oakland." He ran a rag over the counter. "How's working up at the big house?"

"Is that what people call it? It's not that big."

"I just assumed. There's that gate and everything. You didn't answer the question."

"About working there? I don't know. It's fine."

Nikhil swept a squeezed-out lime wedge into the trash. "Your dude's not very popular around town."

"My aunt said something about that." Kate tilted her head, considering him. If there was anyone who knew more town gossip than Louise, it would be the bartender. "She said there are rumors around here about how Miranda died. Have you ever heard anything like that?"

"Like what?"

"Like about it not being suicide."

"Oh, sure. Yeah, people talk about that shit all the time. Especially since they found out Theo was coming back."

"My uncle said some people think he killed her."

"People think a lot of stuff," Nikhil said. "They think he did it, they think her husband did it, they think some crazy cult from upstate did it as part of an initiation rite. I wouldn't stress too much. This town, they like to stir shit up. Especially the older crowd. They remember the town how it was back when, blah blah blah."

"It doesn't sound like you like this place much."

"Well, I like the surfing," he said. "And the people are mostly pretty nice. But I actually live over the hill, closer to Mill Valley. I need some distance."

"You still listen to the gossip, though."

"Of course I do." He grinned. "Job's biggest perk. Is there something in particular you want to know?"

Kate rested her cheek on her hand. "Did Miranda have any friends who are still around? I want to talk to someone who knew her when she lived here. Learn more about what she was like, where all these rumors started."

Nikhil thought for a minute. Then he said, "I know a couple years ago someone did a signing for some book about her. Afterward, a bunch of people came here to drink. They were all from some art gallery. Basically a silver fox convention. Some guy got up and gave a toast all about the honor of creating art with her. That's the guy you should find. Although all I can tell you about him is he ordered a bunch of cosmopolitans and was wearing a yellow plaid suit."

"Good memory," Kate said.

"It was a sick suit." He took her glass, now empty. "You want another?"

"Sure. Thanks."

He went over to pull the draft. A ring of condensation widened on the coaster, warping the surface. Kate imagined some poor archivist someday popping the wrinkled cardboard into an envelope. Evidence of—what?

That she had been here. That she drank beer. Other truths, ones she didn't even know she had told, carried in this tiny paper nothing.

Later that night, while Frank and Louise rewatched the episode of *Madam Secretary* they had fallen asleep in front of the night before, Kate tried to find a listing for the book event online, to no avail. Callinas's web presence needed some work. There wasn't even a Chamber of Commerce page.

Thinking about the guy at the book signing Nikhil had mentioned, she double-checked to see if Miranda had collaborated with any male artists. No record of that either. In fact, most art critics said Miranda had maintained near-obsessive control over her pieces, from using cable releases to take her self-portraits, to developing all of the film on her own. She had never had so much as a darkroom apprentice.

The next morning, as she and Louise walked back from the farmer's market, Kate detoured them into the pay-what-you-want used bookstore off the main drag. Tucked in the Local section, among the bird-watching leaflets and battered Bay Area guidebooks from the '80s, was a thick catalog entitled *Miranda Brand: The Complete Works*. This copy had a gold SIGNED sticker on the spine and an inscription inside that read:

> To Delia—
> With thanks for your CONTINUED SUPPORT
> of TRUE BEAUTY!
> xoxo Hal
> 11/2013

Hal Eggers: Miranda's dealer. He was one of the few people who already had their own correspondence subsection in the finding aid. *Creating art with her* seemed like a bit of an embellishment, but then again, Kate didn't really know what a dealer's job entailed.

She balanced the book on her hip and pulled out her phone. Two pages into an image search for Hal's name, she found a Getty Images photo of a balding man at an art gala in a bespoke yellow plaid suit.

Bingo.

Leafing through the catalog, Kate saw that Hal and Jake Brand had co-written the introduction. The pages were filled with reproductions and essays from critics, and at the end there was an index that listed all of Miranda's known photos. There was a flyer pressed into the book flap:

November 3, 2013

EGGERS GALLERY

celebrates the reprint of

Miranda Brand: The Complete Works

with a special reception

for honored guests

Keynote by:

Hal Eggers

Owner, Eggers Gallery

On the front of the catalog was a photo of Miranda, a black-and-white self-portrait she had done in her late twenties. Angelic face, spill of dark hair. In it, Miranda was wearing a mock turtleneck that sliced her neck in half, and her eyes were huge and dark, looking in the direction of the camera but focused on some point just beyond it.

Kate had seen the photo many times in the past few weeks; it was one of the main image results when you searched Miranda's name online. But this version seemed off somehow. After a moment, she realized what the problem was: in the original photo, Miranda's pupils were dotted with triangles of light, reflections from an unseen window. On the book Kate held, someone had taken a permanent marker and colored over the center of each eye until they looked like paper cutouts. Vacant, dead.

The censored eyes, right under the words *Complete Works*, gave Kate the creeps. But it was the only copy, so she put ten dollars into the tin bucket by the door and slid the book into her shopping tote, next to the arugula.

On their way home, Louise pointed out a shop called Callinas Crystals. Its entrance fluttered with peace flags and hanging planters.

"That's Esme's store," Louise said. "Come on, let's see if she's in. She's a hoot."

That piqued Kate's curiosity. "A hoot" was the same phrase her father sometimes used to describe Louise.

The shop was overly warm, the air thick with incense and the tinny strums of a sitar recording. The shelves were laden with glittering geodes the size of flour bags, tarot decks, and hunks of purple calcite. Although it was filled to the brim, everything seemed meticulously arranged. Kate wasn't generally into the whole concept of the occult. Last year, during a friend's bachelorette, she had gotten her palm read at a basement shop on St. Mark's. The psychic had predicted she would find romance at work. All the Leonard shit had already started to hit the fan, so Kate had yanked her hand away and stormed out.

The cash register at Callinas Crystals was staffed by a man whose skin was so cracked from the sun that he could have been anywhere between fifty and eighty. Bedraggled fringe dangled from the bottom of his leather vest, and his graying dreadlocks were pulled back into a bun.

Esme wasn't there, he told Louise, not sounding very apologetic. Did they want to leave a message?

Louise hemmed and hawed for a minute. Kate had no idea what message she could possibly be thinking of leaving. *Hi Esme, stopped by to show off how weird you are, went home, see you soon, love, Louise*?

Louise must have come to the same conclusion, because she finally declined. Then she said with a Vanna White flourish, "Oh! This is my niece, Kate. Kate, Kid Wormshaw."

"Nice to meet you," Kid said without looking at her. The lines around his mouth were as deep as canyons.

"You, too." Kate set the tote down on the floor and ran her fingers over a pile of black crystals. Tourmaline, the sign said. Good for warding off black magic.

"Kid knew Miranda Brand," Louise told Kate. "He was friends with her—isn't that right?"

He paused. "Right."

Kate raised her eyebrows. "I think you're the first person I've met who was actually friends with her."

"She wasn't much of a people person," Louise said.

Kid grunted in disagreement—or maybe agreement? His face seemed permanently locked in a frown, which made it hard to tell—and started poking around the stick of credit card receipts next to the register. Kate took a step forward and rested her fingertips on the glass counter.

"I'm working up at her house," she said. "Going through her files."

"I heard," he said.

"There's a lot to weed through."

"I bet."

"Remember you signed a nondisclosure agreement," Louise told Kate.

Kate forced a smile. "Thanks, Louise."

Either Louise heard the annoyance in her voice or, more likely, she was distracted by a shiny object, because she drifted away toward the shelves in the back of the shop. Kate barely stopped herself from rolling her eyes. Sometimes her aunt was like a dog with a bone, and other times she had the shortest attention span Kate had ever seen.

When Kate didn't follow her aunt, Kid looked around the store pointedly, as if some other customers might be lurking somewhere. Finding it empty, he asked Kate tersely, "Something you need help with?"

"There's a lot of stuff up there," she said again. "A lot of names, place names, I haven't heard of. I got this book about her"—she gestured to the bag—"but . . . it would be really helpful if there were someone who knows her, someone who can identify some of the names for me."

Kid crossed his arms over his chest. His forearms were iridescent with dehydration, dotted with hematomas. The woven bracelets that encircled his wrists were baggy, like he had recently lost a lot of weight. "Can't her son help you?"

"He was just a kid. He wouldn't have known her business associates."

He snorted. "Whatever you say."

"What's that supposed to mean?"

Kid looked her up and down. When he met her eyes again, his face was sealed shut.

"Listen," he said. His voice was hard and deep, like a hammer striking a barrel. "You just got to town. You're new. But you don't know what you're getting yourself into. If I were you, I'd put your head down, do your job however you need to do it, and get the hell out of Callinas."

Kate let out a shocked, nervous laugh. Kid's lecture plus Theo's warning yesterday made two pseudo-threats in less than twenty-four hours. The last time she had encountered this level of animosity in a source, she was fact-checking a story about a sex scandal that had ultimately gotten a senator thrown out of office.

"If you say so," she said.

Louise came over to the counter, holding one of the salt lamps aloft in triumph. "For Frank's study," she explained.

Kate took a step back to let Kid ring up the purchase. He put the lamp in a box and the box in a bag and tied the bag with a straw bow. He ignored Kate completely. As it went on and on—he was slow with the register, jabbing the touchscreen with one crooked finger—an electric feeling began to web out over Kate's shoulders.

Summers when she was a kid, her grandfather in Pennsylvania would take her out trawling on Lake Erie in his old speedboat. Her favorite job was dropping the anchor. The clunk when it hit solid ground. One time, the anchor went its whole length without ever catching. They must have been floating over some crevasse in the lake bed, her grandfather explained as he helped her haul up the chain. The soil might be a few more inches down, or a few miles.

That was how Kate felt now. Like she had cast down a line and found that she could not reach the bottom.

There was more to find.

A few months before, she had thought her journalistic instinct was dead forever, killed off by medication and exhaustion and unemployment and powerlessness. But now, as they said goodbye to Kid and left the shop, the old thrill bundled in her blood. She had forgotten how much she loved it: the glorious chase. The rush so bright it drowned out the rattle in the track. However deep this water was, whatever was down there, she was going in.

MIRANDA

SERIES 1, Correspondence

BOX 1, Personal correspondence

FOLDER: Toby-Jarrett, Lynn (incl. 12 photocopies of letters from MB, from LTJ private collection)

February 4 1979

Dear Lynn,

Thanks for the birthday card! Sending you back a very belated hi from New York.

I never really understood this city before. There are worlds within worlds here. It's the only place I've ever lived where I feel like I need to expand to fit it, instead of the other way around.

The art community is radical. Performance artists, installation artists, other photographers, some painters . . . It's not just the city that's big. The art is big too. Electronic billboards in Times Square. Dramatic cartwheeling dances. Life-size drawings you would mistake for real people. Everything is huge, bright, intense. Everyone produces so much, so fast. You go out to a club and get as much dope as you want and then you go home and make things. It's a frenzy. I love it. This lustrous city. It's like being in the middle of an exploding star.

How is NM? And your special rocks? I've never been west of the Mississippi. I'm imagining it hot, with rattlesnakes, and you running around in your dorky khaki outfit. I miss you. It's strange to never see you. I hope you don't take it personally when I say it feels like you've died.

    M

2/21/1979

Dear Miranda,

    It's winter, you dork, so no it's not very hot right now. And yes I wear my "khaki outfit" but it's NOT embarrassing, thank you very much, it's FOR SCIENCE.

    Yes there are rattlesnakes. Saw two huge ones mating yesterday on my morning run. I stood there watching them for a long time, the way their scales shone in that weird morning darkness, and thinking how if they hadn't been fucking they'd have wanted to kill me.

    The city sounds amazing. Glad you're so in the middle of it all. It's lonely out here. The only other people I really see are the other team members. This month it's all men, mostly named Mike. Vomit. Sometimes they have literal pissing contests—seeing who can piss farther in the sand. In other words, this might be the last letter you ever get from me. I might gouge out my eyes with my camping spoon before the month is over. But then how will I read your reply??

    Lynn

June 14 1979

Dear Lynn,

    OK, I'm a bad pen pal. My schedule here is crazy since I got a job waitressing. Usually I'm at the restaurant until ten, end up too wired to sleep so I go out for a couple hours, get home and crash, then wake up early the next morning to take photos until I go back on shift at two.

    I'm exhausted. The other day I tried to take my day's tips out of the register and I accidentally took twenties instead of ones. The manager almost fired me for stealing. Which made me think maybe I should steal after all. My tips aren't going to get bigger on their own, and the cops here have better things to do than chase down a diner waitress.

Anyway . . .

Don't gouge your eyes out until you

    A) look in a mirror while wearing the khaki outfit so you can finally admit I am right

    B) discover a new rock and get it named after you

    C) see my latest work.

C is important because I'm making BIG PROGRESS here. I'm in the middle of a new series. Photographing empty spaces with little slivers of women at the edges of the frame. And I have an idea for another series—still working out the details—but the key element is blood. So I've been experimenting with various forms of fake blood, going to all the costume shops in lower Manhattan to get all the different brands. I have to get the texture right, make it shine right in the photo.

    Give my love to the rattlesnakes. Honestly, they probably liked that you were watching.

    M

SERIES 1, Correspondence

BOX 1, Personal correspondence

FOLDER: Brand, Jake (Downtown Studios notes)

Miranda Planchart
Mailbox 19

Miranda,

    Will you go out with me? Check one.

    __ Yes

    __ No

    Jake Brand (Mailbox 4)

Jake Brand
Mailbox 4

September 27 1980

Jake Brand,

I didn't know they rented space to 12-year-olds.

What a rad enrichment program!

Stay in school.

Miranda

P.S. I assume that since you have a mailbox here, you're an artist of some kind. Sadly, I have a strict policy against dating other artists.

P.P.S. Who are you? And how do you know who I am?

Miranda Planchart
Mailbox 19

How do I know who you are? You are the great Miranda Planchart! The vision, the visionary! The household name!

Someday, I trust.

Actually I'm friends with Jimmy. That's why I doubt this claim that you don't date other artists. Poor Jimmy IS an artist, Miranda, even if the miniature-houses-for-mice market is slow at the moment.

I won't tell him what you're implying about his work . . . if you go out with me.

J

Jake Brand
Mailbox 4

September 29 1980

Jimmy and I didn't date. Jimmy and I fucked.

Do you want to fuck or do you want to date?

M

Miranda Planchart
Mailbox 19

Are they mutually exclusive?

I guess I would be happy with either but I would prefer BOTH.

A little about me to help you make up your mind.

1) I'm a painter. I've been renting space here for two years. Before that I was in Italy doing an apprenticeship.

2) I won the Gramercy Award last year.

3) I'm from Buffalo originally. I dream of living somewhere without winter.

4) I smoke too. That's how I first noticed you. My studio has a WINDOW (not to brag) and I saw you smoking outside. You smoke well. Neat little streams out the side of your mouth. You have a good mouth.

Tell me something about yourself.

If you want.

Either way, I still want to take you out.

J

Jake Brand
Mailbox 4

October 2 1980

Jake—

Wow! Now that I know you've been to ITALY and won an AWARD, yes, I would love to go out with you!

Here's something about me. Something real.

I have a brother. His name is Simon. We aren't close but we used to be. When we were growing up, I followed him everywhere.

Then puberty got in the way. I got chubby, awkward. Simon went to high school. Suddenly he was embarrassed to be seen with me. He put a Do Not Disturb sign on his door.

But I took care of it, Jake. That's important to know about me. I take care of things.

The only time I was guaranteed to see Simon was when he walked me home from school. A girl had been abducted that year from one town over, so my parents insisted. Every day, he came over from the high school and waited for me outside the junior high. 3:15 on the dot.

One day after school let out, I hid in the school bathroom, crouching on the back of a toilet until everyone was gone. 3:45, 4. I thought about that abducted girl. Her face had been shown so many times on the news it felt almost like I had known her. I pictured her in the gully where she had been found two weeks after going missing. Wet leaves spidering over her face. Her limbs rigid and smooth as starched silk.

No one remembered her name. We only remembered her as a warning. A worst thing.

I climbed down off the toilet and put on my parka. I walked home slowly. Waiting for the right moment. Three blocks from our house, a car came up behind me. Engine buzzing over the hill. A red Chevy, dented bumper but sparkling paint. When it got close to me, too close to swerve, I stepped in front of it.

I knew I wouldn't die. The speed limit on that street was low, and I had waited for the right car. I just wanted to get a little hurt. Enough so my parents would blame Simon.

I said he hadn't been there waiting for me, so I decided to walk home myself. Of course my parents believed me. Why would I lie? I had a concussion and a leg fracture. No one would do that to themselves on purpose.

He was grounded for two months. And the only person in our house for him to hang out with was me.

So that's who I am.

    You still want to take me out?

    M

Miranda Planchart
Mailbox 19

More than ever.

    Some friends are hosting an installation in a warehouse Saturday night.

Come with me, let me introduce you around. If you don't have fun, you can throw me in front of a car afterward.

J

Jake Brand
Mailbox 4

October 4 1980

Now there's an offer I can't refuse.
    OK for Saturday.
    Meet you in the lobby at 9.
    Check before you cross the street.
    Just in case.
    M

SERIES 1, Correspondence

BOX 1, Personal correspondence

FOLDER: Toby-Jarrett, Lynn (incl. 12 photocopies of letters from MB, from LTJ private collection)

December 21 1980

Lynn,

SO glad one of the Mikes is gone and you finally have another woman at the station. Can you have menstruating contests as retaliation against the remaining assholes? I can always send you my fake blood recommendations. (Turns out the best one is a do-it-yourself. Strawberry Jell-O + Hershey's syrup + powdered sugar . . . It has the right look, a little plasticky.)

Two important men in my life now:

1) An art dealer, Hal Eggers. He works at a good gallery and he's putting a couple of my prints in his next show. Depending on the reception maybe he'd take more for the gallery, or even represent me exclusively. It would be a big break. Not to jinx it.

2) This guy Jake Brand. What a name, right? I wish my last name were something powerful like that. BRAND. Planchart sounds like a kind of wart remover. Anyway, Jake Brand and I are sleeping together. He's a painter. I know, I'm breaking the Richard Rule. But he understands me in this insane way. He's a magnet and I'm a steel filing. He just draws me in close.

In other words, it's been a good year. Sometimes as I'm walking around at night, an immense NOW fills up my chest so full I think I might die of knowing. I look up at the skyscrapers with their lit-up squares of people still working, and down at the candy wrappers spangling the gutters, and around at the people, all the people, and I want to take them all with me, press them into my pockets and bury them in my hair, hold them in my fist as I fly.

M

SERIES 1, Correspondence
BOX 1, Personal correspondence
FOLDER: Brand, Jake (Downtown Studios notes)

Miranda Planchart
Mailbox 19

September 2 1981

Miranda:
  Will you marry me?
  Check one.
  __ Yes
  __ No

Jake Brand
Mailbox 4

September 3 1981

Jake—
  Depends. Are you OK with being a dad in about six months?
  Check one.
  __ Yes
  __ No

5.

KATE

S o romantic," Natasha said. "You can actually *see* them falling in love, on paper. That never happens anymore."

It was Sunday morning and they were FaceTiming. Natasha was stretched out on the sofa in Liam's apartment, and Kate was lying on her bed in Frank and Louise's spare room, Olive dozing beside her. Kate had propped the phone up against the dog's ribs, which meant the screen swayed gently forward and back with Olive's every exhalation. Kate was updating Natasha on work, but Natasha had passed right over the Theo and Kid drama and latched on to some of the early letters Kate had found between Jake and Miranda.

"I'm sure you could go back and find your and Liam's first Tinder conversation," Kate said.

Natasha made a face. "It would probably make me fall *out* of love with him. '*U up?*'"

Olive let out a snuffling snore, and the phone toppled over. Kate righted it and said, "What about the Kid guy?"

"Didn't you say he was old? He probably doesn't even know what Tinder is."

"No, I mean what do you think about how he acted?"

"Um," Natasha said, "I think he sounds like a grouchy old man. And Wormshaw sounds like a fake last name."

"Louise says he's been here since the seventies, and his property is probably worth three million now. But instead of selling it, he's working as a clerk in a magic store."

Natasha rolled over and hung off the sofa, taking the phone with her so that she looked upright in the frame, but the beads on her braids clicked against the floor. "So he has an emotional attachment to his house. Very suspicious."

"I just think his reaction plus the Theo thing is bizarre." Kate propped her chin on her hand. "I want to go up to the Brands' attic. See what's up there."

"What? No."

"Why not?"

"Well, because your boss told you not to."

"I want to know what he's hiding."

"He's probably not *hiding* anything. He's probably just really private."

"He's definitely really private. But there's more than that. His tone was . . . way too much. Scary."

A pause, as if the connection had frozen. Then the screen became a blur of movement as Natasha sat up.

"What do you mean, scary?"

Lawyer voice. Kate immediately realized her mistake. If they had been talking in person, she would have turned away for a second to regroup. What was the digital equivalent? Faking a dropped connection? Too obvious, and too late. Natasha had shifted into concerned mode, ready to test Kate's every word for signs of untruthfulness.

"Not *scary* scary." Kate felt herself slowing down, checking her answers before she said them aloud. "I was exaggerating."

"Are you saying you feel like you're in danger?"

"No. I'm talking about what happened a long time ago. To Miranda."

"You really think your boss shot his mom?"

"No. I don't know." She needed to downplay it. "Anyway, he was eleven."

"Eleven is old enough."

"Old enough for what? Killing her, or hiding it?"

"Both, I guess," Natasha said.

Kate had wanted to talk about the Brands, but not like this, with every question underlaid with concern about her well-being. Hoping to distract Natasha, she slid Miranda's catalog out from under Olive's prone body and began flipping through the pages. "Well, maybe. It's one possible explanation."

"What else is going on?" Natasha pressed. "The town, what's it like?"

"Quiet. Pretty. No subway delays. I already told you the interesting stuff."

"A whole town and there's nothing else interesting?"

"They host a fly fishing tournament in the spring."

Before Natasha could ask anything else, there was the sound of a door closing in the background, and a voice calling out. Natasha raised her hand to wave at someone off-screen. "That's Liam. I should probably go—we're supposed to meet up with Andrew and Susanna for lunch."

"Wait! How are you? How's work?"

"Work?" Natasha squinted at the phone. Only one of her eyes was visible now. "Work sucks, as usual."

"You said they were going to announce the senior partners this week."

"Yeah, and nothing for me. Of course." Natasha exhaled. "I have to find a new job. But I don't know when I'm supposed to look. It's the weekend and I've been working since six a.m. on a stupid deliverable that a paralegal should be doing."

Natasha had been at her law firm for five years. She had been promoted once, quickly, then nothing at all, while less talented white male colleagues leapfrogged ahead of her. For years, she had put in eighty hours a week, slept on the sofa in the women's room, spent so much time on one case that she developed stress-induced blindness. Clients loved her, she brought in business, she had even published an article on securities law for a prestigious law review, yet still no promotion. The justifications were always circumstantial and vaguely backhanded—*limited hiring lines, we want you client-facing, we want to make sure your promotion case is flawless.*

"They want to be able to say they have a black woman as a junior partner so they can get their diversity points, but they don't actually care about promoting me any higher," Natasha said. "They made Dickie a senior partner. *Dickie.* It's 2017 and this asshole is going by *Dickie.*"

"Dickie's the worst," Kate said. "I hate Dickie."

"Everyone hates Dickie. Dickie's wife hates Dickie. Dickie's parents obviously hate Dickie—they named him Dickie. But Dickie is now making a hundred grand more a year than I am, so I guess he's doing okay."

"Let me know if I can do anything to help with job applications. Not that I'm some amazing example of employment."

"You are now!" Natasha said brightly. "You're super employed. Okay, okay, I have to go. Hang in there, okay?"

"You, too." Kate waved at the camera.

"And Kate?" Natasha's other eye came back onto the screen.

"Yeah?"

"Don't go in the attic."

"Have fun at lunch," Kate said.

Oscar and Jemima started camp on Monday. If Kate had never been in the house with them in it, maybe the silence in their absence wouldn't have been so noticeable. As it was, every sound seemed magnified. The settling of the house. The wind outside. She had barely seen Theo since he let her in that morning. Only intermittent bursts of footsteps upstairs told her he was still in the house. She tried turning on music, and it helped a little, but mostly she could still hear the silence sitting awkwardly beneath the sound. When she pulled Miranda's catalog out of her tote bag in the afternoon and opened it, the spine cracked the air like a gunshot.

After talking to Natasha, Kate had spent a little time looking through the book. It was much more detailed than anything she had found online. There was even an index of all of Miranda's known work—an incredible asset, since the dining room boxes were full of photos that Kate didn't recognize.

The editor had arranged the catalog thematically, not chronologically, so it began with one of Miranda's last series, a set of nature photographs called Cruel Mother. As the title suggested, the images were bleak. Leaves that curved sensuously inward only to twist off in a tear. Violent clouds. A coyote feasting on a fallen bird. Then came a chapter on her self-portraits, which spanned a fifteen- or twenty-year range from Miranda's younger days (uncombed hair, baby fat) to her older (cool gaze, no makeup).

The next sections were on Inside Me, Miranda's self-mutilation series. She had slashed different parts of her body and photographed them up close. A hand, sliced open. The inside of a knee, blood pooling from a horizontal slit. An ear with blood pouring out of the canal, over a diamond earring. The gristle and fat and bone of her, torn open into elegant flicks and syrupy drips. Apparently, there was a great deal of scholarly debate about whether Miranda had really cut into her skin or had staged the photographs with makeup. You could see in a later self-portrait, *Found You*, that Miranda had a long scar on her forearm in the same place where *Inside Me #1* showed a cut—but the scar itself could have been makeup.

Brand never revealed the story of the photographs' creation, one critic wrote. *As a result, the viewer remains suspended in the mystery of whether Brand used a knife or a strip of putty to mar her body. The unknowable nature of harm is a persistent theme in her work, in which women resist easy interpretation.*

Inspecting the reproduction of *Found You*, Kate didn't see any indication the scar was fake, or see any reason for Miranda to have faked it. It wasn't even a focal point of the image. But the critic was a man, of course, and men never liked to see a woman permanently marked. Kate herself had a bad burn across her stomach, from a cooking oil accident when she was a child. It had healed badly, and the skin was swollen rigid, purple and white. An ex-boyfriend had dragged his fingers across it pityingly. *You poor thing.* But Kate barely remembered her body without it.

She turned the page roughly to the catalog's next chapter. This one was about *The Threshold*, a self-portrait in which Miranda was standing in a doorway in a floral minidress. Her legs were slim and dimpled, her breasts high, her face terrified. She had lifted her knee as if to step over the jamb, and the photo caught her there, in that perfect moment before she stepped, her bare foot hovering inches above the threshold. Down one leg, out from under the hem of the minidress, snaked a long trail of blood.

The Threshold was Miranda's most famous photograph. The catalog said that in 2005, one copy had sold for $650,000 at auction. Kate had found a signed miniature print of the image the previous week. If that one sold for as much as the one in 2005, her bonus would net her $3,250. All that, for just one photograph. The thought made her dizzy, and she scrambled to her feet, suddenly needing air.

Her knees cracked as she stood: she had been sitting for much longer than she realized. Looking down at the catalog from this higher vantage point, something about the image on the page jogged her memory. She picked up the catalog, carried it into the foyer, and held it up to compare. Yes—it was definitely the same doorway. *The Threshold* had been taken right here, between the foyer and the hallway, in the same door Kate passed through every day.

She knelt down to inspect the floor where Miranda would have stood for the photo. There it was. A brownish stain in the wood grain, right below where Miranda's foot would have been in the photograph. The stain looked like blood.

Footsteps coming down the stairs. Kate slammed the book shut. She must have successfully scrubbed her face of any guilt, because when Theo came into the foyer and saw her, he just said, "Huh," and sat down on the entryway bench to put on his shoes.

"Where are you going?" she asked.

"To pick up the kids."

Kate checked her watch discreetly. It was 2:45. "Where's their camp?"

"Stinson. It's run out of a surf shop there. But they spend most of the day going on excursions, looking at wildlife and stuff. It's a nature camp."

It was more words than she had heard out of him all day, and she blinked down at him. When he looked up at her, his handsomeness surprising her all over again, some unreadable emotion skittered across his face. Maybe he regretted his outburst in the stairwell after all.

She folded the book into her chest and crossed her arms over it.

"I wanted to ask you a question about categories," she said. "Do you want correspondence between your mom and dad grouped together, or separate?"

"What's the difference?"

"Well, your mom and your dad will have different correspondence series that go in different boxes. If I split them up, for example, and put all Miranda's letters to Jake in with Jake's stuff and Jake's letters to Miranda in with Miranda's, it would be more consistent with the rest of the system, but harder for people to see the whole back-and-forth."

"What kind of back-and-forth?"

"I found some notes from when they were in New York together. When they had just met. They're kind of cute, actually. Do you want to see them?"

His forehead creased, and he bent over his shoes again, so that she couldn't see his expression. "No."

"I don't mean right now." She had intended the letters as an olive branch, and his dismissal rankled. She let her arms fall to her sides. "I meant later. Or anytime."

"Maybe." He finished tying his shoes, stood up. "I better get going."

When the front door clicked shut behind him, Kate tapped the catalog against the outside of her thigh. Rude or not, he had unwittingly solved one of her problems. It would take him at least fifteen minutes to get to Stinson and fifteen more to get back again. That meant she would have a solid half-hour chunk alone in the house every day. Plenty of time to get up to the attic.

It was Thursday when Kate finally felt confident enough about Theo's schedule to put her plan into action. When she reached the top of the stairs, half-hoping to find some cramped Gothic oubliette of a space, she discovered instead a vast, sunny room that spanned the entire length of the house. Light streamed from garret windows onto oak beams and honey-colored walls. Like the blacked-out pupils of Miranda's eyes on the catalog cover, the room seemed strangely flat: every surface wore a furry coat of dust, which turned the light milky and dense. There were a few scuffled lines of footprints, presumably Theo's, and although Kate tried to stay on these tracks, her first step forward sent up a billow of dust that drifted through the sunbeams.

The north end of the room was almost empty. Wood plinths and wide rolls of fabric indicated the rudiments of unmade canvases, but there were no finished paintings. Kate paused, realizing now that she hadn't seen any of Jake's paintings downstairs, either. He had taken all his own work even as he had left behind all his wife's.

The scale of the waste struck Kate anew. Okay, so Jake hadn't been able to bring himself to move Miranda's photos in the immediate wake of her death. *Too many memories*, like Kate's mother had said. But he could have come back any time in the last twenty-four years—a year after Miranda's death, two years, five—and saved so many pictures. Instead he had let them decay. He had set up a new life miles away and continued selling his paintings, all while his wife's legacy rotted in the house they had once shared. And now he was dead, too, his intentions gone with him, and there was no knowing whether he had left Miranda's work behind out of too little love or too much.

Kate turned to the other half of the room. Two drafting tables held piles of small objects that were nearly unidentifiable beneath the thick layer of dust. Kate thought she saw film canisters, a cutting mat, a box cutter. The surfaces looked like topographic models of an island chain, bumpy and un-recognizable. Behind the tables was a door with a low, brocade-upholstered sofa next to it. The center of one cushion had split open, and foam extruded from the rupture. Chew marks around the edges, small dark droppings: the telltale signs of rodents nesting. There was a sour smell coming from that general area, like a small animal had died in the wall a long time ago.

Looking around at the untouched room, Kate was suddenly, horribly aware of her own aliveness, her beating heart and her recently showered skin starting to perspire in the stuffy air, and the awareness made her feel sick. Like she had passed over a patch of ice on a highway without incident, only to see in her rearview mirror the car behind her spin out and tumble over a cliff.

She steeled herself and walked over to the door beside the sofa. Like many doors in the house, it required some physical effort to open; the house's sinking and shifting over the years had warped the frame just past the point of functionality. When Kate finally wrenched the door open, she was briefly confused: instead of a room, she saw only a solid black rect-angle, like one of those inky holes Bugs Bunny moved around to thwart the

Roadrunner. She reached out to touch it, and her hand met heavy velvet. It was just a curtain. Feeling stupid, she pushed through the curtain into darkness and fumbled for a light switch on the other side. Two safelights came on, bathing the room in red.

To Kate's surprise, the darkroom was neatly organized, with equipment stacked on metal utility shelves and a long stainless-steel table in the middle of the room. The precautions that had kept the light out had also kept the dust at bay, so that there was only a thin film of disuse. The air had the faint, sterilized tang of a swimming pool locker room. The safelights were hung on cords from the ceiling, and everything above them was a black void, giving Kate the peculiar feeling of having stepped onto a TV soundstage.

She moved slowly around the room, inspecting its contents. Supplier's bottles of undiluted chemicals, funnels, thermometers, glass sheets. One box spat out a crumpled rubber glove, half-dragged from the plastic opening when the previous one had been removed. There was an array of devices that looked like the microscopes Kate remembered from her high school science classes, rows of plastic tubs, and shelves filled with jugs of liquid hand-labeled DEV, STOP, and FIX, in what Kate already recognized as Miranda's handwriting. On one wall were two large sinks, their faucets fogged with cobwebs, and beside them a device like a fax machine and several long ropes peppered with clothespins. A few small prints dangled from these—still drying, after all these years. The place looked the same as it must have looked back in 1993. It was like Miranda had just this morning pinned up her prints and then gone outside to die.

Kate studied the photos on the clothesline. They were black-and-white pictures of a child. He was wearing a dark polo shirt and dark pants and stood against a blank wall, and the contrast between his clothing and the white wall made him look both dangerous and vulnerable. In one photo, he had shoved his hands in his pockets and was looking away, his face in profile, his chin jutted forward stubbornly. In the next, he had looked back at the camera and pouted his lower lip, like a miniature James Dean. The edges of his limbs were spookily blurred—Kate couldn't tell whether that was time or artistry—but his eyes were in focus. In the last photo, he was still looking at the camera. His head was tilted slightly to the side, his hand up and slashing across his throat in a blur. His elbow stuck out like a knife. The universal gesture for *Cut it*. Or—*You're dead*. What a weird hand signal for a child to make. Had he chosen it, or had Miranda told him how to pose?

The boy was Theo, of course. But it was hard to recognize him. He was still a few years short of puberty in these photos, and he had a child's shallow, unformed nose, and his body was spindly and small. Kate had to squint to see the nascent jawline, the early signs of a level brow. She got closer to the photo, trying to make out the expression in his eyes. There was something angry there . . . Then she caught herself. His eyes were just flecks of light in a photo. Staged by Miranda, framed by Miranda, developed by Miranda. His eyes only showed what Miranda wanted them to show. All that these photos proved was how young Theo had been when his mother died. Even if he *had* somehow accidentally shot her, he wouldn't have been able to cover it up. He would have been soaked with blood, traumatized, insensate.

Ignoring a twinge of guilt, Kate ducked under the clothesline and went over to the drying rack in the corner. All the trays were empty except one. She tried to pull out the drawer, but the roller mechanism had rusted, so she wiggled her fingers through the bars of the tray, gently gripped the very edge of the print, and pulled it to her, trying not to imagine how her boss at the museum would have shrieked. She wasn't even wearing gloves.

This photograph had obviously been taken at the same time as the ones hanging from the clothesline. Theo was in it, same outfit, same background, but Miranda was there, too. She leaned down over him, crossing her arms across his chest in a pale X, her mouth cut open in a smile. Theo's head was tilted back, up toward her, his young throat exposed as he laughed.

In all the self-portraits in the catalog, in the prints downstairs, Kate had never seen a photo of Miranda truly happy. Smiling like this, she looked so young. Her face was unlined, her skin glowing. It seemed inconceivable that she could have made this image and then taken her own life. That she could have appeared this joyful and also wanted to die.

Thirty-seven years old. Not much older than Kate.

Suddenly Kate felt a pressure behind her eyes. The photo trembled: her hands were shaking. She slid the photograph back into the rack and knotted her fingers together to hold them steady. It hadn't been so long ago that she herself had lain in her bed, watching the city through her room's single ice-fringed window, and thought about dying. It hadn't been so long ago that she had had in her mind a list of the ways she could make it happen, ranked by how easy or hard they would be for her to achieve, and how messy they would be for someone else to clean up.

More as a fidget than anything, she checked her watch. Already 3:09—shit.

As she slipped out through the velvet curtain, turning off the safelights as she went, she remembered the drawings in the stairwell. Earlier, she had been so eager to get up to the attic that she hadn't even glanced at them. Now she wondered if there was a way to get them off the wall and include them in the auction. Her mood lifted. Drawings by Miranda Brand! Contractors could probably cut out that part of the wall, and a museum could hang it as it was, the way they did with Italian frescoes. She would have to talk to some curators to ask about best practices for transport—you would have to protect the drywall from crumbling, obviously, but also put something down to keep the pencil from smudging . . .

But when she reached the place in the stairwell where Theo's fingers had wrapped around her wrist, she could not find the drawings. She turned in a circle, bewildered.

The wall was a uniform white.

For a terrifying moment, she thought maybe she had imagined the drawings altogether. Their viciousness, the smeared lead, the look on Theo's face when he saw them, like he thought they might reach out and grab him by the neck.

She knelt down to touch the place where the drawings had been. The surface was smooth and hard, with the fluid feel of fresh paint.

Theo had painted them over.

The drawings were gone.

MIRANDA

SERIES 4, Clippings and publications
BOX 18, News clippings
FOLDER: 1979–1984

The Village Voice

JANUARY 27, 1982

■

CAPILLARIES

Adriana Panico

In an otherwise uneven show of new talent at the Patina Gallery exhibition space last night, one artist stood out: Miranda Brand and her photo series Capillaries, which filled the entire back room.

Brand's work will be familiar to night owls at the Palladium and Club 57, where she has shown pieces from her series Empty Spaces. (She went by the name Miranda Planchart until her elopement with painter Jake Brand last fall.) Promising pictures, to be sure, but the works she exhibited last night are in a league of their own.

Capillaries consists of portraits of women in everyday environments, but with a twist: their faces and bodies are caked in blood. A woman and man share a milkshake at a nostalgic diner, but while the man is clean, the woman is drenched head-to-toe in red liquid. A similar fate has befallen the woman sitting in a theater audience, whose off-the-shoulder dress has been stained by the blood dripping from her chin and hair. Brand herself plays the central role in most of the photographs, using the self-portrait genre to toy with the traditional power imbalance between photographer and subject.

Although the photographs' spectacle of horror is visually compelling, what makes Capillaries truly exceptional are the expressions on the women's faces, full of exhaustion, muted boredom, and above all, appeasement. At the diner, the woman's lips curve in a look of feigned attention. While the theatergoer's fellow patrons laugh uproariously around her, she stretches her blood-stained cheeks in a grimace of happiness. Spectacular yet invisible, messy yet controlled, all-knowing yet powerless: this is Brand's vision of the contemporary woman. Think *Carrie*, if no one else noticed anything was wrong.

At the show, Brand, seven months pregnant, curved one hand protectively over her belly as she smiled and chatted with viewers. Although the baby is due in March, she anticipates no change to her production schedule. A relief for her new dealer, Hal Eggers of Patina: he sold all ten of the Capillaries prints on display by the end of the night.

SERIES 1, Correspondence
BOX 1, Personal correspondence
FOLDER: Toby-Jarrett, Lynn (incl. 12 photocopies of letters from MB, from LTJ private collection)

2/10/1982

Dear M,

My cousin sent me a copy of Village Voice from last month and I saw the review of your show. Great review, amazing, but CONGRATULATIONS ON THE BABY!

I think I'm still in shock. You're due so soon! Have to say I wish you had told me. I could have knit you some booties. Not that I know how to knit, but maybe I'll learn. How long are babies in booties? Jesus, never thought I'd be asking you that! It all feels surreal! Part of me thinks maybe you'll call me one of these days telling me it's all a prank.

I hope you and Jake are doing well. I know you're busy with married life, whatever that means. I hope you're not still mad at me. I know I was out of line, and I think you're right, I probably would like Jake if I got to know him. All I care about is that he makes you happy.

Let's talk on the phone soon. Before the baby's born? Need all the news. Plus want to tell you about this cool person I'm seeing. And my trip to Caracas last month—you HAVE to go someday. Think I have the wrong phone number for you, can you mail it to me again? Old one says it's disconnected.

Really miss you.

Lynn

SERIES 2, Personal papers

BOX 9, Diary (1982–1993)

Miranda—

A notebook to keep track of the little one's milestones!

Take time to appreciate the blessings as they come.

Love,

Mom

MARCH 30 1982

The baby is here.

That's the first milestone. The first blessing, right, Mom? That blaze of pain. All those hours of contractions and panting and shitting the sheets.

The labor came on so fast. I couldn't get hold of Jake. He was holed up in a studio somewhere. So the nurse was the one who held my hand through it all. She told me all about her three kids, how the first was the worst and the second two popped out like bullets. She told me I was part of a sisterhood now, made up of all the other women through history who have given birth.

We survive a fire. What is left behind in us is a core, a steel rod. Strong and iridescent.

The thing Jake would have understood, which the nurse didn't, was that I needed my camera. I left the house so fast I forgot it, which was too bad. I would have liked to capture the baby's face when he first came out, streaked with blood and shit, swollen and wrinkled at the same time. That moment when he was weighed and graded and wiped down. A premonition of the final judgment. Had I sinned while he was in me? Had I put him together correctly? I suddenly worried I had done it all wrong, and here there are no rough drafts. But the doctors seemed pleased. My body had taught him how to breathe and how to cry.

MARCH 31 1982

We named the baby Theo.

We chose Theo because BLAH BLAH BLAH! Any sentence where I'm not talking about how much my vagina hurts feels like a lie. Also my tits. The baby won't always latch (latch! like a gate) but the milk keeps coming. It doesn't know it can't get out. I am still in the hospital for recovery and they don't want to send me home until they know the baby will take. Take to the breast, I mean. Take my milk, take me.

APRIL 2 1982

Home now. Familiar sheets with little yellow flowers. How many times did I clutch these sheets as Jake fucked me? How many times did I sweat into them, late in my pregnancy? Every object seems different now, unrecognizable.

My mother was waiting at our apartment door when we got home. She had her suitcase with her. She came up on NJ Transit. Didn't ask permission. "Trust me, Miranda. You need me here."

I didn't have the strength to protest. After all, I just pushed an 8-pound baby out of my body and had ten stitches sewn between my vagina and my asshole. I can barely walk, let alone get a 175-pound woman in a pink sweater out the front door. I went into the bedroom and lay down. When I woke up she was still here. So I guess she's staying.

APRIL 3 1982

Jake likes to hold the baby and say to me, We made him, Miranda, we made him. He's our first collaboration.

But this child is mostly mine. We forged each other in a way Jake can never understand. Even if he had been here. He can never know how, over the past nine months, my body became a thing I shared. It became *our* body. And then, after nine hours of labor, our body split in two. Flesh from flesh. The child and me. And my body, the one that was left behind, is not the same one that started all this. I'm a rounded hill of a stomach with nothing inside.

APRIL 4 1982

Theo

Will

Not

Stop

Crying

My mother comes into the bedroom every morning to read me "words of wisdom" from her self-help book. Today was the PROFOUND and THOUGHT-PROVOKING insight that "every day brings clarity."

Not for me. Every new day that dawns, I feel like I'm dropping into a fog. Like when a plane crashes through the clouds and the windows go white and you wonder whether you're landing or dying.

APRIL 5 1982

Why is he still crying? It seems impossible. Physically impossible. Isn't he tired? Doesn't his throat hurt? Shouldn't he be happy for just one moment? Statistically speaking?

APRIL 6 1982

Mom is gone. I made her leave. I yelled some terrible things. I don't know why. Even as I was doing it, it felt like the words were coming out of someone else. I wanted to turn around and see who was screaming and ask them to please be quiet. But it was me.

Jake is mad at me for making her leave. He says we needed the help. But we'll figure it out. I'll figure it out. People figure it out.

APRIL 8 1982

I'm tired. I didn't know a person could be this tired. But I can't sleep. Even when Theo isn't screaming AND HE IS ALWAYS SCREAMING I can't sleep. My mind runs around and around. Moving backward, wondering what I should have done differently, wondering how I can take this all back.

You can't. Obviously. You aren't supposed to want to.

APRIL 9 1982

I left the house today. I swaddled myself in one of Jake's flannel shirts. I feel cold all the time. I walked down the street to get an herbal tea or some shit that the doctor said I should have. It burned my tongue but I still couldn't get warm.

I took Theo with me in his sling. People kept stopping me to say how beautiful he was. How adorable, how sweet.

I know I should agree with them. I should see what they see. But all I can see is an angry little alien who can't do anything, who shits and pisses everywhere. He's bitten my nipples to shreds and he doesn't even have teeth yet. He's horrible. He's mine, mine, mine, this awful little creature, this mixture of my blood, and I am so full of shame that I can't bear it.

I nod and say thank you. I hear my voice and it is wooden, like a hollow door.

APRIL 12 1982

Women are supposed to love their children. But maybe I can't. Something came loose inside me long ago.

I wish I could go backward. Restore myself to some previous time before puberty smashed me to bits, before I became a creature of flesh. I could be an image of an angel in the stained glass of the church, face frozen, light pouring through me. I wouldn't have to smile. I wouldn't even have to breathe.

6.

KATE

K ate, Kate!"

Jemima streaked through the dining room doorway and ran straight for Kate, leaping on her back and hugging her tightly around the neck. A fine layer of sand rained down onto the papers around them—a pile of Miranda's fan mail, mostly unopened.

"I found a sea searching today," Jemima declared.

"You mean a sea urchin?"

"Yeah, that! What did *you* find?"

"Not much." Kate glanced at the letters on the floor. "Some people wrote to your grandma to tell her they liked her."

"Her friends?"

"Kind of her friends, yeah." Kate loosened Jemima's arms from her neck so she could turn around and smile at her. And so she could breathe. "Did you bring the sea urchin home?"

The kids always came back from camp toting pails full of the day's finds: a miniature pine cone, pebbles from the beach, a shattered coral shell. They arranged these on the edge of the back porch, where the sun would slowly bleach them dry. Jemima liked the collecting part best, but Oscar spent hours considering different ways to order the tiny objects, pursing his mouth as he shifted around the rocks and shells. They usually insisted on giving Kate a tour of the collection before she left, while Theo waited impatiently for her to get off his property.

"Yessssss," Jemima said. "Want to see it?"

"Absolutely."

"Okay, come!" Jemima commanded, and ran out the door.

Kate exhaled and fanned her armpits.

Over the past few days, she had been using Theo's absences to look through the rest of the house. Seeing the attic had not satiated her curiosity the way she thought it would, and now that she had broken that explicit prohibition, it was easy to continue her explorations.

She had started with the rooms she had already been in, the kitchen and the downstairs bathroom, but the cabinets there held nothing more interesting than old hotel soaps and value packs of toilet paper. From there, every day she had moved steadily deeper into the house. The living room, the small guest suite downstairs, with its empty bed frame and a ring of sun damage on the floor. There was nothing more of Miranda's anywhere, and sometimes Kate thought about stopping—but then she would remember the photos drying in the darkroom, or the invaluable drawings Theo had painted over, and a new urgency would seize her.

Today, she had been more brazen and had gone up to the second floor. The first room she entered must have been Theo's childhood bedroom: above a narrow twin bed frame (no mattress), Bruce Willis squinted out of a *Die Hard* movie poster. Faded soccer pennants littered the rest of the walls at uneven intervals. Theo had evidently turned the room into his office for the summer, because it now held two high-end computer monitors and a portable file cabinet. The file cabinet was locked, and after looking around the desk for the key, Kate had turned to YouTube and tried to find a tutorial on how to pick the lock. She was watching a video by someone called breakins881 when she heard the sound of the car coming up the driveway—not the engine, because that damn Tesla was silent, but the gravel beneath its wheels. She hightailed it downstairs, falling down the last few steps and nearly breaking her arm in the process, and planted herself cross-legged on the dining room carpet just seconds before Jemima breezed through the front door.

Way too close.

Anything that led to this tornado of guilt and adrenaline was probably not a good idea. Kate was supposed to be seeking out stability, not running around in a panic at the sound of a car in a driveway.

So she would stop poking around the house. She would stop.

She sighed and rubbed her eyes. She couldn't even convince herself. She knew she'd be up late tonight watching that lock-picking video, and this time tomorrow she'd be up in Theo's study again, trying to pry open that cabinet and get at whatever he wanted to hide.

She found Jemima in the kitchen, where Theo was kneeling at Oscar's feet, untying his sneakers. Oscar was talking earnestly—and somewhat unintelligibly—about some bird they had seen at camp. When Kate came in, Theo looked up at her, then immediately back down. She got that strange, queasy feeling in her stomach again. It seemed impossible that he didn't know what she had been doing.

"I'm going to show Kate my searching," Jemima declared.

"Urchin," Theo said automatically. He managed to pull off one of Oscar's shoes. "Let's get your snack first, okay? Oscar was getting hungry in the car."

"Oscar's always hungry," Jemima said.

Theo raised his eyebrow as he tugged off the other shoe. "So are you."

Oscar and Jemima settled in at the kitchen table, and after a second of hesitation, Kate sat across from them. Theo handed the kids their yogurts and offered Kate one, too, but she smiled and shook her head. Jemima pulled out the promised treasure, a fat purple sphere that was hollow in the middle and missing a chunk from one side. She held it out reverently to Kate, who made the requisite *oohs* and *aahs*. Oscar slid off his chair and came around to look at it, too.

"How was today?" Theo asked Kate as he took the fourth seat at the table. "Find anything interesting?"

"Oh—" She panicked, thinking he knew about her going upstairs, then realized he meant in the dining room. "Um. Some photographs. Not fancy ones, just some Kodak prints."

"Of what?"

"Uh . . . you and your parents." Distracted, she let Oscar take the sea urchin back from her. "Them on their wedding day. I think one is from your birthday—you had a cake shaped like a fire engine. There's one of the three of you in front of this house. They're cool."

Cool was the wrong word, but she didn't know what word would be better. *Awkward, unexpected. Old.* In the wedding photo, Miranda and Jake were standing next to a dour city official in front of some beige wall. Miranda was wearing an ivory jumpsuit and Jake's hair was wavy and down to his chin. The terrible light had flattened the whole snapshot into a grimy yellow, except for Miranda's mouth, which burned brightly under a slash of lipstick. Spots of overexposure spattered across Jake's face, shimmying his expression from view. In the birthday photo, Jake held Theo aloft, big hands bunching the corduroy overalls, both their mouths pursed as they prepared to blow out the cake's five candles. The house photo was awkwardly staged, Miranda's and Jake's expressions nearly catatonic while a toddler Theo screwed up his eyes as if preparing to yell. The background held the lushness of winter, the fuller edge of the pine trees, the sun a sharp and glowing sphere in the upper right corner.

"They're sort of hard to describe," she said. "Do you want to see them?"

"Not right now. You can file them and I'll look later."

She could tell he was making an effort to be polite, but she could also tell he definitely was never going to look. As she tried to decide whether to push him on it, he held out his hand to Jemima for the sea urchin.

"Wow," he said, inspecting it. "This is really amazing. Good find, kiddo."

"It was whole when I found it," Jemima explained. "It got broke in my pocket."

"I think it's prettier how it is," Theo said solemnly.

Kate asked, "Why'd you put it in your pocket? You didn't have your bucket?"

"We aren't s'posed to put them in our buckets," Oscar said. He already had yogurt smeared all around his mouth.

"Oscar!" Jemima jumped up, red-faced.

Theo frowned at Oscar. "What do you mean? They're always in your buckets when you bring them home."

Oscar looked to Jemima for help. "I . . ."

Jemima ran over to him and punched him in the shoulder. "Shut *up*!"

Theo shot to his feet. "Hey! There is no hitting in this house. And don't tell your brother to shut up."

"You suck," Jemima said to Oscar, who began to cry. "You ruin everything."

"Jemima, go to your room," Theo said.

"Because you're a dweeb," she continued, staring Oscar down.

"Now, Jemima. You're grounded."

"You love him more," she sobbed, then ran out of the room.

Theo crouched down next to Oscar.

"You okay?"

Oscar nodded. Tears streamed down his face and mixed with the yogurt. He held his arms out, and Theo picked him up. He carried Oscar around the kitchen, bouncing him as Oscar wiped his face noisily across his father's shirt. Within a few circuits, the tears had disappeared entirely, and the boy wiggled to be put down.

"Finish your snack," Theo said quietly. Oscar sniffled agreement and settled back in his chair, while Theo crossed to the stove.

The whole incident had lasted less than two minutes. A little stunned, Kate leaned down to pick up the sea urchin, which in the commotion had fallen off the table and broken into several large fragments. She carried the pieces over to the kitchen counter and looked at Theo, who was fiddling with one of the burner grates, as if he needed to occupy his hands.

"I'm sorry," she said.

He glanced over at her. "Sorry . . . ? For what?"

"I feel like my question set them off."

"What?" He let go of the grate. "No. It wasn't your fault. This happens a lot. I mean, not the hitting. Jemima's been having a hard time ever since . . ." He seemed to catch himself. He ran his hand over his face. "She misses her mom. Not that there's anything I can do about that," he added, a little bitterly.

Kate had a sudden, horrifying thought. "Is her mom—"

"No," he said quickly, "she's alive. But . . . it's complicated."

She hesitated. "Maybe they could talk on the phone."

He looked over at her again. His expression was almost amused. "You just get in everyone's business, don't you?"

Kate reddened. "I didn't mean . . ."

"A professional hazard," he said, not unkindly.

Again with those eyes that seemed to see right through her. There was a moment when Kate thought maybe she could ask him about the stairwell. Maybe she could get whatever answers she wanted. About him, about Miranda. Then, before she had even figured out how to frame a question, the moment had passed: the opening had closed as soon as she perceived it, like a hologram that vanished when you looked at it straight on.

Theo cleared his throat. "I'm going to go talk to Jemima," he said. "Let me know if you have any other questions about the papers."

Twenty or thirty minutes later, a scream rang out. Kate leaped to her feet and ran to the bottom of the stairs, where she heard Jemima howling, *It's not fair aaaaaaa I hate you eeeeeeee*. Theo said something sharply. The screaming stopped.

Kate was hanging on the banister, debating whether to go up. Then a door closed and several footsteps started down the stairs. She ducked back into the dining room just in time to see Theo frog-marching his kids down the hall. Jemima was still sobbing. Oscar looked like he had a stomachache.

Kate waited until they had rounded the corner into the kitchen, then followed them out onto the back porch, where the kids' daily finds stretched along the edge. Yesterday's shells were purplish and dark, freshly plucked from the ocean; the older ones were white as bone. As she watched, the kids hunched down and began putting each item back into their buckets.

"What are they doing?" she asked Theo.

He rubbed his temples. "Apparently they aren't supposed to take stuff home. Each camper finds an object to show everyone, but then they put them back. It's a lesson in conservation. Whereas *my* children have been hiding things in their pockets and sneaking them out. Now I told them they have to go put the things back. Sticks in there," he said to the kids, pointing at the woods. "Then we'll drive the water stuff down to the beach."

Jemima raised her head defiantly. "At camp, we get to take *one* thing home every day. So we should get to keep one thing for every day. Everyone else got to."

"Everyone else followed the rules," Theo said, unmoved. "But you didn't, so now you have to put it all back."

Oscar stopped and held up the hunk of seaweed. "We can keep this one," he said. "It's already deaded."

"No," Theo said. "It all has to go back. It has to go be with its friends."

"Seaweed doesn't have friends," Jemima said mutinously.

Theo crossed his arms and stared at them. Grumbling, they finished loading everything into their buckets, then carried them down the steps and out toward the woods. Kate looked at Theo to see if his expression had relaxed once their backs were turned. But his face had only grown more fearful. Together, they watched his children walk across the lawn and over the place where their grandmother had died, where the blood had seeped into the soil and taken root.

MIRANDA

SERIES 2, Personal papers

BOX 9, Diary (1982–1993)

APRIL 14 1982

Seventeen days in. I am a survivor of a shipwreck. Floating in the baking sun. Surrounded by undrinkable water. Counting the days since my world ended. Counting the days I can keep treading water. My lips and nipples are cracked and bleeding. Everything in me hurts, from the inside out, as if the baby came out of me and the empty space filled up with pain. I am burned to a crisp. How long can you last? How long can you survive?

APRIL 15 1982

I'm living in white feathers and lizard eyes and dark sludge that pushes up through my throat. When I close my eyes I can feel my blood pouring under the surface of the skin. Where does it all go? If I spill it, I will be lighter, I think. So light I can fly.

APRIL 17 1982

3:06 and everyone is sleeping. Each minute slides past me, too slippery to grip. 3:07 now. See? Soon I will find a way to slow down time and crush open every minute, snap snap. A lobster claw with fresh pink meat inside. The way to do it is to work. Work more. Faster. I have invented a new process. You lay all the sheets of paper all out in a grid, one by one, very specific, and then the light inhabits them, it crawls across the page and nestles in the grain, and then it is at home. Only you must watch the paper very carefully. You must move them when they say they need to be moved. I will stay awake. I will fix it all. I have so many plans.

APRIL 18 1982

Theo is an ugly little beast. He almost looks like an animal. A jaundiced dog, shriveled husk of a human.

Jake snores all night. The sound of it shakes me, gets into my dreams, mows them down. I toss and turn and my ears feel like they are full of glass. And then Theo starts crying and the glass shatters and my head hurts, hurts.

I don't know if I will ever sleep again.

APRIL 18 1982

Every cell is a bloody eye. It blinks and stares at me. The night is an ink wash above me and the ceiling fan drowns out the sound of crying. Lie here forever and soon I will rot to a dandelion wisp and I won't ever have to look at that thing anymore, I won't ever have to pretend I love it.

APRIL 19 1982

There are moments when I catch a glimpse of myself, like bubbles swimming up toward sunlight, like air just beyond my grasp, and I can't understand what I've become. And then away I plunge, down to the ocean floor, to mingle with the other mermaids and trash heaps.

Jake wants me to pull it together but I don't have anything left to pull.

I didn't unravel.

I disappeared.

APRIL 19 1982

Chewing, angry mouth. Blood from my tits. Stitches breaking.

APRIL 19 1982

I hate everyone, every human I've ever met. I want to take them by the shoulders and say, Do you know what you did to your mother when she gave birth to you? Do you know how you broke her? You ungrateful creature.

I've never hated anything this much. My hate wraps around my stomach, squeezes, boa constrictor, you will get no milk.

APRIL 20 1982

I think some part of him is still stuck inside me. An extra arm, a piece of his tongue. Something didn't make it out, and it's festering.

APRIL 21 1982

I am trying. I am trying so hard. Can't anyone see that? Jake moved all my papers into a big pile and messed up the light patterns that I was creating. He says I am acting crazy. Like not cool crazy, he says. Real crazy. Is something wrong?

Of course something is wrong. We have produced a monster. He can't see it Only I can see it. The monster has a cute skin He is very well concealed

APRIL 22 1982

Going to the hospital to have the leftover piece of him taken out of me. They could do surgery. They could rip me all apart and sew me back again. Then my insides will have fresh air and I will understand how to be good again. I could become a marble saint. That is what I would like. I would like to be a cold hard body with worn toes where people rub for good luck. I would like to stand on a tall thing and not crouch down. My eyes will have no pupils and the blindness will make it all more clear. I will rub my own toes.

SERIES 2, Personal papers

BOX 8, Medical records

FOLDER: Nangussett Hospital Psychiatric Unit (hospitalization 4/22/82–
6/23/82)

Psychiatric Unit
Nangussett Hospital
Admission Report

4/22/1982

HISTORY OF PRESENT ILLNESS

Patient presented in ER barefoot and said she was there to have an arm removed from her body. When asked which arm, she said it could be a foot. She said it was inside her. Intake noticed deep scratches on her arms, apparently self-inflicted with fingernails. When asked, Patient said that she was trying to make the surgery easier. Nurse tried to put slippers on Patient's feet and Patient became agitated.

Vaginal exam showed recent childbirth. When asked about the location of her child, patient said he was at home with her husband. Social work referral to verify.

Psych evaluation ordered. Psych evaluation demonstrated lack of short-term memory, hallucinations, extreme sensitivity to pain, shortness of breath, and delusions of grandeur. Admitted to psych emergency on an in-patient basis for an indefinite period.

VITAL SIGNS

HT: 64 in. WT: 115 lbs. T: 98.0 SITE: oral P: 78 RHYTHM: regular R: 18 BP: 110/70

REVIEW OF SYSTEMS

GENERAL: fatigue

EYES: normal

EAR/NOSE/THROAT: minor nasal congestion

CARDIOVASCULAR: chest pain, palpitations

RESPIRATORY: shortness of breath

GASTROINTESTINAL: unclear

GENITOURINARY: normal w/ remaining trauma from recent childbirth (3/28/1982)

MUSCULOSKELETAL: joint pain, joint stiffness

SKIN: pruritus

NEUROLOGIC: normal

PSYCHIATRIC: abnormal, history unclear, requires fuller evaluation

ENDOCRINE: weight loss, cold intolerance

HEME/LYMPHATIC: anemia (resolved)

ALLERGIC/IMMUNOLOGIC: hay fever

SOCIAL WORK REPORT

Patient arrived postpartum. Medical records indicate gave childbirth 3/28/1982. Social worker confirmed safety of child over the phone with husband who was unaware wife had left the house. Request filed with police for non-urgent welfare check.

INITIAL PSYCHIATRIC EVALUATION

Performed by Warren Sands, MD, second-year resident in psychiatry, with supervision by Raymond Zielinski, MD, attending.

Initial psychiatric evaluation began with questions about the circumstances preceding her arrival at the ER. Patient frequently lost strand of thought but suggested that the scratches had been self-inflicted and that she believed some part of her child was still stuck inside her. Patient requested to be turned into a "saint," "statue," or "crackling noise." Requested interviewer touch her feet. When request was denied, Patient became upset and began to hallucinate "ball of light" in the corner of the room. Hysterical crying. Patient had to be sedated and interview was terminated. Pupil dilation and shortness of breath consistent with use of stimulant drug, will require monitoring to determine if paranoia is psychiatric or drug-induced.

Contacted husband and instructed him to come to psychiatric unit tomorrow during normal visiting hours, without child.

Patient considered a danger to herself and others. Recommend inpatient evaluation and psychiatric hold of at least 96 hours, continuation dependent on re-evaluation.

7.

KATE

"This traffic is terrible," Louise said, nudging her car almost up to the bumper of the car in front of them. "Crap. I hate tourists."

Over the past couple weeks, Kate had learned that tourists were a favorite scapegoat in Callinas. Complaining about them was the fastest way to establish yourself as a local. The resentment had deep roots. Callinas had been just a few small farms until the '70s, when an oil spill prompted an influx of environmental activists who wanted to help with the clean-up effort. After the spill was as gone as it would ever be, the activists traded in their tents for houses and an "intentional community." When San Francisco started sprawling farther north, the residents knotted together under a banner of esoteric bylaws about water systems and zoning patterns, trying to keep outsiders away through infinite red tape. Kate had done her fair share of moaning about tourists in New York, but the Callinas residents were on a whole new level. Many people still refused to put up house numbers or street signs, and some people had started icing out anyone who had the audacity to list their house on Airbnb. Frank and Louise spoke in disgusted tones about the San Franciscans who came up to use the beach and left behind plastic toys, dog shit, cigarettes, sandwich wrappers, soggy books, and invasive species. To hear Louise tell it, it was only thanks to the hard work of devoted volunteers that Callinas hadn't been embalmed in beachgoers' refuse, like Pompeii beneath a layer of frozen ash.

"Tourists!" Louise cried again now, banging one hand against the steering wheel in frustration as the car ahead of them slowed to get around a sharp turn.

"I don't think those people are tourists," Kate said. "They have a Berkeley decal."

"Day-trippers. Same thing."

"Didn't you used to come up here for the day? Before you moved here?"

"That was different," Louise said.

"Why?"

"Because we truly appreciated it. We weren't disrespectful like these people."

Kate suppressed a smile. She had discovered a certain satisfaction in goading her aunt into contradicting herself. There was an art to it: Kate had to play a little dumb, so that she didn't seem to be challenging Louise, but she also couldn't sound too dumb or Louise would realize she was mocking her, which would ruin the game. And would be mean.

"Did you call ahead about your prescriptions?" Louise asked, for the dozenth time.

Kate's smile faded. "The doctor called it in."

"Sometimes they don't fill it unless you're there. Then you have to stand in line with all these strangers sneezing all over you. It's very unhygienic."

"So I'll use hand sanitizer."

"No!" Louise said, horrified. "Antibacterials create superbugs."

Kate sighed and leaned her head against the window. She had wanted to borrow the car and run to the Mill Valley pharmacy herself, but Louise had insisted on coming along so that she could return a gallon of milk to the grocery store, even though they had already drunk half of it. It had gone bad too fast, Louise said. Kate wanted to say that it was probably because Louise had left it out on the counter overnight. But she couldn't. There were a lot of things you couldn't say when you were staying in someone's house for free.

These days, she lived her whole life in other people's spaces, bouncing back and forth between Frank and Louise's cottage and the Brand house. Weirdly, she almost preferred the Brand house, as lonely and creepy as it could be. At least there she had some privacy, some time alone. Some autonomy.

So far, she hadn't found much else of interest. The file cabinet lock had thwarted her—no matter how many times she watched that instructional video, she couldn't figure out how to pick the lock without leaving scratches—so she had moved on to the other rooms on the second floor. The children's bathroom was smeared with glittery blue toothpaste and strewn with sodden towels that Kate desperately wanted to pick up and hang on the towel rack. The kids' bedroom was also a disaster, with tiny clothing heaped in tiny piles, a reusable grocery tote overflowing with chapter books, and Legos covering Oscar's bed. He was sleeping on the twin mattress that was missing from Theo's office, while Jemima got the full bed that must have come with the room. There was a pineapple-shaped nightlight plugged into one wall outlet, and above it, Jemima had cut a photo of Theo and a dark-haired woman—presumably their mother—into a heart and taped it on the wall.

Kate had studied the photo for longer than she meant to. Rachel Tatum was one of those women who looked like they could run a marathon without breaking a sweat. Her hair dark and shining, her smile wide, dimples at the corners of her mouth. She was leaning against Theo. He looked different, too. Younger, bulkier. He was, believe it or not, smiling.

So maybe his rudeness to Kate wasn't about his parents at all, or about being back in his childhood town. If he wouldn't even let Jemima talk to Rachel on the phone, the divorce must have been acrimonious. Maybe he was still reeling from the split.

Or maybe he just really disliked Kate.

"Kate? Can you get out and look?"

They had gotten to the town center and Louise was trying to parallel park. Kate jumped out and guided her aunt into the space, a process that took Louise about seven cycles of reversing even though the spot was big enough to fit a minivan.

After the ordeal was over, Louise pointed across the town square. "The pharmacy is over there. Do you want me to come with?"

As if Kate needed an adult present. "No, thanks. You return your milk. I'll meet you back here."

Weekend foot traffic filled the adorable streets. The Mill Valley police had set up a biker safety tent in the middle of the square, and many slender men in aerodynamic helmets were standing around it with their bicycles, chugging water and sweating through their skintight neon suits. Outside an espresso bar, two identical Lhasa Apsos strained at their leashes as they waited for their owner to emerge. As Kate crossed the square, something seemed off. After a moment she realized what it was: no one was stopping to look at her, no one was recognizing her and waving. She was anonymous.

The pharmacy had a Fourth of July display up front, shiny blue stream-ers around flag-patterned toothbrushes arranged in the shape of a heart. Kate headed straight for the prescription window at the back, where a guy who looked about sixteen was standing in a wrinkled white coat. His tie had a picture of a wolf howling at the moon.

He took her name, typed it into the system, and shook his head. "No go," he said.

Kate frowned. "What do you mean?"

"There's no prescriptions under that name."

She rested her hands on the counter and tried to lean forward. The pharmacist swiveled the computer screen away with an admonishing glare.

"My doctor was supposed to call them in," she said.

"Our answering machine was out last week. Have him try again."

"What if my doctor's a she?"

The guy looked at her. "Are they?"

"No," Kate admitted. "But they could be."

Outside, she wandered back to the car to wait for Louise. She'd have to make another trip here. Forty minutes each way. An hour if you got stuck behind a tractor-trailer. There was a pharmacy in Stinson, but the owner was a friend of Frank's. He was a nice guy, but Kate would rather get her mood stabilizers from someone she would never have to see again. Forty minutes wasn't that far, she reassured herself, and she still had eight days of pills left. She'd just come here after work this week. Maybe Tuesday.

She leaned against the hood of the car and gnawed at her thumbnail's ragged edge. The whole thing was annoying. She didn't even like the pills. They made her groggy and slow. She had gained weight. And the truth was, she had no conviction that the medication was working, would continue to work. Even on the best days, she felt there was something teeming under-neath. There was something strapped down.

Rifling through the master bathroom at the Brand house, she had found, in among Theo's few masculine accoutrements (shaving cream, a razor, generic shampoo, unscented deodorant), a bottle of Klonopin. The prescription was dated a month ago and made out to Theo. TAKE AS NEEDED. How often did that mean? He didn't seem like someone who would need anything. Aside from an attitude adjustment.

The sun was beginning to give her a headache. She shielded her eyes and looked across the square. Louise was striding toward her with a new gallon of milk in one hand.

"Success?" Kate asked as her aunt got close enough.

Louise waved a receipt triumphantly over her head. "Success. Should we go for lunch? Did you get your prescription already?"

"There was a screw-up. I'll come back later this week."

Louise clucked. "Have them transfer it to Jerry in Stinson. You'll save so much time."

"It's fine." Kate wanted to talk about anything else. She took the milk from Louise and put it in her tote bag. "Yes to lunch. My treat."

On Monday, Kate's furtive investigations took her into the last room in the Brand house: Theo's bedroom. Once Jake and Miranda's. The room had walls the color of smoke. The furniture was all pine, like a Swiss chalet, more traditional than Kate would have expected. The sheets were tangled on the bed where Theo must have kicked them away upon waking. On the floor were a couple shirts and a pair of black boxer briefs. Kate stared at these for a moment, then flushed and turned away. The closets and dresser drawers were empty except for his clothing, an unremarkable mix of monochrome T-shirts and jeans.

On the nightstand were two books. *The Alienist* and a copy of *Miranda Brand: The Collected Works*. Theo's copy was shiny and new, the glint in Miranda's eyes unmarked by pen. A couple pages were dog-eared. One about Jake and Miranda's move to California. Another in the middle of an essay about Hal Eggers and how he had shaped Miranda's career, discovering her young, pricing her high even when others scoffed. There was a photo of them deep in conversation at one of Miranda's early shows. Hal must have only been in his early thirties, but he was already paunchy and thin-haired. Miranda wore a patterned dress and gestured broadly with a plastic cup of wine.

Kate set the catalog back down as she had found it and opened the nightstand drawer. Aside from a vial of eyedrops, the only thing inside was a small blue notebook. The cover was leather and embossed with a starfish. It was the kind of notebook you could find at any stationery store, displayed next to hand-stamped birthday cards and jars of fake beach glass. What was strange about it, what set Kate's skull buzzing before she even picked it up, were the dark spots on the cover—the same foxing that had ruined entire batches of photographs down in the dining room.

She lifted the notebook out of the drawer and opened it. Its pages rippled like gooseflesh under the pressure of all colors of ink, black and blue and red. The handwriting was Miranda's. Bold, spiky, with a surprisingly curvaceous lowercase s. Kate had seen so much of that handwriting; she had noticed the other day that the shape of her own k had begun to shift in an unconscious imitation.

Reading Miranda's handwriting was always a struggle, and much of the notebook's ink had blurred, making it borderline illegible. But the book was divided into entries, and each entry was dated.

March 30 1982
March 31 1982
April 2 1982
April 3 1982
April 4 1982

A diary.
Miranda's diary.
Kate sat down on the bed. Her muscles had gone slack. She felt light-

headed, nearly faint. She locked her legs together, positioned the notebook on her lap, and stared down at it. 1982. The year Theo was born. Miranda would have been twenty-six. Kate tried to remember what she had been doing when she was that age. Spending her tiny paycheck on nightclub covers, mixing rice with sriracha and calling it a meal, taking time off work to go with college friends to Costa Rica, where she spent most of the time making out with someone's brother in a grimy hot tub. And here was Miranda, same age, becoming a mother. Writing this diary, not knowing what would come next.

Kate had been right after all: Theo *had* been holding something back from her. Not just something, but *the* thing.

She checked her watch. It was 3:11. She needed to go back downstairs. She had an irrational urge to take the notebook with her. After all, the stairwell drawings had vanished in a matter of days. A notebook was even easier to eradicate.

Why *had* he painted over those drawings? Kate had come up with some possible explanations, but none felt sufficient. Fine, the house eventually had to be salable. But those drawings had been worth hundreds of thousands of dollars. Now they were gone forever beneath a sloppy coat of Benjamin Moore. And he had hidden away this diary specifically so Kate wouldn't find it.

She had been trying not to think about the rumors, but now she let herself take out an idea and consider it, as if she were trying to distinguish salt from sugar by touching it to her tongue. Theo had killed his mother. No, that sounded too harsh, like it had been intentional. Theo had pulled the trigger. No, that was wrong, too. It lost Miranda altogether. Kate didn't know how to phrase the action without starting to come down on one side or another. She didn't know how to think about the possibility without starting to believe it.

Either way, it seemed increasingly likely that when he had asked her to tell him about anything "sensitive," he had been talking about evidence.

The diary's pages were wrinkling under her grip. She forced herself to relax her fingers.

The therapist in Connecticut had given her a bunch of phrases she was supposed to pull out whenever she felt herself slipping. *Thought distortion.*

Catastrophizing. Kate tried to string them together in a way that might apply to this situation, but instead she wound up reciting them to herself like a mantra—*thought distortion catastrophizing thought distortion catastrophizing*—until they lost all meaning.

It was 3:13 now. She put the diary back in the drawer exactly as she had found it. Theo had destroyed the drawings only after he knew she'd seen them. He didn't have to know she had found the journal. She could just leave it here, exactly as it had been. Theo would think it was safe from her, and that was how she would keep it safe from him. She would read it the way Miranda had written it: bit by bit, a little every day.

"Frank," Kate said after dinner, as she was helping her aunt and uncle clean up, "the other day you said you had a friend who was a detective on Miranda Brand's case."

Frank nodded. "Victor Velázquez. Good guy. We play tennis sometimes."

"So he still lives around here?"

He spread his arms. "Why would anyone ever leave Callinas?"

"Fair enough," Kate said, although she could think of a few reasons. "Could you ask him if he would talk to me?"

Louise paused in the act of loading the dishwasher. "What about?"

"Some stuff about the case." Kate opened a cabinet and pretended to search for a water glass. "You know. The inconsistencies you mentioned."

Behind her, there was another brief silence. She could practically hear Frank and Louise exchanging looks. Then the clanging of plates and silverware recommenced.

"Well, remember he's retired," Louise said. "And I know he and Leah are visiting their son in Tahoe for the next few days. But sure, I think he would talk to us if I asked him."

Kate spun around. "You don't need to come with. I can talk to him on my own. It could take a while."

"Oh, sweetie." Louise thrust a knife into the dishwasher as if she were spearing a live animal. "Of course I'm coming with."

MIRANDA

SERIES 2, Personal papers

BOX 9, Diary (1982–1993)

JUNE 25 1982

Back from Nangussett.

What do I do now?

I remembered making something incredible right before I left for the hospital. I didn't remember the details, didn't even remember what it was, but I remembered the pride filling me up inside.

My whole time in That Place, I thought about that photo, and what it would be like to see it for the first time. Putting all the negatives out on the light table and lowering the loupe. I thought it would hit me like a sack of bricks. I thought it would show me some secret truth I'd forgotten. The reason I went through all this.

I looked for it for so long. I developed every roll of film I have.

All I found were photos of the ceiling fan. My pillow. My hand. Photos of Theo, cherub cheeks, looking like a baby clothing ad. Blurry shots. Empty rolls.

There was nothing.

I have nothing to show.

JUNE 26 1982

Theo is bigger than when I left. They say they grow so fast, but you don't know until you are locked up for six weeks and get out and the person you pushed out of your body has doubled in size. His skin is milky, not red, and his wrinkles have smoothed, like a raisin plumped up with water. He smiles now. What is there to smile about? You have a crazy person for a mother. You don't know what life will bring you.

I can't nurse yet, they say. Which was fine when I was inside, but now that I am back with Theo my tits are leaking everywhere. They think they're needed.

I am afraid to be alone with him. In the hospital I thought (or I hoped) maybe I had imagined it all. That I would come home and everything would be easy. I even thought maybe I had imagined the crying. But he still cries. I twitch when I hear him. He knows something is wrong. He knows I am not supposed to be here.

SERIES 2, Personal papers
BOX 8, Medical records
FOLDER: Prescriptions and refills

Prescription issued 6/28/1982
Continued regimen: 1800 mg lithium as 900 mg 2x/day.
150 mg zimelidine. 1 pill 1x/day.
Call prescriber or emergency room 911 with any symptoms.
<<*Duane Reade! We fill generics AND brand-names!*>>

SERIES 2, Personal papers
BOX 9, Diary (1982–1993)

JULY 2 1982

Jake ran the calculations, and after all the hospital bills we have enough money for me to not produce a single thing for three months. Three months. I'm on parole. Yes, you can get your life back, if at the end of the time you make a perfect image, something that proves to your dealers and your husband and your buyers that you are the same as you ever were. If you mess up, back in the box you go.

While I was gone, my mother moved into our second bedroom to help Jake with Theo. Now she is staying to help me "manage."

Another set of eyes watching me. Looking for signs of weakness. Waiting for me to fail.

JULY 19 1982

I lose time. Yesterday I looked at the clock and it was two in the afternoon and then I looked at it again and it was nine p.m. and I hadn't moved from bed.

When Jake came in later, I told him I don't know if I can meet the deadline. It seemed like plenty of time a few weeks ago, but I've never had this blankness before. I've never had *no* ideas.

We fought about it for a while. Me saying I couldn't. Him saying I needed to try harder.

Finally he asked, Why are you like this?

What happened to you in there?

Where did you go?

I have no answers.

AUGUST 1 1982

My mother called Dr. Pottle about me. Without asking, of course. Why ask? I am a child passed between adults. No, I am a ball passed between children. I only know she called because I overheard her thanking him when she hung up the phone. I confronted her and she said she was worried about my fatigue. I think Jake put her onto it. Sometimes they're so buddy-buddy I can't stand it.

Pottle called me later to ask how I was doing. He pretended like my mother hadn't said a thing. I said I wasn't great and he said it was an adjustment period. If I'm still feeling the same way in six weeks, we can talk about changing medication.

Six weeks! Six fucking weeks.

I told him about my deadline. He didn't understand.

You're very talented, he said. I'm sure you'll be able to make a photograph in time.

I could almost hear him thinking, Just click the fucking button.

After that I spent the whole day on the sofa. Holding Theo, listening to him breathe against my tummy. Mom stayed there to watch me, which was humiliating.

SERIES 2, Personal papers

BOX 8, Medical records

FOLDER: Prescriptions and refills

Prescription issued 9/25/1982

1200 mg lithium as 600 mg 2x/day. Taper from 1800 mg: 800 mg 2x/day for first 3 days, 700 mg 2x/day for second 3 days.

150 mg zimelidine. 1 pill 1x/day.

Call prescriber or emergency room 911 with any symptoms.

<<*Duane Reade! We fill generics AND brand-names!*>>

SERIES 2, Personal papers

BOX 9, Diary (1982–1993)

OCTOBER 2 1982

Pottle finally changed my dosage. He says come back in four to six weeks to discuss results. Why is everything four to six weeks? Is that how long it takes the human body to regenerate? Or is it just some magic number the doctors figured out to appease people—long enough you don't bother them, short enough they keep getting their co-pays?

Meanwhile, my three-month deadline expired today. I've made nothing new. Fortunately, Jake sold a painting. Only $1000, but at least it was under the table. A month extension for me. You should see him strutting around. So proud, like he saved us all.

I promise him I'm trying. I'm honestly trying.

OCTOBER 8 1982

I can't tell if the new dosage is helping.

I can't focus, I can't come up with any work.

I sweat all the time. I go through three shirts a day.

I'm so dizzy I can barely stand.

I can only eat toast.

On the phone, Pottle said, "It's better than being in the hospital, isn't it?"

Yes. But that's a low bar.

SERIES 1, Correspondence

BOX 1, Personal correspondence

FOLDER: Eggers, Hal (incl. 39 photocopies of letters from MB, from HE private collection)

October 12 1982

Dear Hal,

Thanks for your letter. I'm doing better. No, I still haven't had any new ideas. The medication is slowing things down. Don't worry, I'll adjust soon and then I'll be back at it.

In the meantime should I print extras of Capillaries? Would you be able to sell them? J and I could use the money. Diapers are fucking expensive. I can do reprints easy. It's more the new stuff I'm having trouble with.

Also can you fast-track the payment from summer sales?

Talk soon,

M

10/19

Dear Miranda,

Poor thing. Glad you're on the mend. Have asked assistant to send over sales stats and check, thanks for reminder.

About new work, remember: YOU ARE A SUPERSTAR! Take a deep breath. It's all like the tide, in and out, in and out.

Extras from Capillaries would be great. Esp. #2, which has sold like hot-cakes. Just don't do too many or the value will depreciate and past buyers will start complaining.

Hal

October 21 1982

Hal,

Thank you for the advice to breathe. That had never occurred to me before. Now that I have inhaled and exhaled I feel able to confront the day! Please see enclosed new photograph.

M

10/28

Miranda,

New photograph needs work. The middle finger should be extended directly through the center line to create symmetrical composition.

The breathing exercise was recommended to me by a famous Siberian shaman who has become a good friend. So don't knock it!! I want you to TAKE CARE OF YOURSELF. Just let yourself relax and the ideas will start to flow.

Hal

SERIES 2, Personal papers

BOX 9, Diary (1982–1993)

OCTOBER 30 1982

Hal thinks he knows everything there is to know about creating. He always thinks he can make the process more efficient. Faster. More profitable. He doesn't understand that we're not machines. He can hire a machine to make art if he wants, but it would be a different kind of art.

Before Theo, before Nangussett, I felt creativity almost as a physical presence inside me. I remember feeling like my veins were expanding to hold another creature, a powerful creature. Sometimes I felt like I was communicating with the universe.

But the meds are fucking with me. I'm numb. My veins are frozen in their same size. It's been over four months since I left the hospital, one month since changing dose, and I haven't developed a single roll of film. I don't know where the days go. The hours.

When it comes down to it, I have two choices.

Create or medicate.

The sharp pain.

Or the dull lack.

8.

KATE

The diary soon shaped Kate's days. She used every possible second of her secret sessions, running upstairs as soon as Theo had left, then huddling on the floor of his bedroom with the notebook open on her knees. Despite the diary's intensity, it was slow reading. Miranda's handwriting was even worse when she was writing just for herself, and Kate could only get through five or six pages before she had to dash back downstairs, where she read documents twice as fast to make up for the time she had lost. Between squinting at the diary and squinting at the materials she was actually supposed to be reading, a headache pinched her temples by the end of each day. She considered it an appropriate penance.

When she wasn't at work, she was trying to track down Kid, the only person who claimed Miranda as a friend. He was never at the crystal store when she went back, but she did meet Esme, the store's owner. Esme was a delight. She was in her late forties, short and round and beautiful, and always looked like she had just come from having multiple orgasms and a rejuvenating cleanse. She was as talkative as Louise but less critical. She was a hugger—had hugged Kate the very moment she met her, in fact, and welcomed her exuberantly to the shop. Every time Kate visited the store, she was overcome by a feeling of warmth and ended up spending large quantities of her newly earned money on the various remedies that Esme promised would turn her "sickly yellow" aura into a confident blue. A week later, Kate had a pile of candles, herbs, and crystals sitting on her nightstand, but she was no closer to finding Kid.

"Dude, go to his house," Nikhil said on Friday night.

Kate slumped over the bar. She had become something of a regular at Pawpaw's, mainly to avoid Frank and Louise's helicoptering, but also because Nikhil was the only person in Callinas with whom she felt like she could have a normal conversation. He lived with his girlfriend and two roommates in a shared house over the hill, the local term for what was actually multiple hills separating the beach towns from the rest of Marin. Probably because of that distance, he took a *chill out, man* attitude to everything in Callinas, including the Brand drama.

"I don't know where he lives," Kate said. "Esme won't tell me. She says she has to respect his privacy. But I think actually she just wants me coming back to the store. She makes, like, fifty bucks every time I come in."

"You buy something every time you go there?"

Kate frowned at the small paper bag on the stool next to her. "It always seems like I need it."

Nikhil snorted. "If Esme won't tell you, ask Louise," he said, draping his bar towel over his shoulder. "Louise knows everything."

Kate shook her head. Louise would want to tag along, which would be a nightmare. They were supposed to go visit Chief Velázquez tomorrow, and Kate was already unsure how to manage her aunt while also getting the relevant information out of the retired cop. She would have to be extra careful with her questions, to avoid revealing too much about the Brands (Louise would definitely tell the rest of town) or about her fascination with them (Louise would definitely tell Kate's mother). And if Louise went off on one of her beloved tangents about Kate being delicate . . .

"Do you ever get sick of it?" she asked Nikhil, turning her pint glass in her hands.

"Of what?"

"It. This. Callinas. It's so . . . small."

He shrugged. "I think it's sort of cute. Everyone looking after each other."

"I guess I'm just tired of being looked after." She was thinking about the past months in Connecticut, the solicitous concern constantly affixed to her parents' faces.

"Oh, come on." Nikhil grinned. "You've only been here a month. It can't be that bad yet."

She looked up, surprised. She kept forgetting that Nikhil didn't know how she had ended up here. Everything that had happened back on the East Coast was invisible to him. She should have felt relieved by his cluelessness; this had been the whole appeal of California in the first place. But instead she only felt exhausted, like she had been ripped in two, and part of her was still all the way across the country, and she only had half her energy to work with.

Behind her, the bar door opened, and two women came in. One was in her late fifties, one in her thirties, and both were wearing athleisure. When they came up to the counter, Nikhil introduced them to Kate as Roberta and Wendy.

"Three-time champions of the Point Reyes mother-daughter 5K," he said. "And two of my best customers."

"We come here after yoga every week," Wendy explained to Kate. "To undo all our hard work."

Kate recognized Wendy as one of the yummy mummy crew that was always stroller-jogging around the neighborhood, a type more likely to drive to the wine bars in Sonoma than make do with Pawpaw's house red and house white. So she was not exactly surprised when Wendy whipped out an antibacterial wipe and swiped it across the barstool's seat.

"I've been dying to meet you," Roberta said to Kate as Wendy ordered two vodka sodas. "I'm friends with your aunt. She's been *so* excited to have you here."

"I'm excited to be here," Kate said. She wondered if Louise knew about the antibacterial wipe situation. She would have a field day.

"We have *lots* of questions about what you're doing up at that house," Roberta said, wiggling up onto the stool.

"Oh, yeah?"

"Yes." Roberta did not elaborate. She simply stared at Kate, waiting for information.

"I can't really talk about it," Kate said, apologetically.

"It's not like we're strangers," Roberta said, even though they were, of course, strangers.

"You know, I went to school with Theo," Wendy told Kate, leaning forward to talk around her mother. "Actually, we got paired on a lot of projects, because our last names were next to each other alphabetically."

Kate's ears pricked up. "Were you friends?"

"No, not exactly. He didn't really have friends, per se. He was sort of a weird kid, you know? Like super quiet."

"But we went to their house once," Roberta said. "Theo had been over to our place a bunch of times for other projects, but this assignment was to make a diorama, and I figured, who better to help with an art project than two famous artists?"

Wendy rolled her eyes. "You just wanted to see inside their house."

"Okay, so I was *curious*," Roberta said. "Sue me. Anyway, I drove Wendy up there to drop her off, and oh my God, what a pigsty. All these papers piled everywhere. And Miranda's photos, really gross stuff, right where Wendy could see them. Plus, there was just a weird feeling about the place."

Nikhil planted his elbows on the counter. "You don't think you're maybe just saying that now?"

"No, it was spooky. His parents didn't even come to the door. I asked Theo where they were, and he said they were working I couldn't exactly invite myself in, could I?"

"*I* would," Wendy said. "If it were Texas at someone else's house."

Kate looked at Nikhil like, *She named her kid Texas?* He shrugged.

"It was the nineties," Roberta said. "Things were more laid back."

"Anyway, Mom left, and Theo went to get his markers and the poster board from upstairs. I sort of stood there by the door waiting for him to get back. I started messing with a photo from one of the piles, which I thought was hilarious because it had a naked woman in it, and then I heard a noise from above me. It was Miranda. She was standing on the stairs, staring down at me." Wendy's voice dropped to a confidential tone. "I thought she was mad about the photo, so I started apologizing. She waved me away, like"—Wendy made a shooing gesture—"and then she said, 'What are you doing here?' I said

I was here to work on the school project. And she said, I'm serious, 'Fuck the school project.'"

"To a child," Roberta put in. "A child!"

"I was, like, dazzled," Wendy said. "I was nine. *Maybe* ten? I had only heard the word a couple times from someone at school. And while I was trying to figure out what to say, she just *sat down* on the stairs and lit a cigarette. I thought she had forgotten I was there, but then she started talking again, saying something about how I shouldn't do what other people say. How that was an important lesson to learn, because I was a girl, and soon I would be a woman, and it would get harder to say no. So I should practice now. Practice saying no.

"And I said, thinking I was so smart, 'Well, if I shouldn't do what people say, then I shouldn't do what *you* say.' And she put down her cigarette and smiled at me. It was the weirdest, most incredible smile. It was like she saw right down inside me. And she said, 'No, of course you shouldn't. I'm the last person you should listen to. Haven't you seen?'"

When Wendy didn't go on, Kate asked, "What did she mean? Haven't you seen . . . what?"

"I don't know. She never said."

Wendy sat back with a flourish, signaling that the story was over, and lifted her glass to her lips.

Kate picked up her drink too, mostly to hide her frustration. The story was plausible, but too specific to be true. Surely no one remembered a random incident from their childhood in such detail. Kate's own memory was far fuzzier. Puberty, first kiss, first drink, first rejection letter, first breakup, any number of the tiny humiliations that felt like public shamings—sure, she remembered those more watershed moments, but she still wouldn't be able to piece together a coherent narrative. It was as if a fire had broken out in her memories of her youth, leaving behind only weird ravaged fragments that had fused together into a smooth, stonelike mass.

Wendy obviously didn't have that problem. Maybe she rehearsed. Woke up every morning and recited five stories about herself, the way job-search guides recommend you do before an interview. Or maybe she had been dining out on the story for years, and had slowly shaped it into the perfect version of itself.

The more Kate thought about what Wendy had said, the more meaning-less it seemed, like a broken piece of chalk that crumbled when you picked it up. She could have learned that Miranda was eccentric just by reading her Wikipedia page. And yet the story also made Kate ravenous. The vision of Miranda sitting on the stairs, smoking, lecturing a nine-year-old.

Haven't you seen? If Miranda had been using it as an idiom, she would have said *Haven't you heard?* So she must have been referring to some-thing in particular. No, now Kate was reading too much into it.

"Want another?" Nikhil said, breaking into her thoughts.

Kate looked down and saw, to her surprise, that her glass was empty. Roberta had gotten a text and was asking Wendy how to open it on her phone. Kate agreed: the same again, please.

Victor Velázquez lived just a few blocks from Frank and Louise. His house was a tidy two-story Craftsman decorated entirely in shades of brown. He was in his sixties, thick-framed, with a large black mustache straight out of *Magnum, P.I.* Other than the mustache, he didn't exude an ex-cop vibe. He seemed like most of Frank and Louise's friends: genial, un-worried. After ushering Kate and Louise into the living room and settling them on a tan jacquard sofa, he put a plate of cookies down on the coffee table. His wife was trying to get on a baking show on TV, he explained. The audition was in a few weeks, and she had been practicing nonstop.

"The dough is a little bland," Louise said after a bite of a snickerdoodle.

"Tell me about it," Velázquez said. "Leah's on a crusade against pro-cessed sugar. She won't even let me buy Gatorade anymore. What do I have to live for if I can't drink Gatorade?"

Kate ate her cookie without comment as she studied the gallery wall next to the sofa. Like most gallery walls, it worked better in theory than in practice. The focal point was a staged portrait, at least twenty years old, in which the Velázquezes and their two sons posed in matching outfits against a dreary pastel backdrop.

"So," Velázquez said, sitting down in the leather recliner opposite them. "What's all this about, Louise? You were very mysterious on the phone."

Louise opened her mouth to answer, but Kate intercepted her. "I actually asked Louise to introduce us," she said. "Maybe you heard I'm working up at the Brand house?"

"Oh, right. You having fun?"

That was the first time anyone had put it like that. "It's a good job," she said.

"She signed a nondisclosure agreement," Louise said to Velázquez, as if Kate wasn't there. "So I don't know half of what's going on up there. Did you hear how rude Theo Brand was to Marjorie on Thursday?"

Kate, who had already heard this story, tried not to roll her eyes. "Well, in Theo's defense"—words she never thought she'd hear herself say— "Marjorie *did* try to break into his front gate." Apparently the woman had pulled so hard she had almost broken the hinge.

"She wasn't breaking in. She was bringing him cookies. Neighborly cookies." Louise took another one of the cookies on the table and held it up as an example. "Marjorie's are very flavorful. Leah might want to ask her advice. If she's serious about the baking show, I mean."

Kate pushed ahead. "Anyway, Chief Velázquez—"

"Please, call me Victor."

"Victor. Louise told me that you worked Miranda Brand's case. And I wanted to hear about it from your perspective. To make sense of what I'm finding up there."

He raised his eyebrows. "Why? What are you finding?"

"Papers, letters, photos. That kind of thing."

"Huh," he said. "Well, I'd love to help you. But I don't know anything about art."

"You don't have to. I'm more curious about . . . Well, everyone talks about her death, but I don't know any of the facts, you know? Just rumors. And I don't want to ask Theo about it. For obvious reasons. But I'd like to understand how she died."

Victor frowned. "Didn't Frank tell me you're a journalist?"

"I used to be." She didn't bother to correct her job title. "Not anymore. But this isn't for a story."

"So it's off the record."

"Sure. Totally off the record." It was an easy promise. She couldn't imagine what newspaper would take any story she wrote.

Mollified, he leaned back in his chair and ran his hand over his mustache.

"Well, where should I start?" he asked.

"Start with finding the body," Louise said.

He grimaced. "God, it was awful. It was only the second dead body I ever caught up here. I was a rookie. I had been working the traffic beat in Fresno. Saw some car crashes, but this . . . As soon as I saw her, I actually ran back to the car and threw up. Not my proudest moment. The problem was, I had met her before. It's a lot harder when it's someone you've seen alive."

"So you recognized her," Kate said.

"More or less. I mean, half her head was blown off. But I had recognized the address as soon as we got it off the scanner. The dispatcher said the victim was a woman. I pretty much knew what we'd find."

"Who called it in?"

"Theo. He found the body."

"So she was dead when you got there."

Victor gave her a look. "Like I said. Half her brain was missing."

"Oh, God," Louise said, her eyes bright with morbid curiosity.

"Right away it looked like a suicide," Victor continued. "The gun was next to her. Everyone knew she had troubles. Still, the sheriff's office sent Barb down as a matter of protocol. We're a local police department. We're not equipped to do that kind of investigation."

"Barb?"

"Barbara Lippland. She was the lead on the case."

"Where does she live?"

"She died of ovarian cancer two years ago. Very sad. Although I will say, she was a real terror on this investigation. She brought some other officers down here to help, and she had us all running around. Interviewing people. Trying to establish Miranda's state of mind. Things like that."

"So she didn't think it was a suicide," Kate said.

"Well, she was dotting her i's and crossing her t's. It was a high-profile case, and there was a lot of pressure on her. And she was always a real by-the-book type. She was hung up on this idea that legally speaking, for a suicide verdict, you need evidence of a desire to self-harm. She wanted to know why the gun was clean, whether Miranda had left a suicide note."

"Had she?"

"No. But most suicides don't."

"And what do you mean, the gun was clean?"

"It didn't have any fingerprints on it. Even Miranda's."

"*What?*"

"You know, I think there was a case like this on *CSI*," Louise said in a hushed voice. "And it turned out the murderer had burned all his fingertips so he wouldn't leave any prints. Did you check people's fingers? To see if they had burned them?"

Kate and Victor turned to stare at Louise. Sometimes Kate wondered if her aunt was secretly trolling her.

"Everyone we talked to had fingerprints," Victor said at last.

Kate pointedly turned her head back to him. "Where did the gun even come from?"

"Jake had bought it. He said he wanted to put it in some painting he was working on. Of course, Barb asked him why he couldn't just use a plastic one, which really shocked him." Victor chuckled. "He said he would paint it differently if he knew it was plastic. It wouldn't have the same . . . what was the word he used? 'Menace.' Barb didn't like that explanation. She had one of us do a bunch of calling around, asking about Jake's artistic process. I guess it checked out in the end. Anyway, he didn't keep the gun locked up. In fact, he left it in his studio, which he and Miranda shared. So that's how she got it."

Kate didn't like this explanation any more than Barb had. "You questioned him, though, right? Did he have an alibi?"

Something changed about Victor's posture. Kate couldn't put her finger on what it was, exactly, but suddenly it seemed like he was sitting on a steel chair rather than a recliner, and she was thinking, *Oh, right. He's a cop.*

"Of course we questioned him," he said. "No, he didn't have an alibi. I wouldn't expect him to. She died at five, six in the morning, so he was asleep. But listen, Jake was a good guy. I knew him for a long time before Miranda died, and I saw how he acted after. He was torn up. She had been everything to him. He had been through a lot, taking care of her, making sure she was okay."

"He sounds like a really nice guy." Kate let just a touch of skepticism leak into her voice.

"He was."

So he wasn't budging on that. Kate changed tack. "What about Kid Wormshaw?" she asked. "Louise told me they were friends. Did you talk to him?"

Now Victor looked really annoyed. "Yes, we talked to Kid. We talked to everyone. We did our jobs, okay?"

"Of course you did. I'm sorry. I wasn't trying to imply otherwise. I was just wondering what Kid . . . what everyone said about Miranda."

"The same stuff," he said, and she wanted to ask, *Same as what?* But she held her tongue.

Instead she said delicately, "I heard some people think Theo was involved. That there might have been an accident."

Louise had been mostly quiet so far—a pleasant surprise—so Kate hadn't called her out directly. But Victor let out a huff and turned to Louise anyway.

"Is this about what I said to Frank at bingo?" he demanded.

"What?" Louise clapped a hand to her chest. "No! No, not at all. I don't know what Kate's talking about."

"You know, this kind of stuff really ticks me off." Victor passed his hand over his forehead. "These rumors get so out of control. I mean, Frank told me Theo was coming back, and I started saying some stuff I shouldn't have. You know how strong Chuck's margaritas are. But I never said Theo had done it. He was just a kid."

"Accidents happen," Kate said.

"Trust me. That gunshot was no accident." He mimed a gun with his hand and held his finger to his skull an inch above his ear, pointing diagonally down. "The bullet went in right here, then down and out through her chin. The coroner told us it was fired no more than a few inches away. That's why her brains were all over the place."

"Victor, please," Louise said. Kate couldn't tell whether she meant "please stop" or "please go on, in great detail."

"I know what people say about Theo," Victor said. "He was . . . different as a kid, even before all this happened. But I also know what boys are like at that age. I have two sons." He gestured at the family photos Kate had been looking at earlier. "And if you think an eleven-year-old could kill his mother at close range, see her body in the shape it was in, then call the police and fake tears like that, all without getting blood on his clothes . . . No. No way."

Kate had thought something similar when she was looking at the photos of Theo in Miranda's darkroom. How young he had been, how innocent. But it was Victor's first words that caught in her mind. *I know what people say.* How many times had Kate imagined hearing those words about herself? How many times had she walked into a room and heard the chatter stop for a beat, as if passing over a speed bump? She had been so quick to judge Theo. The truth was, a part of her had been relieved that someone else was the focus of speculation.

"So what about someone else?" she asked, pushing aside her discomfort. "Maybe she went out that morning to meet someone. She was standing there talking to them, it got heated, she turned away, and they shot her. Then they wiped the gun off after. It's possible, right? They just would have had to get through the gate."

Victor rubbed his eyes, tired. "The gate wasn't like it is now. Jake had that put in after they left town."

"So *anyone* could have come in. I know how many people disliked her. You really never had any other suspects?"

For an instant, Victor's face seemed to shudder, as if it had been wrenched sideways. A light went on in his eyes, then out.

"No," he said. "No one important."

"People from her childhood? From the art world?"

"I am not going to name everyone we investigated," he said in what Kate now thought of as his cop voice.

Before she could push him any further, he looked at the clock and said, "Well, all right. I better get back to my day." He picked up the plate of cookies, which Louise had mostly demolished, and held it out to them. "One for the road?"

At the front door, as Louise moseyed out to admire Leah's new mulch, Victor patted Kate awkwardly on the shoulder.

"You're asking good questions," he said. "I'm sorry it wasn't what you wanted to hear."

Although he meant it kindly, Kate didn't like the way he phrased it, as if she were a child who had been denied a second scoop of ice cream. She turned back to him. "I forgot. Earlier, you said they couldn't rule it a suicide unless they could prove Miranda's state of mind. So what happened? Did you find proof?"

"Oh, we didn't have to." He gave a dismissive wave. "We had all her photographs. Self-mutilation. Blood everywhere. Her hospital admission, her list of prescriptions. That was all the evidence we needed. In the end, the investigation was just a formality."

As Kate and Louise walked down through the pink clouds of the Velázquezes' manzanita bushes, Louise asked, "Did you see his face when you asked about other suspects?"

"Yeah," Kate said, surprised her aunt had caught that. "Do you know who he was talking about?"

Louise shook her head. "No," she said sadly. "I haven't heard anything."

"At least we know Theo didn't shoot her," Kate said, mostly to herself.

Louise nodded sagely. Then she added, as if she couldn't help it, "At least not by accident."

"Aunt Louise!" Exasperated, Kate stopped at the end of the walkway, so fast her aunt bumped into her. "Did you see how Victor was holding his hand, imitating the gun? I've seen photos of Theo from back then. There's no way he could have gotten the gun up anywhere near high enough."

"Okay, but—"

"Besides, I think Victor's right," Kate continued, a little more loudly. "Would an eleven-year-old really be able to shoot his mother point-blank and lie about it?"

"No, you're right, you're right," Louise said. She exhaled and clapped her hands together. "Well! That's a relief. So nervous over nothing."

Kate tugged at the end of her ponytail. "I guess so. But now I feel kind of bad."

Louise frowned. "Why?"

"For thinking he did it." Kate gave her a pointed look. "Don't *you* feel bad?"

"For what?"

"For spreading the rumor."

"I didn't spread any rumors."

"Aunt Louise."

With a huff, Louise started walking again, in the direction of home. They walked like that for a while, Louise a pace ahead, Merrells crunching over the maple seeds that littered the sidewalk. The air was bright and clean, and daylilies spiked yellow through the fences, but all Kate could think about was that dim November morning so many years ago—the sticky tumble of Miranda's hair, the police lights spinning red and blue through the fog.

"The Fourth of July party," Louise said suddenly. "Is Theo coming?"

"I don't know. It's a party, so . . . probably not."

"Get him to come. We'll make sure he has fun."

"I'm not sure Theo is really a 'fun' kind of guy," Kate said.

"You said you felt bad. I'm giving you a way to fix it."

Seeing Louise's profile from this angle reminded Kate of their resemblance. It was strange, seeing your features on someone else. Like looking into a hall of mirrors. One long genetic *mise en abyme*. Your real self could get lost in all the reflections.

"Okay," Kate said. "I'll see what I can do."

MIRANDA

SERIES 2, Personal papers

BOX 9, Diary (1982–1993)

NOVEMBER 20 1982

Pottle says I should write about Nangussett. "A step in the healing process." Unfortunately it's harder than you would think, to explain how you went crazy. Even flipping back through this book, I can barely piece it all together. The words blur and jump on the page and I get this heavy sick feeling in my stomach and it ruins me for the rest of the day. Focus on getting through the day, that's what they tell you. Like you're drunk and stumbling along some policeman's yellow line and you're supposed to focus on walking. But the problem isn't that I'm not focusing. The problem is that I've forgotten how to walk at all.

My memory of that night starts with me telling Jake, I have to go in. He said to wait until the morning. His voice was flat and firm. I never wanted to marry a kind man, that was never important to me, but in that moment I wished he were kinder. It was late at night and I had looked at the baby and thought about running a blade through his tiny heart and I knew I could not do this anymore.

So I pretended I was going outside for a smoke and instead I walked to Nangussett, which was only ten blocks away. I started feeling so far away from the baby, and I thought about how I should have taken him with me. Only if I had brought him I would have had to bring so much fucking shit, the pacifier and the toy and the baby jacket and the stroller and the diapers, and then I was thinking this is my whole life now, I will never not have this baby, I will never not have to walk under the burden of endless plastic shit. This is the last time I will leave the house alone. Should I have brought him? Half of me thought he would be safer with me. Half of me thought if I picked him up again I might crush his little skull into the ground.

The whole time I walked, I was scratching at my arms because it felt like there was something stuck inside me and I thought if I opened up my skin it would come out. The scratching hurt so much but once the blood started coming all the pain disappeared. It seemed to take forever to get to the hospital. I went to the emergency room. The woman at the desk had her hair all wound up onto her head like a magical beehive. I told her I needed to see a doctor and she looked at me, then at my arms—I forgot my coat, why hadn't Jake made me take my coat?—and she called out over her shoulder, "PSYCH EVAL" in this bored voice, like she had seen a hundred of me that night. After a while, I saw a doctor. He listened to what I said, mm-hmm, mm-hmm, and then he asked, Where's your baby? Like maybe I had actually killed him. I said he was with my husband. He called Jake and told him to come down in the morning for visiting hours. I was staying overnight.

The rest of the time there was so much noise. Screaming and wailing. People begging to get out. Quiet sobbing—like mice snuffling in a kitchen. But the silence was no better. Then I lay in my narrow bed and my thoughts hung over my head like an ornately woven carpet, the motifs brawling with one another for my attention, ravens and roses and tigers. There was a pattern but I couldn't figure it out. The carpet was musty and so close to me. At any moment it could fall and cover me. It was the kind of carpet you would use to hide a body. Roll it up nice and tight, heave it in the trunk of a car. That's what Nangussett felt like—like someone was driving me around rolled up in a carpet, so I couldn't see what was happening, I could only feel when we hit a bump and my body collided with the side of the trunk.

The smell of shit and piss—all this time I had spent reading about the abject and I barely understood. I had never lived with the sourness of my insides. I had never known how bitter we smell. All the blood in my photos was fake.

Not now. From here on out, the blood is real.

The people in there were all crazies but I divided them into two types. One: the greasy, believed-they-were-chickens, skin-scratching, screaming, self-pissing people. The Chickens grabbed your attention first. They made you afraid. One woman put another in a chokehold and crushed her windpipe. One woman followed another one around trying to pluck out individual strands of her hair. Eventually, once all that chaos passed, you saw that there were other people too, flat cardboard people, faces drawn shut, sallow and pudgy. Ghosts.

It's easy to know whether other people are Chickens or Ghosts, but it's harder to figure out which one you are. The chokehold lady, for instance, thought she was on the verge of getting out. Even as they dragged her out to the isolation wing, her victim still as a rock on the floor, she screamed, Why me? Why are you picking on me? I keep to myself. I do what you ask. I behave.

Sometimes I was a Chicken. One time Jake visited and I saw him recoil from me. Greasy and unshowered, my arms bandaged from scratching, sobbing and talking in equal measure. I thought I was a saint. I asked people to kiss my toes.

Other times I was a Ghost, and people looked right through me.

I wasn't progressing. They wanted me to move toward sanity at a steady, decent rate, like a cable car going up a mountain. My cable car got stuck. It was bouncing around in the wind. So they took me to a little room and shocked me with electric currents. Buzz, buzz. Prodding the cattle. Get the cow to move.

A tube down my throat tasted like a tin can.

The tube came before the ECT.

The order of things is hard to remember now.

There were forms to sign. Jake was there. He visited sometimes, but my brain can't remember how often. He says it was pretty much every day so I guess we'll go with that. Even if it's not true, it's nice to hear. Anyway, Jake was there and asking us about the ECT. I tried to speak but I couldn't. My throat hurt from the tube. So yes, that must have come before. I was so tired. I had this feeling that if I opened my mouth at all, to talk or to eat, all my ideas would come rushing out in a black mess, and I would have nothing left. So I said nothing. I stayed quiet to protect who I am. Not that it mattered. Jake was in charge now.

I remember him looking at me, and a kind of cold wonder dawned on his face. Like he understood it was all on him now. He had total control.

I consent, he said.

Chicken or Ghost? Maybe it doesn't matter. To people on the outside, we were all the same.

9.

KATE

H ey."
Kate spun around, startled.

"Sorry," Theo said. "I didn't mean to scare you."

"Oh, no. It's fine." She hit the space bar on her computer to pause the music and wondered how long he had been standing there. It was early afternoon, and she had been trying to get through her usual post-lunch slump by bopping along to a '90s hits playlist, which she now realized might have looked less than professional. "Was I too loud?"

"Well. I did enjoy your Whitney rendition." When she didn't reply, he held out his hand, palm facing her, as if he were approaching a skittish raccoon. "I'm kidding. I mean, I did hear you. But only because I was down here anyway, and I thought I would ask if you needed help with anything."

Kate didn't like when he was nice. It made her feel worse about sneaking around the house and reading his mother's diary. Although, she reminded herself, she wouldn't have had to do that if he had shown her the diary in the first place.

"I'm fine," she said. "Thanks, though."

"What are you working on?"

She couldn't tell if he was testing her or if he was just curious. She had to look down at the table to remember what she had been doing before he came in.

"Oh," she said. "Your sketchbooks."

"*My* sketchbooks?"

She lifted one up off the pile and showed him the inside cover. *Theo Brand*, it said in a child's wobbly letters. He looked surprised.

"Good cursive," Kate remarked.

He came forward and stood next to her. He smelled good, she thought, and was immediately horrified with herself. It was probably just his soap. Dr. Bronner's peppermint. Which she only knew because she had searched his entire bathroom. She wanted to sink into a hole in the floor.

Instead she said, "I like your drawings."

"I was terrible," he said, smiling.

"All kids are terrible."

He ran his finger down the coil of one spine. "My parents wanted me to be a prodigy. They thought their powers combined would create some miracle. But I had no sense of color. No artistic spirit."

"Oh, come on," Kate said.

"Hand to heart. Their exact words."

Kate opened her mouth, then closed it. Frowned. It was such a cruel thing to say to a child. True, Miranda had a reputation for brittleness, but her pictures, even the violent ones, were so sensitive to light, to the weight of her forms. They showed tenderness. Theo was making it sound like she had been kinder to her photographs than to her own son.

"There was something I wanted to ask you about," she said, changing the subject. "Here, let me find it."

She put on her gloves and went to one of the boxes she had been transferring photographs into. She lifted each one out until she found what she was looking for. It was a print of *The Threshold*. She had found a few by now. On the back, Miranda had written three lines. In red pen:

MB 1990

And then, in black Sharpie, as if it had been added later:

All I ever wanted was a life that meant something.

I thought wanting it would be enough.

Miranda had written on other prints, too. Not names or places, but mysterious phrases that did not describe the photo's contents. *Gray tendrils, heavy salt*, she had written on the reverse of an image of dried seaweed. On a self-portrait: *I am time, I refuse myself.*

"Are the words supposed to be part of the art?" Kate asked Theo. "Or are they just notes to herself?"

He studied the writing. His good humor faded, leaving his face severe. He reached out to touch the edge of the picture, and although her instinct was to flinch the paper away, she let his finger graze it. It belonged to him, after all.

"I don't know," he said at last, dropping his hand. "I guess we'll have to wait to see what Hal says."

"Hal Eggers?"

"Yeah. He's the one in charge of selling the stuff. He was my parents' dealer."

"I've seen his name." Kate studied the print. "This must be worth a fortune. It's in perfect condition. Plus the inscription. What'll it sell for? Six hundred grand? Seven?"

"Why?" Theo asked. "Are you planning to steal it?"

Kate was so taken aback she almost dropped the picture.

"Of course not," she said. "I would never do that. Even if I could get away with it, which I couldn't."

She set about returning the photograph to its box so that she didn't have to look at him. Who the fuck *was* he, thinking everyone was out to get him? She had spent so much time this weekend wondering if she had misjudged him, and he kept tossing out these stupid accusations.

"I'm sorry," he said. "I shouldn't have said that."

"You know, I get that you have this whole dark and brooding thing going on," she said, waving her hand in his direction. "But number one, it's not working for you. And number two, it's not working for your kids."

"What are you talking about?"

"Jemima and Oscar need friends. That's why she's been stealing things at camp. She needs to distract herself because she doesn't have anyone to hang out with. And Oscar goes along with it because he doesn't know anyone, either."

"I put them in camp so that they would make friends."

"Yeah, but then you hole up here and ignore everyone in town. The parents start talking shit about you, and their kids hear it. Then no one wants to hang out with Oscar and Jemima. And you aren't friends with anyone in town, so there's no chance of a playdate. You do know what a playdate is, right?"

"Yes, I know what a playdate is," Theo said wearily. "I do actually have friends, you know. They just don't live in Callinas."

"So find some new ones."

"We're only here a couple more months."

"You don't have to swear a blood oath of fealty to anyone. Just make some acquaintances."

Theo raised his eyebrows, but he didn't protest. He was no longer projecting his usual doom-and-gloom vibes, so Kate forged ahead.

"The town is having a Fourth of July party on the beach," she said. "They have it every year, I guess. My aunt is helping organize it. Obviously it's going to be extreme. And kind of stupid. And your worst nightmare. But you should come."

Now he looked almost amused.

"Should I," he said.

Probably people didn't volunteer to help him very often. Either they didn't think he needed help, or they were afraid to offer.

"Yes," Kate said firmly. "I insist."

MIRANDA

SERIES 2, Personal papers

BOX 9, Diary (1982–1993)

DECEMBER 9 1982

William from Downtown Studios has the new disease. I saw him today when I was coming out of my studio to go home and he was unlocking his door to go in. He looked fine to my eyes, maybe a little thin, until he pulled his collar down to show me the dark patches on his neck.

He said he didn't know how long it would take. He just wanted to do as much work as possible before the end.

A literal deadline, he said, and then we began to cry.

I have to try.

I have to try harder.

SERIES 2, Personal papers

BOX 8, Medical records

FOLDER: Prescriptions and refills

Prescription issued 1/2/1983

1200 mg lithium as 600 mg 2x/day.

300 mg zimelidine. 1 pill 2x/day. Taper up from 150 mg: take ½ extra pill for 1 week, then switch to full dose.

Call prescriber or emergency room 911 with any symptoms.

<<*Duane Reade! We fill generics AND brand-names!*>>

SERIES 2, Personal papers
BOX 9, Diary (1982–1993)

JANUARY 27 1983

I'm starting to see things again: the light against someone's nose; a shapely leaf; the thick rippled veins on the grocery clerk's arms, dotted with old needle marks.

I can take the subway again. I only lose a couple minutes here and there.

I see Theo again. I see his fat little body, his elbows puffed up like rice, his wet mouth. I have started to breastfeed him again sometimes, though it feels strange, like he is sucking out all my power through my breast. I can do this—I can be his mother.

I no longer think terrible things when I look at him. I only think about how tired I am and how I love him and how he needs a change of diaper. I hate changing his diaper. It makes me think of Tina smearing shit across the walls in Nangussett. Hieroglyphs. The stench.

I am not there anymore, I remind myself.

I am here. I am out.

Sometimes Jake and Theo and I are eating dinner and I see our reflection in the window and for a split second I think, that family across the way looks happy, and then I realize it's us.

FEBRUARY 4 1983

Today I saw:

A reflection on the lake in Central Park. Clouds moving above, swish swish, their dark vulnerable stomachs turned down to the water.

A homeless woman with bubblegum rain boots.

Two safety razors Jake threw out, crossed in the garbage can in the shape of an X.

And I saw Theo as I think other mothers must see their children: a circle of small miracles. Each breath he takes, the soapy smell of his heart. Each precious delicate finger, curled up against my chest. His big green eyes. How far he had to travel to get into this world. Down through my womb, or else out from a distant galaxy of exploding stars.

FEBRUARY 28 1983

Today I went to my usual guy down the road to get sour coffee and a rolled-up *Times*. His papers are always a little damp. I don't want to know why. I read the paper in a certain order: the Arts section, which I skim because it's bullshit; then Business and Sports, which I don't know anything about but that relaxes me; and then finally the actual important news, because by that time I'm bored enough by the idea of news that I don't get so freaked out by whatever the government is getting up to.

I never got to Cal Ripken Jr. or the Soviet Union though. I never even got to the *Times*, because when my usual guy was handing me my crap coffee I saw a tabloid with a headline in the corner saying: ART WORLD DARLING MIRANDA BRAND NEARLY KILLED HER OWN CHILD.

I bought it even though I knew I shouldn't and I brought it back here and read it with shaking hands. And now . . . now the phone is ringing. FUCK this fucking SHIT.

The Squeal

FEBRUARY 28–MARCH 6, 1983

Miranda Brand, 27, has captured attention as a rising star in the New York art scene. When she vanished from public view last year, her fans assumed she was working on her latest important project—raising her infant son. However, *The Squeal* has now learned that Brand's disappearance had darker roots. Far from playing the doting mother, Brand spent two months in the psych ward after a psychotic break during which she tried to strangle her newborn.

Located on the Upper West Side, Nangussett Hospital's infamous Psychiatric Unit claims to treat disorders ranging from schizophrenia to sociopathy. Nurses are required to complete training in restraining violent patients. An inside source says that Brand received multiple treatments of electroshock therapy. During group therapy, she described detailed fantasies of killing her son and said she believed the child had been injected into her body by aliens.

After two months of sustained treatment, Brand was released and returned to her Midtown apartment, where she now raises her child with her husband, the painter Jake Brand. Jake, 32, has undoubtedly borne the brunt of his wife's illness, as he must now raise an infant son and grow his own artistic career while monitoring his unstable wife. Rumor has it that Miranda is not even allowed to be alone with the child, for fear that she will relapse.

It is unclear what impact Brand's mental instability will have on her burgeoning photography career. While her output has been limited since the hospitalization, a source close to the family reports that she has been working on a new series that will offer a window into her troubled mind. That is, if she lives long enough to finish it.

SERIES 2, Personal papers
BOX 9, Diary (1982–1993)

MARCH 12 1983

A source, a source. No one will tell me who it was. I've called the tabloid a thousand times. I told them I'll sue them. They won't budge. Apparently you get to keep your privacy even when you destroy someone else's.

MARCH 21 1983

William died. Went to the funeral. Third one this year. We brought Theo. Big mistake. Everyone stared at me like I might drop him on his head. I started sweating. Eventually I pinched Theo's leg to make him cry, then took him outside, as if to calm him down. We stood in front of the church watching the taxis pass, our tears mixing. Grieving is a wet process.

MARCH 27 1983

Lynn put me in touch with a lawyer who said I can file a libel lawsuit. He asked me which parts of the article are untrue.

I said, The photo of Capillaries #3 they put in, they misaligned the dots while printing, so now it looks like shit. When actually it's a great piece.

He said he more meant what they wrote.

I said, Where to start?

I mean, I can be left alone with Theo. Jake leaves me alone with him all the time. He has to go to his studio, go to events on our behalf. Now he'll have to go to even more, I guess, to tell people I'm not crazy. Damage control.

Also, I don't know about the nurses' training, but I wasn't violent. I wasn't that kind of Chicken. (I tried to explain Chickens and Ghosts. He didn't get it.)

He said, OK, that's great. What about the psychotic break? The electroshock? What about these fantasies? What about you wanting to kill yourself? Is any of that true?

He sounded so convinced it was all made up. I didn't know how to break it to him that yes, I am just as fucked up as they say.

I said, It's the way they put it together . . .

What we have to focus on are the factual inaccuracies, he said.

I thought for a moment.

Well, I never tried to strangle Theo. I only fantasized about it.

That's it, he said, relieved. Perfect. That's what we'll focus on.

MAY 14 1983

The past few months have made me want to blow my brains out. The calls, the letters, the newspaper articles. Lawyer updating me about the lawsuit, like the lawsuit can undo that heartbeat after people recognize me, when their eyes fill with fascination, disgust. I don't even think about going to the gallery openings, the parties. I can't handle how everyone looks at me. They see me through a frame I didn't make.

No, but think of the good news, Miranda! The shrink says I have to lead with the good news before letting myself get to the real shit. (Not his exact words.)

Good News: Apparently if people think you might kill yourself any day, the value of your works goes way up and your dealers sell out of everything they have. So suddenly you've finished paying the medical bills and your bank account is bulging and you have all the time in the world to create something new, because whenever you finish it, it will surprise people that you are not already dead or in jail.

Good News: Hal is happy.

Good News: Jake is happy. He sold a painting recently, a decent chunk of change. Of course then the tabloid happened, and now money's not an issue, but selling work puts him in a good mood. Which makes the days go smoother.

Good News: Theo is happy. Cooing and cuddling. Talking gibberish words. A sweet boy. A good phase.

Bad News: Someone sold me out.

Bad News: Everyone knows I'm crazy.

Bad News: Maybe I'm still crazy.

Bad News: You never really know for sure.

10.

KATE

There was already a crowd at the Fourth of July party by the time Kate, Frank, and Louise hauled their wares over the rise of the dunes. Folding tables had been set up in the middle of the beach, and they were fully laden, their middles bowed by stoneware tagines and large aluminum trays. Red, white, and blue balloons snapped in the breeze. The mayor was blending margaritas in a battery-powered travel blender. Louise had also gone all out, making a watermelon salad and a leek soufflé that she had been worrying about ever since it came out of the oven that afternoon. Now she set it down on one folding table with an audible sigh of relief.

"Your cake's not here," Kate said. Her aunt had spent hours the previous day baking an elaborate cake with alternating layers of blue- and red-dyed batter, but she had transferred it to her friend Nora to decorate.

"Nora has it in her car. We're going to bring it out as a surprise," Louise said.

The party was much bigger than Kate had expected. There must have been two hundred people there, easily. Women in woven ponchos and men in quarter-zip sweaters. Women with clipped blond bobs and men in Hawaiian shirts. Star-spangled knee socks. A baseball cap that said *Make America Gay Again*. Babies swaddled to their mothers' chests. Children building sandcastles, children crying. Kate had never seen so many Callinas residents in one place.

Her palms began to sweat. She had been so distracted with getting Theo to come to this thing, she hadn't thought about what a party would mean for her. How many people there would be.

This was different than parties in Brooklyn, she reminded herself. It *had* to be different. Here, the curious looks had nothing to do with her. People wanted to know about Theo, about Miranda, about the house. She was a means for getting the gossip, not the target.

Still, when the mayor handed her a margarita, her clammy hands slipped a little on the cup.

"You're sure they're coming, right?" Louise asked as she hid someone's rival soufflé under a pile of paper napkins.

"Theo said they were."

"I guess there's still time. The fireworks don't start until nine. No, Katie, don't eat that. Benny only uses some bizarre fake sugar substitute. One time he made a flan and it gave Frank diarrhea for a week."

The party swirled and heated. Beer and food made tanned shoulders sweaty even as the temperature dropped and dusk came in from the ocean. Loud chatter about property taxes and Lake Tahoe, kombucha starters and quinoa chips, the problems with Whole Foods but also how it offered so many *options*. Weed smoke in the air.

Everyone Kate met wanted to talk about the Brands. One guy who had been on the zoning board in the '80s said that when Jake and Miranda moved to Callinas, they had wanted to construct an outbuilding to use as their art studio, but it would have needed another water line, so the town had declined their proposal. The Brands made a huge fuss, he said, "but we won in the end." A librarian told Kate that Miranda had once checked out forty books from the library—books she could certainly afford to buy!—and returned them stained and defaced with notes *in pen* in the margins.

Roberta, Wendy, and Wendy's husband were there, twelve-month-old Texas hoisted on Wendy's hip. It seemed they had used their best Brand story the other day, because now they just kept listing expensive nearby restaurants, as if Kate could afford to spend ninety dollars on a tasting menu. Kate was trying to steer the conversation away from Wendy's Whole 30 diet when a force collided with the back of her leg, almost buckling her knee.

"*Kate.*" Jemima sighed happily and wrapped her arms around Kate's midsection. "*There* you are."

Kate turned awkwardly, dragging Jemima in a circle with her. Theo and Oscar were coming in from the parking lot. Theo was handsome in a black windbreaker, his face tanned and angular in the setting sun. She felt a strange, piercing relief to see him, which she attributed to knowing she wouldn't have to field any of Louise's complaints later.

As they got closer, Theo said, "Say hi to people before you run into them, Jem."

"It's not people," Jemima replied, still clinging to Kate. "It's Kate. She's my friend."

"You still have to be polite to your friends."

Jemima sniffed. "You didn't say hi to her either."

Theo smiled at Kate. "Hi."

"Hi," Kate said. She realized that she had never seen him off his property, and out here he looked larger, more alive, as if the house had been slowly squishing him into a small cube.

"I thought maybe you guys had decided not to come," she said.

"They really wanted to. And I thought about what you said." He looked down at Oscar, who was sucking his thumb as he stared in wonder at the balloons. Theo reached down and gently pulled his son's thumb out of his mouth. "So here we are."

Kate wanted to ask what he was so afraid of, then realized that an hour ago, she had been stressed about the party, too. She felt less stressed now. She actually felt kind of light, like she was levitating. She looked down at her margarita cup and saw it was empty.

"This is Roberta and Wendy," she said. They were standing at attention, eyes trained on Theo. "I guess maybe you knew each other when you were younger?"

"Did we?" Theo smiled politely at Wendy. "Nice to see you again. Listen, I better help get the kids some food."

He took Jemima's hand, too, and the three of them walked toward the picnic tables like they were heading into battle.

Once he was out of earshot, Wendy turned to the others and widened her eyes. "Well, hot damn. He turned out all right."

"You know, I'm right here," her husband said.

Wendy smiled at him. "Yes, and you're *much* nicer."

"Like mother, like son," Roberta said.

Kate said nothing. She didn't know how to explain to them what it meant for Theo to come here. That what felt like a brush-off . . . well, *was* a brush-off, but for good reason. Just think what they had been saying in Pawpaw's the other day. The knot inside Kate seemed to grow another loop, and as she changed the subject to local hikes, she clutched her plastic cup until it began to crack.

Nikhil was at the party with his girlfriend, Sabrina, a rock-climbing instructor who was wearing a fanny pack unironically and somehow pulling it off. They had brought along their roommate Josh. Josh was the kind of guy who would describe himself as "sarcastic" on a dating app. His main redeeming quality appeared to be that he had stopped drinking alcohol for his keto diet, so he was a good designated driver.

"Wait, you used to work for the *Tribune*?" he asked Kate. "And now you're here? Why?"

"I needed a change of pace," Kate said.

Even though he had asked the question, Josh didn't seem to be listening. Instead he sat down on the sand, pulled a tiny baggie of weed and some artisanal filter papers out of his pocket, and set about rolling the world's most pretentious joint.

"Yeah, that journalism stuff is crazy, man," he said. "Round the clock, am I right? Actually, I know someone from college who works at the *Tribune* now."

"It's a big company," Kate said.

"Landon McDowell?"

Kate paled. She knew Landon. Not well—he worked on sports reporting, which she had barely ever touched. But he definitely knew her. He was close friends with one of Leonard's protégés, and one of the people who had signed the company letter in Leonard's defense.

Sabrina seemed to see something on her face, because before Kate could reply, she said brightly, "Oh my God, not the name game. How's California? Our weather is better than New York, right?"

"Definitely," Kate said, throwing her a grateful look. "It's been in the nineties all week back there."

"Anyway, Miranda Brand is cool," Josh continued, as if Sabrina hadn't spoken. He had finished rolling the joint and now got to his feet. "Total commitment to her craft. Even how she died."

"What does her craft have to do with that?" Kate asked.

"Didn't she do all those pictures of, like, cutting herself? So suicide was like the culmination of her work." He put the joint between his lips and pulled a lighter from his front pocket. "Now she's famous for it. She's a fucking household name. A feminist icon."

"To some people," Sabrina said.

Josh looked at her, surprised. "You don't like her? You're the biggest man-hater I know."

Sabrina rolled her eyes. "I don't dislike her. I just don't really care. Like, of course she was successful. She was pretty, white, rich. People love to see women like that go crazy. They think it's romantic. Like all those ladies lounging around with pneumonia in nineteenth-century paintings."

"Odalisques," Josh corrected, although Kate wasn't sure if that was actually correct.

"My point is, Miranda Brand got famous doing a lot of stuff that other women do and never get credit for. Women of color—we don't get put in the Guggenheim for being insane. If we threaten to kill our kids, we sure as fuck don't get to keep the kids. No one cares if we cut our bodies open. That isn't shocking to anyone. You see what I mean?"

"Yeah, I see," Kate said. "It's a good point."

Nikhil had been observing in silence, but now he spoke up. "I don't know, Sab. You can't judge her by the standards of today."

"I can't? Why not?"

"It was a different time."

"Intersectionality had *happened*, Nikhil. Combahee River Collective, Audre Lorde. I don't know that much about art specifically, but I'm sure there was the same thing in photography. But Miranda got the press coverage. Most of what she got famous for had already been done better by other women, only they weren't the kind of women who get profiled in *The New Yorker* or whatever."

"Okay, okay," Nikhil said, holding up his hands.

Sabrina shook her head, frustrated. "You can't just say *okay*."

"Well, this shit got serious," Josh said. He snapped his fingers and called out to an imaginary waiter: "Another margarita for the ladies?"

As if the alcohol could slow everyone's hearts, clean out all their wounds. As if Sabrina, or Kate, or any woman, just needed the world to be a little blurrier, and that would put their pain at the right level, a level that was tolerable and small.

As Nikhil laughed, Sabrina and Kate exchanged glances. When the pretend waiter didn't materialize, Josh grabbed Nikhil's half-full cup and passed it to Kate. That was some part of the gag, she guessed. She waited for Nikhil to take it back. Only he never did; in fact, he seemed to forget about it as soon as it left his hand. She felt stupid for taking it. She had accepted it automatically, and now she was stuck holding it, not wanting to drink the watery tequila, not wanting to dump it out in case one of the men accused her of being high-strung.

As she was looking around for a way to get rid of the cup, she saw Theo emerge out of the crowd. She had spotted him from afar earlier, holding a paper plate stacked with ribs as the residents circled him like hungry sharks. Now it looked like one or two had taken a bite out of him. His expression was harried, and he was walking a little too fast. Maybe it had been wrong of her to leave him to the scrum. She forced a smile and waved him over.

"Theo, this is Sabrina, Nikhil, Josh," she said, gesturing around. "This is Theo. Brand. My boss." She added the extra words to mask the fact that they had been talking about his family, but the explanation made it worse. Theo's eyes flicked to her.

"Hey, nice to meet you," Theo said to the others. He and Nikhil shook hands in that casual way men sometimes did, bringing their elbows out and almost slapping their palms together. Kate had never figured out where men learned that. Maybe the same place she learned to apologize for interrupting, or to rephrase her ideas in a meeting to make them sound like they were someone else's.

"Did you compete?" Theo motioned to Nikhil's T-shirt, which Kate now saw advertised a surfing championship from last year.

Nikhil brightened. "Yeah. I didn't place or anything. But I think maybe next year I will. Do you surf?"

That set off a conversation about surfing that Kate struggled to follow. Not that she would have participated even if she had known anything about surfing: she was too surprised to see Theo speaking with such ease. She had thought of him as a cranky shut-in, had assumed his keeping away from town had been due partly to his general discomfort with socializing. And he was still stern, of course. But outside that memory trap of a house, talking about a hobby, some of his brusqueness washed away, and he seemed . . . likable. It was as if she had let a tiger into a living room, thinking a bloodbath would ensue, only to discover that the tiger was vegetarian and would happily watch *Dancing with the Stars*.

Something like disappointment snuck up her neck. Kate realized that all this time, a part of her had liked that Theo was awful, because it meant that there was someone worse than her. Next to Theo she had been a goddamn sunbeam.

She must have been staring, because as Nikhil and Sabrina started talking about a beach a ways north, Theo turned his head slightly to look at her. The low sun settled comfortably on his cheekbones; the wind had tumbled his hair into dark waves. As always, his direct gaze was disconcerting, penetrating.

Her face reddened, and she buried her nose in the collar of her borrowed fleece to hide it. What was *wrong* with her? It had been several years since she had been attracted to someone that she also disliked. She had thought that phase of her life was over. She was thirty now. She was supposed to be attracted to reasonable, thoughtful, appropriate people.

When she looked down, to her relief, she saw Oscar edging his way into the circle between her and Theo. He wore his usual worried expression, but his cheeks were red from running around and his mouth was stained Popsicle blue and he wasn't crying, so it seemed like everything was going well. Kate squatted down to say hi.

"Are you having fun?" she asked.

Oscar shrugged. "I had two macaroni and cheese."

"That sounds delicious."

"And watermelon."

"Yum. Did you make any new friends?"

He hesitated. "Everyone's looking at us."

Kate glanced up. It was true. People had gathered closer to their circle without her realizing it, and they kept sneaking looks at Theo and Oscar. Inspecting them, recording them for later analysis.

"Jemima said it was because I had a big spot on my face," Oscar said, rubbing his cheek. "She said it looks like I have another nose."

"Oh, Oscar," Kate said. "She was just teasing you. There's nothing on your face except your face."

"No spot?"

"No spot. Pinky swear."

Oscar nodded and reached for Theo's leg, pinching the fabric of his father's jeans between two fingers, as if he were afraid of being left behind.

"Hey, squirt." Theo rested his hand on Oscar's head. His fingers were long enough to encompass his son's entire skull. "What's up?"

"I want to go home," Oscar mumbled into his leg.

"We'll go soon. We haven't even been here that long."

"We've been here a million and five years," Oscar said, but he wrapped his arms around Theo's leg and seemed to give up the argument. Kate patted his back, trying not to laugh.

When she glanced up at Theo, he was smiling down at her. A real smile, tentative, like he thought he might be happy but wasn't sure. She blushed again and looked away.

That was how she saw it—a ripple going through the crowd. A collective rumble of anticipation. Her blood went cold, her body guessing what would happen before her mind did.

She instinctively stood up and searched the crowd for the source of the commotion. When she found it, her heart sank. Louise. Of course. Her aunt and Nora and the mayor were all carrying a tray across the beach, struggling to keep it level as their feet sank into the sand. They came to a triumphant stop just a few feet away from her.

"We made this for you," Louise said to Theo. "To say welcome."

She and the mayor lifted the cake higher, and Nora peeled back the tinfoil. It was the sheet cake Louise had been making, only now it was frosted. Or rather printed—with a photograph of Miranda.

The photo they had chosen was the same one on the cover of Miranda's catalog, her familiar face carefully pixelated onto the vanilla buttercream frosting. The pupils weren't blacked out on this one, but it was worse: some genius had stabbed two striped candles straight through Miranda's eyes, so that they protruded like barber poles from her eye sockets. Other candles lined the border of the cake, and Louise swooped in with a grill lighter, flicking it over one candle after another until the cake glowed like a small sun.

At the top of the cake, white frosting spelled out *WELCOME BACK*.

A horrified laugh bubbled up in Kate's throat, viscous and sour, and she coughed to hide it. This was what Louise had meant when she said she would make it up to Theo. This was why she had wanted Kate to get him to come to the party. So she could present him with a cake with a photo of his dead mother while everyone stared at him.

And Kate had made it happen.

Beside her, Theo had gone perfectly still. As if he thought that if he didn't move, didn't even breathe, he might be teleported out of the moment.

"Thanks," he said.

Kate knew how fast grief could strike. She remembered it from when her grandfather had died of lung cancer, and when her best friend in high school had been hit by a drunk driver on the Sawmill Parkway the day before their graduation. All those weeks of thinking you were getting better, getting through it, and then a sharp wind came and you learned you had been walking a tightrope this whole time. The line slackened. You went tumbling. You were cast back, suddenly, to the minutiae of their dying—the unsteady drip of urine into your grandfather's catheter, or the satin lining of your friend's casket, the injuries sewn shut and covered with foundation for appearance's sake.

The rope was trembling beneath Theo now, and although he moved instinctively to balance, Kate saw how his weight shifted, searching for ground. The early morning ambulance. The spread of blood on a damp lawn. He had done such a good job hiding it, all these weeks; she had almost thought he didn't care.

Now she saw that she had been wrong, and the twist of recognition inside her was so painful she actually thought for a moment that she could feel his grief, that she had somehow pulled it into herself.

"Blow them out!" Louise said, meaning the candles. "Before the wind gets them!"

Theo looked up at a point slightly above everyone's head, as if hoping a meteor might swing close enough for him to jump aboard. Then he sighed and looked back down at the cake. Lowered his face, pursed his lips, and blew.

MIRANDA

SERIES 2, Personal papers
BOX 9, Diary (1982–1993)

OCTOBER 18 1983

I've been working, working, working, all the time. There's a lot of demand and Hal says I have to meet it. He says you never know how long you will be the hot thing. You have to live like you're always about to fall off the edge.

So I've been making prints of some old stuff, and booking models for a new series. I've been reading this whole series of books about ancient Egypt. I like how the figures are always in profile, always moving forward into the next part of the mural. The god Ra's eye is a woman who can run away from him and become her own goddess. The Eye of Ra. But he gets angry and chases her, and brings her back, and once she is his again, controlled, order is restored.

I don't know if any of this research will amount to anything. That's a new fear. I used to be good at pushing forward, focusing on the process, creating, creating. Now I am sometimes paralyzed by the fear that I will have to throw everything out. Terrified that months of my life will disappear again. Added to the fog.

I don't know if it was the ECT or the meds, but many of my days feel like dead weight. They pass before I know they are gone. And the next day

I cannot remember them. The last year exists for me in bolts and flashes, a club with bad lighting. Memories bouncing off a disco ball.

I am no longer the person I was, and I am also not the person I dreamed I would be. If you asked me two years ago where I would be right about now, I would have said I'd be thin again, propping a toddler on my hip as I went between gallery shows, eyes dark with kohl, making cutting comments, teaching people to love my art.

Well—that didn't work out.

That said, if I am not where I thought I would be two years ago, I also am not where I was one year ago, and that is a relief.

NOVEMBER 12 1983

How do you talk to other people, afterward? After the worst, I mean. After your brain swells you up and spits you out, a saliva lump of a human being. How do you communicate with people who spent that entire time in charge of their own mind?

This was something they never taught us in Nangussett.

They assumed we would be restored by the time we got out.

Reset to defaults.

And we would have no memory of what had happened to us in the meantime. No memory of our parts failing. No memory of the screams, the night checks, the boredom, the loneliness, the ways we accommodated the fear that we might never leave.

NOVEMBER 17 1983

Jake has been busy. He got offered a course for the spring semester. A good job, but between the class itself and his commute and his moving his studio over there, he's gone a lot during the day. Then at night he goes to openings or parties, drinks, does what you have to do in this industry.

On weekends, we go together to funerals. Five friends dead this year. I wear the same dress every time. Put it on, take it off, throw it in the hamper, wash, rinse, repeat.

The days Jake is teaching, I have all this time alone with Theo. I didn't realize how much I have avoided being alone with him. Just not trusting myself. And then I have all these long days, just me and him. There's a nice girl in the apartment downstairs who comes to watch him when I need to be in the darkroom. But otherwise I spend the days pushing him in a stroller through the streets, like maybe that will make me accountable somehow. The buildings rising around us in black smudges, like prison bars.

Everything is more dangerous now that he's walking. Clumsy steps. Careening back and forth like a drunken sailor. He's scared of grass—fortunately we don't have much of that around. Now everything in the apartment is a hazard. My mother came to visit and put zip ties around all our cabinet doors, cushioned the table corners, things I never even thought of.

At night I stay home staring at him sleep, watching his chest rise and fall, checking to make sure he hasn't died. Checking to make sure I haven't killed him.

I'm holding a ticking time bomb, and I have a shaky grip.

Jake doesn't have to be gone so much. He's avoiding me. But I can't blame him. I've changed. He chained himself to another Miranda, and she pulled a bait-and-switch. Now he has a worse version. Unstable. Uncertain. Stomach doughy and striped.

So let him roam. I don't know what we would do without him. It's better to give the dog a longer leash than to risk that he pulls himself free.

It won't last for long. We've been talking about leaving New York. Moving in the spring, using the libel settlement as our down payment. Jake has always wanted to live out west, and I like the idea of going somewhere by the sea. Somewhere with new views and inspiration. Somewhere quiet, where maybe I will improve. Maybe Jake will relax, and I will go back to being the person he married.

11.

KATE

Theo had stopped a hundred or so feet down the beach. Far enough away that the noise was dulled, close enough that he could not technically be said to have left. The wind had quieted, and the sun was preparing to move below the horizon. The organizers had set small electric lanterns around the perimeter of the party, but Theo had moved just beyond their glow, so as Kate approached, she only could see the shape of him, a dark rectangle against the cobalt sky, a lump in the middle where Oscar had fallen asleep in his arms. Then she, too, crossed the line of light and could see that Theo was watching the sun intently, as if he could keep it from slipping down.

She came to a halt a few feet away from him, not sure how to continue, or if she should. Her sneakers were damp and half-filled with sand. Behind them, the cake had been handed out. Slices of Miranda's face, the frosting ridging up where the knife cut it, the layer of raspberry jam streaking redly across the plates.

Kate had refused any cake, even though her refusal made Louise's eyebrows snap together. Theo had accepted a slice, but he hadn't eaten it. Instead, he had held the paper plate in one hand as Louise talked to him excitedly about the cake design, about how Kate had told her all about him, about how nice it was to meet him *at last*. As he conversed politely, he flipped the cake over, frosting-side down, and tore off little bits of the red-and-blue sponge and handed them down to Oscar. Jemima was off running around, gray icing smeared across her mouth. She had been given a whole corner of Miranda's face and had eaten it happily.

The whole time, Kate had wanted to scream. It was all the guilt she had felt after learning he couldn't have killed Miranda, and then some. Seeing Theo in that moment, seeing the clarity of his grief, had cracked something open inside her. Now she understood why he had been so rude before. Why he hadn't come down into town, why he had been so paranoid she would tell people anything about his parents. His fear was not dissimilar to the fear she had felt back in New York, where people knew about Leonard Webb or about her breakdown. It was the fear that people—strangers!—could, any time they liked, peel open this painful scab you had, just because they thought it was interesting, or just so they could tell you what they thought about your blood.

"Hey," she said at last, "are you okay?"

He didn't startle or turn when she spoke, so he must have heard her coming. "Why wouldn't I be?"

"Well. Because . . ." Kate gestured vaguely back at the party. But he was still facing out to sea and couldn't see her, so she came forward a few more steps, until she was standing right next to him. "My aunt. The cake."

"It was nice of her." His voice was emotionless.

"It was fucked up." Kate was getting on her Louise rant. "She never thinks things through. She never thinks about how anyone else feels."

Theo snorted and shook his head, like he wanted to say something else.

"What?" she demanded.

At last he turned. And she saw that he wasn't emotionless at all. He was furious. At her.

"What you do isn't any different," he said. "You get that, don't you? You show me these photos of my mom, my dad. The drawings in the stairs. My sketchbooks. And you want me to give you . . . I don't know what you want me to give you. Cold facts? You want me to cry? I don't know. I never know."

"I want you to act like a human being!" Kate cried, losing her own patience. "And treat *me* like a human being. Maybe I don't have all my shit together like you do, but I'm trying. I'm doing all the dirty work you didn't want to do."

"You think I have my shit together?" Theo looked incredulous. "I'm a single dad with two kids, an extra house full of *crap*, and a town of people who think I'm some kind of zoo animal!"

He pointed at the party behind her, and she turned to see that a few people were staring at them. Great. As if she hadn't already been constantly interrogated about what it was like to work for Theo. Now people would want to know why they were fighting, too.

She turned back to him. "I came out here to check on you," she hissed. "Not to get in some competition over who has it worse."

"I never said I had it worse than anyone!" As Oscar started to stretch and kick in his arms, Theo lowered his voice. "*You* said I was condescending to you."

"You have been! You *know* you have been." Kate stamped her foot, which was less than satisfying in the soft sand. "Don't act like you don't know what I'm talking about."

"I'm trying to create boundaries."

"Why? Because you think I'm going to steal stuff?"

"No," he said, sounding agonized.

"The other day you asked if I was going to."

"I was overreacting. I apologized for that."

"Then what are you so afraid of?"

"What do you *think*?"

As soon as the words left Theo's mouth, he flushed a deep red that was visible even in the darkness.

For one beat, two, Kate didn't understand what he meant. She stared at him, uncomprehendingly, until he looked away.

Then it all came together. His blush, his sharp tone. The shock almost made her fall over.

All this time, she had thought he hated her, but that wasn't it at all. He *liked* her. He was attracted to her, too, and he was afraid of crossing a line.

"Oh," she said.

She felt like she had been listening to their whole argument through a stereo whose electricity had suddenly been cut. She sifted through her memories of the past few weeks, trying to square them with this new revelation. That first encounter in the foggy backyard; his defensiveness about the sketchbooks, the stairs; how he had seemed to avoid her at all costs. She had sensed that the attraction wasn't completely one-sided, but she had never imagined that he might be conscious of it—that he was trying to set her away from him.

She had an odd, dizzy feeling, as if she had held her breath to get rid of hiccups, and had thought they were gone, only to open her mouth and have her body jerk with a *hup* of air. Without meaning to, she began to laugh. Not cruelly: giddily, confusedly. Theo swung his head around.

"I'm sorry," she said, covering her mouth. "It's just . . . I thought you hated me."

He threw her a baleful look. "I don't hate you," he said.

His voice was calm, but his shoulders had a slight defensive hitch. He didn't want her to say anything else about it. Good. She had no idea what she would say. The surprise had melted away her anger, and maybe some ligaments in her knees, because standing up suddenly seemed exhausting. She sat down cross-legged in the sand.

When Theo didn't move, she tilted her head up at him expectantly. After a moment, he sighed and sat down next to her, setting Oscar down between them. The boy immediately stretched out on the sand, his head cradled against his elbow.

"So loud," Oscar said sleepily. "Shh."

"Sorry, bud," Theo said.

Kate turned her attention to the sand beside her. There was a little pink shell there, and she brushed sand over it again and again, until a small pyramid rose up over it.

"Listen," she said to Theo. "Putting all that aside for a second, I came over here to say I'm sorry. I didn't know what Louise was planning."

"I know." Theo's lip quirked up at the corner. "The look on your face . . . I thought you might pass out."

She laughed again, this time in relief. "*I* thought I might pass out."

Theo scratched his temple. "It wasn't the cake that bothered me. It's just—it's weird being back here. Where it all happened. All this stuff I try to ignore. We came down to this beach once for my dad's birthday, when I was little. We brought a cake and everything. Lit the candles, sang him happy birthday, ate it. And then he . . ." He seemed to catch himself. "Well, it just reminded me of that, you know? The crowd, the candles. I got thrown back." He sighed and dropped his hand. "That's why I got upset in the stairwell that day, you know. I hadn't seen those drawings in years."

"I could tell you were surprised," Kate said carefully.

"Growing up, we didn't have people come to the house. So when I see you in there, sometimes there's a reflex. That you're not supposed to be there. I know that's not an excuse."

For a second, Kate was comforted by the apology. Then she remembered all the things she had done that he didn't know about—her footprints in the attic, her fingerprints on his nightstand—and her hand trembled, accidentally knocking over the sand pyramid. The shell emerged again, white and pink and smooth.

"Why did you come here?" she asked. "I understand why you hired me. It's a big job. You couldn't do it yourself. But you came up here for the whole summer. You brought the kids."

There was a silence as Theo thought about her question. Beyond him, the water slapped gray and hungry against the beach. The sunset's last orange glow lit up the lines around his mouth, making him look older.

"I guess it was kind of a dare," he said at last. "To myself. I avoided this place for so long. Then my dad died and I had to take care of it. I thought it could be a good change for the kids. And I thought, I'm thirty-five, I should be able to go back. So I did." He cleared his throat. "And you? Why'd you come all the way out here for a job?"

Kate smiled. "Because it was a job. You haven't been unemployed before, have you?"

"Not in a while," he admitted. "But this seems like a long way to come, for someone with your experience. There wasn't anything in New York?"

Kate gathered her sweater tighter around herself. The party's laughter wobbled and refracted against the vast emptiness of the beach.

"There might have been," she said slowly. "But something happened . . . at my last job . . . and it made it hard for me to get hired. I mean, I didn't *do* anything," she added, worried he might misunderstand. "But—well, it's complicated. I guess I just wanted to go somewhere new. I thought it might clear my head."

"And has it?"

"Sort of. Maybe." She smiled a little. "Your parents' stuff, it's not exactly head-clearing."

"No," he agreed. "No, my parents were kind of a mindfuck."

It was a bizarre thing to say about your parents, especially about your dead parents, and Kate wanted to ask what he meant. But she found herself hesitating. Some thread of trust had stretched between her and Theo just now, and she didn't want to break it with questions.

"I'm sorry," she said again. "Really. I haven't been fair to you. I've been taking my stuff out on you as much as you've been taking your stuff out on me. Maybe more."

Theo tilted his head, studying her. Then he said, "Truce?" and held out his hand.

Kate laughed. "Fine. Truce."

His hand was surprisingly warm, his palm rough, his grip firm. It was much larger than hers, and it seemed to trap hers inside it. Not unpleasantly. A shock traveled up her arm and then down her spine. For a moment, she could feel their pulses beating against each other, uneven, out of sync.

Kate pulled her hand away and tucked her hair behind her ear, suddenly self-conscious.

"The fireworks should be starting soon," she said. "My uncle said they would set them off at nine thirty."

Theo checked his watch. "Fifteen minutes."

"Fifteen minutes," she agreed.

Time dripped past, slow as molasses. In the distance, the party continued in a vibrant circle of light. Up close, it would have been too bright and too loud to make anything out. From their hollow in the chilled sand, though, everything was Kate's. She could see the whole scene. The guide light of the fireworks boat as it motored out over the waves. The lanterns shining on sweaty faces. Oscar's snores fluttered against her thigh.

At last, the fireworks screamed up to the sky and split apart in a rain of gold. The bang, the smoke, the streaks of ashes shading into darkness. Theo was beside her through it all, glowing like an electric field.

SERIES 4, Clippings & publications

BOX 18, News clippings

FOLDER: 1979–1984

ARTnews

JUNE 12, 1984

■

In Miniature:
Jake and Miranda Re-Brand in Northern California

Martin Granberg

The New York City art scene will soon lose two more major players: Jake and Miranda Brand are relocating this month to northern California. Rumors of their move have been swirling for some time, but *ARTnews* has learned that they have officially purchased a home in the small hamlet of Callinas, an idyllic yet underdeveloped beach town in Marin County.

New York art savants may not feel the absence as strongly as they expect. While her infamous hospitalization raised her public profile, Miranda has distanced herself socially from the art scene and has not released a major series since the Capillaries show that first put her on the map. Meanwhile, Jake has struggled to break out of the pack of painters trying to expand upon Pop Art. With any luck, the new home will provide the inspiration necessary for Miranda and Jake to develop their promising voices.

Both artists are represented by Hal Eggers, who recently left Patina to form his own gallery.

SERIES 2, Personal papers
BOX 9, Diary (1982–1993)

AUGUST 14 1984

We live in California now. We're West Coasters. House bought in May. Moved in June. I keep hoping I'll understand it more, that our life will settle around me like dust. We must have decided on Callinas somehow, we must have weighed other options, we must have bought the house and discussed the renovation. The truth is I don't remember any of that. It feels to me like we arrived here by magic. Borne on a dark cloud.

The absence disturbs me. I looked back in this journal for clues, like I'm an archaeologist excavating my own past. But all I turn up is bits of ground-up bone.

So let the bones lie buried. What matters now is that we are settled in our high house with the sea anchored in the distance and the smell of fresh paint slowly fleeing through the windows. I have room for a darkroom in the attic, mine all mine. It's bigger than my shitty studio in New York, and I can set it up however I want.

From our bedroom window you can see the water. Limitless here. The end of the earth.

SEPTEMBER 14 1984

Callinas is a weird place. Reminds me of college in some ways. Its smallness. The town has three restaurants and one bar. When we're out, everyone comes over to our table to see how we're doing. The parents at Theo's preschool are always making excuses to talk to me. "Wanted to welcome you to the neighborhood." More like overshare about their mediocre kids. Arrange car pools.

I try to say yes. Part of me wants to order Chardonnay with them, go camping on the weekends, wear that same brand of jogging suit they all own, the kind that whispers when you walk. Renounce whatever I used to think was lame.

But as soon as I open my mouth, words flash through my mind. *A source close to Brand.* I need to be careful. Someday I will be strong again. Strong enough not to care. Not to divulge.

For now I am scared.

There are fewer people here, but more are watching.

DECEMBER 10 1984

Sometimes I think I am like a nocturnal animal who got yanked out of its cave into the sunlight. A raccoon, a possum maybe, good at hunting for trash, but cursed with a naked wriggling tail and needle teeth.

New York was hard in its way, but at least I knew how to move around in the darkness. It was easier to conceal myself in the rush and pitch of it all. The subways open all night, the police sirens wailing through the time before dawn. Wee hours, they say. Like they are so little. But I always thought of them as bigger than the other hours, stretched out until they were thin as film, holding so much time they sagged in the middle like an overburdened net. Full of possibility. Belonging only to you.

Here it always feels like daylight, and I am disoriented. The fame has followed me here like a dead rat caught on the raccoon's tail. In New York, I could get lost in the crowd. Here I am such an outlier. So recognizable. Who else would that woman be, with the stroller on Main Street, black turtleneck and black slacks?

The raccoon. Trying to stay unseen.

Blend in, Jake says, when I complain about it.

Wear brighter colors.

Make an effort.

JANUARY 30 1985

Every time I develop any film of Callinas, all I have is empty beauty. There should be a touch of violence in everything. But if any slender knife ever wedged its way into this paradise, these people would sew up the wound immediately. They would stuff themselves inside it, soak themselves in gore, just to save this place.

From what, I don't know. Lately I think they want to save it from me.

The problem is these people have no depth. They are painted shells around a plaster center. They think not putting up street signs means they're moral beacons. They meditate to stop thinking. They think surfing is a religion because the ocean makes them feel powerless.

I want to say: You want to hear about powerlessness? Let me tell you about being a prisoner. Let me tell you about looking around and seeing only darkness and knowing that you are its agent. Let me tell you about fearing yourself, about breathing in air and thinking it's poison, about hearing things. About thinking your baby will stab you in your sleep.

Let me tell you about a wave coming up under you when you think you are floating, when you think you have made it and that you have nothing else to lose.

JANUARY 31 1985

As for the art. Ideas come to me as if out of the deep ocean—shadowy, groping through darkness. Slimy when they arrive. Glistening, like a newborn child.

12.

KATE

The sauce was impressive," Kate remarked as she put her plate in the dishwasher. "Very . . . tomatoey."

Theo smiled. "Good save. Hey, kids, time for bed."

Jemima poked Kate in the side. "Kate, can you stay in our room tonight? You can share my bed. It's a big girl bed."

"I'm not staying overnight," Kate said gently. "I have to go back to my own house."

"Oh." Jemima let her face collapse into a pout.

"Come on, come on, tooth-brushing," Theo said, and shepherded the kids upstairs.

It had been a week since the Fourth of July party, and her truce with Theo had held. He left the front door open for her now, instead of her having to ring the doorbell. They joked around with each other. Sometimes they ate lunch together, talking about news stories or movies over the weathered kitchen table. Tonight, Louise and Frank were having the neighbors over again; when Kate had admitted to Theo earlier that she was dreading the whole dog-and-pony show, he had invited her to stay for spaghetti.

There was a strange cast to it all, a net drawn tight beneath their interactions. Because although the dinner had been fun (Jemima and Oscar on their best behavior, Theo turning out to be sillier than she had expected, at one point putting a metal bowl on his head and chasing Oscar around, pretending he was a space monster), Kate was also always aware of that tacit admission, out on the beach, that he was attracted to her. She was even more aware of her own attraction to him, which was easier to admit now that she understood the dynamics. Now that he was kinder to her. Now that she could be kinder to him.

And then there had been that moment, earlier, after she had drunk a couple glasses of wine, when he had been ready to drain the pasta and had asked her to pass the colander. For some reason (God, it was humiliating to recall), she had grabbed the colander and ducked under his arm, caging herself between his body and the sink. She wasn't thinking: it was reflex. He had tensed behind her, and she was embarrassed, and then his body relaxed somehow, and he emptied the pot into the colander. As he turned away, he placed his hand on her lower back, and for the space of a single heartbeat, she felt the outline of each finger against her spine. Then the hand was gone, and the steam from the draining water coursed up, clouding around her face.

Too much. Too complicated for anyone, especially someone with her history. She hadn't been joking when she told him his sauce was good, but she hadn't really known, either; she had eaten without much attention to what was in front of her. Her stomach had dropped when he asked her to stay for dinner, and it had dropped again just now, when the kids went to bed. It was like she was on a roller coaster, hearing the clack-clack of the gears inching her closer to the top, waiting for everything to fall away.

I'm not staying overnight, she had told Jemima—but a part of her wondered.

Now she should leave, only Theo and the kids had disappeared upstairs, so instead she went around the kitchen, tidying up. From overhead, she heard the noises of kids getting ready for bed: floorboards creaking, drawers opening to get out pajamas, little voices protesting their toothbrushes. A murmured conversation, a giggle. Soon there was nothing left to clean in the kitchen. Trying not to fidget, Kate opened the fridge, stared blindly into it. Closed it again. Her mind was running and running but going nowhere. On a treadmill, zoned out.

She wandered into the dining room and flipped on the lights. She had never seen the room at night before, and she was surprised at how much smaller it seemed. The light from the avant-garde chandelier turned the papers tungsten, shadowy. It pressed in on all sides, like a trash compactor, shrinking and shrinking the piles until they just looked like blocks of paper, mashed-up trees.

So silly, to care so much about these papers. These people. But how could she stop?

"Kate?"

There it was. The drop. Kate started, her heart jamming up under her ribs, then went back into the kitchen.

"Hey." Theo smiled. "Thought I lost you."

"Just checking my chickens." She gestured back to the dining room. "All down for the count. I couldn't find the wine."

"Right." He opened the fridge. The wine was on the top shelf; she must have stared right at it. Theo took it out and a beer for himself. Kate found a wine key in the silverware drawer, and, by silent agreement, they took the drinks out onto the porch.

The air had cooled and hardened, an iron being removed from the forge. The silhouettes of the trees were still crisp where the branches pricked the sky's blue background, and stars were visible, like tiny punctures in a tent.

Theo sat on one end of the porch swing, Kate on the other. The distance between them was like another person, warm, made out of shadow.

"Is it always like that?" she asked.

"What?"

"Dinner. Like—it was such a party. So energetic."

"I try to make it fun. That was something Rachel and I wanted to do, have family dinners every night. To give the kids structure."

"Did you have family dinners as a kid?"

"No." He laughed. "Not at all. My dad worked best in the afternoon, and my mom liked to be in the darkroom at night. Sometimes we would have breakfast together."

"At that same table."

"At that same table," he agreed.

Kate rocked her wineglass back and forth. "Where is Rachel?" she asked abruptly. "Why do you have the kids this summer?"

"I have the kids all the time," Theo said, his voice neutral.

"That's unusual, right? For the courts to give the dad full custody?"

"Well. Technically we share custody, but she lives in Switzerland now, so."

"*Switzerland?*" Kate was startled. "I'm sorry, I know I'm prying. But what happened between you?"

Theo rubbed the back of his head. "It's complicated. Or maybe not. I guess it's the same thing that happens to a lot of people. We got married too young. We had kids too young. She hadn't lived life enough. She met this guy, Hans, and they fell in love. He works in the Swiss government, so she moved there to be with him."

"And she just—left the kids behind?"

"Yeah. That's the hardest part, to be honest. I mean, being cheated on sucks, don't get me wrong. That still hurts. But I guess I've processed it, or something. And going through a divorce, you see some ugly parts to people. I don't want to be married to her anymore. But the kids don't understand. They ask about her all the time. We Skype sometimes, but it's hard on everyone. She gets upset, they get upset, I get upset . . . I can understand the cheating, you know? I can process it. But I don't know what to say to the kids when they ask if their mom is dead. Or if she doesn't love them. Because maybe she doesn't. Sometimes she talks like she doesn't."

"I'm sure she does."

"I don't know. Sometimes parents don't love their kids."

His expression was bleak. Somehow Kate knew he wasn't only talking about Rachel. She thought of Miranda's journal. *I won't ever have to love it.* She felt suddenly off-balance, as if she had been looking down into a hole, thinking she had seen the bottom, and only just discovered that it was much deeper than she had realized.

"How long has it been?" she asked. "A year or two? She might realize. Make more of an effort."

Just a month ago, she had been so desperate to get out of New York. It was nice to think that if she had had something keeping her there, something like children, she would have stayed, but she wasn't sure. The decision to leave hadn't felt like a decision at all; it had felt like a physical pull. She understood the desire to escape your current life, at any cost.

"I did think about moving the kids to Switzerland," Theo said. "But the immigration is really hard. The kids know their school here, they know their teachers. They'd be going back and forth between houses, and Rachel and Hans are gone a lot of weekends at races. They do ultramarathons."

"Ew," Kate said.

He shook his head as if to clear it. "Anyway, what about you? Where'd you grow up? Do you have siblings?"

"Connecticut. No siblings."

"I knew you were an only. Or the oldest."

"What? Why?"

"Because you're bossy."

"Excuse me. You mean I have a leadership mentality."

"Yes," Theo agreed. "That's it. A leadership mentality."

She refilled her glass. She must have drunk a whole bottle tonight. Her tongue dry from the tannins. The grapes stormy and ripe.

How odd to be listened to so closely. Teased. It had been too long since she had gone out on a date; she had forgotten the hot rush of being heard. Not that this was a date. Still, she was acutely conscious of her thin sweater, the flush that had spread across her chest and wouldn't leave, like an allergic reaction. Her eyes had adjusted to the darkness; now she could see his face, grainy and blurred, and the way the light from the window slid along the planes of his shoulders. One leg crossed over the other, ankle to knee, a triangle. One foot on the ground, rocking them.

"You know," she said slowly, "I spend all this time in your childhood home, looking at things from when you were young, but I don't know what any of it was like for you."

The slightest hitch in the movement of the swing. "What do you mean?"

"You know what I mean." She gestured to the house, the yard. "Tell me something. A memory from when you were a kid. Anything."

It took him a while. Kate watched his long fingers move across the grain of the wood as he thought.

"All right," Theo said. "It's from the beach."

"Your dad's birthday. You mentioned it the other night."

"No. A different time. Same place, though. I was seven, maybe eight.

You know that spot, over by the cliffs, with the rocks? We were having a picnic there, and I went over to look at the tide pools. I loved those tide pools. I could stay there for hours, watching everything inside. Barnacles, crabs. I was kneeling, just staring, when all of a sudden I see this sparkle. It was just this normal little fish, only it had swum through a patch of sun, and the sun made its scales look like a rainbow . . . I thought it was so magical. This beautiful secret. All you had to do was see it from the right angle. Then I realized why it was swimming back and forth like that: it was stuck in the tide pool. It couldn't get out.

"I was watching it when a wave hit me. It was like a truck—it lifted me up and pulled me back into the ocean. I hit a rock, I didn't know which way was up. Then my shirt caught, and I was out of the water. My dad had seen me fall in and pulled me out. His face was so pale. He took me back to the towels and my mom was crying. But that was the happy part. Seeing how relieved they were that I was alive."

But first he had to almost drown.

Kate knew something about the kind of happiness that came only after terror, the kind of breath that came only after suffocation. She felt the opposite now: yanked from the pleasant hum of alcohol into clarity. Not by the story, but by the wonder in how he had said the last part. *How relieved they were that I was alive.* As if he hadn't always known that. As if he had once feared that his parents might want him to die.

She didn't know how to respond. She couldn't pretend she thought it was a happy story, and yet she knew Theo well enough to know that any sign of pity would shut him down. They were alike in that way.

"It's good they were there," she mumbled at last.

Cicadas singing. The night around them bending back and forth.

Theo said, "Can I ask you a question?"

"Okay."

"The other day," Theo said, and his voice sounded a bit faded, too, as if he also might have drunk too much, "you said something happened at work."

Kate had forgotten she had said that. Actually, she had temporarily forgotten the thing itself, which surprised her: it had occupied so much of her mind and her time, these last few months.

"Yeah," she said.

"So what was it?"

It wasn't as fun, being on the other side of the questions. She stared at her wine. Through the curve of the glass, the surface was a thin liquid line of reflected light. Yellow against black.

"You know what it is," she said. "You know the story. Didn't they tell you, when you called my references?"

"I dug around," Theo admitted. "But they were cagey. They wouldn't say why you had been fired. But when I asked if you had done anything wrong, they went over the top, saying no, you hadn't. Then they got off the phone."

"Theo, come on. I know the resources you have. It wouldn't be that hard to find out. It was supposed to be anonymous, but word got around fast."

"I heard *a* story," he said stubbornly. "But I don't know if it's the same one."

Kate blinked. Plenty of people had asked her what had happened. Some, mainly women, waited to hear her side of it before they decided what to believe. Men like Theo (white, handsome, domineering) usually came to her ready to poke holes in her story.

"First tell me the version you heard," she said. "Then I'll tell you my side."

"Okay." Theo leaned back. "There was a sexual harassment case against a senior editor. He had been making inappropriate jokes, sharing inappropriate materials. Groping. There wasn't enough evidence to bring a lawsuit, but he ended up resigning. You were the main accuser. How does that sound?"

"Familiar. And correct, sort of."

"So tell me the sort of."

"You really want to hear it?"

"Unless you don't want to talk about it."

She shrugged. "Talking about it doesn't matter. It's just not really, like, fun to hear."

"Tell me," he said.

She exhaled and looked out into the darkness. "His name is Leonard. Leonard Webb. He was a few rungs above me. I worked with him on a bunch of projects. We all knew he was kind of a creep, but I guess I thought he was a harmless creep. He would say I looked good in a skirt. He'd ask me what I had done over the weekend, but in a weird way; he'd ask if I had gone out, gone wild. If I wore any tight shirt, he'd stare at my boobs. Normal stuff."

Theo frowned. "Not normal."

"Normal for women. You see it all the time. I mean, not *every* dude does it, obviously, but it's not unusual. For a couple years it was manageable. Then, I guess around two years ago, he got a divorce, and that's when it started getting worse. I got assigned more of his stories, so I had to spend more time with him. He would tell me the kind of porn he liked, ask what porn I liked. Ask if I would let guys do certain things to me. One time he squeezed my thigh in a meeting, under the table. When I went into his office, he would have his computer open and there would be porn on it. He kept it open so I would see it. I asked some other people about it and they said, Well, that's just Leonard. I even sort of went to HR asking what they could do about it, or if I could stop working with him, but they said if they reported it, there was no way to guarantee my anonymity. And I didn't want it to get back to the other bosses. I mean, I wanted a promotion. I was due for one. I hadn't been promoted in four years." She felt her eyes getting hot. "There was an opening, but to apply for it, I had to get evaluations from all the main people I had worked with. I sent Leonard the form and he sent back that he would fill it out but first he wanted to meet about the opportunity. That's what he said. 'Meet about the opportunity.' So okay, I went into his office. He was sitting at his computer. There was no porn up and I remember thinking, Thank God, okay, I don't have to deal with this today. He's serious about this. He sat me down across the desk and steepled his fingers and said, 'I think you're a great candidate for the position. I think you're really talented. You do good work.' I said thanks. I was waiting for him to ask whatever questions he wanted.

"Then he said, 'Come over here for a second.' I don't even know why I did. I knew whatever he wanted couldn't be good. But it was like someone was controlling my limbs. I walked around his desk and stood in front of him. And he looked me in the eye and unzipped his pants and took his dick out."

Theo let out a little hiss of surprise. Kate couldn't look at him.

"He asked what I thought of his dick," she said, hearing the flatness in her own voice. "I said it looked fine. He asked me if it was a big fat dick. I said, I thought this was about the promotion. He said, 'It is. There are several candidates and you're on the cusp. But you can help yourself out.' And then he started touching himself."

She dug the heels of her hands into her eyes until it hurt. "I froze. It was obvious what he wanted me to do. I thought . . ."

She had thought all kinds of things. She had thought about screaming. Or laughing in his face. She had thought about how the desk was between her and the door, so if she lunged for the door he could grab her. For a brief splinter of a moment, she had thought about killing him; grabbing one of the ballpoint pens on his desk and sinking it into his heart. But the worst thought—the thought she hadn't told anyone, not even her therapist, and certainly couldn't tell Theo—was that maybe she should do it. A part of her brain started to rationalize it. She had given plenty of blow jobs in her life: what was one more? She thought about the raise, about how she could start working on different kinds of stories. About how her career could take off, if only she did this one little thing.

"I really think he thought I wanted it," Kate said. "I think he thought he was giving me a choice. An opportunity."

Theo snorted. "No. He knew what he was doing."

"You don't get it," she said. "I didn't do anything. I just stood there while he . . . I could have left. I should have left."

The report doesn't make sense, she had overheard someone saying in the office kitchen one day, when they hadn't realized she was right outside. *If he had really done that, would she really have just stood there? I mean, why didn't she just leave?*

"I didn't leave, and I didn't tell anyone," Kate said. "So of course he did it again. And again. It went on for months. Different kinds of things . . . I don't need to get into it. But I kept going back to his office, I kept letting it happen. I only reported it when I found out he had started doing the same shit to, like, three other women. I always wonder if I could have prevented all that, if I had reported it earlier."

"Kate, you can't blame yourself for what he did. He was a fucking predator."

Theo was saying the things you were supposed to say, the same things she would have said if she was hearing the story, and for some reason it made her angry.

"I don't blame myself for what he did," she said, harshly. "I blame myself for what *I* did. I was twenty-eight when that started. One of the other girls he did shit to was an intern. She was nineteen. You think she's going to have some big career in journalism after this?"

Theo let it drop. "What happened when you told HR?"

"There were a lot of interviews. All different levels of HR. Writing up timelines and everything. The problem was, I didn't have any proof. I hadn't gotten that promotion after all, and people started saying I made the whole thing up as revenge. I don't actually know if Leonard opposed my promotion or not. But that's the story that got around." She swallowed. "It split a lot of the company in two. Who they believed. Leonard had a lot of friends around town. *Has* a lot of friends. There was some retribution . . . I stopped getting certain assignments. If I put lunch in the fridge, people would throw it out. Dumb stuff. I thought if I worked really hard, if I did really well, I could make it up to them. So I threw myself into my work, and I—"

But no. That was too much. Theo hadn't said he knew anything about what came after, and she wasn't about to bring it up. The Leonard story alone made her feel flayed, exposed, like she had taken out all her organs and laid them on a rock to dry overnight.

"I couldn't get over it," she said instead. "So I quit."

"You quit, or you got fired?"

"Does it matter? I didn't want to leave, and I left."

"If they fired you because you reported sexual harassment, that's grounds for a lawsuit."

"I've been down that road. Another girl and I were looking into a lawsuit, and into pressing charges, but we didn't have enough evidence. We didn't write anything down at the time, we didn't tell anyone . . . My friend Natasha explained what it would involve, how long it would take, and that we'd probably lose. We were already so exhausted. And we didn't have enough money to try."

She expected Theo to press the issue. Tell her she should try anyway, tell her she would win. But blind optimism wasn't his game, as she had learned. There was a long, uncomfortable pause.

"I told you it wasn't a pretty story," Kate said, making her voice light, trying to break the tension.

"No, it's not," he agreed. "I'm sorry. I'm just thinking. It's terrible, what happened to you."

Not *what he did*. It was a small difference, semantics really, but in some ways Kate thought it felt more true. Because although she hated Leonard and even hearing his name made her stiffen and sweat, it was not his actions alone that had hurt her, but rather the whole series of events. The system crashing down upon her.

She had tried to become someone who took action, who was *empowered*, and eventually the people who didn't call her a bitch called her brave. But even after all that, she didn't feel powerful. She felt like she had been thrown into a whirlpool and had gotten out the only way she could. Banged up, bleeding. And as angry as she was at her own helplessness, as much as she feared pity, hearing Theo say those words—*what happened to you*—in his low, solemn voice soothed some part of her she hadn't known existed. Some part, deep down, that wanted someone to recognize that she had never asked for any of this; that the whirlpool had reached up and grabbed her, and now that she had crawled out, she still didn't understand what had gone on inside.

"Thanks," she said.

"It was brave of you, to report him."

Back to being brave. Half helpless, half courageous. Maybe she would always be split in two.

"I guess so," she said.

He looked down at his beer bottle and began to fray the damp label into tiny pastilles of adhesive.

She had the sense he was working up to say something. She turned on the bench, tucking her knees up to her chest so that she faced him. Her bare toes almost grazed his hip.

At last he said, quietly, "I hope I haven't put you in that position."

How easy it would be to ignore him. To pretend that she hadn't understood what he meant on the beach about creating boundaries. Or that she hadn't felt the attraction uncoiling between them jerkily, like a stiff cable that had been tied up too long. Yes, it would be easy to pretend. It would be wise.

Her skin pricked to life, sparking, tugging her muscles up and away from her bones. She had a sense of vertigo, not unlike on that last night in New York, when she looked down from the balcony and imagined falling.

"No, you haven't," she said. She leaned forward over her knees and said urgently, "Theo. That's not what this is."

He looked out at the backyard. His profile was one shadow against another. Her feet were still only millimeters from his thigh. All the muscles in her back stretching as she canted her body forward. A few moments ago, she had felt like he understood her. She wanted that synchronicity back again. But he had gotten the story out of her, and now was, perhaps unconsciously, assigning her to a new category: victim.

So she was not surprised when he sighed and said, turning to her, "I should get to bed. The kids will be up early. Let me drive you home."

Kate realized with a start that he had only had that one beer, all this time, while she had drunk more than half of this bottle of wine, on top of what she had at dinner. Presumably he had done it knowing he would drive her home, in which case it was good someone was thinking ahead, but an irrational part of her felt betrayed somehow, like he had done this on purpose. To get her drunk and trick her into divulging everything.

"Okay," she said.

The short drive to Louise and Frank's was quiet in the cocoon of Theo's car. The woods slipped past in the glare of the headlights, the trees as buttery-soft as the leather seats, the engine's purr drowning out any rustling leaves. As they spun around one bend, Kate saw two silver circles in the night—an animal's eyes, a deer maybe, maybe a coyote—but then they swung past, the headlights moving on, and the animal melted back, indistinguishable now, a stroke of ink in a bottomless night.

MIRANDA

SERIES 2, Personal papers

BOX 9, Diary (1982–1993)

APRIL 18 1986

I've been giving more lectures lately. When Hal asked me to do the first one last year, down in the city, I was skeptical. Some days I can barely talk to the grocery store clerk without breaking out in a sweat. How could I do a lecture? The first one was hard. I stumbled over everything. I hate stumbling.

But now that I have the format all figured out, I like the talks. They have a pattern. I put on the same black velvet suit, I stride out on stage, I hit my mark. I say thank you, I turn on the slide projector and one of my photographs blares up onto the screen. It is magical to have my pictures behind me, next to me. Bigger than me. I feel like I am inside them, like I am in the darkroom making them again for the first time. Even the ones I hate now, like Margins, seem somehow precious in this space. 30 minutes and questions. I am in control.

Afterward, riding the high, I don't even remember to be nervous talking to all the doe-eyed college students who dream of making it big. Sometimes I even believe they *will* make it—based on nothing, just the wattage of their smiles and the purple dots of the spotlights still patterning my vision.

SERIES 2, Personal papers

BOX 7, Lecture notes and ephemera

FOLDER: Mills College (March 1986)

Thank organizers Pamela Thomas, Roxanne O'Hara, Cecilia Patterson—
Mills College Art Club, Mills College Student Fund

Title: "Photography and the Female Gaze"

1. *Empty Spaces*
   Whose gaze hunts for the woman?
   We want her in the middle. We want her easy to pin down.
   (Slides ES #1, #4, discuss)

2. *Capillaries*
   Women at center. Self-portraiture—couldn't afford models.
   Tell the story about fake blood staining theater seats (funny?)
   Smiles are secret—men in photo don't see them—implies female viewer
   (Slides Caps #3, #6, #17, discuss)

3. *Mothering as method*
   (Slides: Birth Unit #5, Called Child #8, #10, discuss)

4. *Male gaze, female photographers*
   Laura Mulvey, 1975, on male gaze in cinema:
   women = "to-be-looked-at" / men = "bearers of the look"
   Women only as desired objects, not as desirers
   Female photographers reverse that formulation
   addressing it, adopting it, forcing it (ref. Cindy S)

5. *Photography lets us control our surroundings*
   Susan Sontag: "To photograph is to appropriate the thing photographed.

It means putting oneself into a certain relation to the world that feels like knowledge—and, therefore, like power."

Men control so much of women's lives—homes, finances, sex, happiness, work
Photography lets women exert control
construct new worlds where we reimagine our intimate relationships
use utopias as blueprint for equal partnerships—as J & I have done

Thank organizers again

Q&A
Remind about SPARKLING water for stage and NO questions about Nangussett

SERIES 2, Personal papers
BOX 9, Diary (1982–1993)

JULY 12 1986
Jake has been working, but he won't show me any of it. Most days I wrap myself in my darkroom, or I wander down the hill and into town and along the beach with my camera, looking, looking. It's quiet. The people from town mostly leave me alone. Except Kid, a hippie guy who lives on the mesa. Sometimes we run into each other and chat. People walk by us and stare like they just saw two tarantulas hugging.

AUGUST 20 1986
Hal asked me if I would consider going across the country for lectures. Other cities—Denver, Minneapolis, Chicago, Philadelphia. Same thing, he promised. Just more places.

I don't know if it's a good idea. Jake worries about the travel. The attention, the crowds. Will I get tired? What if something happens? And what would we do with Theo? Because of course Jake would come with me.

The talks themselves bother him, too. He thinks they seem fake. Rote. Spitting out a chewed-up version of feminist theory. Watering down my work, he says. Why explain what you do? Why tell them what to think about it?

Men aren't afraid of misinterpretation. It's not dangerous to them. Women, we know bad things can happen when someone misreads you.

Jake doesn't like to be told he's part of the problem. He prefers to keep the problem theoretical.

I'm trying to start fewer arguments, so I just tell him (and it's true) that I like the pretending part. I like manufacturing an illusion.

But that's all photography is, Jake says. You can do that from home.

SEPTEMBER 15 1986

I go over to Kid's trailer sometimes just to talk and hang out. He moved here fifteen years ago to help clean up the oil spill, and he likes to tell me about what it was like to live here before it was a real town, when it was mostly just the volunteers. It hasn't changed much, he says. But it will. It will go the way of Sausalito and Tiburon and Petaluma.

He sounds so solemn. Like an oracle auguring birds in ancient Rome.

Truthfully, I don't give a shit if Callinas changes. I have no attachment to how it is now. But when he says stuff like this, I nod like I agree, because he is my first and only friend here. Two years here, and one friend. And although I'm rusty at friendship, I know it is easy to make men like you, if you say you believe what they believe.

13.

KATE

"Louise says you were rude the other day," Kate's mother said. "Something about a cake?"

Kate rolled her eyes. She turned her phone to speaker and placed it on top of a pile of folders in the middle of the dining room. She had woken up to a text message saying HAVEN'T HEARD FROM YOU IN A WHILE CALL ME THIS AFTERNOON NO EXCUSES.

It wasn't that Kate had been avoiding her mother, exactly. But she wasn't sure what they could talk about. Darcy obviously would want to go into detail about Kate's "condition" and medications, which Kate had zero desire to discuss. As for work . . . Kate had already broken the nondisclosure agreement for her mother, who was much better than Louise at keeping secrets, but she couldn't tell Darcy she had been searching the house without worrying her, and she didn't want to lie to her outright. Nor did she want to talk about Theo. She had barely seen him the last few days, anyway. He said he was in the middle of some big project and had to work through lunches, but it felt like he was avoiding her.

No Theo, no Miranda, no psychological check-ins: there were a lot of things Kate didn't want her mother to mention right now. In a desperate effort to find topics for today's conversation, she had spent her lunch break poring over that day's newspaper headlines and weather reports. She had actually *studied* for a phone call with her mother. It was almost as bad as that time in college when, having recently lost her virginity, and convinced that her mother would somehow be able to intuit it from three hundred miles away, she had pretended for several weeks that she had shattered her phone while sledding down a local hill.

Maybe the Fourth of July cake debacle wasn't such a bad topic after all.

"I don't think I was rude," Kate said. "Louise just did something stupid, and I told her she shouldn't have."

"What did she do?"

"There was this party, and she made a cake for Theo, my boss. But it had a picture of his mom on it. And she made him blow the candles out and everything, and then everyone ate pieces of his mom. His *dead* mom."

"Well, not literal pieces of her body."

"Obviously, Mom. But Theo doesn't like being in the limelight. I think the whole thing was really hard for him."

"He probably sees his mother's photo a lot."

"I know that. I just—it wasn't very sensitive of Louise. That's all."

Oh, how awful for him, Louise had said dryly when Kate told her that she had misstepped. *Getting a cake. Blowing out candles. Birthdays must be the end of the world.*

"She means well," Darcy said.

"I know, I know."

"And remember, she's letting you live with her for free. You can't criticize her all the time."

"I don't," Kate said, trying not to roll her eyes again. "You asked me what had happened, and that's what happened. I wasn't rude to her. Maybe she took it that way, but you know her interpretations can be . . . off."

"Kate."

"Mom." Kate turned her attention back to the pile of photographs she was sifting through. "Is this why you wanted me to call? So you could yell at me?"

"I'm not yelling at you. And no, I just wanted to chat. You haven't called in a while. Dad and I worry about you. We like to hear what's going on."

"Nothing, really." Kate ran through the list of forbidden topics again and shook her head. "Just work."

"Okay, but how are you feeling about work? You know what Dr. Nesbit said, about how important it is to be in touch with—"

"I'm feeling great," Kate said. Only after she said it did she realize it was true. She had been so weary when she had arrived in Callinas, so drained. Limp, like overkneaded dough. Now there was a little crackle of energy inside her. A flicker of yeast, starting to rise.

"I think you were right," she continued. "All I needed was some sun."

"I didn't say that was *all* you needed," her mother said. Her voice had taken on that frayed tone she got sometimes, and Kate could picture her fidgeting with the sleeve of her cardigan, the way she did when she felt like a conversation was swooping out of control.

"No, I know." Kate tried to sound soothing. "I'm trying to say I'm doing well."

"Okay, but let me read you this article I saw in *Psychology Today*—wait, let me find it . . . here, I'm looking in the dining room, I think it was on the table . . ."

As Darcy continued narrating her movements, Kate's phone pinged with a message. It was from Nikhil.

Hey Kate, breaking the BARTENDER'S CODE OF SILENCE to tell u Kid just walked into PPs. If u still want to talk to him.

God bless Nikhil. Kate had still been checking at Esme's store from time to time, hoping to find Kid again, with no luck. The surly old man seemed to have vanished into thin air.

"It's not on the console," her mother was saying.

"Mom, I have to go," Kate said, reaching out to hang up the call.

She checked the time. She didn't get off work for three and a half hours, which was a lot of hourly pay. But she had been trying to find Kid for days, and if she waited until she normally left work, he would be long gone. She flipped her phone over and over in her hand, thinking hard. Then she sighed and got to her feet. She went down the hall, through the living room, to the base of the stairs.

"Theo?" she called out.

The squeak of his desk chair being rolled back. "Yeah?"

"I'm not feeling so well. I think I'm going to go home early."

There was a pause, then footsteps. Kate tried to look sick just as Theo appeared at the bend in the stairs.

"Are you okay?" He looked concerned. "Do you want me to drive you home? You shouldn't hike alone if you're not feeling well."

"I might throw up," she said. "I'd be embarrassed."

"If that's all . . ." Theo started down the stairs. "I have two kids. One of them likes getting the other to eat crayons. I've seen a lot of vomit."

"Theo!" Kate held up her hand. Now she felt like she might actually be sick. "Thank you. But I really just want to walk home on my own."

Theo stopped and rested his hand on the rail. His brows knit together. "Okay. But can you at least text me when you get to your aunt and uncle's?"

"As soon as I get there," she promised.

When Kate walked into Pawpaw's, the place looked empty, except for the same rotating group of barely legal surf bros who were always parked in the biggest booth, and of course Nikhil, who had contorted himself halfway across the counter to watch the soccer match playing on the bar's only TV. Kate thought Kid might have already left. Only when Nikhil—not taking his eyes off the screen—pointed to the corner did she see the skinny, cargo-pants leg sticking out from behind the nonfunctional jukebox. She gave Nikhil a mock salute and wove through the tables.

Kid was alone, doing a newspaper crossword and nursing a dark beer. He had brought in some Chinese takeout, and the gluey brown sauce dripped from the takeout container onto the plastic bag. His scarecrow body barely fit into the tiny nook he had chosen. It should have looked ridiculous. Yet there was something defiant about the way he sat there, his knees scrunched almost to his chest, his pen scratching across the pale gray paper.

"I used to know someone who wrote those," Kate said brightly.

Kid looked up and frowned. He didn't look especially surprised to see her.

"Big whoop," he said, returning to the crossword.

She tried to look kind and nonthreatening. "Do you have a moment to talk? I've been trying to find you."

"I know." He started filling in a blank square. "Esme told me."

"It won't take long."

"I told you before, I don't want to talk about Miranda."

"I didn't say it was about Miranda."

"Do I look stupid to you?"

"No," Kate lied. The truth was, she did think his white-guy dreadlocks looked stupid, although maybe old hippies got a pass. "Is there some reason you don't want to talk about her?"

"Is there some reason I *should* want to?"

Well, this tactic wasn't working. Kate pulled out the chair across from him. The cheap foam seat hissed as she sat down.

"Excuse you," he said.

She ignored him. "I've been finding references to you in Miranda's files," she said. "Your name keeps coming up."

That startled him. "In what context?"

"She talks about meeting you. You being the first friend she made here. From what I've heard, maybe you were the only friend she ever made. You meant a lot to her."

He huffed. But he seemed to be wavering. He stuck the cap of his pen in his mouth, worrying it with his teeth as he waited for her to go on.

"She said that she was lonely," Kate continued, "but you were the bright spot for her in Callinas." Okay, that last part was embroidered a little, but so what? The implication had been there, in the diary entry, if you read between the lines.

"That doesn't sound like her," he said, but he sounded unsure, and Kate knew she had hooked him.

"Listen, I know it's probably hard to talk about her," she said. "I'm really not trying to make you go back to any difficult stuff. But I'm going through all these boxes of hers, all these things she wrote . . . I just want to talk to someone who really knew her. As far as I can tell, you're the only friend she had." Remembering Victor's hesitation, she added, "All off the record, of course. I won't even tell Theo."

Kid frowned, his bushy eyebrows nearly meeting in the center of his forehead. He seemed to be considering the offer, so Kate averted her gaze. It was a trick an old coworker had taught her: if a subject is about to talk, give them the illusion of privacy, of autonomy, and let them come to the decision on their own. It had backfired on Kate about as often as it had worked. Still, she dutifully studied the jukebox behind Kid, with its sheaves of song choices walled off behind scratched glass.

When she finally looked back at him, he sighed and said, "I wouldn't even know where to begin."

She tried not to smile. "Well, what did you do together? Where did you hang out?"

"My trailer, mostly. Sometimes she would bring Theo over, and he would build little houses out of sticks, and we would have a beer and shoot the shit."

"About what?"

"I don't know. Random crap. I was Buddhist back then, and Miranda really respected that about me, even though she was an atheist. She liked to debate big philosophical things. Free will, all that jazz. Or she would tell me about what she was working on, ideas she had."

As he talked, his face softened with affection. He had been in love with Miranda at some point. Kate was sure of it. But if Miranda hadn't returned the feelings, Kate couldn't blame her. Kid was a piece of work.

"Sometimes she would tell me about places she wanted to go," he continued, lost in the memory. "You know she never left the country? Her photos went all over, but she didn't go with them. She used to give lectures and stuff nearby, but by the time I got to know her, she had stopped all that. Said it was too much time away from her work, away from Theo and Jake."

Something about the way Kid said Jake's name—clipped, like he wanted to get it over with—made Kate ask, gently, "Did you and Miranda ever become more than friends?"

"What? No. *No.*" Kid spat the pen cap out into his hand. It was squashed nearly flat, riven with teeth marks. "Who said that?"

"No one. I just wondered."

"Well, don't. We were just friends. That can happen, you know. A man and a woman being friends."

Now that she had yanked him back from the edge of reminiscence, his eyes were losing their warmth.

"Was Jake okay with you and Miranda being friends?" she said.

"If he wasn't, he never said anything to me. But then again, I didn't know him very well."

"Even though you were so close to his wife?"

"Are you friends with all your friends' husbands?"

She thought about Natasha's boyfriend, Liam. Kate had spent hours upon hours with the guy, but all she knew about him was that he was a Celtics fan and worked in video game design. Or was it video game marketing? "I guess not," she admitted.

"There you go."

"Okay, but even if you didn't know him personally, Callinas is a small place. You must have met him, right? Often enough to know whether or not you liked him."

"I don't see what difference it makes," Kid said. "I don't like most people. And it's not like I went over to their place for dinner parties. Miranda was private. She kept everything divided."

Her bag buzzed against her hip. Fuck. Her phone. She had forgotten to text Theo when she "got home."

TB: Home ok?

KA: Yes, sorry. She hesitated, then typed quickly, *Threw up. Forgot to text.*

TB: Feeling any better?

KA: A ton.

TB: Do you need anything? I can stop by before I pick up the kids?
Fuck fuck fuck.

KA: I'm actually about to take a nap.

KA: But thank you. I appreciate it.

KA: I'll see you tomorrow.

TB: Don't rush it. Whenever you're feeling better.

Kate scowled at the phone. It was almost like he knew she had been lying and was trying to maximize her guilt.

Kid had been watching her, and when she put her phone back in her bag, he said suddenly, "You know who I don't like?"

"Me?" she said, half-joking.

"Besides you. Her dealer. That Hal guy. He was up here a couple years ago, yammering on about some book he wrote. What a blowhard. Miranda was always complaining about him. He was greedy. Impatient. Rushing her to finish things. She called him a vampire."

"If she hated him so much, why didn't she change dealers?"

"She was always putting things off. My point is, she loathed that guy, but in the end he got filthy rich off her. So if you're going to be harassing people, you might as well go harass an asshole like Hal, instead of bothering regular people who are just trying to go about their business." He picked up his crossword again and glared at her. "*Now* will you go away?"

K ate was making dinner with Louise, spooning minced chicken into homemade ravioli wrappers, when her phone rang. Theo. She wiped her floury hands on a dish towel and stepped away from the counter to answer it.

"Hey, what's up?" she asked.

"You sound like you're feeling better," Theo said.

She had forgotten she was supposed to be sick. "A lot better," she said. "The nap really helped. I think I'll be okay to come back to work tomorrow."

At that, Louise looked up from her own ravioli assembly. Kate frowned and ducked out of the kitchen, lowering her voice.

"Everything okay with you?" she asked Theo.

"Great, thanks."

There was an awkward silence.

"Listen," he said. "I was wondering if you wanted to come to Finley Lake with us this weekend. It's about half an hour away. We're just going for the afternoon. Walking down there, swimming a little. Maybe we'll see if we can find an In-N-Out. Anyway, I know you have the weekend off, but the kids would love for you to come."

"Sure, that sounds fun." She smiled. "You didn't have to call me for that. I don't exactly have a bustling social schedule."

Theo paused, then said, "I guess I wanted to ask you off the clock. Since it's—personal."

A few seconds slow on the uptake, Kate realized what was going on. Her stomach tightened.

"Oh." Did her voice sound higher than before? "Yeah. Yes. Thanks."

When she went back into the kitchen, Louise looked at her curiously. Kate went to the sink and turned the water on full blast, washing her hands in silence, avoiding her aunt's gaze.

MIRANDA

SERIES 2, Personal papers

BOX 9, Diary (1982–1993)

OCTOBER 11 1986

Five years married.

I didn't think about how being so far from everyone else would also mean being so close to Jake. In New York, he would go out with his friends, go to shows, disappear for whole nights sometimes, and I hated it. But here even though our house is bigger, our world is smaller, and we are breathing down each other's necks.

We are special, of course. Tied together in a way that no one else would understand. Sometimes I have a thought and he says it out loud, like he has leaped into my mind and come out with a wriggling piece of gold. I used to think this was a magic trick. It used to turn me on.

The timing has changed, though. Now sometimes the thing he says I think, I don't think until he says it.

But what was I thinking before? Was there only a blank space in my head until he opened his mouth and filled it? Who was I, what did I believe?

FEBRUARY 24 1987

Jake is working on a new painting. He's feverish about it, so I've been doing Theo's pickups and dropoffs while he fills the whole house with the crystal smell of turpentine and linseed. He gets upset when I try to see his work before it's ready, but today when I came up into the studio, he looked happy, calm, so I peeked over his shoulder. Put my hand on his back.

At first I didn't understand what the painting was. He's been doing that, experimenting with shapes, lines, so that you could look at something you see every day and you could have a moment of not recognizing. It's a photographic impulse, actually. The decontextualization. Though don't tell Jake he's photographic because he would make it a whole thing. All I saw, when I saw the canvas, was a series of white slabs, gray lines. A spill of shit-colored brown in the corner.

It's different than your other stuff, I said. Rougher.

It has to be, doesn't it, he said distantly. To convey the reality of the place.

What place?

Nangussett, he said.

I was confused. Then I looked back at the canvas, and it rearranged itself somehow, some planes slipping up and others slipping down, until I saw that it was a room, a white room, with a bed with a gray blanket. The brown was the color of shit because it was supposed to be shit.

You didn't recognize it?

I couldn't tell if he was pleased or displeased.

It doesn't look anything like it, I said. I mean—that's not what the rooms look like. You never saw the rooms.

Sure I did. Near the waiting room, there were some open.

Those are day rooms. They aren't the same. I backed away. My head was spinning. Why are you painting Nangussett?

He swiveled around on his stool. What's wrong?

I don't . . . I don't want to look at it.

So close your eyes. You're the one who came over here.

People will see it.

I hope so.

But it's not . . .

Not what?

It's not your story.

Jake frowned.

It is my story, he said. You were in there for two months. I was alone with Theo the whole time. It was hard for me too.

(False. My mom was with them, too. But we've had that argument before. We've had most of our arguments before.)

Fine, make a painting about that, I said. Not this. This is fake. It's not what it looks like. It's a lie.

Like your photos aren't lies? You make blood with *food dye*. You stage it all. Then you change everything again when you process it. You lecture college kids all day about how art is fiction!

I don't lecture them anymore. You told me to stop.

He put his paintbrush down on the palette, then the palette down on the floor. He did it all so slowly I took a step backward. He only moves slow like that when he's angry.

I knew it was bad for your career, he said. And I wanted to help you. Which is more than I can say for you. I'm finally making a painting that moves you, that produces emotion, and you can't handle it. You don't want me to be successful.

This isn't about success, I said. Unless this is why you left me in there so long, why you let them shock me. So you could have something to paint.

He got up and walked toward me. I backed up and tripped against a frame. I heard a snap, and I knew the glass had broken under my heel, and maybe cut the photo beneath, too.

He reached out to grab my arm and I winced, but he didn't squeeze as hard as I knew he could.

I let them shock you because I thought it might fix you, he said. But it turns out you're still fucked up.

I am sitting in the bathtub as I write this. Not taking a bath, just sitting here, I like how cold the ceramic gets. We had sex just now. Afterward, Jake apologized for yelling. He said he'd divide the attic into two sections so I wouldn't have to look at what he's working on.

Then he got quiet. Waiting for something.

I'm sorry too, I said.

One of the bathroom lightbulbs overhead has burned out. The other one still works, which is how I saw the bruises on my arm. Five delicate ovals. Four little ones on my forearm. A fifth by my elbow.

They could have come from anywhere. I bruise easily these days. All the marks coming up to the surface of my skin. I might have a vitamin deficiency.

It was stupid of me to get so angry. Jake is right. The painting doesn't really matter. Art is supposed to upset you.

Art is supposed to make you feel afraid.

14.

KATE

I thought this was a day trip," Kate said, leaning through the window of the packed car. "Should I go grab some ice skates? A few pieces of Elvis memorabilia? What else do you need?"

Theo hefted a tote bag of snacks off the passenger seat and gestured her inside. "Welcome to the wide world of children. Very glamorous, full of whining."

In the backseat, Jemima glanced up from her chapter book. "I do *not* whine."

Theo lowered his aviators to give Kate a look. She laughed and opened the door.

The road to Point Reyes spun through mottled hills that glowed with orange poppies. The ocean rose in and out of view, white and immense in the noon sun. Kate led the kids in a game of I Spy, until Jemima got mad at Oscar for not understanding the game and they switched to listening to the *Frozen* soundtrack. Jemima insisted on holding Kate's hand the entire car ride, meaning that Kate had to loop her arm backward over the center console; after a while, her arm fell asleep below the elbow, but she could still feel the ghost of Jemima's hand in hers, sweaty and small.

The day before, she had read an entry in Miranda's diary about arguing with Jake over his painting of Nangussett. It had made Kate uneasy, and she had wanted to read on, but her phone alarm had beeped and she had to run downstairs before the Brands came home. Now, as she looked over at Theo, his eyes fixed on the road in front of them, she felt torn: guilty about reading the diary in the first place, and desperate to go back to it. She tried to adjust her grip on Jemima's hand, but the effort sent spikes up her arm.

The parking lot was busy, although most of the people were there to get to the hiking trail along the coast. Theo led them down another path, dim and comparatively empty. They passed a couple people, including a woman who smiled at Kate and said, "Beautiful children." It was only when Theo said a hurried *thanks* that Kate realized the woman had thought that they were a family and she was Oscar and Jemima's mother.

At last, they pushed through a slightly overgrown section of trees and popped out onto the edge of the lake. It was narrow and glassy, shaped like a footprint, as if a giant had stepped there and left an indentation to fill with rainwater. The drought had lowered the water height—a tan stripe of rock ringed the lake like scum in a bathtub—but it was still deep enough that fish flickered beneath the surface. There were a few people in brightly colored swimsuits far off on the opposite side of the lake, apparently jumping off a rope swing. Otherwise, the place was empty.

"It's so quiet," Kate said.

"I guess it's sort of a local secret," Theo said as he took off his sunglasses. "They don't make it easy to find. My dad used to take me here when I was little. He loved swimming."

"I want to go off the swing," Jemima declared, pointing at the people across the way.

"Yeah, no," Theo said.

"Please, please, please."

Theo pretended to think about it. "Still no."

"*Pleeeease.*"

"The rope has cooties," Kate told Jemima. "You put your hands on it and then they crawl up your arms and—*poof*!" She wiggled her fingers. "That's why everyone is falling off it. The cooties pinched them!"

"Ew," Jemima said, horrified. Shaking her head, she pulled off her shorts and scrambled into the water.

Theo helped Oscar into a tiny yellow life vest, while Kate sat on a rock and dipped her feet in the water. It slushed with broken pine needles and small particles of dirt. Her feet gleamed pale and alien through the water.

"California is so beautiful," she said to Theo as he guided Oscar into the lake. "All these lakes and mountains and the ocean. Do you ever get used to it?"

"I grew up used to it. I thought everywhere looked like this. The first time I left the West Coast was when I went to college in Boston. The brick, the brownstones . . . I felt like I was living in a dollhouse. But then I got used to that. When I moved back here after college, I hadn't seen California in four years. That was the first time I saw it the way you probably see it."

Four years away from California—even though Kate knew Jake had been living in L.A. since Miranda's death. She filed this information away to consider later.

"Do you think you'll ever leave?" she asked.

"Not any time soon, I don't think. The kids have a good school. And the Bay Area is a great place to live."

Kate smiled. "If you have enough money."

"Right," he said, embarrassed.

They watched Oscar paddle out to Jemima and splash her. Outraged, Jemima swung her arm back as if preparing to deliver a tsunami in return. Then she glanced over at her father and reconsidered. She brought her arm closer and splashed Oscar just enough to make him giggle. Kate was moved by this demonstration of self-control.

Beside her, Theo had grown pensive. "What do you think about the kids?" he asked.

"They look fine to me. I think it's still pretty shallow over there."

"No, I mean, do you think they seem spoiled?"

Kate turned to him, surprised. "What? No."

"I worry about that. How would I know how to be down-to-earth? I've always had everything. At least in terms of money. I try to set rules with them, but I just worry they don't . . . understand."

She remembered how upset he had been about the shells and pinecones the children had taken home from camp. His overreaction when he had found them looking at the drawings in the stairwell. Now that he was raising them on his own, every choice was his and his alone. For a moment,

Kate felt his fear, dense as mercury: that he had chosen badly for them, that he had done it all wrong.

"I'm no expert on kids," she said. "And probably not on what it means to be down-to-earth. I grew up in Greenwich. Like, my high school had a meditation room. But I think Oscar and Jemima are good kids, and you've done a good job getting them through a difficult time."

Twenty feet off, Oscar bobbed in his life vest and Jemima turned somersaults in the water. She had never thought about what they would be like as adults, and thinking about it now made her a little sad.

"They really like you," Theo said. "They say you can make a really good dolphin noise."

That made Kate laugh. She wiggled her toes in the silt. "Is that why you like me? My dolphin noise?"

"No," he said automatically. "I like you for other reasons."

She hadn't consciously been angling for a compliment, but his words sent a shudder of satisfaction through her. She suddenly noticed how close they were. He was leaning back, his hand on the rock beside her. If he extended a finger, he could graze the small of her back.

"Like what?" she heard herself ask.

He looked over at her. His eyes crinkled as he smiled. "You're smart. You're sharp. You're brave. You're kind. But a little mean."

Kate let out a startled laugh. "That's not good!"

"Sure it is. I don't trust people who seem all good."

"Go back to the nice stuff. This isn't as flattering as I imagined."

Theo paused. His eyes flicked from her head to her toes and back again. Then he said softly, "I can flatter you if you want."

Kate's whole body seemed to twist and untwist, as if she were being wrung out.

"It's easy to say," she said. "You don't know the worst parts about me."

He raised an eyebrow. "Like what?"

She could tell him. She *should* tell him. Her illness. The real reason she had lost her job. The fact that she was sneaking around his house, that she spent every afternoon in his bedroom reading a diary that he obviously hadn't wanted her to find. She kept forgetting how much she was lying to him.

But. But, but. It had been so long since she had felt this way. And this thing between them wasn't a lie. She felt like a pot that had almost reached a boil. A firecracker on the brink of exploding. And it had started even before she had begun keeping secrets, even before she had said a single thing . . . it had been there the moment she turned around in the backyard and saw him through the fog and a part of her had seemed to split apart. Shock, fear, recognition.

So she didn't answer his question. She stood up and started taking off her dress.

"I'm going in," she said.

His eyes followed the hem up, over her thighs and her bikini and her stomach and her breasts. When the dress was off and he had gotten to her face, he saw that she was watching him watch her, and he flushed a little. Her chest went as red as her swimsuit, and she dove into the water.

As she swam toward the kids, she heard a splash behind her: Theo jumping in. He surfaced nearer to them than she expected. He surged out of the water in a single fluid movement, water rolling off his shoulders, his dark hair stuck all sideways to his head. Jemima leaped on his back and Oscar paddled frantically to them, clutching at his father's arm, and the three of them rowed in circles until the kids fell off him laughing.

Kate lowered herself until her mouth and nose were submerged beneath the water. Until she was only a pair of eyes, watching, not even breathing, living off the air stored in her chest. The tingling in the back of her knees when his mouth moved a certain way. The way her heart seemed to beat harder near him, like a fish yanking for its life. Only—someone having their hook in you was dangerous. It hurt when you wiggled against it. It hurt when it was removed.

In the past year, she had learned some limit of herself she wasn't meant to know. It was as if, in the middle of a ballet, entranced by the dancers whirling and streaming a thousand bright colors, she had glanced the wrong way and seen the area offstage. The aged scaffolding, the curtains pushed to the side. Joy was an illusion, she had learned, held up with masking tape and rusted pulleys. You had to make yourself watch the show. You had to make yourself ignore what was waiting in the wings.

She saw that dark part of herself now, glimmering on the edge of this beautiful day. Shading everything, making the happiness more beautiful and more menacing. She ducked briefly beneath the water, trying to clear her head, then came back up and gasped for air.

"Let's play Marco Polo," Jemima said, paddling to her like an eager dog. "Daddy, you be Marco."

"Marco," Theo said obediently.

"You have to *wait*!" Jemima said. "And we all close our eyes!"

Theo smiled and spat an arc of water at Oscar, who giggled. He gestured for Oscar to close his eyes and then swam away from the kids, to Kate.

"Marco," Theo said. His eyes were still open. Kate gave him a look.

"Polo," the kids squealed.

She mouthed: *Close your eyes!* But he didn't listen. He was close to her now, treading water a couple feet away. If she reached out she could touch him.

"Marco," he said again.

"*Polo!*"

He went under. Kate thought he was diving toward the kids. Then she felt a cool pressure on her rib cage and Theo surfaced right in front of her. His hands were on her hips, under the water. She couldn't breathe. His eyelashes were spiky and his irises were dark. She rested her hands on his shoulders, on the triangular muscle above his collarbone. Her entire body filled with one impossible wish: to be merged with him, to be one person, to never be let go.

"Marco," he said, looking at her.

"Polo," the kids shouted, their eyes sealed shut.

She kissed him.

Quickly, on his warm mouth. He tasted like the sun. A quick start ran through his body. Underwater, he tightened his hold on her, his thumbs pressing into the soft flesh just inside her hip bones. She gasped and opened her mouth to him.

She didn't know which one of them broke the kiss. Letting go of him felt like a loss, felt like switching off the television in the middle of the show. She slipped under the water and backpedaled away from him.

Her boss, her boss, her boss. *No. Yes.*

They swam for another hour. The people on the other side of the lake were still swinging on the cootie swing, unaware that everything had changed. Her mind replayed the kiss again and again until she had to sink her face into the cold water. She wondered what would happen next, and for once the wondering didn't feel painful, it felt like being scooped up as you fell, carried aloft by the wind.

Exhausted, the kids scrambled back onto shore and set about playing restaurant with twigs and pebbles. Theo swam out to the center of the lake, long powerful strokes until he was just a splash in the distance. Then he turned around and came home.

They drove through the sunny evening to the Point Reyes Lighthouse, an egg-blue hut perched on a spindly point. The stairs were closing soon, but they squeezed past the guards and dashed down the thousands of steps to find themselves on the balcony around the lighthouse, face-to-face with the rocks and the expanse of sea.

Every cell in her body had been polarized toward Theo, was aware of him even when he disappeared behind the other side of the lighthouse with Oscar.

"Kate!" Jemima tugged on the hem of Kate's dress. She placed her hands around her mouth to call up to her, as if the sea were loud enough to drown her out, which it wasn't. "Is this the end of the world?"

"The end?" Kate turned her to face the horizon. That stream of impossible blue. "Of course not. It's the beginning."

They were almost back to Callinas, the kids snoring contentedly in the backseat, when Theo spoke.

"You should come back for dinner."

She glanced up. He turned away from the road to look at her with that

vivid hunter's gaze. His cheekbones were lightly sunburned. He had absorbed the outdoors—she could smell the salt on his skin and see a crest
of sand beneath his jaw—and even inside the car, with its sleek upholstery
strewn with toys, he seemed half wild.

This time there was no mistaking what he wanted.

She said yes.

They got back to the house at seven. After a feast of cheese sandwiches,
Theo put the kids to bed and Kate set about unpacking the bags. When
Theo came back downstairs, she was washing the Tupperware.

"You don't have to do that," he said.

She brandished the sponge. "Almost done."

He went to the fridge and pulled out a bottle of wine. She listened to the
rustling as he found wineglasses, the quiet *pop* as he uncorked the bottle.
He came over to her and leaned back against the counter, so that they were
facing in opposite directions. She rinsed the last container. He waited until
she had dried her hands, then handed her a glass.

It was good wine. She could taste the mineral edge. Peach and stone.
And the color, as she tipped the glass, was like dissolved gold.

"We should talk," he said.

Kate took another sip of wine and watched the soap bubbling down the
drain, the light glinting off the wet knives in the rack. Talking meant lying
or telling the truth, both of which seemed like bad ideas.

"Why?"

"Kate."

"Theo."

"We should talk because this is complicated," he said.

She thought of that start in her gut when she had first seen him. His
eyelashes sweeping down over his cheeks as he listened to her. His honesty,
his severity. The way he left the door open every morning and let her into
his life, a secret life, a walled-off life, a place people weren't supposed to go.

She looked up at him. Her lungs felt tight, airless. "Is it?"

He opened his mouth. Closed it. Then somehow they were kissing again, the wineglasses shoved clumsily onto the counter. His hands ran over her, bold and tender. The rasp of his breathing, like being chased. No talking. No lying.

It was a bad idea.

Of course it was.

She knew this.

And yet.

And yet she followed him to his room, the same one she sat in every afternoon to read his mother's diary, and pretended like it was the first time she had seen it. She watched from the shadows as he locked the door and put on music, a low blaze of jazz that would muffle any noise. She let the night swamp her, let her knees fall open. The music jowled through her veins, a throaty mix of longing. Loss being invented chord by chord, riffed on and remade. Light from the single lamp on the nightstand that held Miranda's diary. The sex was hard, her hair falling in her face and his fingers denting her thighs. And when she came, it was dizzying in its brightness, in its self-destruction. It felt, unaccountably, like a species of love.

MIRANDA

SERIES 2, Personal papers

BOX 9, Diary (1982–1993)

MAY 4 1987

Jake came downstairs this morning with a bandage on his finger. I asked him what happened.

You're kidding, right? he asked.

No, I said. Why? Should I know?

He said I had gotten home late last night, missed dinner, and we had gotten into a fight and I slammed his finger in the door. Now he would have to go to the doctor and ask for a splint.

I don't remember any of it, which isn't exactly a surprise. Lately, I forget things I've done. Big things and small. Jake has to tell me after the fact that I was in my darkroom for twenty hours straight, that I refused to go on a camping trip by throwing a tantrum, that I was the one who finished the bag of snack mix. I've stopped asking him when I notice something off, because it's too humiliating to not remember.

I wish I remembered the argument. Where would I have been, that I got home so late? Maybe I was at Kid's, or out at the beach, maybe it grew dark and I didn't even notice, not even when I had to change the exposures or when I drove back through purple tunnels of sky.

I'm sorry, I said.

It's okay, Jake said. It was an accident.

JUNE 28 1987

I find myself thinking a lot about that Diane Arbus portrait of a headless woman draped in a silky printed sheet. She is sitting in a big chair, like Abraham Lincoln at the D.C. memorial, and the fabric pours from her shoulders down over her arms and pools on the floor—this is how the illusion of headlessness is created. All you see of her, actually, are her legs, ankles and knees pressed together, feet shoved into black flats. Her arms are dead and waxy. Propped up on the chair, fingers dangling down like elegant sausages. You can see she has breasts but they are high and unlikely. She's on some kind of stage.

She makes sense to me, this pile of parts. There must be a real woman buried under there somewhere. She is sweltering beneath the display, the clothing and the fake shoulders, contorting her arms to sit just right, to create the impression of a person. Arbus shouts at her to make her fingers look natural but she can't manage it.

She really does look headless. But the breasts give her away.

JULY 14 1987

Ups and downs. I am a boat on a bumpy ocean.

I wonder if I am suffering wrong.

I want to do the glamorous kind.

I want to suffer in bursts and splats and scintillations. Something more than lying awake at night running my fingers along my veins, wondering which one is the most fragile, wondering which one would be the first to break.

SEPTEMBER 19 1987

Dr. Grady switched my medication again. One of my old ones was recalled. As if just putting out the notice could recall it from my body, could take out all the weeks and months and years I've absorbed it into my bloodstream, into my brain. But no. That drug is a part of me now. I must live with the consequences.

RECALLED. My medication has a better memory than I do.

The new medication, unrecalled, unremembered, makes me sleepy and still. I spend hours sitting at our bedroom window, watching the knife of the sea in the distance and the leaves of the trees brushing the sky. Wind comes and flips them over like a thousand gold coins. Hours, days up there. Jake is getting angry. He's always worried I'm not producing enough. Like we'll run out of money. But we're drowning in money.

Does the medication keep me from making art? It's hard to say. Let's break it down:

Made When I Was Good
    Capillaries
    Bottle Girls
    Empty Spaces
    Rancid

Made When I Was Bad
    Tricksters
    Zero
    Fever Dreams

Four and three. Some more, I can't remember where they fit. But which ones were better? That's what is hard. Four is not necessarily greater than three when three includes Fever Dreams, "today's TOP SELLER!"

Hal asked me if I ever think about quitting my meds, if I think I'd be OK without them. OK enough to live, he implied, but not so OK that my art is mediocre.

I would never tell him this, but I worry he's right. You hear so many stories about these crazy artists, their depression, their alcoholism, the wives they killed. And the masterpieces they made in the meantime. Suffering for their art. You know who I mean.

But those are men. Men are always better at being crazy. Better at being forgiven. The blood on their hands can be real, not imagined. They can be bought and sold and still no one thinks they are owned.

Creation ≠ sanity? If I am too medicated then I have no energy, and my work is not good. If I am too happy then I have no perspective, and my work is not good. If I am too far gone then I spend days scratching my arms apart instead of making pictures, and my work is not good. And then the world calls me a killer, a bad mother. They look at me like a specimen in a jar. But my sales rise. My name builds.

I must figure out how to be exactly the right level of insane.

15.

KATE

Kate woke up early, starting awake from a bad dream. The sky outside the window was like the inside of an oyster shell, shiny white, blue at the edges. She was briefly confused by the presence of another body in the bed. Theo had taken most of the covers and huddled them around himself like a burrito, squashing his face into the pillow. Somehow, this made Kate embarrassed, as if he had been the one to catch her sleeping. They both smelled like sex. She needed to shower.

In the bathroom, she saw the same details she had absorbed all those weeks ago, when she had first started nosing around the house: the utilitarian green bar of soap, the carefully stored electric toothbrush, the medicine cabinet that hid his pills.

And now he was out there, thinking she had never seen any of this before. Thinking he had let her into his private world, when she had been there all along. She swallowed and turned the shower on extra hot.

When she walked back into the bedroom, Theo was waking up.

"Shh," she said, in response to his inarticulate groan. "Go back to sleep."

He stretched his arms over his head. "You don't have to go."

"Yes, I do."

He encircled her wrist with his fingers—a perfect fit—and pulled her to him. Kate let herself fall, but not all the way, catching herself on the mattress with her free hand. She laughed as he kissed her lips, her throat. In the bathroom mirror, she had discovered a hickey there, the flesh still darkening to a bruise.

"Stop." Wiggle away. "The kids will be up soon."

Theo fell back onto his pillow and groaned again. "The kids."

Outside, the fog grasped Kate like a handshake, like an old friend. She wrung her hair out over the porch and smiled as the flagstones darkened beneath her, the water bringing forth the stone's hidden veins.

When Kate walked through Louise and Frank's front door, she found her aunt in the kitchen, anxiously chewing her thumbnail. Bathrobe and shearling slippers. She jumped up when she saw Kate, her face pure relief.

"Thank God," she said fervently. She went into the living room and called down the hallway. "Frank! Katie's back!"

Frank skidded into the kitchen and gathered her in a hug. "*There* you are. Are you all right?"

Kate hugged him back, bewildered. Fatigue rolled over her.

"What's wrong?" she asked. "Is everyone okay?"

"You didn't come back last night." Louise wrung her hands. She wasn't wearing any makeup. Seeing her without it (the pale eyelashes; the tiny capillaries that threaded through her cheeks) made Kate feel vulnerable by proxy. "Didn't you see our texts?"

"My phone died. I didn't think . . ." She trailed off.

It had never occurred to her to tell Louise and Frank that she was staying over at Theo's. After all, at what point should she have called them? While Theo was reading his kids their bedtime stories? While he was going down on her? And what should she have said? *Sorry won't be home—busy fucking my boss?*

She was used to living in New York, where the weekend subways were filled with people saggy-eyed from getting banged into oblivion the night before. Every time someone left her apartment after dinner or a party, she said, "Text me when you get home," but half the time they forgot. It was an air kiss: you did it for show, not contact.

"I didn't mean to worry you," she said.

"We thought maybe there was an accident coming back from your lake trip."

"No, there wasn't any accident." Kate tried to keep her voice patient. "It just got late and I stayed the night."

They kept staring. She wondered if she would have to spell it out for them, or if she was supposed to pretend that she had stayed in the spare room. That was ridiculous. She was thirty years old. It seemed a little late in life to be lying about having sex. But admitting it outright would mean opening it up for conversation, which she didn't want to do.

Then, just as Kate was preparing to make up an elaborate story, Louise got it, in a crash of realization that turned her face red.

"All right, fine," Louise said rapidly. "We shouldn't have gotten worried, anyway. Like our parents, aren't we, Frank! You should take Olive for her walk now. She's going to pee in the corner."

Frank said, "But she already—"

Louise glared at him. Frank gave a little *aah* of understanding and shooed Olive out the door. Kate wanted to head for her room, but she had the feeling she wasn't off the hook yet. She scraped her hair back in a ponytail as Louise started tidying the kitchen. Lining up the pepper shakers, putting a spoon back in its container.

"Kate . . ." Louise adjusted a dish towel on the oven handle. "Are you sure this is the best idea?"

"Is *what* the best idea?"

Louise threw her a pained look. "Theo Brand."

"I thought you liked him. You said he was nice at the party."

"I do. I mean, I did. But he's your employer. Your mother would—"

Kate flattened her hands against her thighs. "Louise," she said, "I can't tell you how grateful I am that you're letting me stay here. But I'm *an adult*."

Pink spots rose in Louise's cheeks. "You're also my niece, and I'm supposed to be watching you. You worked so hard to get this job. What if it ends badly? What if he fires you, or won't give you a recommendation? What happens then?"

Anger bubbled in Kate's throat. *None of your business*, she wanted to say. But of course it was, because she was living in Louise's house. What she saved in rent, she paid for in obligation.

"I think it's terrible that he took advantage of you like that," Louise said. "Especially with what happened at your job in New York and—"

"Please stop."

"You're getting too wrapped up in that family."

"Louise, *stop!*"

Her aunt fell silent. They sized each other up. Kate couldn't tell if Louise was really concerned for her or if she just wanted to prove a point.

"I'm exhausted," Kate said at last. "Can we talk about this later?"

Louise threw up her hands. "Fine."

"Great. Thank you." Kate made to march past. Louise stopped her.

"On your—" She broke off, gesturing to Kate's collarbone. The hickey. Kate flushed and clapped her hand over her neck as she fled the room.

When Kate woke up for the second time that day, it was in fits and starts. Sleep clawed at her eyes. The sun had shifted and the room was stuffy. Her dream had been sickening Technicolor, a spinning carousel that left her dizzy and panting for breath. Tucked beneath her body, her left arm had gone completely numb. She fumbled for her phone and saw that it was almost noon. She had a missed call from her mom and twenty-three messages in a group text about a GIF of a panda sneezing. When she got out of bed, she tripped and caught herself against the sewing machine in the corner.

She had to get out of this place.

Louise had gone to yoga, thank God, but Frank was working on some gadget project in the living room. When Kate asked if she could borrow his car, he paused for a moment—she presumed that hesitation meant that Louise had filled him in on the fight—then nodded.

In the car, she smeared concealer across her hickey. It only left a bigger pink patch across her neck, as if she had developed a strange rash.

Although she had planned to go to the beach or one of the other small towns scattered around the area, she found herself heading south on the coastal route, the sea shining at her back. She drove past the Muir Woods turnoff, the Mill Valley exit, until she was joining the sluggish line of cars marching south on the 101. The traffic made her angry. She wanted to drive fast, she wanted to flee.

Images of the previous night kept coming back to her. Theo bending over her. Her stomach quivering. The gentle kiss he had placed on her hip. The next one, on the inside of her thigh.

The memory of the sweetness caused her physical pain. Theo had cut a flap out of her, unveiled her. Plenty of people could be vulnerable like that, could gaze down at their dissected self and marvel at what they were learning. Kate wasn't like that. She needed a layer between. Already she wished there were a way to cover back over the parts he had unpeeled. It was as if her happiness were a scab, and somewhere in the sweat and murmurs and skin, it had gotten torn off, and beneath it was a wound that bled both tenderness and fear.

And Louise was acting like it was her fault, which Kate guessed it was, and acting like Kate could pull back, which Kate guessed she could. It didn't feel like she could. It felt like the Brands were a planet and she was some space junk that had been set in orbit around them. Kept close by a gravitational pull.

The San Francisco and Oakland skylines were a relief. Spindly skyscrapers, acres of flat roofs, the staggered add-ons of new developments: these sights were familiar to her. Every car that slid through the toll carried other people with other problems. Only five, six weeks away from New York and already she had forgotten the fury of cities, the elation and anger and sadness that coursed through the air. A million hearts bouncing off walls and buildings. The joy of living in other people's echoes.

When she got across the bridge, she pulled over into a parking spot and took out her phone. She loaded the spreadsheet of names, dates, places, every jumbled piece of information that she had gathered to make the finding aid, and scrolled through it until she found the address she was looking for. She fed it into Google Maps, her knee jittering against the steering wheel. The red slash of the Golden Gate rose behind her like a lipsticked mouth, or like a wound in the sky.

E ggers Gallery was on a busy street off Union Square between luxury shops and outposts of European café chains. Two black pillars framed a span of square windows. On the massive metal door, the initials EG were inlaid in gold. The door looked heavy, so Kate put all her strength into the handle. It flew open, nearly hitting her in the head.

A gallery attendant with pink hair intercepted her as soon as she entered.

"Can I help you?" she asked, grimacing at Kate's chest.

Kate looked down and discovered a coffee stain sprawling across the front of her shirt. She didn't know when that had gotten there.

"Yeah." She swiped ineffectually at the stain. "I'm looking for Hal Eggers."

"This is his gallery."

"I know. Is he in?"

"Do you have an appointment?"

"No." Kate suddenly remembered it was Sunday. "But I work for Theo Brand."

The attendant's expression changed.

"Oh," she said, in a much kinder voice. "Your name?"

"Kate Aitken."

"I'm Samantha. Let me see if he's available."

As the attendant called Hal on a sleek landline hidden in an alcove, Kate surveyed the rest of the gallery. The front room was filled with expressive oils, including a six-foot portrait of a man in a prison uniform and a grid of colorful shapes that might be an original Ellsworth Kelly. In one corner, a noose hung from the wall, with broken glass piled artfully beneath it.

"Djiamnolski," the gallery attendant said, coming to stand beside Kate. "A new Czech artist. Very talented. Mr. Eggers discovered him himself at Art Basel a few years ago. He's becoming quite well known worldwide, but he's loyal to the gallery."

"Did you get through to Hal?"

"He'll be over in fifteen. He wouldn't normally meet with visitors, but of course he always has time for Theo. He said I should show you around in the meantime. Are there any artists whose work you'd like to see?"

"Do you have any from the 1980s? Like, anyone from Miranda's circle."

"Oh, sure. Hal represents that whole crowd."

Samantha led Kate through a series of rooms to a bright space illuminated by a skylight. There was one other couple in the corner, talking quietly to another attendant about a sculpture the size of a Lego figurine. Samantha showed Kate black-and-white portraits of children playing in 1980s Harlem, psychedelic finger-paintings, stills from a performance piece of a woman swathed in white tulle. At last they arrived at a photo Kate recognized: Miranda, stepping through a doorway. *The Threshold.*

Samantha said, "One of my favorites," which she had already said about several other pieces in the room.

"Do you still sell a lot of her stuff?" Kate asked.

"We could sell more. But there aren't many of her prints left on the market. A lot of them have been acquired by museums, or their owners are keeping them as investments. Her value is still going up—which is interesting, because some of the other eighties stuff hasn't aged well." Samantha added, "If you work for Theo, you probably know that he's taking care of the Callinas estate now. I think Hal's hoping he'll find a couple more prints up there."

"Fingers crossed," Kate said. She nodded at the *Threshold* print. "How much is this one worth?"

"This? Well, it's from the second run, and it's actually damaged on one corner. You can't see that right now because of the frame. But this particular photo always sells well. We don't have a set price on things like this, but I think it will probably go for around four hundred thousand."

"Jesus."

"I know. Just think how I feel. I have to handle them!"

Kate smiled, a little awkwardly, and moved on to the next work.

"That's Jake's," Samantha said, following her. "*Fishing.*"

The painting was about three feet tall and five feet wide, done in geometric shapes and shades of greenish yellow. The paint was flat, exact, no brushstrokes visible, every line smooth. In it, a boy was standing on a pile of rocks, his arm upraised, holding a wriggling fish aloft in one fist. The angles were off somehow, making the whole picture a little warped, so that the longer you looked at it, the crueler the picture became and the sicker you felt. The more you felt like the fish itself, struggling for air.

Kate realized with a start that the boy was around eight years old: the age Theo had been in the story he told her the other night. Only in his story, he hadn't touched the fish, and it had survived.

"The perspective is supposed to be like that," Samantha explained, misreading her expression. "Jake liked to put the viewer off-kilter, confuse them a little. I think this is one of his more successful works. Supposedly the boy is modeled on Theo."

So much had happened in the last two days that Kate had half-forgotten about Miranda's diary, but now, as she studied the painting, she remembered the last entry she had read, the fight about Jake painting Nangussett. *Art is supposed to make you feel afraid.*

She asked, "Is Jake's value still increasing, too?"

Samantha seemed to choose her words carefully. "Well, I think most critics would agree that Miranda was the bigger force in the couple. But we at Eggers really love all of Jake's work. I think it's just a matter of waiting for his viewpoint to come back into style."

Kate was about to ask Samantha another question when someone exclaimed from behind her, "Kate *Aitken!*"

An egg-shaped man with very thin legs, Hal rushed to Kate like she was an old friend. His suit was beige linen; his tie and his glasses were both neon blue.

"Hello, hello, hello," he chirped. "Ms. Aitken. *So* good to see you. I see you've met one of our lovely assistants?" (Obviously not remembering Samantha's name.) "De*lighted* to welcome you to Eggers Gallery."

He talked quickly but with long vowels, like a Kennedy on speed. He mopped his perspiring brow with a monogrammed handkerchief, then took her hands and circled around her. Beneath the performance of bonhomie, his eyes were like bullets.

"Now," he said, "how can I help this lovely young woman?"

Kate thought he was talking to her, but she wasn't sure why he was using the third person. She carefully pried her hands out of his.

"I wanted to talk to you about some of Miranda's work," she said. "Could we go to your office?"

"Of course, of course. Do you take espresso?"

"Uh, sure."

"Perfect. Darling"—this to Samantha, whose name he apparently still hadn't remembered—"could you bring us two espressos?"

His office was at the back of the gallery, overlooking a courtyard filled with lemon trees. Priceless artworks covered the walls. Kate spied the telltale sheen of Klein Blue in the corner before she returned her attention to Hal. He directed her to sit in one low-slung leather chair, and he took the other, crossing one leg comfortably over the other.

"So, Ms. Aitken. You want to talk about Miranda's work."

"And her life," Kate said. "Theo hired me to help him turn over the Callinas house. I'm going through old papers. Trying to trace names and so on."

"Yes, of course. Theo told me he had hired someone. I can imagine it's very tedious. Miranda was always a bit of a hoarder. So? What have you found?"

A subtle, avaricious glint in his eye. Kate opened her mouth, then was interrupted by a faint knock at the door. Samantha glided in with two minuscule gold-leaf cups on matching gold-leaf saucers and placed them on the table.

"Yours has sugar," she said to Hal. To Kate, she said, "Did you want any? Or a splash of milk?"

"I'm fine. Thank you."

"Yes, *thank* you, you're an absolute gem," Hal agreed. Too effusive. It felt like a power play—against her or against Samantha, she didn't know.

When the door had closed behind Samantha, Kate said to Hal, "I should be clear. I'm not here to talk about any specific photographs. That's up to Theo. I just have some questions about her life. To help me get a handle on what I'm finding."

"Of course." Hal picked up his cup with a bland smile. "I'm here to help. That's why I wanted to know what you've found."

"Well, I know you worked with her for a long time. You corresponded a lot. Your letters—so far, I think I've found more letters from you than anyone else."

Hal nodded. "Miranda hated talking on the phone. And she could be quite forgetful, especially after Nangussett. Letters were better for her to remember what we discussed." He laughed. "Their most frequent visitor must have been the mailman. Or postal worker, I guess we say now? I'm showing my age."

"I found some letters where you wanted her to write about her life. Like a memoir. Did she ever take you up on it?"

Hal gave her a patient smile. "Darling, if Miranda had ever written me anything like a memoir, you'd have known. It would have sold a million copies. Many people don't know this about her, but Miranda could *write*."

"Did she ever *think* about writing it?"

"I save all my letters. I have hers stored somewhere. If you like, I can have some of them photocopied. You can see exactly what she told me when I asked. Which was, more or less, *Go fuck yourself.*"

"I'd love to see them."

"I'll have an assistant take care of it. Is there anything else you wanted to know?"

So, so much. The curiosity strained at Kate, rising up from deep inside her, pushing aside her confusion about what had happened with Theo last night . . . pushing aside everything. That shaking feeling was back, the one where her bones felt like leaves in the wind. She had to be careful with Hal. He liked toying with others. He liked thinking he was winning.

"Listen," Kate said, in the same deliberate tone he had used. "I'll be honest. Theo's been asking my advice about a lot of the papers. Whether to auction them off or just donate them. What to do with the photos we've found . . ."

Hal sat up straighter. "He can't just donate the photos. What about Miranda's will?"

Kate shrugged. "I don't know anything about any will. All I can tell you is what he's asking me. For me, it's an ethical issue. How can I tell him if he should make money off this deal, when I don't know what Miranda wanted? I don't even know how she died."

"What do you mean, how? She shot herself. That's how she died. You can Google that."

"Were you surprised when you found out? Had you seen it coming?"

Hal sighed and put down his espresso cup. It clinked against the glass tabletop. "Ms. Aitken."

"You can call me Kate," she said, smiling.

He waved this aside. "Kate. You have to understand. Miranda had always had . . . difficulties. It became worse after Nangussett. But even when I first scouted her, when she was doing Capillaries, she was intense. Devoted to her work. Erratic about everything else. Many artists are like that. You think they work on their own? They don't. I'm there. I'm a therapist, I'm a punching bag. After she got out of Nangussett, some of her tendencies were exacerbated. She kept me in the dark. I would go months without hearing from her, sending checks along without so much as a peep in response, and then *voilà*, twenty new prints would show up on my doorstep. She'd agree to give a talk somewhere and then cancel last-minute. So yes, I was surprised when she died. Everything she did surprised me. Which meant nothing did."

Kate felt a swish of unease. She wished she had brought a notebook, so she could have something to do with her hands.

"I saw you have one of Jake's paintings out there," she said, gesturing toward the door. "You represented him, too, right?"

"Yes."

"What was he like?"

Hal sighed again. Kate had the feeling he was getting bored with her. "Enthusiastic. Lively, charming. Unrealistic. He didn't understand the art market the way Miranda did. Not that Miranda was particularly interested in the market," he explained, "but she understood it. Jake dreamed a little too big. He was constantly trying to get me to drive up prices for his work. I think he had a bit of a complex about Miranda being more successful than him, and he had an idea that if I raised his prices, he could make more of a name for himself." Hal gave a wry smile. "Well. His name had been made—

by Miranda. I think sometimes he regretted her taking his name, to be honest, because it was a very good name, very *brand*able, if you'll forgive the pun, and then once it was linked to her, he could never unlink it. Anyway, I couldn't just raise the prices on his work arbitrarily. I have a reputation to protect. You have to respond to demand, and there wasn't much demand for his work. Until he started painting Nangussett."

Kate raised her head. That last diary entry she had read. She had intended to look up the painting Jake and Miranda had fought about, see if it had ever been finished or sold, but then yesterday had happened, and she had forgotten.

"Have you seen the Nangussett work? No?" Hal got up, went over to one of the bookshelves. Pulled out a thin volume. "This is the only catalog anyone's done of Jake's work. It didn't get published very widely. And now most of the Nangussett paintings are sitting in a vault in Switzerland—a Chinese collector bought them all up about ten years ago, thinking they'd be an investment. Smart move. They're probably Jake's most valuable work. Ah. Here."

He found the page he was looking for and set it down in front of Kate. Her head was ringing a little, overstimulated by the caffeine and the bright light from the courtyard, so it took her a moment to understand what she was seeing. Like the painting out in the gallery, this one's perspective was all off, the ground shifted sideways. It made Kate feel unsteady again, even seasick, but she couldn't quite look away.

"Is that what the hospital rooms really looked like?" she asked.

"I assume so. I know he visited Miranda."

"It's . . ." She searched for the right word. *Good* was too light. *Dark* too simplistic. *Nauseating* sounded like a criticism. *Interesting* meant nothing.

Hal seemed to understand what she meant. "It isn't just voyeurism that makes the Nangussett paintings sell," he said. "They really are some of his best work." He closed the book and walked over to put it on his desk. "But most people are like you. They want to know about Jake because of Miranda. It's always been like that, ever since Capillaries took off. That was hard for him. And for her."

"How was it hard for her?"

"I think she felt responsible for his unhappiness. She wanted him to succeed."

"Did she put pressure on you to sell his work?"

Hal leaned against the side of his desk and crossed his arms, bunching the sides of his expensive jacket.

"Why all these questions?" he asked.

"Well. It's my job."

"Is it? You aren't a fact-checker anymore."

"No, but I—" Kate broke off. She hadn't told him that she had been a fact-checker.

"Yes," Hal said. "I know who you are. When Theo mentioned he'd hired someone, I did some digging. You were going to be handling so many photographs. I had actually asked Theo to hire someone from our gallery, someone versed in conservation, but he ignored me." He added sourly, "So who knows what dismal condition the photos will arrive in."

Kate bristled. "I've been very careful," she said. "I did work in a museum once, and—"

"I know why you were fired from your last job," Hal said.

A cold shiver coursed over her body. There was a chirping noise outside the window. Her eyes darted to it, then back to Hal. Birds in the courtyard. She became vaguely aware that her mouth was hanging open, and she somehow managed to close it.

"Okay," she said.

"Have you told Theo?"

"Yes."

"All of it?"

"Yes."

He knew she was lying.

"Maybe you should," he said. "Because seeing you here . . . I've known people like you. Bright-eyed. Focused. Obsessed. Do you know you've been bouncing your leg the whole time we've been talking?"

Kate looked down and discovered, to her surprise, that he was right. She put a hand on her thigh to still it.

"That doesn't have anything to do with you," she said.

"You're in my office," he said slowly, as if he were speaking to a small child. "You're asking me about one of my top clients. Trying to find out about her marriage, her secrets. Of course it has to do with me."

His condescension enraged her. She wanted to tell him she knew who he was, too. So what if he had talked to her old colleagues, or even to Leonard? She had read his letters to Miranda. Thirty, forty, fifty missives from him. She had him in his own words. She had a record of him.

She could have screamed all that, but that morning's fight with Louise had exhausted her, and now she was distracted trying to keep her knee from jiggling, trying to slow down her words. He had only brought up her past to show her that he was in charge. If she fought back, he would go to Theo and tell him the rest of what had happened at the newspaper. Whatever version he had heard. Even if he had the facts right, it was a story Kate didn't want anyone else to tell.

"I'm sorry," she said instead, trying to make her voice deferential. "You're right. You're doing me a favor, meeting with me."

Hal inclined his head. "In that case, why don't you tell me why you're really here? Talking about depressing subjects on such a beautiful Sunday afternoon?"

The birds were clamoring at the window again. Steam had stopped rising from her espresso. Kate bit her lip, then leaned forward.

"I'm here," she said, "because I think Miranda was murdered."

MIRANDA

SERIES 2, Personal papers

BOX 9, Diary (1982–1993)

DECEMBER 12 1987

When I worked at the restaurant, we had a sign in the break room. SMILES = TIPS. So I smiled, taped my blisters, drank five Diet Cokes a shift to stay awake, counted my tips, and smiled, smiled, smiled.

These days there's no motivation to smile: I don't need the tips anymore, and people don't expect me to be happy. In fact, the more I smile, the more confused people get. I tried to be friendly to one of Theo's teachers the other day and I swear she nearly ran away.

Of course, I like not living off tips. I like not having to bow and scrape. But I do miss having people smile back. I got a jolt of their happiness. Like those batons they hand off in relay races. Some days I just want someone, anyone, to pass me a baton.

FEBRUARY 19 1988

Jake hasn't sold anything in months. Needless to say, he's angry. He's been thumping around the house for days. Whenever I see him, it's like coming across a wild bear. Lashing out, claws extended.

I don't know what to do when he gets like this. He doesn't like it when I yell back and he doesn't like it when I am too quiet. So I experiment with the in-betweens. Every time, I adjust my tone a little. Like a volume dial on the stereo. Notch by notch.

One of these days, I'll find the exact right tone, and I'll mark it with a line so I can find it again every time. Then I'll have the good part of my husband back, and everything will be easy.

MARCH 8 1988

Jake in a worse mood than ever. He stopped by the gallery last week and saw that the painting he sent Hal isn't even hanging up. Disaster ensued. Complete Feral Animal.

I try to spend my days in the darkroom. Working until my eyes are stinging and the drying line is full. If Theo isn't at school, I put him under one of the counters with some Legos and he builds tiny sculptures in the dark. I mentioned this to Kid and he asked if the chemicals were bad for children. I guess probably they are. But I don't want Theo getting in Jake's way when he's like this. Today I tied a bandanna over his face like a mask. I told him we were playing cops and robbers.

MARCH 14 1988

Lunch with Hal today. Restaurant near the gallery. White tablecloths, wine and water in matching crystal goblets. Hal's tastes have gotten expensive since we've gotten richer. He ordered octopus and it came in its original shape, head lopped off, eight tentacles spread across the plate, dangling off the rim. Tiny suction cups curled and blackened.

I arranged the meeting. Called down yesterday to tell Hal I wanted to talk about that show in Nebraska. Obviously that wasn't the real reason. When the octopus only had four tentacles left, I asked Hal why he still hadn't sold Jake's painting.

Hal said no one was going to buy that painting. It wasn't in style, it wasn't developed enough. He didn't sound concerned.

Have him send me something new, he said.

New?

Whatever he's working on now.

He's between projects.

That's his problem, Hal said. He needs to work faster. You need to grab him by the shoulders and shake him. Tell him to put something on the goddamned canvas. Anything.

It isn't my job to make Jake work, I said.

You're right, he said. It's not. So why are we talking about it? Why aren't we talking about YOUR work?

No way to answer that without the whole thing exploding. Windows bursting out in slivers of glass, survivors diving for cover as the bomb goes off.

Listen, I said to Hal. What's the painting going for? Ten thousand?

More or less.

Okay, so let's say twelve.

He paused. What?

I'll buy it. Take twelve out of the next check you cut me, before you send it to me. Then give the painting to one of your interns, or—no, don't do that. Burn it. Just destroy it.

Hal stared at me for a minute.

You can't just give up twelve thousand dollars, he said.

I'm not. I'm giving up six thousand. You'll send Jake his half, pretend it was a buyer from Switzerland or China.

Miranda, we have records, protocols . . .

So you can't do it? I should find another dealer?

His face went red. We've been together since the beginning, he said. Eight years.

Seven, I said. And if that's too long, then just let me know.

"We've been together since the beginning" is one of Hal's favorite lines. He probably wants his name listed alongside mine on every museum label. But no one's been with me since the beginning but me.

I'm trying to help you, Hal said. This is a bad business decision.

Is it? I picked up my fork again. Solving this problem was bringing back my appetite. If you don't think you would sell the painting to someone else, then it's kind of like I'm giving you six thousand dollars. My faithful representative. I smiled at him with all my teeth. Think of it like a Christmas bonus.

It's March, he said.

Gemma Linsdale from Koyo sent me flowers last week. She wants to add me to her list. I feel like it might be good for me to get a new perspective?

Hal shoved his plate away. He was so angry he didn't even finish his tentacles.

Fine, he said. I'll do it. But you need to sort out your marriage, Miranda. Or he's going to be the hill you die on.

16.

KATE

The word *murdered* echoed through the office, bouncing off the tiger-wood paneling and priceless canvases.

"Ah," Hal said. His expression didn't change.

To hide her nerves, Kate picked up her lukewarm espresso cup by its tiny handle and raised it to her lips. "You don't sound surprised," she said.

"I'm not. But I like the conspiracy theories. They're part of what keep me in business." He smiled. "Free advertising."

"Do *you* think she killed herself?"

Hal shrugged. "Like I said—everything she did was a surprise. I've stopped thinking about it, over the years."

"Where were you when she died? San Francisco?"

His smile faded. "Are you asking for my alibi?"

"I'm just curious."

"Yes. We discussed your curiosity." He uncrossed his legs. "You're some detective. But if you think I might have killed Miranda, it was stupid of you to come to my office alone."

She raised her chin. "You won't attack me next to a Bacon." She nodded at the painting hanging a few feet away from her. "The blood might stain the canvas."

Hal tipped his head back and laughed. The laugh went on a little too long, and when he looked back at Kate, his eyes were hard.

"You're cute," he said. "Yes, I was in San Francisco when she died. At my apartment around the corner from here. Which is only about an hour away from Callinas at that time of day, so yes, I certainly had the opportunity. But in 1993, Miranda provided most of my income. I wouldn't have shut down her production for anything."

"Prices go up when artists die," Kate said. "Like when the story came out about Miranda being in Nangussett, and everyone thought she was about to kill herself. Her prices doubled then, didn't they?"

"I believe so. I don't know the exact numbers. It was a long time ago."

"It just seems so convenient that the story came out when it did. I mean, a year after she left the hospital, suddenly someone decides to talk? And in such detail. Before that story, she was still up-and-coming. After it was published, people couldn't get enough of her." Kate cocked her head. "It was a big turning point for you, too, wasn't it? You started your own gallery the next year."

Hal's face darkened. "I'm not sure what you're trying to say."

"Just that galleries are expensive. And it's nice when things work out well."

Actually, until coming here today, she hadn't been sure Hal had been the tabloid's source. True, the list of candidates wasn't long: the tabloid must have had a lot of confidence in its source to risk the lawsuit, and as far as Kate could tell, Miranda had barely corresponded with anyone after leaving Nangussett. Now Hal's expression told her everything she needed to know.

"I work hard for my artists," Hal said. "I do what needs to be done."

"Oh, absolutely." Kate widened her eyes. "I'm sure Miranda would agree. Did she ever find out you were the one who leaked the story?"

Hal turned his wrist over and glanced at his heavy gold watch.

"Look at the time," he said curtly. "It's been a pleasure chatting with you. But I have a client meeting I need to get to. Give my love to Theo, won't you?"

Kate put her cup down and stood up. She felt a little shaky, as if the coffee had held something stronger than caffeine.

"Of course."

Despite her victory, there was something too familiar about how it felt to cross that thick silk rug, backtracking to the door she had come in through. Leonard's office; the flat berry-colored carpet, the diplomas on his wall. Her stomach knotted, then knotted again, folding in on itself. She had just reached for the door's chrome handle when Hal said from behind her, "Oh, and Ms. Aitken?"

She turned and waited.

"You met Samantha out in the gallery?" Hal said.

So he had known the attendant's name after all. Kate nodded.

"Theo dated her for three months last year. And he's slept with half the Young Trustees at SFMOMA. As far as I can tell, he's been working his way through Miranda's fans. So if you think fucking him makes you special, I'd think again."

Kate's hand dropped, banging against the door frame. Hal was smiling at her with the satisfied look of someone who had just reached checkmate.

"That's none of my business," she managed.

"Maybe not," Hal agreed. "Then again. You did say you were *curious*."

Flustered by the meeting, Kate got turned around trying to get back to Marin and wound up driving half an hour south, into Daly City, where the highways spiraled over one another like elastic bands and big-box stores lined the exits. She had just reoriented herself when the traffic ground to a halt and a series of emergency vehicles flew by on the highway shoulder. As their sirens faded into the distance, the car speaker started playing her ringtone full blast, and she nearly jumped out of her skin.

"Hello?" she said, jabbing at the dashboard buttons.

"Kate?" Natasha's voice came through staticky and uncertain. "Can you hear me?"

"Yeah, what's up?"

"Did you still want to talk today?"

Kate didn't know what Natasha meant, and then she remembered that they had a phone date for today, two o'clock her time. She glanced at the car clock. It was 4:19.

"Shit. I'm sorry," she said. "I forgot."

"Did you get my texts?"

"I don't know. Maybe. I didn't look at my phone."

Natasha was silent.

"What?" Kate asked, a little impatiently. Up ahead, someone in the next lane over put on their blinker to get into her lane, even though no one was moving.

"I don't know," Natasha said. "You just sound a little off."

"It's probably the Bluetooth. I don't really know how to work this car speaker."

"Oh—I didn't know you were driving. You want to talk later?"

"No." Kate put the car into park and rested her elbow on the window. "No one's moving anyway. I think there's an accident. Go on, how are you? How's work?"

"Work is . . . shitty." Natasha laughed. "As always. The other day a senior partner called me into her office and said I was getting too emotional during depositions."

"Emotional how?"

"She said I was too angry. Because I told the opposing counsel his client had to start showing up on time, not an hour late. Apparently that seemed *angry*."

"Fuck. Seriously?"

"Seriously. I cried for thirty minutes in the bathroom afterward. Which I hope no one found out about." Natasha sighed. "I really am thinking about quitting. But I don't know if it would be better anywhere else. Anyway." She put on a more cheerful tone. "What were you doing in the city? Did you see Michelle?"

An acquaintance from college. "No, I haven't gotten in touch with her yet. I was visiting Hal Eggers. Miranda's dealer."

"I thought you got weekends off."

"It wasn't for work. I mean, it was related, but I did it on my own time."

"Kate! You should bill for that shit."

"It's complicated. It doesn't really have to do with the archive. I just wanted to know if he knew anything."

"Knew anything about what?"

"About Miranda. How she died."

Another, longer silence from Natasha. Kate could practically feel the judgment radiating through the car audio system.

"I thought you were giving that stuff up," Natasha said at last. "Like. Investigating."

"I'm just poking around. There are a lot of holes in the story, you know? Not just conspiracy theory stuff. Like, real inconsistencies. Natasha—I found her diary. I mean, I don't know everything it says. I can't read it all at once. Since I'm not really supposed to be reading it at all."

"What do you mean? How do you sort it without reading it?"

"Well. It's not part of the collection."

"So how'd you find it?"

"I looked for it."

"Yeah, but where was it?"

"In Theo's bedroom."

"His *bedroom*?"

"Now I feel like *I'm* in a deposition," Kate said, annoyed.

"Why were you in his bedroom? Did you sleep with him?"

"I'm serious, cut it out with the questions," Kate said. "You're in lawyer mode, and it sucks."

"Excuse me if I'm a little concerned. After all that stuff you went through with Leonard? Why can't any of these dudes keep it in their pants?"

"It's not like Leonard at all. Trust me. It's an unusual situation." At least she had thought so, until Hal had said that stuff about Samantha and the other women.

"I don't get how unusual it can be. He should know better."

"Well, I know better, too," Kate said, shortly. "And it happened and I chose for it to happen. Okay? Are you done lecturing me on my poor life decisions yet?"

There was a silence on the other end. Then Natasha exhaled in a *whoosh* of static that filled the car.

"I'm sorry," she said. "I'm stressed out because of my own stuff. But I know you're an adult, you can make your own decisions."

"Thanks."

The brake lights of the car in front of Kate turned off. The traffic was starting to move up ahead.

"Just tell me you're taking care of yourself," Natasha said.

"I'm taking care of myself." Kate took the car out of park.

"Your meds and everything."

"Of course," she said, automatically. Only after saying it did she realize that she still hadn't managed to fill her prescription. She had called the doctor's office two more times earlier that week, but both times the call had gone to voice mail and no one had called her back. She hadn't checked with the pharmacy yet to see if they had received the fax. If this continued, she would have to find a new doctor out here, one that took the shitty insurance she had bought after her COBRA expired. She tried to remember how long it had been since she had taken her last pills. Not very long. A couple days? Certainly less than a week.

"I'm fine," she said. "Don't worry. And I do appreciate you asking. And I'll be careful with Theo."

"Okay. Thank you."

There wasn't much place to go from there. They chatted for a couple more minutes, robotic nothings. Kate was relieved when Natasha said her food delivery had arrived and she had to go.

The cars crawled forward slowly, a collection of left blinkers going on as everyone converged into a single line, like a chain of shiny ants marching along under the bright sun.

First a fight with Louise, then with Natasha. Kate was sick of their worry, their oppressive care. *Obsessed*, Hal had said. Well, so what if she showed symptoms sometimes, she thought angrily. She would never be perfect. That didn't mean she was powerless.

It was another fifteen minutes before Kate could even see the accident. A pickup truck had sideswiped a red sedan. Somehow the sedan had emerged mostly intact; the driver was standing by the side of the road, answering a police officer's questions and shivering as she stared at the huge dent in her passenger door. But the pickup, maybe trying to correct its course, had crashed into the guardrail, and its front had crumpled like an accordion.

There was glass everywhere, and a hundred feet ahead, the emergency crew was preparing the jaws of life.

A policewoman signaled Kate through a narrow gap between orange cones. Even once they were past the police cordon and the lanes were clear, the traffic was slow with rubberneckers watching the accident in their rear-view mirrors. For a mile or so, people drove carefully, cautiously, newly aware of the risks, holding their lives with a delicate grip. Then, as if on cue, everyone forgot why they had been afraid, and almost in unison, each driver pressed the gas.

MIRANDA

SERIES 5, Jake Brand

BOX 24, Correspondence

FOLDER: Eggers, Hal

9/2/1989

Dear Jake,

How delightful to receive yet another marvelous painting from you. I particularly like the play between emerald and pink and I agree with you that the earlier experiments with texture were not that successful. The flatness really ADDS something.

Truthfully, I am wondering whether you might consider going back to some of your work about fatherhood, home life, the Nangussett material? I feel this representation was RAW and shows you at your most VULNERABLE which always plays well with buyers.

As for your questions about Miranda, I very much would like to share that information with you, because I know we both care so much about her, but unfortunately it is confidential. Oh, rules!

Hal

SERIES 1, Correspondence

BOX 1, Personal correspondence

FOLDER: Eggers, Hal (incl. 39 photocopies of letters from MB, from HE private collection)

9/2/1989

Miranda, my darling girl,

   Ravishing news—Inside Me is officially a HIT! I have already sold 3 cop-ies of each print from the original run (except #5 of your knee, I think the knee is not a very interesting body part from a thematic perspective) at $22,000 each and am now hoping I can convince you to do a second run of 3 each.

   I also would not be OPPOSED to you doing a second set of Inside Me altogether, maybe based around the body parts that are more SYMBOLI-CALLY meaningful—the first ones to sell were #2 (hand), #4 (sternum), #8 (thigh), #9 (unidentifiable). Exploring more PERSONAL areas would prob-ably go over very well.

   As I said over the phone, I remain EXTREMELY excited about #8 being acquired by MoMA and I feel certain that we will be able to command even greater prices after that show.

   Your sincerest fan,

   Hal

SERIES 2, Personal papers

BOX 9, Diary (1982–1993)

SEPTEMBER 4 1989

A HIT, Hal said. Fuck you, Hal. Do you know what a hit feels like?

   The initial shock, the shame, the recovering bruise?

I was in the darkroom tonight and smelled burning. Theo had been hungry and had raided the cupboards. He tried to make pasta but didn't know to put water in first. He had pulled up a stool to the stove so he could cook. The entire kitchen filled with smoke and he was crying and crying. Jake was nowhere to be seen. I threw the pot outside and fanned some of the smoke out with a dish towel and then sat down and let Theo climb up onto my lap. He cried into my shoulder for a long time. I held him and held him. His rib cage felt so small against my hand.

I wanted to make him feel better so I told him we could make a secret together. We went upstairs and drew little drawings all along the baseboard.

You have to sign them, he said. So they're worth more.

He has learned that already. He is not even eight.

MB MB MB.

Guilt churns in my stomach. Churns acid. Churns out work. Produce. Produce. Produce.

Go deeper, they say. Cut something else out.

17.

KATE

Kate entered the Brands' clammy foyer on Monday morning with a lump in her throat. As she toed off her sneakers, she heard footsteps banging down the stairs. Theo popped out of the dark stairwell, wearing his usual jeans and T-shirt. Kate had spent the whole hike up the hill thinking about the situation, rationalizing it, gaming out possible scenarios for this conversation. Now that he was here in front of her, smile creasing his eyes, soft cotton stretched over his broad shoulders, her logic sputtered and died. She remembered lying in his bed Saturday night, boneless, tacky with sweat. Trumpets mewling from the stereo. The thin crack in the ceiling paint, branched like a vein. He had brushed his thumb over her bare shoulder once, twice—her exhausted nerves prickling each time. Now his hands were in his pockets, and still her whole body was zinging, like she had touched a hot stove.

"Hey," he said.

"Hey," she said. "How are you?"

"Good. You?"

"Good."

They stood there awkwardly for a minute. Kate shifted her weight, left to right and back again, her tote bag hitting her hip each time. (The blue sweep of the night, the taste of his sweat.)

At last Theo said, "You want coffee?"

"Please," she said gratefully.

In the kitchen, she sat down at the table while he got the coffee machine started. There was something intimate about watching him make coffee, maybe because he didn't seem to be very good at it. He couldn't find the pack of filters; he opened the coffee bag from the wrong end. The kitchen looked more dated than ever. For once, there was no morning fog, and the undiluted sunlight picked out every crack in the tile floor, every inch of stained grout.

"I'm sorry I didn't text yesterday," Theo said, pouring the grounds into the filter without measuring. "I meant to. But it seemed—I don't know. I thought it would be better to talk in person."

"No, I agree," she said. The nuances of morning-after texting belonged to her life back in New York. What could she have said? Still, she didn't like how he enunciated each word clearly, as if he were practicing in front of a mirror. She had the distinct sense that she was about to receive a speech.

He started the machine, then turned around and rested his hands on the counter behind him. His expression was inscrutable.

"I don't know," he said again. "I guess I wimped out."

Kate's throat tightened. The more he talked, the worse it sounded.

"You can just say it." She could hear a new hardness in her voice. "You don't want it to happen again."

"No, wait," he said, looking alarmed. "That's not it at all."

He let go of the counter and came over to sit at the table.

"It's just that I know I'm your boss," he said. "And I'm worried that . . . well, it's an ethical issue, right?"

Kate wanted to say, *You should have thought about that before*, but she knew he had. They both had. Preparing to jump the hurdle didn't make the hurdle disappear.

"I went to see Hal yesterday," she said.

"Who?"

"Hal Eggers. Your parents' dealer?"

"Oh." His brow furrowed. "Why?"

"I met Samantha."

"Huh?"

"Hal said you dated her."

Theo shifted in his seat. "Yeah. Briefly."

"So there wasn't any ethical issue there?"

"Well, she wasn't my employee."

"What about the women on the SFMOMA board? Was that ethical?"

"What, did Hal give you a list of everyone I've slept with in the last two years?"

"It sounded like it would be a long list."

He was silent for a moment. "I guess I don't know what you want me to say," he said at last. "Yeah. I got divorced and I went on the rebound. Are you worried that's what I'm doing with you?"

"I'm just saying, it seems like you have a pattern of sleeping with women who work under you."

"No." Theo sounded annoyed now. "None of those women worked under me. Yes, I met them through things related to my parents. I have to deal with a lot of stuff with the estate, so that's the main way I end up meeting people. Otherwise I'm at work or with Jemima and Oscar. But I've never slept with any of my employees. Until now."

"So I'm supposed to think I'm special."

"Yes." Color rose in his cheeks. "You are special. Anyway, I thought this was mutual."

In the background, the coffee machine was making its spitting noise, and the room was filling with the familiar smell. Kate looked at his hands on the table—strong, tanned, square-cut nails—and then at her own, paler, smaller, blue ink flowering over one knuckle from a broken pen at the bottom of one of Miranda's boxes.

Then she groaned and buried her face in her hands. "I'm sorry," she said through her fingers. "It is mutual. I don't know why I'm giving you such a hard time. I think I'm just nervous."

"Because of what happened at your last job?"

"Maybe. No. I don't think so." She inhaled and lifted her head. "I guess I'm scared. Aren't you scared?"

"Yes. Of course." He hesitated. "I don't want you to do anything you don't really, a hundred percent, want to do. That's what I'm most scared of. If you want to go back to normal, pretend Saturday never happened—we can do that. Anytime, we can do that. It's a standing offer. It's whatever you want."

Whatever you want. What didn't she want? She wanted everything.

She wanted to fuck him and also get paid, but not for the fucking. She wanted someone to come along and smooth over her entire life, and she wanted to stand on her own two feet and stare the world down. She wanted to know all his secrets and share none of her own.

She wanted the entire world to open itself to her, full of promises and creatures, teeming with every ragged desire that had chased her ever since she had first pried open her infant eyes and watched the colors blur and shake into shapes.

She wanted it all.

She knew she couldn't have whatever she wanted. Not everything, and not forever. And yet, in this moment, poised on this threshold, *yes or no*, part of her rose up, rebelled: Why *shouldn't* she try? Other people did.

He was too good for her, of course. But if you stumbled upon a diamond in the street, did you throw it in the gutter for someone else to find? No. You clutched it tighter. You held it for as long as you could.

Before she could talk herself out of it, Kate rose from her seat and went over to him. While his eyes were still surprised, she swung her leg over him and straddled him, so that they were chest to chest, forehead to forehead. She was too close to see his expression shift into understanding, but she felt it in the way his muscles loosened, his shoulders going slack and his hands, those hands, coming to rest on her hips.

She remembered seeing him in the backyard the first time. The sensation that had fallen across her skin, like frozen fingers being thrust into warm water. At the time, she had thought it was fear. But perhaps it was a deeper kind of startling.

"Hi," he said, and she laid her mouth to his before he could finish shaping the word.

Sweat, musk. Late morning through the windows, warming a square of sun on the bed as they lay there getting their breath back. Theo hadn't changed the sheets since they had abused them on Saturday, which Kate—usually a laundry fanatic—found strangely comforting. She liked being better at something than him, even if that something was laundry.

"I hope you know I'm not counting this toward my hours," she said, propping her chin on his forearm. "Ground rules."

Theo hesitated, then nodded. "Ground rules," he agreed. "And when Jemima and Oscar are around, we'll be . . ."

"Discreet."

"For now."

For now made Kate think about the future, which she didn't want to do.

Theo must have sensed her discomfort, because he changed the subject, saying instead, "So you met Hal yesterday."

"Yeah."

"What did you think?"

Kate thought for a moment. "Smart," she said finally. "Slippery. He puts on a whole show, but the show is like an inside joke."

Theo nodded. "He likes to seem a little fake. In a way, I think it's better. You know what you're getting. He uses you, but he doesn't make a secret about it."

Kate wasn't so sure Hal was as straightforward as Theo thought. But she wasn't going to argue the point.

"Why did you go see him, anyway?" Theo asked.

She tilted her head to look up at him. It was hard to read his expression from this angle, but she thought the question was genuinely casual. He was staring into space, idly running his fingers up and down her arm. When she didn't answer right away, he looked back at her face, his gaze sharpening.

"Kate?"

It would be easy to lie. She had already lied so much to him. But she was still all twisted up inside from the sex, wrung clean. She pushed herself up to lean against the headboard.

"Theo," she said, "do you ever think your mother might have been murdered?"

The words sounded so strange, so distant, coming out of her mouth. Theo blinked at her once, twice, and then his face grew solemn.

"No," he said flatly. "I don't."

She already knew she had made a mistake. Still, she pressed, "Really? Because you must have known there were issues with the case, right?"

"Did you watch that *60 Minutes* special or something?"

"No. I mean, yes. But that's not why I'm asking."

He rolled over and swung his legs off the bed. Kate continued, "It's just, looking through her papers, she doesn't seem like . . . it doesn't seem like she would have killed herself."

"No? You know she spent two months in a psych ward, right? For threatening to kill me?"

"Right. Yeah, I know. It's just . . . wait, will you look at me?"

He turned his head to look over his shoulder. The muscles of his back moved as he twisted. But he didn't turn all the way, and she could still only see his profile, backlit by the bright window behind him.

"I'm sorry," she said. "I wasn't trying to bring up something difficult. I just meant, that's why I went down to see Hal. I wanted to see what he was like. If he could have . . ."

"And? You think he did?"

"I don't know," she said honestly.

Theo sighed. He stayed sitting on the edge of the bed for a moment, as if he was thinking about what she had said, or maybe what he should say back. Then he shoved his hands through his hair and stood up.

"My mother wasn't murdered," he said, his tone final. "And I don't want to talk about it anymore. I'm going to take a shower."

With that, he went off into the bathroom, leaving Kate alone in the bed. She folded her legs and leaned over them, arms outreached as she stretched her spine. Her bra was at the end of the bed, and she snagged the strap and pulled it toward her and put it on. She felt strangely exposed, almost like she had never been here before, when of course she had been spending afternoons here for weeks, crouched right next to this bed. Next to this nightstand. Kate ran her finger along the drawer's wood grain. She could almost feel Miranda's journal radiating into her hand.

No. She yanked her hand back. If she was going to do this—thing— with Theo, she would have to stop sneaking around behind his back. God, fifteen minutes ago they had been having sex; now he was showering in the next room over.

On the other hand.

She had upset him with talking about his mother, obviously. But she had gone about it the wrong way. She hadn't had any evidence. He didn't know she had been reading the journal. She had the information from Victor, she had the feeling in her gut that something had happened to Miranda, but she didn't have any conclusive proof. She didn't even have a specific suspect. She hadn't liked that last diary entry she had read, where Jake and Miranda fought about him painting Nangussett, but one argument six years before Miranda's death was hardly a smoking gun. If she wanted Theo to believe her, she would have to back up her suspicions, introduce them at a better time, when they hadn't just had sex, when they knew each other better. And she would have to know everything he knew—which meant she had to finish reading the diary.

The toilet flushed, and then the shower turned on. Kate held her breath for a second, then huffed impatiently and reached out to open the drawer. She could at least *see* the journal. She could at least remind herself it was there.

She had pulled that drawer open so many times, knew its contents so well, that it took her a moment to realize that anything had changed. There was the same curled rubber band in the corner, the same single bent bobby pin, grubby at the points . . . and nothing else.

The journal was gone.

MIRANDA

SERIES 2, Personal papers

BOX 9, Diary (1982–1993)

NOVEMBER 21 1990

Lynn is out here for Thanksgiving.

She and Candace arrived two days ago. They made a trip of it. They spent three days camping in Big Sur and arrived all dusty. When I saw Lynn, I almost didn't recognize her. Her hair was different. Her face was rounder. I was glad she was so dirty: I pretended that was why my eyes slid over her for a second. But it shook me. It's just been so long.

Candace is . . . fine. She seems smart. She seems to love Lynn. She touches her automatically, instinctively. I never really care about whether people are nice, but I found myself wanting her to be nice. She wasn't. Lynn doesn't like nice people, I guess. Because I'm not nice either. As we know.

Jake made dinner. It felt weird. I don't remember the last time we had guests. Candace and Lynn exclaimed over Theo, even though he didn't do much, just sat there silently, pushing vegetables around his plate. I guess I forgot to enroll him in some after-school thing, and now it's filled up. Eight years old and already so good at resentment.

After dinner, I showed Candace and Lynn their room. Candace wrinkled her nose when she saw the pile of magazines in the corner but I have things to do besides cleaning.

Candace wanted to read and Jake had gone upstairs, so Lynn and I went out on the back porch and had a smoke. Like traveling back in time. She told me she had seen one of my Inside Me photos at a show. Thinking of her looking at my pictures put this sudden weight in my throat—like I had swallowed a lead ball. I don't know if I was more worried that she had seen through them, or that she hadn't.

You look different, I told her.

It's been four years, she said.

I did the math in my head. I keep meaning to come out to Boston, I said.

She gave me this pitying look and said, I know you're never coming to Boston.

She said it lightly. But you could tell she meant something more by it. Like I had failed some kind of test, not just now, but over years and years. I should have tried to explain to her—about my memory, about Jake, about all of it—but that would only have made her pitying look brighter, and I was already sweating with shame in its glow.

If I already failed the test, then why did she even come here? To rub it in my face?

NOVEMBER 22 1990

THANKSGIVING DAY

We haven't had guests in a while, so I didn't remember how disruptive it is. It turns out we have so many ingrained routines I just forget about, take for granted. With them here we are so much more careful about everything. We tiptoe around our own house. It makes me feel like I am living a different life. Jake is a wonderful host, of course, so friendly, but I know he is fed up. Part of me is desperate for Lynn and Candace to leave, just so we can get it over with, whatever's coming next.

Thanksgiving dinner was full of food. Candace is a good cook, she and Jake took over the kitchen, and Theo was throwing a tantrum so Lynn and I took him to the beach to get him out of their hair.

A cold day, so no one was out except the surfers. We were sitting on the sand, Theo working on a sandcastle, me and Lynn talking about the people we had known in college and what they were doing now, when Lynn said, At least Richard Rohber finally got what he deserved.

I asked her what that meant, and she said he had a heart attack while he was fucking some undergrad. Last year. You really didn't know?

I haven't talked to anyone from Falkman in a while, I said.

Lynn told me about how it was hushed up anyway, but I barely listened. I was thinking about the girl. How she must have felt, thinking she was in control, thinking how close she was to power. His thrusting, and then the sudden spasm, a choking noise, his full weight falling on top of her.

I said, I hope it doesn't ruin fucking for her.

Lynn was shocked for a minute, then she laughed and said, Sometimes I don't think you've changed at all.

Then she said, You'd tell me, right? If you needed help. If anything was wrong.

I think my heart's in good condition, I joked.

I mean if you need any help with Jake.

I was speechless for a moment. Jake and I had been so careful, the past few days. I thought we had played our parts. I thought we had tricked Lynn. All this time, she had been able to see down into the heart of me. The truth of the matter, even if she didn't know exactly what it was. This awful feeling came over me, like a thundercloud in my chest. Terror, shame.

I told her she was out of line. She said she was trying to help.

I said, You have to get over the Jake thing. So what if we didn't invite you to the wedding? We didn't invite anyone. We eloped.

This isn't about that.

Sure it is, I said. You're taking your jealousy out on me.

My jealousy? she asked.

You always had a crush on me. You wanted me, and you're jealous of Jake for getting me.

She stared at me. I'll never forget the way she stared at me. You've always been a real bitch, she said. But I never thought you'd be a bitch to me. I've never been in love with you. I've never even been attracted to you. I'm not some kind of shark circling for scraps. Is that what you think? That I follow you around waiting to make a move?

I said, Well, that's why we haven't seen each other in so long, right? You couldn't handle being close to me.

No, Miranda. We haven't seen each other because I have to call you ten times for you to call me back once. You disappeared to California. You disappeared into Jake and Theo and your art, always your fucking art. And now I ask you how you are, and you come at me acting like I'm a predator. That's why we don't talk. Because you're a shitty friend.

She got up then and went over to Theo and bent down to look at what he was digging. Eventually we went back to the house, ate turkey, laughed, on the surface we returned to normal. I know she'll never forgive me. For what I said, and for not trusting her with the truth.

I know I was wrong to say it. But I had no choice. If I hadn't distracted her, she would have kept pushing. She would have gotten me to tell her about what Jake does sometimes. And there are days when I think the only thing holding me together is the fact that no one else knows.

NOVEMBER 23 1990

Lynn and Candace left at last. Dust behind their wheels, the last particles of trust.

No rain here for days. I was waiting for the storm and it came. I triggered it: I poked at Jake about his painting, how it was coming along. Sudden fight about how he couldn't work with those people in his house, how I made him do all the work, how I'm an ungrateful cunt. He hit me across the face, which he never does because it leaves marks. I fell down on the floor. I tried to pull myself up using the dining table. My hand closed over the letter opener Hal sent last spring in honor of some milestone. For a moment I thought I would use it. I could imagine it so clearly: the opener up to its hilt in his chest. His surprised face. Pulling it out, the metal slick with his blood. The monogram would catch the blood like ink in an engraving plate. Burgundy red: MB.

My hand relaxed. I released the table and fell back onto the rug. Sometimes it's easier not to try. When I looked over my shoulder, Jake was leaving the room, and Theo was watching from the door.

Yes, Lynn, I am different now. I didn't know fear before. I didn't know how it could shape you. Make you do things you didn't want to do. I didn't know how it lives in you like dye, like a stain that will never come out. How it works its way through you until your blood is made of it, until it is fear that pushes oxygen through your veins, fear that pumps your heart, open and shut, open and shut. The fear has no subject. It has no ground. It has only me, and some days it eats me alive.

18.

KATE

As July slipped over the cusp into August, Kate's days changed shape, like a bubble distorting in midair. By unspoken agreement, she and Theo came to a schedule of sorts. They worked separately through the morning, then spent the lunch hour in bed. Despite the routine, the sex still felt spontaneous, urgent, inventive. After, they lay talking about anything and everything unrelated to his family—what they had been like in high school, where they wanted to travel, whether they believed in God. Food was an afterthought: cold sandwiches while hunched over spreadsheets, protein bars devoured on her walk home.

"I haven't had fruits or vegetables in three days," she told him one day. "I'm going to be the first person in the world to get scurvy from having sex."

"Rotted flesh," he said. "Hot."

"That's leprosy."

"Yum."

The next day, she found an orange sitting on the dining room table. An imperfect sphere, dimpled like a golf ball, practically glowing. When she bit into the first wedge, it was juicy and almost spicy, like liquid gold.

It had been so difficult, that morning when Theo came back from the shower, towel around his waist and his wet hair ridged by a comb, not to demand he tell her what he had done with the diary. The shock of its disappearance was quickly followed by fear—did he know she had been reading it? Was that why he had moved it?—and then, in the days that followed, by a sense of resolution. Surely he would have mentioned if he had known she was reading it. He had probably moved it for another reason, maybe to keep Oscar or Jemima away. So her task was the same as it had been: figure out what had happened to Miranda.

Not having the diary wasn't the end of the world, Kate knew. She had an entire room full of Jake's and Miranda's papers, some still unsorted. Every day she found new photographs, new letters, new records. The archivist's equivalent of rolling around in a pile of hundred-dollar bills. The layperson's equivalent, too, when you thought about how much all that stuff was worth. But now that Kate knew what she had had, she missed the diary acutely. It had been so orderly, so *chronological*, and she had been so close to the end. Sometimes she had sensed in Miranda's words an acceleration toward that final moment, November 16, 1993. It was as if speed of light and speed of sound were reversed, and Kate had heard that gunshot like a roll of thunder in the distance, and was only waiting now to see the flash of the bullet discharging.

She wondered whether Miranda had sensed that acceleration, too: whether she had known the pieces of her death were being put into place, and whether she had known who was responsible.

Kate felt the long reach of destiny in her own life, too. Her doctor had finally faxed the prescription. But when she drove to the pharmacy to pick it up, the pharmacist told her that she had reached an insurance cap and would need to have her provider call the insurance company and ask for an exception. Or else she could pay for the drug out-of-pocket. One month of pills would cost $1,240. He didn't blink when he pronounced the number, not even when Kate let out a short, squawking laugh. She left the pharmacy empty-handed. Called the doctor, left him a voice mail. It would probably be a few days before she heard back. So whatever. She had gone most of her life without any medication.

And right now, everything was aligning. Her body seemed sped up, lit up, her movements quicker than ever. She, too, was moving toward her future. Fate filled her; she was its vessel. She felt, for the first time in a long time, certain that everything would work out.

O utside the Brand house, the world was less peaceful. Wildfires raged across the state, vast, uncontrollable, decimating. Footage of the fires was all over the local news: hills consumed by orange pockets of flames, the burned-through patches turned into black spots against the infernal blaze. Mobile homes melted into the ground in metallic pools. People burned alive in their cars. When the wind turned, you could smell the smoke. The fires smelled different than Kate had imagined: not like a campfire, but acrid and angry, as if the scale of the destruction had shaped the scent itself. From the Brands' hill, a low gray line hovered near the horizon, a distant and invisible beast.

Callinas was not at risk, but the locals were consumed by talk about the fires. Acreage destroyed, rescue efforts, which areas had been spared and which had been flattened to ash. The number of questions Kate was asked about the Brands dwindled. The bottomless human hunger for tragedy had been filled, and Miranda had been temporarily forgotten.

Although Kate followed news of the fires, the locals' sudden apparent indifference to Miranda bewildered her. They had asked so many questions when she arrived, and now that she was finally starting to understand the obsession with Miranda, and was considering a more flexible approach to the nondisclosure agreement, no one cared. When she hung out at Pawpaw's, she started dropping little hints for Nikhil, baiting the hook with references to what she had found that day; he only shrugged and changed the subject.

Even Frank and Louise had stopped asking questions. Louise was still mad about the argument and was constantly shooting Kate plaintive looks, while Frank, burrowing further into his feigned obliviousness, steered around the topic of the Brands with all the deliberation of a ship's captain avoiding an iceberg.

As a peace offering, Kate helped Louise organize a collection drive to support the firefighters. They recruited donations from half of town, filling the living room with sunscreen, bandannas, Gatorade, until one morning Kate was flicking through the local news on Frank's iPad and reported to Louise, "The fire department says not to send any more donations."

Louise glanced up from a pile of gauze she had been folding. "What?"

"It says they're overwhelmed. They can't get anything done. They're having to move donations around instead of sleeping between shifts."

"We sent so much we shut them down," Louise said proudly. Then she looked around the living room, and her smile faded. "So now what do we do with all this?"

Plastic bags of unsorted donations were everywhere. One chair was piled with tiny bottles of Vaseline. It looked a little like the Brands' dining room, although that was also because the Brands' dining room looked more respectable these days, thanks to Kate's new wave of energy.

"I don't know," Kate admitted. She put her hands in her pockets and took a deep breath. "Listen. Aunt Louise . . . I was wondering, have you told my mom?"

"Told her what?" Louise was still distracted by the mess around them.

"About me and Theo."

Louise's eyes flicked to her, then slid away. "No."

"Because I've been getting weird texts from her. Or at least a lot of texts. Checking in."

She had woken up to three messages from her mother:

Hi, how are you feeling today?

Did you get that refill you were worried about??

Are you maintaining a PROFESSIONAL DISTANCE from your work??

"Well, that's not because of me," Louise said. "Maybe there's some other reason she's worried. She's probably looking for warning signs."

"Warning signs of what?"

"You know."

"Why?" Kate asked, her voice coming out a little accusatory. "Do you see warning signs?"

Louise threw up her hands. "I don't know, Kate. We don't know each other that well, do we?"

The comment nicked an artery. It was one thing for Kate to sense a gulf between her and her aunt, for her to realize how little time they had spent together before this summer, and another thing for Louise to acknowledge it. Kate felt both guilty and wounded, like all the effort she had put in so far that summer—all the errands run together, all the episodes of *Madam Secretary*, all the times she had helped Frank untangle his dumb radio wires or studiously ignored Louise's thoughtless comments—had gone unrecognized. Had disappeared under the weight of the little things she had done wrong: the times she had delayed coming home after work by going to Pawpaw's, or when she told Louise to lay off Theo, or when she forgot to call. Kate wondered how the calculations worked, sacrifice versus selfishness. If only there were a spreadsheet she could consult to tell her who was right or wrong.

"I'll help you figure out what to do with these when I get back," Kate said, gesturing at the donations.

"Fine." Her aunt waved her away. "Have a good day at work." A touch of bitterness in the final word, as if Louise had noticed halfway through the sentence that it was past its expiration date.

MIRANDA

SERIES 2, Personal papers
BOX 9, Diary (1982–1993)

FEBRUARY 24 1991

The other night on TV there was a news special about battered women. Battered: a ship in a storm, taking on water. High winds tattering the sails.

Disappointed in myself because I don't remember much about the women they interviewed. I mainly remember the interviewer. He pulled each woman's story out of her with such dexterity. A question, a question, a question, and then the story slipped out all at once, like a blood clot after a nosebleed. He was talented, that man. He cried on command at each story. As if removing their clot made his own eyes water. But personally I wouldn't be surprised if he gets home and unbuckles his brown leather belt and lays into his wife. I suspect most marriages involve a little hitting.

I've been trying to call Lynn. Candace always picks up and she always has an excuse prepared. Lynn's at work, Lynn's out for a run, Lynn will call me back.

Candace, I've known Lynn longer than you have. I knew her when we were young, which is the truest way you can know someone, before life has had a chance to chip away at you, refine those rough shapes into features.

I knew Lynn when we were only clay. So I know Lynn won't be calling me back anytime soon.

Of course what I said to Lynn at Thanksgiving was cruel. I don't dispute that. People like me, cruelty rises within us, blood tide, pushing at our skulls. The only way to relieve the pressure is to drill a hole. Lynn doesn't understand this, but Jake must. He must feel it when he hits me. How can I fault him for that, really, when I know I'm the same way?

No one is a good victim. Not really. If they dove into any person, if they slipped between the walls of you and took you out, pinched you between their fingers, they would see you are not worthy of your pain. Our past like shrapnel inside us. It shreds our veins.

MAY 3 1991

Theo's school had a parent show-and-tell. I never do that kind of thing, but Theo asked me to. His eyes wide and questioning and with a look in them like, *I know you won't*.

It's true I was terrified by the thought. His teacher wanted me to get up in front of the whole class of shouting children, not to mention their parents, waiting for me to fail so they can tell all their friends.

But I had to try. Theo had asked me to.

I made it to the school. Which itself was a bigger success than these idiots realize. I was shaking, I was coming apart inside. I handed my slides over to the teacher, Cassie fucking Davenport, and said Here you go and tried not to sweat. She held them up through the light and squinted at the shapes. Then she brought them down and gave me a tight-lipped smile.

Miranda—you can't show these to the children.

There's no projector?

There's a projector. She handed me back the stack. But they aren't appropriate.

It's art. It pushes boundaries.

They're offensive.

There's no violence. I didn't choose any of the ones with blood.

Yes, but the nudity. It's too much.

I stood there in the front of the classroom and a huge anger rose up in me. I wanted to shake her. All the talk these people give about wanting to raise well-rounded children. Natural everything, no chemicals, no dyes, wearing handwoven shawls $200 each. And then they come to me and say breasts are too much for these kids.

It's nothing against *you*, she said. You can still present without the slides.

Her mouth like a crocodile. The children started filing in. Theo hovered at the door. His face so full of hope.

No, I said at last. My head split open with a terrible ache. I don't think I can.

I didn't stay to see the other show-and-tells. Or Theo's face. I walked home. My shoes gave me blisters, I had bought new shoes for those bitches, and no one even looked at my feet.

When I told Jake about it, he said, I don't know why they invited you in the first place. It's not like your recent stuff is any good.

MAY 4 1991

When we left New York, I thought of it like disappearing. I would make the art and leave it open to interpretation. Let people see whatever they wanted to see, without me as a distraction. I wanted their eyes off me. Their feverish, scratching eyes. I figured the pictures could handle the scrutiny. They had glass to protect them. Security guards.

But still, after all these years of exile, every place I go, every clipping about an exhibition I'm in, says right up front—Miranda Brand, recluse. Miranda Brand, nutcase. My plan has backfired. The pictures can't escape me.

I worry about what I will leave behind when I die.

19.

KATE

L ibrary day!"

Startled, Kate nearly dropped her mug on the kitchen floor. She had slept poorly the night before. A bad dream. She couldn't remember the details—only the horror of something bleeding in front of her. Organs spilling from a vertical slit, liver and intestines and kidneys all glistening in an unholy light. It felt wrong, remembering this dream now, with Jemima standing before her in her sandy camp clothes, emanating a sugary smell of sunscreen and child's sweat and holding a reusable Trader Joe's bag full of books. Her shins were streaked with gray mud from that day's nature explorations.

"Aren't you supposed to be taking your bath?" Kate asked.

"Oscar's going. Anyway, I'm the librarian, and librarians don't need baths."

"But baths are where librarians get their magic," Kate said.

Ignoring this transparent propaganda, Jemima began hauling books out of the bag and arranging them on the kitchen table. "What book do you want?"

"Huh?"

"It's a library. You have to choose a book."

Kate set down her mug and went over to look at the selection. *Miss Twinkle and the Venus Fly Trap. Dried Up: A History of Droughts in Southern California*—Theo had been reading that recently; Jemima must have taken it out of his room. *Toot Toot the Engine. Prima Ballerina: A Ballet Stars Story.*

Kate tapped *Miss Twinkle*. "How about this one?"

Jemima wrinkled her nose. "You're too old for that."

"How old do you think I am?"

"I don't know. Fifty?"

Kate laughed and held up her hands. "Okay, you pick the book. They all look so good."

Jemima took the question seriously, stepping back to consider her array. Kate watched her downturned head, the thin line of scalp shining up through her center part. Jemima was such a big personality that sometimes Kate forgot how small she was. Kate squatted down to be on her level.

"Hey, Jemima. Can I ask you something?"

"Yeah." Jemima wasn't listening. She had picked out a copy of *The Giver* and was busy riffling through the book's pages in a pantomime of a librarian looking for the borrowing card.

"Does it bother you," Kate asked, "that I come over here so often? Besides work. Like when I come over for dinner, or to hang out with your dad." Even though she and Theo were still keeping their distance around the children, Jemima was smart; she would know something had changed, even if she didn't understand what.

"No," Jemima said, wiggling away to pick up her notepad. "You're my friend. I have lots of friends. For sample, Devon. Isabella. Cohen. Madeline. Other Madeline. Leaper."

"Leaper?"

"He likes robots," Jemima said, as if that explained his name.

"Well, I'm happy to be your friend, too," Kate said. The squatting was making her thighs burn. Life with the kids had made her aware of vertical space in a whole new way: she was always sitting or kneeling or lying down, letting them crawl all over her.

Jemima wrote "THE GIVER" in large, awkward letters on her notepad, then scribbled on another piece of paper, put it inside the book, and handed the book to Kate. "Here. The man on the cover will make you look smart."

There was a lot there to unpack. "Cool, thanks," Kate said, taking it.

Jemima gave her a big smile. "Oscar stinks," she said. "I can't wait to have a sister."

Kate coughed. "A—what?"

"When Daddy adopts you. We'll be sisters."

"Oh, Jemima . . ."

As Kate was trying to figure out what to say to this, Theo appeared in the doorway. His shirt was splattered with water, and he had the frazzled expression that came with wrangling a small unwilling being into a soapy tub.

"Bath time," he said to Jemima.

"Librarians don't need baths," she repeated.

"Librarians who want to go out for ice cream do," Theo said.

Jemima's expression changed. "Really?"

"Really. But only if you finish your bath in time."

Jemima hightailed it out of the kitchen.

"Sometimes I feel like being a parent is just running one elaborate con after another," Theo said. "You got a library book, I guess?"

"I did. And she told me about her friends back at school. Is there really someone named Leaper?"

"Yeah. Like a reindeer." But Theo looked at her curiously. "She said he was her friend?"

"Yeah. And Isabella and Cohen. What is it? You look worried."

He reached up to scratch the back of his head. "I don't know. Leaper and Isabella are the names of two kids who were bullying her last year. I had, like, four mediations with their parents. I don't know why she's saying they're her friends."

Kate was surprised. Not that Jemima had lied—Jemima liked to lie, although she usually confessed right after, all in a rush, like she had suddenly downed a vial of truth serum—but that there was this whole backstory she hadn't known about. She and the Brands had become so entwined with each other the past few months that she sometimes forgot they had this entire life a couple hours south, full of PTA dramas and kids' karate classes and long work hours for Theo and an entire house Kate had never even seen.

Looking at the mess of books on the table, Theo grinned. "Just like the dining room."

"What—?"

But Theo was already out the door, heading back upstairs to help Jemima with the bath. When Kate looked at the table, she realized that Theo was right: Jemima hadn't been copying any imaginary librarian. She had been imitating Kate going through the papers.

Kate opened the book and found the slip of paper Jemima had stuck in the middle. DUE AUGSUT 28. The date sent a jitter through her. August 28 was just over three weeks away. She didn't know when the kids' school started again, or when the Brands were planning to head back to Portola Valley.

When she had arrived in California, three months had seemed like such a long time. Now the summer was almost over, and she didn't know what she was doing next. She hadn't even started looking for jobs.

In the living room, the television flicked on, followed by the dulcet sounds of Oscar's favorite cartoon theme song, a ditty that always made Kate feel like her brain was dripping into her spinal column. Kate put back the date slip, tucked the book under her arm, and took her mug of tea to the dining room to get back to work.

MIRANDA

SERIES 1, Correspondence

BOX 1, Personal correspondence

FOLDER: Toby-Jarrett, Lynn (incl. 12 photocopies of letters from MB, from LTJ private collection)

November 18 1991

Dear Lynn,

Happy belated birthday!

I keep thinking about what happened at Thanksgiving last year. I feel terrible about what I said. I want to talk about it. Will you call me?

M

February 4 1992

Dear Lynn,

Found an article I thought you would like. See where it talks about the strata in the rock, the calc deposits? It sounds up your alley. Or maybe the intersection of our two alleys. Maybe someday we should do what we used to talk about, go down to Utah or Arizona, you can take your weird measurements and I'll take my photos. We can camp out and listen to the lizards rumble through the sand.

Miss you—

xo M

[*clipping attached:* "New State Park Opens in Utah—and It's a Gem," *San Francisco Chronicle*, February 3, 1992]

March 11 1992

Dear Lynn,

    Thought you would like this book.

    Will you please write back?

    xo Miranda

[*mailed with:* Clive and Claire Daneborn, *Art Rocks: The Intersection of Painting and Geology* (Mooser Press, 1990)]

SERIES 2, Personal papers

BOX 9, Diary (1982–1993)

APRIL 14 1992

Last night he yanked off my clothing and held me down and fucked me. I was not wet and it felt like I was being scraped open. Burned alive. I was quiet. I didn't want Theo to hear. I lay there in the dark and let Jake do what he wanted and at last it was over. He held me gently after. It was a relief to fall asleep. That beautiful void.

SERIES 1, Correspondence

BOX 1, Personal correspondence

FOLDER: Toby-Jarrett, Lynn (incl. 12 photocopies of letters from MB, from LTJ private collection)

April 15 1992

Lynn,

    Do you remember that day after my final printmaking critique at Falkman? You came over to the art building to celebrate and we got a few cases of beers and stayed around the critique space drinking, so drunk, you high off your ass and Caleb being a dick in the corner and everyone laughing, so relieved. Everyone except you was disgusting because no one had showered in days, prepping for the critique. But we were all disgusting together, and I remember you and I sat on that low wall outside the building, it was dark already because it was winter, I was all wrapped up in my coat and you were in a T-shirt. We were watching the shapes of people's heads through the lit window, we couldn't see much of them because of the angle, but you could tell there was joy and relief and youth in that room. You finished your beer and cracked open a second bottle you had in your pocket and before you drank from it you clinked our bottles. Cheers.

To friendship, you said. To your art.

I was happy then, I think.

To friendship and art.

Lynn, I need help. I need your help.

Write me back.

M

SERIES 5, Jake Brand

BOX 24, Correspondence

FOLDER: Toby-Jarrett, Lynn (1 photocopy of letter from JB, from LTJ private collection)

5/2/1992

Lynn,

    Miranda mentioned that she has been writing to you and I just want to make sure you are paying attention to her mental health in what she is writing. As you know, she has been through a lot and she does not always see things clearly. She gets very angry for no reason at all and makes bizarre accusations. Sometimes I worry that she has misunderstood very basic things.

    If she says anything unusual, please let me know. I am keeping an eye on her to make sure she does not need to return to a hospital. Please help me with this because I know we both care about her a lot.

It was nice seeing you for Thanksgiving and I hope we can do it again soon when Miranda is well.

Jake

SERIES 1, Correspondence

BOX 1, Personal correspondence

FOLDER: Carpicci, Candace

5/23/1992

Hi Jake and Miranda,

This is Candace, Lynn's girlfriend. You have sent several letters/packages addressed to Lynn (I didn't open them) so I think you might not know that Lynn is on a research trip / humanitarian mission in Mongolia. She left in April and she'll be back sometime next year, depending on how the surveys go. I've attached the address I have for her, but I know they only check it occasionally and the mail is not very reliable, so letters usually take 1–3 months.

Hope you are well.

Candace Carpicci

SERIES 2, Personal papers

BOX 9, Diary (1982–1993)

MAY 28 1992

Lynn is in some distant country. I've lost her.

If I ever had her. Increasingly I think friends are illusions of love our younger selves create. The links between us are so breakable. No legal documents, no custody arrangements, no joint accounts. The only sign it's over is that the mail never comes.

Candace addressed the letter to me and Jake. He wrote to Lynn, too?

Maybe I'm seeing things that aren't there. Except . . . knowing the things are invented doesn't make me see them any less.

All these years later, I still remember that moment in Nangussett. *I consent.* I talked to Dr. Pottle once about how those words swirl around my head at night, and he said lots of people feel that way. Betrayed by the person who sent them there.

But I sent myself there. I went there on my own.

Jake only saw me when I was weak and pressed down on me like a bug.

Sometimes the only reason I want to live is that I still have so much art to make.

20.

KATE

The second Sunday in August, Theo arranged for one of the camp counselors to watch the kids for the day, and he and Kate drove down to a small beach south of Muir Woods so that she could go surfing for the first time.

She was bad at it. Even with Theo there to guide her, the whole thing was so foreign: the board banging up and down as she paddled out over the waves, the opaque rhythms of who got to go when, the complete impossibility of levering her body up at the right moment. Theo said when she caught the wave it would feel like a train beneath her, but that never happened. The wave always crashed over her, catching some odd angle of her board if she so much as moved a muscle. Again and again she was pounded down into the tide, her legs smacking water and seaweed and the board. And yet it was fun, in a weird way, the surrender, the momentary panic every time the water closed over her head, Theo's too-detailed descriptions of the physics concepts involved.

At last, after one wave had pulled her (half-clinging to her board, half-scraping against the sand) all the way to the shallows, she hauled herself out of the water, laughing, and dropped the board on the ground. Theo was somewhere out in the water still, one of the many ink-black figures straddling their boards on the waves.

Wiggling out of her rented wetsuit, Kate gazed at the rest of the beach: people in bikinis and sweatshirts and parkas and tank tops; children waving pink shovels; dogs making mad dashes for any abandoned food; chatter burning the cool air. She could already feel the bruises forming on her shins, and in each place where the board had clanged into the bone, over and over, the blood seemed to pulse more intensely, glittering, trying to get out.

She didn't know Theo was behind her until she was already up in his arms, hoisted under the armpits the way he would pick up Jemima to see ice cream flavors at the store. She shrieked in delight, and he threw her over his shoulder and marched them back down the beach.

"Wait, wait, wait—" she said, laughing. Waist-deep in water, Theo shifted his weight as if he were about to throw her in, and she locked her legs around his torso so that they both toppled over.

The water was ice. An octopus of limbs, they pulled and fought each other and the tide. She twisted away into the clean oblivion of the sea. Each wild wave folded around her, hugged her, told her, *You are home.*

They surfaced. Kate first, Theo next, shaking his hair and throwing diamonds of water onto her. She swam to him and wrapped her arms around his neck and her legs around his waist.

"You're crazy," she said.

"Yes, guilty," he said, grinning back at her.

It was like that first kiss at Finley Lake. But he was different now, she realized: looser, at ease, as if the sea had sloughed off all his earthly hesitations. The past few weeks had relaxed him, too—he had become comfortable with her, the same way she had become comfortable with him.

She kissed him again and again, digging her fingers into his shoulder blades to find the bone beneath the neoprene. Her body was in emergency. His mouth was warm and salty. His eyelashes stroked her cheeks like a wet paintbrush. She was breathless, weightless, free.

Who cares that you are shivering? That your heart is overloaded, shutting down? If you die now, you die in joy. His hands were possessive and sure on her breasts; by now he knew their curves. Under the waves, he tugged aside her swimsuit and slid a finger inside her. Hard, familiar. Lightning striking the sea. A wave hit them and she came up spluttering and started for shore.

They made it to the car, barely. Bodies wet, towels thrown in heaps in the trunk, wetsuit slung down to his hips, board strapped haphazardly to the roof, inviting a ticket. Sand fell from her feet to the carpet and stuck there. It would be there for months. She liked that idea.

"Drive," she said.

Theo drove until they found an abandoned fire road, ankle-deep in weeds and lined with leaning eucalyptus. He crashed open the door to get out and she climbed over the center console and into the backseat. She took off her swimsuit and waited while he peeled off his wetsuit outside the door. Every part of her shaking, every cell banging against each other for release. He crawled in over her, his long body contorting to fit into the cramped space. Something bit her beneath the knee: a toy princess, her tiara dented beneath their weight.

Theo ran his hands over her breasts, between her legs, and she was wet so he slid into her without any elaboration. When he did she mouthed, *Thank God*, or maybe she shouted it, who could tell, what did it matter, every inch of that car was theirs theirs theirs. She cried out and only Theo and the woods heard it, only the ancient trees nodding to one another: *Them again. Those fools.*

A re you awake?"

"Barely. I might be dead."

Her heart winging up and down, like an injured bird.

"I like you, Kate Aitken."

"You're okay." *Flap, flap.* "I don't know about surfing."

"You didn't like it?"

"I did. But I'm not very good at it."

"You have to do it more to get the hang of it."

"Mmm, *do* I."

"Ha, ha."

They turned so they were lying on their sides on the narrow backseat. Bent knees, bent elbows, wrapped around each other. Sweat dried on their bodies and made their skin tacky. Her mind felt clearer than it had in days. The sex had briefly quieted her wildness, the rippling and shuddering. Even the idea of Miranda, of Jake, seemed to exist at a muted distance from her and Theo.

"I want to tell you something," she said.

"Okay." He drew a finger down her arm. "What is it?"

They were too close for her eyes to focus; his face was only a tan blur. She twisted her head to look up at the car's ceiling instead.

"When I told you why I left the newspaper, I didn't tell you the whole story. I mean—I did. In a way. This isn't about Leonard. But I told you it was more complicated than that, them firing me."

"I remember," he said.

"After I reported Leonard—things got really messy. Half the office wouldn't talk to me. Even some of the women. Everyone liked him a lot. He had won some mentorship awards. People started doing these tiny little things. Like if I came back to my desk, they would have changed the height of my chair. Or they'd mix up my files. Or they refused to meet with me alone. It made me so tired. Going to HR about it would make it worse. But I thought if I just put my head down and worked I could get through it. I had been there so long already. I started staying later at the office. Getting there earlier." Kate began picking at her cuticles. It was hard to look at him. "For a couple weeks, maybe a month or two, I was so productive. I would stay at the office until midnight, one in the morning, even when everyone else left at six p.m. But I wasn't tired at all, and even when I went home I couldn't sleep."

All through January and February, a tingling feeling had striped her entire body. The world was crisper, more vibrant. Colors fell off trees. Skyscrapers seemed to vibrate around her as she charged down the sidewalk to work. Smells were intense: urine-soaked subway platforms, rotting trash, clouds of June rising from the out-of-season tulips parked in furled bunches in the bodega's doorway. Her body felt like it was skipping, skipping, skipping, like she had swallowed five cups of coffee in a row, which sometimes she had.

She had swum in that sensory sparkling before in her life. In college, in the years after. The episodes always felt like a streak of luck. Like she was finally in touch with the world. Like a skin had been peeled back and now she could see life's flex, its flesh. Looking back, she could see now that it was strange to forget to eat for two days while working on an essay, or to stay up until four a.m. organizing spices. But her social circle prized erratic behavior. Every party she went to, people were boasting about juice fasts and Marie Kondo-ing. It was easy to chalk her triumphant moods up to caffeine, astrology, her new spin class, and uncouple them from the darker periods, the fatigue and indifference that so readily slid their arms around her. So the winter episode wasn't Kate's first manic episode. Just the first one anyone called by that name. The worst one, and the best one, and the first time it ruined her life.

"One time I stayed at the office all night," she said. "I didn't sleep at all. My coworkers came in the next day and one of them realized I was wearing the same clothes as the day before. I had to make up some lie. Then I started thinking I was having these breakthroughs—I thought there were codes hidden in the stories I was being sent, and that I needed to crack them. That was when stuff started getting bad, because people noticed something was wrong. I started missing deadlines. My desk was a mess. Some of my coworkers were still acting like dicks, but some others were worried, I think, or at least they said something to HR. But HR was terrified of me because they were already trying to avoid a lawsuit about the Leonard stuff. Maybe someone would have helped me somehow, but then the depression hit, and I stopped going to work at all. I didn't even leave the house. I think everyone was probably relieved when they had a real excuse to fire me."

That voice mail, like someone was reading off a script. *In accordance with our absenteeism policy, and pursuant upon our previous emails to this effect, we are terminating your employment . . .*

"They called me. I never even replied. I couldn't. I didn't even leave the house. I wasn't eating anything. Finally my friend Natasha called my mom, who came and picked me up and took me back to their house and then to the doctor. Otherwise I don't know where I would be.

"People throw it around so casually. 'Oh, she's so bipolar.' Like it's nothing. Or like you're totally unhinged. But neither one is right. It destroyed me. But it also *is* me. And"—she heard her tone grow defensive—"I could have told you earlier, but I didn't know how. And it was managed. It is managed."

Theo had been silent, barely even moving, but now he cleared his throat. "You didn't have to tell me any earlier."

"I should have. Your mother . . ."

"You aren't the same as my mother," he said.

He sounded so sure, and Kate would have argued, except that she wanted so badly for him to be right.

"I have panic attacks," he said. "I almost failed out of college because I was smoking so much weed just to get through the day. We all have things."

"I'm sure you handled it better."

"What? Why?"

"I don't know. I bet you turned yourself in."

"Turned myself in?"

"I mean asked for help."

"No," he said mildly. "My girlfriend dragged me to the counseling center. Then I was so grateful for her help I ended up marrying her and having two kids before I was thirty. Not that I regret Jem and Oscar, obviously. But it was stupid, objectively. Gratitude is a dumb reason to stay with someone."

"It's not dumb," she said. "I understand."

"You don't want to make a run for it?"

He was joking and not joking. He would deny it if she pressed, but she heard the thread of insecurity in his voice. Which didn't make sense. Obviously he could do better than her.

"Not yet," she said, her tone light. "I'm too tired to run."

She had to tell him about the diary. About searching the house. The secret felt like an animal wriggling between them, pressing them apart. But she was the only one who could feel it.

She laid her fingers on his collarbone, and he turned his head and smiled. As their eyes met, a shock rippled through her. It felt like someone had reached inside her chest and clasped her heart, her messy heart with all its frantically pumping chambers, and squeezed. In retrospect, of course, she could see that the defibrillator paddles had been up against each other for weeks, building their charge. Still, in that moment, the miracle seemed to strike out of nowhere. She was brought to life in the backseat of that stupidly expensive car.

She tucked her head into the hollow of his throat. The animal writhed silently. Through the window, they watched a vulture rise in the sky, painting circles with its dark wings.

They went to an early dinner at a fish restaurant on a harbor thirty miles north of San Francisco. The water of the marina was almost still, the wind barely rippling the surface. Palm trees dotted the shore, permanently lopsided from the wind coursing against them. The harbor was crowded with gleaming white masts connected to gleaming white boats whose bows slid forward into elegant points. The only noise was a reggae-style playlist blasting from a speaker above the door. It was the kind of place that made suffering unimaginable. Callinas, with all its shadows and secrets, seemed a thousand miles away.

As they waited for their order to come out, Theo asked suddenly, "What are the warning signs?"

"Of what?" Although she knew what he meant.

"Bipolar. What happens before an episode?" He picked up the plastic number on their table and flipped it back and forth. "It would help you out if I can watch for it, right? Since we're—seeing each other."

He was trying to sound casual, but the words came out a little too formal. Kate didn't know if the awkwardness was about the bipolar part or about the "seeing each other" part, and her throat closed a little.

"I guess it depends," she said. "I mean, for depression, I guess, sleeping too much, not getting excited about things. The mania . . . I don't know. It starts with hypomania. Like a mini version. Talking faster, getting distracted."

"You always talk fast," he said. "It's the New York in you."

She managed a smile. "The early stuff is more in my own head than anything. But that's nice of you to want to look out for it. Hey—I'm going to go wash my hands before the food comes."

The bathroom was single-occupancy, with a cracked concrete floor;

it smelled like fried fish. Kate locked the door, went to the mirror, and gripped the sink with both hands. Her face was pale, her hair still tangled and salty from the ocean.

Warning signs. Louise had used the same expression the other day, and Kate had dismissed it. But hearing Theo ask about it now . . .

She had attributed her happiness these past few weeks to Theo, to her work, to the relief of feeling like she finally had a purpose again. But it was impossible to be sure. Even now, her skin prickling and hurting, she did not know where the glowing feeling was coming from, and whether it was a real, normal reaction to having had sex an hour earlier with a wonderful man, or whether it was a harbinger of a storm.

Given everything she had lost this winter, she had nodded along with the doctor in Connecticut when he said the mania was unhealthy. But she had forgotten how *good* it felt when you were in it. How bright, how remarkable. Several years ago, during what she now knew had been a manic episode, Kate had gotten a small raise as reward for her hard work. Even Natasha had said, just a couple weeks before Kate was fired from the newspaper, how upbeat Kate seemed, and what a relief it was that she had regrouped so quickly after the Leonard shit.

People loved you, right up until the moment they feared you.

Her hands were shaking. She let go of the sink and (making her movements as slow as possible, just to prove to herself that she could) washed her hands with the generic pink hand soap. Then she splashed her face with water for good measure and dried it with a paper towel.

Theo was facing away from her and didn't see her return to the deck. Their order had arrived, still glistening from the fryer. She came up behind him and just looked at the nape of his neck where his hair curled, where skin met shirt collar. There was a faint red mark where she had bit him an hour earlier. He looked large and vulnerable and dangerously alive.

The animal rose again, shaking the bars of its cage. Tell Theo what Kid said about Jake, tell him you've been reading Miranda's diary, tell him you lied to him. Go back on your medication. Call a new psychiatrist. Ask for help.

But doing any of that would mean releasing whatever this feeling was—

happiness, mania, love. It would mean choosing to return to the struggle and self-doubt that had been her whole reason for coming to California in the first place. It would mean losing Theo, when certainly, almost certainly, she could figure out another way to get out from under all these secrets.

She put her hand on Theo's shoulder.

"Oh, the food came," she said, and she leaned in to kiss his neck.

MIRANDA

Dear Mom and Dad

Hi from camp it's pretty nice here. I like the fish in the lake.

Yesterday I went for a hike and then I learned to make keychains.

Wednesdays are the day to call. The number is 850-390-8819 in case you forgot.

Dont worry I am making lots of friends.

love

Theo

JULY 2 1992

It happened again. I tried to say no. I did say no. I said it loudly. With Theo at camp there was no reason to be quiet. It hurt. By the end Jake made me come and it was awful, it fractured me, the way my body spasmed without me telling it to, so that I didn't even know anymore what I wanted or didn't want. When I went to pee later there was blood on my underwear. I don't know if I can stand it anymore. I need a break, I need to leave, just for a little while.

SERIES 1, Correspondence

BOX 1, Personal correspondence

FOLDER: Camp Derrico (Theo Brand summer camp)

Dear Mom and Dad

In case you lost our address it is Camp Derrico, 400 East Route 73, Derrico, CA 91109. Make sure you use a stamp because my counselor said that might be why my letter got lost last time!

I have many, many friends. My favorite one is Luke, who is SO! FUNNY! Bob (my favorite counseler) called him a hoot. I said like an owl? So Bob said I was a hoot too.

love

Theo

PS Mom, Bridget (my 2nd favorite counseler) wants me to ask if you can write your name on a photo and send it to me. Can you please do that? She says you are her idle.

SERIES 2, Personal papers

BOX 9, Diary (1982–1993)

JULY 18 1992

Packed a bag last night. Unpacked it this morning. I overreact a lot, I am sick, my brain is dissolved. Obviously I can't leave Jake. We have built a life together. My photos are here. My equipment is here. Theo is here. I couldn't raise Theo alone. I would never have time to make anything.

Not that the courts would even grant me custody.

Look at my track record.

Baby-killer Brand.

So my husband fucked me too hard. So what? He probably thought the no was a game. He probably didn't even know it hurt. I can't expect him to read my mind. After all, I can't read his, and his is the normal one.

Being married to someone, you think you know them. You think you have seen everything there is to see in the world, you think you have plumbed the absolute night. But you learn there is always something deeper and blacker, something harder.

Jake learned that lesson when I went to Nangussett. I am learning it now. We trade it back and forth like children taking turns in a game. You're it. I'm it. You're it.

JULY 24 1992

I tried to talk to Jake about what happened last week. I worked myself up to it. I kept my voice reasonable. I prepared for him to yell, hit me, anything. But he only stared at me blankly and said he didn't remember that. He said he thought maybe it had been a dream.

SERIES 1, Correspondence

BOX 1, Personal correspondence

FOLDER: Camp Derrico (Theo Brand summer camp)

July 28, 1992

Dear Mr. and Mrs. Brand,

We hope you are having a restful summer. We are writing in regards to your son, Theo, who is in our Dolphins 8-week sleepaway group at the central Derrico site. We have tried to contact you by phone but have not received a response. Would you please verify your phone number by return mailing?

We would like to talk to you at the soonest possible moment to discuss

Theo's experience at Camp Derrico. Overall Theo is an inquisitive and helpful child. However, he has been involved in several fights with fellow campers. We do not believe that he instigated any of these fights (except one), but we are concerned that continued participation in the camp experience may be uncomfortable for him. He did sustain an injury to his left eye, but the eye has healed well, with only some minor bruising. This is why it is important for us to have your accurate contact information.

Theo also mentions that he has not received any letters from you, and we would like to remind you that we consider contact with parents to be beneficial to the campers as they learn to adjust to life away from home.

Please call us back at the number on the letterhead so that we can discuss Theo's continuation at camp.

Thank you for your time, and "alla maluha!"

Genevieve Diburton

Director, Camp Derrico

Dear Mom and Dad

Hope you like this stamp. I am excited to see you in 5 days!!

This camp has been fun and I am glad that I am part of the Dolphins. I don't know if I want to come back next year though.

When I get home can we get a dog? I know probably not.

I miss you!!

love Theo

21.

KATE

As the month wore on, Kate's nightmares got worse. As soon as she dropped into sleep, they sloshed across her, thick and tarry. Sometimes they were about Miranda—standing upright with her head half shot off, mouth set firm, a gun in her hands, pointed at Kate. Sometimes Kate was facing down an unswimmable sea, or the sun was burning her skin to crisped tissue, or she would open her mouth and her teeth would pour out into her hand, tiny white pills with bloody stumps.

She would come awake with a gasp, her shirt soaked in sweat and Olive anxiously licking her arm. It happened three, four, ten times a night. When she woke, sleepless and disoriented, Kate sometimes thought she was back in New York. Thought she might be in her Brooklyn bed, unable to move, staring at the window. Caught between sleep and waking, her mind spun out images of herself locked in her own body, her hair turning gray, her nails curling into long scoops as time passed.

Sometimes in those half-world moments, she wondered if Miranda had infiltrated her somehow. If she had breathed in so much dust in the dining room, so many skin cells, dropped eyelashes, dead hair, that Miranda was growing inside her, like a tumor or a child.

In the mornings, she caked yellow concealer over the shadows beneath her eyes, the same way Theo had hidden the drawings beneath that coat of white paint. But there was no such thing as a perfect cover. Whatever you did left traces. The fear showed through.

MIRANDA

SERIES 2, Personal papers

BOX 9, Diary (1982–1993)

AUGUST 22 1992

Went to Kid's today. At first, usual stuff: we sat out on the stoop of his trailer, drank some beers, smoked a joint. We talked shit about the people in town. I act braver when he's around. I feel more like my old self. Then all of a sudden he leaned over and tried to kiss me.

What the fuck, I said.

Miranda, he said. Do you ever think . . .

No, I said. I don't. Come on, Kid.

He inched away from me. His frown came on.

Fine, sure, he said, but I could tell he was upset.

We sat there for a while, watching the trees. I got madder and madder at myself for not knowing. Or not noticing. The signs must have been there, and I got too comfortable to bother reading them. Story of my life: missing the warning signs.

The silence was awkward. I thought about leaving, but if I left, it would be hard to come back. Another story of my life: not leaving.

I picked up the joint again. Birds were crying in the trees.

Tell me again that thing you heard about Roberta, I said, as if nothing had happened. Tell me what she did wrong.

SEPTEMBER 14 1992

The fan mail accumulates. Letters all have the same format. Woman—it's always a woman—tells me how she first saw my work, how I changed her life. Then she asks me to change her life again: she's struggling, she says, she needs inspiration, she wants to live authentically. She wants me to tell her what to do.

As if I know. It makes me sick, thinking about the lectures I used to give. Appearing in public, presenting myself as some kind of visionary. Let me tell you about feminism, I said, about women, I said, and all along Jake was watching me from the back of the room, his arms crossed.

Imagine if they really knew who I am, what I've put up with. Miranda Brand, a feminist! Took a man's name, took his punches, let him hold her down. Then she turned around and told us she had it all figured out.

My photos are lies.

I never meant them that way. I cut deep into myself, I took myself apart, the way you have to, to produce anything. I thought what I pulled out was the truth. It felt like the truth: intestines, dark and swollen, coming out of the slit space, widening me. Maybe I was tricked by the pain.

SERIES 4, Clippings & publications
BOX 18, News clippings
FOLDER: Jake Brand

Contemporary Art

SEPTEMBER 1992

THE OTHER BRAND

Jake Brand, 43, is best known to the art world as husband to photographer Miranda Brand, who took his name when they married in 1981. But Jake himself is a talented painter. We talked to Jake about his upcoming San Francisco show, The Low Down (opening at the Chaminska Space on September 20); his artistic process; and, of course, his wife.

Contemporary Art: How does it feel to have your first solo show?

Jake Brand: I'm enormously excited. The Low Down shows the whole range of my career, from my "plastics" series to the landscapes I've been working on more recently. It's humbling to look back and see how you've evolved over the years.

CA: The show also includes a series you call the Nangussett paintings. I presume that's after the institution where your wife, Miranda Brand, was hospitalized for postpartum psychosis in 1982.

JB: Yes. Those paintings are based on what I saw inside the hospital when I visited Miranda. The places Miranda slept or ate, the people she met. It took me some years to feel able to tackle that subject. What Miranda and I went through during those years . . . the memories are still very raw. It was a traumatic time for me. She was so inaccessible. As a husband, I felt very helpless. Producing these paintings was therapeutic for me.

CA: I was struck by how explicit the paintings are, given that Miranda has been so private about the experience. She sued the tabloid that ran the initial story for quite a bit of money, didn't she? But she was fine with you putting these paintings out there?

JB: Look, there's a big difference between a tabloid running a story and your husband working through his memories in an artistic medium. Miranda understands I need to process my feelings about that time. She would never interfere with my self-expression.

CA: Miranda obviously looms large in contemporary art. Does that create pressure in your relationship?

JB: You know, it actually doesn't, because we are trying to accomplish such different things. We work in different media, different subject matter. We do happen to have the same dealer, which is just the luck of the draw, that he saw something in both our work. But that doesn't create tension so much as it helps us stay in the loop about each other. We really understand what the other is going through. In that way, being married to another artist is an incredible gift. The art world is so dog-eat-dog. You can be here one minute and gone another. It's a relief to know you have someone you can trust. Someone who's watching everything you do.

SERIES 2, Personal papers
BOX 9, Diary (1982–1993)

SEPTEMBER 26 1992

New theory: no image is complete without a clue to its continuity. A line that moves beyond the edge. The shadow of an unseen object. A pattern extending outward.

Something suffering beyond the edges of the frame.

22.

KATE

The dining room was looking pretty good. Kate stretched her arms overhead as she surveyed the scene. She had gotten through the first and second passes of all the boxes and sorted the documents into twenty-two main categories. Now she was doing a third pass on some of the problem areas—like the mail crates full of fan letters, most of them unopened. Slitting apart these envelopes felt violent somehow, even with the sleek silver letter opener she had found in a kitchen drawer. All morning she had been tearing into one *Dear Miranda, I know you might never read this but* after another, and the sound of paper ripping felt so anathema to the care she had taken with all the other documents. But Theo wanted it done. After a final upward stretch—an audible *pop* as she managed to crack that one persnickety vertebra in her spine—she reached for another envelope.

This one wasn't sealed. It wasn't addressed, either; just a crinkly white envelope with a blue line around the edges. Kate opened the flap, and a set of photographs tipped out into her hand.

She flipped over the first photograph and froze.

It was a color photograph of a man in his fifties. His eyes were oversaturated blue, glowing up from sun-ravaged skin. He was wearing only an undershirt, so thin from washing you could see his wiry chest hairs pressing against the fabric. He had a bandanna pushed back over his sweaty hair, and thin leather bracelets on his wrists.

Kid.

That Miranda had photographed her friend was not exactly a surprise.

It was the setting that came as a shock. He was sitting on a bed, framed in front of a familiar headboard—large, rectangular, made of gray oak.

It was the headboard of the bed upstairs.

Kate flipped to the next photo and instantly blushed. Kid was on his back, the camera above him, pointing straight down. He wasn't wearing a shirt, and his arms were tensed forward, as if he was holding the photographer by the hips. His eyes were screwed shut in pleasure. There were four more photographs, apparently taken at the same time. Six in total. Different expressions on Kid's face. His eyes open. His hand reaching up behind the camera, and black tendrils falling into view as he gripped Miranda's hair. In one, her thigh had moved into the frame, cutting off the corner of the image. It was close enough to the lens that you could see the cellulite. The bluish tint of her skin.

That was as much of Miranda as you got. The rest was all Kid.

Kate sat back on her heels. It seemed monumentally stupid of Miranda to store photos of her lover—her lover *naked, in her bed*—in the house she shared with her husband. Maybe Jake had found the photos. Or found the two of them together, gotten angry.

Or maybe Miranda had tried to end the affair, and it was Kid who got angry, Kid who had hurt Miranda. That would explain why he had been so aggressive with Kate, and so worried about what she would uncover.

Drumming her fingers on one knee, Kate thought about the virulence in his voice that first day at Esme's shop, the hidden threat . . . And how he had pointed her to Hal . . .

She couldn't sit still. The light through the window was turning the room hot and stale. She glanced up at the ceiling—the master bedroom above, the bed where the photos had been taken. Sweat under her arms. Bug under a magnifying glass. She put all the photos back in the envelope and got to her feet.

Theo was in his office. He didn't hear her approach, so she had a moment to lean against the door frame and watch him. He was hunched over his keyboard, lit blue by the computer screen and framed by the remnants of his childhood. The soccer participation pennants, the wrinkled movie posters. His long legs blocked the file cabinet she had tried to break into, all those weeks ago. The monitor rippled with lines of code, and his fingertips flew across the keyboard. His lips moved slightly as he typed.

Fondness stabbed her, so sudden it was nearly painful. It felt like longing. Which made no sense. He was still here.

She knocked on the door frame. "Yoo-hoo," she said.

He turned in surprise, then smiled. Sometimes when he looked at her, she felt like a stained-glass window, bright and translucent, scattering light as the sun passed through her.

"I've hit a stopping point," Kate said. "I thought you might be ready for a break."

His smile widened. "Yes. A hundred percent."

He launched himself up from his chair. Came to her, wrapped his arms around her from behind, a kiss on the side of her neck as her face pressed against the beveled door frame. She felt his hand at her hip, nudging her down the hall to the master bedroom.

"No," she said. The image of Kid and Miranda in that same bed was still fresh in her mind. "No, not there. Here."

"Here?" He frowned. "The bed doesn't even have a mattress on it."

She gave him an arch look. "I didn't know you were so picky."

They fell together onto the unswept floor, laughing, kissing, his hands sliding down her arms.

A few hours later, preparing to go home, Kate lifted the box where she had stored the photographs of Kid. She took out the most compromising image, the one where you could see Miranda's thigh, and gazed at it for a moment.

Then she put the photo into a new, separate box, and slid that box into her tote bag, resting her jacket gently on top. She walked out the front door and down the lawn to the path through the woods. The box banged against her hip with every step.

MIRANDA

SERIES 2, Personal papers

BOX 9, Diary (1982–1993)

JANUARY 13 1993

I started sleeping with Kid. I'm not even sure when. Three weeks ago? Four? It was the holidays that got to me. Going with Jake to the mall to buy presents for Theo. How happy he was, picking out what we would get. I loved him then, his bulk, his charm, his love for his son, and for some reason, I went to Kid's trailer a few days later and slept with him. That feeling of loving Jake made me angry, made me want to get back at him for what he's done to me. Only of course I deserved it all, I started it all, so now I've been doubly bad. I guess what I'm trying to say is I don't know why I've done anything I've done, ever. But I do know what I feel when Kid touches me. Not pleasure, exactly, but relief, like a migraine disappeared.

JANUARY 18 1993

Jake wants another child. He's been bringing it up for months, even though the idea makes me sick.

He said once that he believed you weren't really a man until you've had a child or killed someone. Given birth or death.

But men don't give birth, I told him. Women do.

Men think children are proof of virility.

For women, children are only proof of pain.

Even when Theo makes me laugh, or does something sweet, one part of my brain looks at him and sees how he ruined me. Tore me end to end. The doctors cannot fix that break inside us. When they stitch us up, it is only a surface repair.

A woman down in town has recently given birth. I know her but I forget her name. I keep passing her. In the street, in the grocery store. The baby nestled high against her volcanic breasts. Its round, red arms. Her smile as she looks down at that tiny shrub of a human being. Her smile.

She knows I am a bad mother and she flinches away from me. Walks circles so that we don't cross paths. But sometimes she's too late, and I walk near her, and across the space of air I can smell the talcum rising from the warm skin and the delicate stench of vomit, unsuccessfully scrubbed dry.

I say to Jake: Maybe, honey. Maybe maybe. Maybe baby maybe, maybe.

JANUARY 19 1993

I figured it out: Kid's boring. That's what I like about him.

The threads of the screw coming apart, letting out whatever gas had been stored up inside. A loosening that drugs you bit by bit. An inertia that comforts, mainly by numbing.

JANUARY 26 1993

Jake bought a gun.

I asked, Why?

He said, It's for a painting. A still life.

It's dangerous to leave that around Theo.

I'm not going to put it where he can get it, Miranda.

JANUARY 27 1993

Fears cross my mind. Back and forth. Zigzag.

My mind is a castle, a ruined one. Rusty suits of armor. Dungeons with faulty locks. In the dark, a slithering noise. My horrors never stay locked away for long. Every time I round a corner, they resurface, an eye watching me from a shadow. A gleam of mucus. Sometimes I turn a light on too fast, and there it is, skittering back into darkness too slowly, the light reflecting off its brown carapace.

I was born to be miserable. I have always been an arrow aimed for some darker life. I flew along that path straight and true and now that I've landed I might as well learn to love the place I've stayed.

It's fuel for art, is all it is. Is all.

23.

KATE

Kid lived on a large plot of land on the northern edge of town, up on the mesa and close to the sea. His property was not marked with his name, a street number, or even a mailbox, and Kate—who had finally weaseled the directions out of Esme by saying she had something for Kid from Miranda—drove back and forth several times before she spotted the turnoff. She followed the dirt road until it dead-ended in an oak grove with a battered silver Airstream trailer. Through the winding tree limbs, the sea shone a murky pink, topped by the incoming evening fog.

Kid was already standing in the trailer's doorway when she parked the car. As she approached, carrying the photo box, he scowled and braced his elbows against the narrow oval door. She was struck again by the ropy, undernourished look of his arms, sticking out from his short sleeves like orange pipe cleaners.

"How'd you get my address?" he demanded.

"You're in the phone book," she said.

"I am not."

Kate lifted the box higher. "Can I come in? I have something to show you."

He chomped on his gum, studying her. At last his curiosity won out, and he tossed his head. The movement sent the beads on his dreadlocks clattering.

"Fine," he said. "But you better be fast."

Inside, the trailer was short and cylindrical and smelled faintly of

patchouli. At one end, the wall swooped into a curve that held two uphol-
stered benches and a laminate table. The kitchenette was tiny, with two
propane burners and a miniature hood. Kate could see through an accordion door to a bed beyond. Everything was painstakingly neat, like a
ship's berth. Over the sink, two dog tags dangled from a nail. Ex-military.
Funny—she had had him pegged as a conscientious objector.

They sat on the benches, and Kate took the photo out of its box and
set it on the table between them. Kid looked at the photo, then up at Kate,
then down at the photo again. She felt him slide back into the memory:
Miranda grinning down at him, the camera hovering inches from his face.
There was a moment when the two Kids blurred together for her, when the
vulnerability of the Kid in the photo seemed to transfer to the Kid who was
examining it.

"You lied to me," she said. "You told me you and Miranda weren't sleeping together."

"Yeah." Kid sat back on the bench. "I did."

"So what is this?"

"It's just a photo. I modeled for her." His hands were shaking a little.

"So this is all staged," Kate said.

"Yeah."

"Okay, great." She made as if to gather the photo back into its box.
"Well, I'm sorry I was confused. I'll just add it to the list of photos to send
off to the dealer, and—"

"Wait." His hand shot out, trapping her wrist. "Dealer?"

"Yeah." Kate shook off his hand and painted a smile on her face. "All
the new photos I find go to auction. It's great for me, actually, since I get
a percentage—and some of these museums are willing to pay a lot for an
original print, especially something like this, where it's one-of-a-kind . . ."

"Museums?"

"Big ones. International."

"Wait. Wait." Kid looked distraught. "You can't put that in a museum.
It's private."

"You just said she wanted it exhibited."

Kid's face reddened, his eyes going bluer and bluer in contrast to his flushed skin. He knew she was manipulating him, but that didn't mean it wasn't working.

"What do you want from me?" he asked, pained. "What do you want to know?"

"I want to know what happened to Miranda," Kate said.

"I don't *know* what happened."

"Then why did you lie to me?" She pointed to the photo. "Why are you hiding this? It doesn't make sense. It's an affair that happened twenty-five years ago. Her husband is dead. Most people in your position would be proud to tell everyone they slept with a celebrity."

"I'm not most people," Kid said. His words were jagged, each syllable punched through with anger. "And your tricks won't work on me. I know them all. You make me think you're on my side. That you know how to keep private things private. You give me hot chocolate, no food, just sugar. You get me talking about anything. About how I moved here. Then you start calling me a home-wrecker, calling her a whore. I get upset. Then you buy me some hot food and placate me, and it all starts back over. And eventually . . ." He ran his hand around his throat. "I've been through it all before. In the interrogation."

Kate blinked. "What interrogation?"

"The police interrogation," Kid said. "That's why you've been hounding me, right? Victor told you. I've been wondering whether he would start telling people, now that the Lippland bitch is dead." His voice rose. "I guess it's only a matter of time before everyone is knocking down my frigging door. As if they care. As if they would really listen." He smacked the edge of the table.

Now Kate was completely lost. She had asked Victor if he had questioned Kid, and he had said yes, but he hadn't called it an interrogation. Had he?

After the ringing noise of the smack vanished from the air, Kid drew his hand back, put it under the table as if ashamed. No—he *was* ashamed. His shoulders caved in as he met her eyes. Her theories wavered, then broke apart. Whatever he had been hiding was close to the surface now. The secret was a spasm on his tongue.

"Start at the beginning," Kate said, as gently as she could, even though her heart was beating faster and faster in her chest. "When you and Miranda met."

They went over what he had told her before about how he and Miranda had become friends. That had all been true, he said. It was only at the end that things had started to change.

"This"—he pressed his index finger into the table below the photo— "didn't last very long. A few months. She ended it. She didn't really say why, which was confusing to me. I think she wasn't ready to leave Jake, but she was developing feelings for me. I treated her better. I was kinder. But I was the one who had to go.

"It hurt, but I got over it. I ran into her a few times that summer, and she seemed distracted. I figured she was working on something. She was always working, always thinking. Then my dad got sick, and I went back to Iowa to look after him. He died. I organized his funeral. We didn't have any of this social media junk back then," he said with a sniff, "and I wasn't following the newspapers. So it was only when I got back here that I found out Miranda was dead."

Kate imagined him stepping off the plane, exhausted from the caretaking and the funeral arrangements, telling himself at least it was over and he could return to his old life now. And then overhearing someone, maybe a stranger in the airport, saying, *The Miranda Brand investigation is a waste of taxpayer money. Anyone with a brain knows she killed herself.*

"I'm sorry," she said. "That must have been devastating."

"Two days. I missed her by two days."

He lifted his hands to his face and, with a shuddering breath, drew them down his cheeks.

"I went to the police as soon as I found out she had died. I wanted to tell them she hadn't been happy with Jake. That they weren't getting along. But when I said that, the cops got suspicious of me. They got it out of me that we had been intimate, and then, ka-bam, I was suspect numero uno. Once I saw what they were up to, I stopped cooperating. They kept going, kept bugging me. They just wanted to get a confession out of me. They didn't care if it was true. I got mad. Believe it or not, I had a temper then. I said some stuff they didn't like. They threw me in a cell overnight—that one cell they have at the Callinas police station, where they let drunks sober up. The night guard was one of these sheriff's department guys they brought in to investigate the case, and he was a real son of a bitch. He had a chip on his shoulder. Like I said, I had a temper. I started saying stuff. About his mom, his daughter, calling him names, the usual crap. I couldn't do anything from behind those bars, you know? I was just talking. But later in the night I guess he'd had enough, because he opened up my cell and came in and started beating me.

"Next thing I know, I wake up and I'm pretty sure I'm dying. I'm still in the cell, only the guard is gone and it's Victor Velázquez and Barbara Lippland with me. My tongue was so swollen in my mouth . . . every time I breathed it felt like someone was stomping on my chest. Later I found out I had four broken ribs, a concussion . . . I got fifteen stitches in my head. One of my fingers was shattered. I still can't move it right." He extended his hands as evidence. When he tried to curl his right hand in a fist, the ring finger barely moved. "That's why they closed up the case so fast. They were worried it was going to get out, what that guard did to me. A Vietnam vet beat to shit in custody? They figured they better just end it all before I sued them."

He pushed himself out of the booth and went over to the sink to pour himself a glass of water. There was a movement in the corner, and Kate started: but it was only a cat, slinking out of the bedroom door and leaping onto the bench Kid had just vacated. The cat had probably been black once, but the sun had bleached its fur chestnut red. It eyed Kate skeptically, then turned away and began licking its paws.

"Why didn't you report it?" Kate asked.

Kid let out a humorless laugh. "Report it to who? The police? Anyway, I wasn't in any shape to make any complaints. My dad, Miranda, the beating. It was too much. I couldn't deal. I got hooked on the painkillers they prescribed me, then on heroin. I got arrested for distribution and went upstate for a couple years. It took me five more years after that to clean up, and even then, things weren't easy. You know how hard it is to get a job as an ex-felon?" He scoffed. "Sure, I thought about calling the newspapers, but I knew from Miranda how things could get twisted in the press. And then everyone would know about Miranda and me, and I didn't want to do that to her, when she was gone and didn't have any say in it."

Kate had no response. She knew better than anyone the reasons why someone wouldn't go public about an attack. They sat in silence for a while, neither of them really looking at each other. Although she had more or less forced her way into his trailer, now she had the strange sense that he didn't want her to go. The afterglow of confession, before the defensiveness set in; the part where the person thought the way out of the vulnerability might be to tell more, and more, and more. Leonard had always said it was the most important time in an interview. The cat jumped off the bench and wove around her legs in a silky figure eight.

"You said Miranda and Jake weren't happy," Kate said. "Did she tell you why?"

"No. It was just a feeling I had. Like I told you the other day, she never talked about him." He scratched his eyelid and sighed. "I always thought he was a real asshole, even though he had everyone else fooled. She was so tense all the time. I tried to tell that to the police, and they wrote it down. But they also said, and I guess they could be right, that the tension might be because of Theo."

"What do you mean?"

"He was always getting into fights at school. He got suspended for bullying someone that spring, I remember. She didn't worry too much over Theo, but she was upset about that. I guess he broke someone's nose. Just slammed his fist into someone's face in the middle of the classroom."

Kate started to feel cold. She didn't want to listen to this. She reached out to take back the photograph, but Kid clapped his hand over it. The broken finger was crooked, like a divining rod.

"I have to take it with me," she said calmly. "It belongs to Theo."

"It's mine. That's *me* in it."

"Yeah. But it's also worth a lot of money."

"So—what? You're going to put it in the auction?"

"I don't know. That's up to Theo."

Kid's temporary goodwill had vanished now. As his face became stubborn again, his wrinkles puckered deeper. "So you're going to take what I told you and go off and enjoy your day. Glad I could provide you entertainment."

"I didn't say anything about enjoying it," she said, her nerves starting to fray. "But I have to keep the photo, because of professional ethics."

He sneered at her. "Professional ethics, my ass. At least when I slept with a Brand, the whole town didn't know."

The barb went straight through Kate and out clean on the other side. While he was distracted by insulting her, she slid her fingers under his hand and grabbed the photo. It could have ended badly, with fingerprints across the surface or the paper ripped in half, but they both moved deftly, delicately, guided by a shared instinct to protect the picture. Within seconds, Kate had the photo back in the box and had risen to her feet.

"Thanks for telling me your story," she said. "I'll see you around."

As she left, he called out, "You're just like everyone else. You know that, right? You're all the same."

In the short time she had been inside the trailer, a mist had already started crawling in from the sea. It wrapped around the trees' spidery branches and filled the divots in the rutted driveway. She balanced the box on one hip as she fumbled Frank's car keys out of her bag and tried to hit the unlock button. A scraping noise startled her, and she dropped the keys in the dirt. She looked back at the trailer, but Kid hadn't even come outside to watch her go. She set the box on the hood of the car and knelt down to pick up the keys. Only when she stood back up and tried the lock again did she realize the noise had come from the keys themselves, jangling against one other in her twitching hand.

MIRANDA

SERIES 2, Personal papers

BOX 9, Diary (1982–1993)

MARCH 16 1993

Jake still on the baby idea. Unending.

> He says another child could be different.
>
> This time it could go well.

I want to say: Or it could not. It could be the same. The lizard skin and feathery panic and hidden hell of my own mind.

> I want to say: How can we grow this family when we both know it is rotten at its core? Don't you see the way Theo looks at us? Don't you think it's bad that we forget him so easily?
>
> I want to say: How can I want to make a new life when I barely want my own?

APRIL 9 1993

My birth control pills are gone.

> I've looked everywhere. Emptied every trash can.

Jake says maybe I threw them out. But I can't have done it. It can't have been me. If it was me, it was a me I don't know.

It's fine, we can do this, he said. Meaning a baby. I'm sure he can but I know I cannot.

I said no. You need to use condoms.

He left a bad bruise. When I move, it feels like someone is playing the piano on my ribs.

I wish I had known when I was young that there is no limit to what someone can do.

Hate, like love, will multiply to fill an allotted space.

Jake has that gun, and still no painting.

APRIL 10 1993

He went to the city today, and while he was gone, I tried calling to get birth control refills but they said I would need a new prescription. I tried calling the doctor and the doctor asked what happened to the old ones.

I hung up.

APRIL 21 1993

People always want to know whether I really cut myself for Inside Me. The answer is that it varied. I remember mixing the blood in the kitchen sink for some of them. I remember wiping down the steel afterward, and how many sponges I ruined trying to get it clean. But I can also see the scars that other pictures left. The silvered cross on my palm, a stigma.

Honestly, I've forgotten which are which. I look at the place on my thigh where the scar of #8 should be, and sure enough, there's a swollen white line. From another angle, it looks like a stretch mark. Sometimes your body lies.

I do remember the one on my forearm. #1. The start of it all. Jake had grabbed my arm and the clasp on his watch gouged a line down my arm. The next day, I played with the scab that was forming. I pulled the sides of the flesh farther and farther apart. Right after Theo was born, I was convinced other things were hidden inside me. I hadn't tried to check in years. I was relieved to learn that it was only blood. I took the photograph as proof.

All the others in that series, real or not real, were all trying to re-create that first one.

In a way, you could say Jake was the real mastermind behind it all. He was the one who thought to grab me.

On the other hand, it was me, scratching my arm open on that walk to Nangussett, who first had the idea to break my skin.

APRIL 26 1993

Went to Theo's soccer game today. He was bad. The coach only put him on the field when the game couldn't be lost. He subbed for the sub of the sub. Him playing was a kindness, a mercy. He kept looking up at me in the stands. It was like he could see inside me. Like from a hundred feet away, he could see deep into the cold staves of my brain and see how my mind buckles under the weight.

My killer child: the child who killed me. Who tore my world out and threw it down the sink. Nine months sucking at my very blood, pounding his feet against the walls of my stomach.

I have failed him in every way.

There was one moment today where he might have made a goal. The ball was between his feet. His sweet knee socks. The hard plastic plate bent around his shin. And his eyes, Jake's eyes, cutting across the sky at me. Wanting something I don't have and don't know how to give.

Is it any surprise he missed?

APRIL 29 1993

I haven't seen Jake start that painting yet.

24.

KATE

Kate stopped speaking mid-sentence. She had glanced over at her aunt to see that Louise was eyeing her with a strange, uncharacteristic solemnity. Her hands were frozen in the act of cutting, her fork and knife hovering over the cooling tuna casserole.

"What is it?" Kate asked.

"Nothing." Louise didn't move. "I'm just having trouble following what you're telling me."

Kate felt impatient. "Okay, which part?"

"Well, this diary you're talking about," Louise said. "It's Miranda's diary? She wrote it? And you saw it, but now it's gone?"

Kate hadn't planned to tell Frank and Louise about everything that had happened at Kid's trailer. But as soon as they sat down to dinner, Frank had asked her where she had taken the car, and suddenly it seemed so *stupid* to lie. Louise was her aunt, and if she spread the story around town, so what? By the time it got back to Theo, Kate would have figured out what had happened to Miranda, and she would have told him herself. She was so *close*, she knew it: she could taste the discovery on the back of her tongue, a rusty, musky taste, like old blood.

She only needed a little more information, and if anyone could get it for her, it was Louise.

So Kate had launched into it. She had explained about the photographs she had found of Kid and Miranda, and what Kid had said about Jake and about the police, and somehow the diary had come up. But now, seeing

Louise's confused face, she was starting to regret it. It was too complicated to explain in one go. Louise wasn't keeping up.

"Theo took the diary away before I finished it," Kate said. "But I don't know if he knew I had been reading it. He could have moved it for any reason."

"Aren't you two, you know, hanging out?" Frank asked.

"Yes. Anyway"—this to Louise—"the more important thing is what Kid said today. About how maybe Jake was hurting Miranda. Have you ever heard anyone say that?"

"No," Louise said. "And I haven't heard anything about this police business. But you know, I would take what Kid says with a grain of salt. He has a bad attitude."

"I checked his story," Kate said. "He was at his dad's funeral when Miranda died, just like he said."

Using an NYU Law alumni log-in Natasha had given her years ago, she had searched the obituaries of Iowa newspapers from the week of Miranda's death. Thomas Wormshaw had apparently been enough of a figure in DePront, Iowa, that *The DePront Daily News* had described his funeral in detail, right down to his son's emotional eulogy.

"But you're right," Kate went on. "I do need more information. I was thinking of going back to Victor's house tomorrow afternoon, actually. You could even come with," she added generously.

Louise looked over at her husband, obviously trying to communicate something, but Frank had his phone out and was typing something on the screen. Kate was quickly learning that Frank had the basic emotional response of an ostrich. Any sign of discord only made him crouch lower over whatever tech device was closest to hand.

"No, thank you," Louise said to Kate.

"It won't just be about Kid's interrogation," Kate reassured her. "I'll ask him about that, obviously, but mostly I want to push him again on why they didn't investigate Jake. Last time he went on and on about what a good guy Jake was, but was that all? Did they have any evidence that let him off? What if Miranda was—"

"No more Miranda, okay?" Louise said loudly. "Please. Let's just change the subject."

Kate felt like she had been slapped. She drew back and stared at Louise. Louise stared down at her food. For a long moment, the only sound in the room was the fake clicking noise of Frank typing on his phone.

"Frank," Louise said, her voice strained. "I thought we agreed, no sudoku at the dinner table."

"It's not sudoku." Frank gave her a wounded look. "I was checking on the kayak raffle."

"And?"

"I didn't win." Frank turned off his phone and slid it back into his pocket. "But these things are always rigged."

Kate paced back and forth in the street, a few doors down from Frank and Louise's house. The heat wave had broken a few days earlier, and now the air was cold and loamy, so damp it was nearly solid. Each inhalation felt like someone was sticking icy fingers up her nostrils. Even though it was almost dark out, she had gone far enough that, should her aunt try to watch her from the window, the neighbor's trellis of clematis would block her from view. She needed *privacy*, that was all. Louise and Frank had talked about the stupid raffle for the rest of dinner. *You didn't win, forget it*, Kate had wanted to shout, and only through great self-restraint had she managed to sit there through it all, jiggling her leg and listening to them parse the entry odds for what felt like hours, when all she really wanted was a little space to think.

So now she was out here, chewing her hangnail, treading back and forth over the same bumpy patch of road behind the trellis. Victor had been friendly the first time around; she still thought he would tell her more about the investigation, maybe even the interrogation, if she asked the right way. Although now that Kate thought about it, who was to say the cover-up stopped at the assault? It could have been just a piece of the story. Maybe the police had known who killed Miranda, and Kid had been a pawn all along. The whole thing could have been a cover for Jake—Jake, obvious and yet somehow untouchable, an automatic door that moved aside whenever you got close enough.

"*Fuck*," she said out loud, pressing her hands to her temples and bending over. Her head was spinning, well and truly dizzy. All the hypotheticals made her want to vomit. It was like her body was rejecting knowledge, or rather, the lack of it.

"Kate? Are you okay?"

Kate uncurled halfway from her crouch and rested her hands on her knees. An athlete wiped out after a sprint. It was Frank, his fleece zipped all the way up against the chill.

She stood up. "Oh, hi. Yeah." She tried to sound normal. "What's up?"

"Coming out to check on you."

"Oh," she said again, surprised. "Well, I'm fine. Thanks. Just . . . you know. Thinking."

She waved around at the empty street, and Frank glanced around thoughtfully, as if the shadowy gardens and crumbling curbs might actually explain whatever was going through her mind.

He had the same pensive look on his face that her dad got when he wanted to have a Serious Conversation. But the idea of Frank initiating such a conversation was bizarre, like watching a kitten try to take the SAT. Over the past couple months, he and Kate had honed a list of mutually acceptable conversation topics. Tidal schedules. The hardware store's opening hours. Louise's potholder collection. Traffic on the 101. You kids these days. That one time he had met Cher. More than ten weeks living in the same house, and he hadn't asked her anything more serious than a crossword clue. If Louise ever complained to Frank about Kate—which she must have, considering how often she complained to Kate about Kate—all Kate could imagine him saying was, *It's your family*, maybe followed by a shrug. *You can handle it however you want.*

But now he said carefully, as if he had been rehearsing the words since dinner ended, "Louise loves you, you know."

"I know," Kate said. Belatedly, she remembered to add, "I love her, too."

"You should tell her. She'd like to hear it."

Kate ran her tongue around her teeth.

"Okay," she said. "I will."

"It's hard for aunts and uncles, you know. We see you when you're so little." Frank put his hands together to indicate the size of a baby. "And then you grow up, and you don't remember us."

Resentment pinched Kate's mouth shut. She and Frank weren't related by blood. He had siblings of his own, and they had kids, but when it came to her, he had stumbled into this uncle thing by chance. Kate hadn't even met him until his and Louise's wedding fourteen years ago, and her main memory of that event was throwing up stolen champagne in a glorified porta-potty. In her family's stories, he was a flat character, an aside. Now he was telling her how she should treat Louise.

It's our family, she thought. *We'll handle it however we want.*

"Kids change so fast," he continued, reminiscing. "I remember with my brothers' kids. It's just so funny. Seeing these personalities grow out of nothing. Feelings, emotions, opinions."

"I bet."

"You've gotten to know your boss's kids pretty well, right?"

"Yeah." Kate felt a twang, thinking about Oscar and Jemima. "It's been nice. I never spent much time with kids before. I feel like they know things I didn't know at that age. The other day I asked Jemima if she wanted a glass of juice and she said, 'Let me go analyze.' Who knows the word *analyze* when they're seven?"

Frank grinned. "I did all kinds of pranks when I was little. But it was easier back then. Parents weren't as overprotective as they are now."

This comment sounded promisingly close to *You millennials,* one of their established topics of conversation. Kate was relieved. She just had to prepare a few laughs in reaction to whatever stories Frank wanted to tell, and then he would go back inside.

"Like, I was ten the first time I shot a gun," he said.

Her head jerked up.

"A BB gun, I mean," he clarified. "My dad gave it to me to shoot squirrels in the backyard. I thought I was so old at the time, so mature. Now I look back and think, what on earth was I doing with a gun at that age? I could have hurt someone."

Kate stared at him. She had started smiling in preparation for a joke, and now her face had frozen like that, cheeks cramped up at the corners.

Theo, age eleven. Old enough to hold a gun.

Young enough to misfire.

No, Kate, you're being ridiculous, she told herself. Remember the forensics. It wasn't an accident. Think about anything else. Anything. The sounds in this silence. The click of a dog's nails on asphalt as someone walked down the street. The steady call of the wind. The plucked, rattling sound of cicadas strumming the air.

"Good thing you didn't," she said, swallowing. "Hurt anyone, I mean."

Frank clapped his hands together, like he had finished some important job. "Okay, well. I guess I'd better turn in. I'm playing tennis with Victor in the morning."

Her skin pinged to life. "Victor Velázquez?"

"Yep. Neither of us are that good," he said with a confidential wink, "but we get competitive. I have to rest up. Psychologically prepare."

Her heart lifted. *Ah-ha.* So Frank hadn't been coming out here to launch some big intervention in her relationship with Louise. He had been listening during the dinner conversation after all, and he knew Kate wanted more information. So he had come out to plant a clue for her, tell her where to find Victor. He was sending her a message. Here, in the shadowed street, where Louise couldn't see or judge or criticize.

"Sounds fun," Kate said, casually. "What time?"

MIRANDA

SERIES 2, Personal papers

BOX 9, Diary (1982–1993)

JUNE 18 1993

Theo is home with us this summer. Camp Derrico wouldn't take him back after I fucked everything up last year, and I never got around to finding a new place. I wasn't sure it was right to send him away anyway. He's bad with other kids. We haven't taught him right. On the other hand, I would rather he was far away from this house, from what happens here. One of his teachers last year said he was having "outbursts." I never know how much he sees or doesn't see. What a terrible person I am— wishing for my child not to see.

I began a tally last month. Incidents with Jake. Three. Fewer than I thought. Everything grows too large in my mind.

I don't know what I thought I would do with the tally. Eventually I threw it away. Anyone who finds it will think I was just testing the pen. Ballpoint almost out of ink:

I I I

Lately I think about my uterus regrowing its lining without the pills to stop it. All the places eggs might rest now. Bury themselves within me, emerge again as children. Emerge as a trap.

I produce no art. I put my camera to my eye and wheel around like a drunk.

My mind scrabbles to stay standing. It finds no purchase.

JUNE 22 1993

I told Kid I can't do it anymore. He was starting to look at me with a kindness in his eyes that I can't take. I think he's in love with me. At least, some image of me. He isn't looking closely. He never notices any bruises. He only sees a placeholder for me. The genius, the artist. He's proud of his conquest. I'm just territory.

Anyway, the boredom doesn't help at all anymore. I've become too accustomed. That's my problem: I build up a tolerance.

I made prints of the photos I took of him. A kind of farewell rite. Part of me hopes Jake finds them. I want it to happen, I want him to annihilate me, I want this fear to be achieved, and then be gone.

JULY 2 1993

Still impossible to work. Nothing shows up when I tap on the chamber. A snake hides in the grass and waits to strike.

Instead of working, I spent the day at the window, watching each minute leaf flutter in the wind like a tiny flag. The leaf is latched on to its twig, which is latched on to a branch, and the latches are what will break if the wind gets too strong, which it hasn't. Yet.

JULY 7 1993

When I met Jake, we were so young. We were mostly formed, but not quite. I think if I had been stronger in some ways, if I had resisted better, or if I had resisted less, perhaps he would have become a different man.

As it is, I think he sensed all my soft spots and he grew into them. He became accustomed to pushing and getting. He grew to like the feeling of struggle.

He could have been anyone, that first date, the warehouse party. He was just a kid, twenty-seven and hungry, too handsome for his own good, used to getting his way. He could have met anyone that day.

I'm thinking of that tree near the grade school, the one that got sick and had to be taken down. I saw it cut, the trunk carried off . . . on the outside, it looked like a whole tree, but on the inside it was a mush of rotting wood. That is what Jake sensed in me. It's why he loved me. It's why I loved him.

Sometimes at night I hear a noise outside, a whishing, a crackling. I think it is the woods growing around me, growing to cover me tight and keep me here.

JULY 19 1993

Jake, Theo, and I watched two movies today. *A Fish Called Wanda,* then *Edward Scissorhands,* back to back, as the afternoon waned. It was too hot but we clung to each other anyway. Limbs pressed against each other. A single heartbeat flowing elbow to knee to elbow. We laughed. I microwaved a frozen pizza for dinner. Jake told me, Good job. Theo asked me to tuck him in.

There are days like this.

AUGUST 8 1993

Last night, he pushed into me even when I said I was tired.

This morning, he was kind. He said I was beautiful, he said he didn't deserve me.

AUGUST 16 1993

What have I accomplished in my life?

I have captured. I have produced. I have seen things no one else has seen.

I have made money. Money that poured from my eyes and knit me a reputation, a child, a house, a cocoon.

I have used. I have been used.

I have dived into the green ocean, caught seaweed around my ankle, I have flashed through the waves with seals and sharks. I have floated on salt, I have drowned in the air.

I have burst under the intensity of the sun.

AUGUST 18 1993

I got my period today. Every time it comes as a relief. The routine of tampons, the brackish blood.

I love Theo but I hate the way he looks at me. When he sees me, I see myself. If he weren't here to witness, maybe I'd never have to admit what I am: the wan shriveled husk, hunched in the corner, holding up her hands in surrender. Or fighting back and losing. Imagine being the kind of parent whose child gazes at you in wonder. How rich you must feel, how holy.

Mostly you could blame me for what I have become.

Maybe you could blame Jake.

But it was Theo, too.

Theo was my atom bomb.

That devastation was only the immediate explosion, and all these years since, the aftermath has been multiplying inside me. A shortness of breath. A red and cancerous mass.

Dying slowly, thinking I survived.

SERIES 4, Household documents
BOX 21, Receipts
FOLDER: Miscellaneous receipts

Dolly Pharmacy
We live to please!
Mill Valley, CA

10/23/1993

Item	Price
Kool-Aid Pouch	
2 @ 3.99	7.98
Bic Razor	
1 @ 4.99	4.99
Quik-Read Pregnancy	
2 @ 21.99	43.98
Medication Co-Pay	
1 @ 18.79	18.79
Mondavi Pinot Noir	
2 @ 8.99	17.98
Subtotal	93.72
Tax Alcohol 4%	0.72
Total	94.44
Paid Cash	$100.00
Change	$5.56

Thank You For Shopping Dolly Pharmacy!!

25.

KATE

Heat wiggled up from the tennis court's red clay. The men's shirts were patched with sweat on the rise of their bellies, and their like-new rackets shone in the morning sun. When Kate waved, they let the ball drop and came over to the sidelines, their foreheads dripping.

"Good game?" she asked.

Victor mopped his brow with a small towel. "Your uncle's a monster. You play?"

"Not really. Here, have some Gatorade." She fished two matching bottles out of her bag and held them out to the men.

"Contraband!" Victor took the bottle happily. "Good Lord, I've missed this stuff. You know Leah won't let me drink it anymore?"

Kate nodded. "I remembered you saying." She made herself wait until Victor had taken a sip. Then the words burst out of her: "Actually, I wanted to ask you a couple questions."

Beside her, Frank paused in the act of twisting off the orange lid.

"Me?" Victor said, surprised.

"Yeah." She smiled at Frank, trying to communicate that his job was done now, he had arranged the meeting and now he could go home, but he didn't seem to get the hint. To Victor, she said, "It's about Miranda."

"Oh." He shrugged. "Okay."

She didn't like how cavalier he sounded. She had to make him realize how important this was. Only where to begin? Everything was moving so fast in her head.

"I know Miranda was afraid of Jake," she said. "She wasn't happy in her marriage."

"Okay," Victor said again, and waited.

Rage slid through her, like loose rock tumbling into a landslide. He seemed so indifferent, as if he hadn't thought twice about Miranda since Kate had first come to see him.

"I talked to Kid Wormshaw," she said, and there—finally—something flashed across his face. Panic? "He told me he had been having an affair with Miranda before she died. And that he told you that Miranda was scared of Jake, but you never looked into it."

Victor raised his eyebrows and glanced over at Frank, as if checking that it was okay. "Of course we looked into it. But we couldn't find any evidence."

"What kind of evidence do you need?" Her heart began to race. "I can find it. There's so much stuff up there. Letters, photographs, sketchbooks, diaries—" Fuck, she hadn't meant to mention the diary. "Whatever it is, I can find it, I've organized almost everything, and I just need to look a little closer. I just need a little more time."

"Kate . . ." Frank said, tapping his racket slowly against the bench. "Are you feeling okay?"

Kate released a frustrated breath and swiveled toward him. "What?"

"You seem a little . . . flustered."

She shook her head, confused.

"I'm fine," she said. "I'm just really involved in this, you know?"

She looked over at Victor for confirmation. He would know what it was like to get so into an investigation. What it was like to care so much about an answer. But he wasn't nodding along with her.

"You know, Kate," he said, "I wonder if maybe I gave you the wrong impression when you came to my house. I like being retired. I don't have any intention of reopening the case, and I'm absolutely sure the sheriff's office doesn't have any intention of doing so, either."

"Why not? If there's new evidence? There's no statute of limitations on murder."

"Who do you want them to investigate, exactly?" Victor asked. "Jake? He's dead."

"Still," she said stubbornly. "People need to know what really happened to Miranda. She deserves that, doesn't she? Or maybe you don't want to ask the hard questions, because it's easier to call her crazy."

Victor frowned. "It's not politically optimal for them," he said.

He sounded like Theo, shutting her down when she got too close. She was tired of being underestimated, pushed out. How many times now had she needed to convince a man to talk to her about Miranda? Victor, Kid, Theo, Hal. Men holding all the stories, doling them out to whomever they judged worthy.

She took a step closer to Victor.

"You mean because of what happened to Kid?" she demanded. "You don't want it to get out that a police officer beat a guy so badly he put him in the hospital?"

Victor's whole face went blank.

"Frank," he said to Kate's uncle, who was looking increasingly nervous. "Can we have a minute?"

Frank blinked. "Uh. Sure." He stepped down the court and started bouncing a tennis ball off the ground with his racket, periodically glancing in their direction.

Victor took a long chug of Gatorade. Buying himself time.

"Fine, yes," he said at last, wiping his mouth. "When we were holding Kid for interrogation, there was an . . . incident. We were supposed to let him out the previous day—we hadn't charged him with anything—but he didn't have a lawyer, so Barb said, What the hell? Keep him overnight. In the morning, she got word that Kid's alibi was solid, and we went in to let him go, and found him half-covered in blood." He paused. "Last time you and I talked, you wanted to know why we closed the case so fast. That's why. It was a PR mess waiting to happen. We had to finish up the case, so the journalists wouldn't start sniffing around."

"So when you told me the investigation was just a formality," Kate said, "you mean you *made* it into a formality. It could have gone on for weeks.

You don't know what you would have found out about Jake, because you decided to help cover up an assault."

Victor bristled. "I did what I had to do. If that crap got out, heads were going to roll. I couldn't lose that job. I had two kids at home."

"You weren't the one who attacked him. Why would you have been fired?"

He sighed. "I was new on the job. The only Latino on the force. I know how these things work, Kate. And I think you do too."

He didn't say it outright, but Kate heard the subtext, and her face heated. Leonard. The newspaper. None of it was as secret as she had thought it was. Would she never escape that disaster? The worst part was, it *had* changed the way she heard these stories. Her whole life, she had thought people who didn't come forward were cowards. Now all she could see were these infinite layers of power pushing against one another, holding everyone down.

"What that officer did to Kid was horrible," Victor said. "And the rest of my life, I will feel ashamed that we helped him get away with it. But I promise you, even if we had kept the case open a little longer, we wouldn't have found anything on Jake. That man loved his wife. His whole life was taking care of her, protecting her. When she died, he was destroyed."

"But I found things up in the house. Like this one time, she confronted him one time about his paintings, and he got angry at her—"

"Did you find proof that he killed her? Hard evidence?"

Kate opened her mouth, then closed it. The diary. If only she had been able to finish reading the fucking diary.

"If that's all," Victor said, "I'd better get home."

He waved goodbye to Frank, then picked up his gym bag and started across the court. After a moment, Kate ran after him. It was easy to catch up with him, but her muscle memory reminded her to cut her pace right before overtaking him. Men didn't like it when you overtook them. It made them defensive.

Sweat had drawn a dark cross on his back, and Kate spoke to it when she said, pleading, "Miranda is important to me. I don't think she killed herself. You said you did what you had to. Well, I'm doing what I have to. I know a lot of people want to talk about the case and come up with theories and make it into some story. I don't care about that. I won't tell anyone anything. Not about Kid. Not even about Miranda. I just need to know how she died. *I need to know.*"

Victor slowed, then stopped. Kate barely avoided tripping over him. When he turned around, it was hard to tell whether his expression was one of sympathy or pity. It didn't matter. Kate was beyond caring. Her pulse was fast, so fast, so very fast.

"You might not be happy with what you learn," he said.

She almost cried out in relief. "So you do know the answer."

"No. Not an answer. An instinct."

"Okay, an instinct. Go on."

He folded his arms.

"Your boss," he said. "Your boyfriend. Whatever he is to you."

"Theo?"

Victor nodded. "There was something weird about the way he acted when we took his statement. And this stuff we turned up about him bullying kids at school, getting in fights. Violent stuff. But Jake didn't want us to interview him, was worried it might cause psychological damage, and Lippland thought it was stupid to look at him anyway. Kids act weird, she said. She thought it was a waste of time. I didn't push it. It wasn't my place, first of all. I was just supposed to be following orders. But also . . . I had sons. Whenever I looked at Theo, I saw them, and I thought . . . if they had grown up differently, if they hadn't had a good mother—what might they do?"

Kate was speechless for a moment. Then she shook her head. "At your house, you told me Theo couldn't have done it."

He lifted his shoulders, dropped them. "I didn't want to accuse anyone without proof. Especially with your aunt sitting there. I know she likes to talk."

"But he *couldn't* have done it." Her voice came out high-pitched. "He was shorter than Miranda."

"So?"

"So, you showed us the angle the bullet went in. He couldn't have reached that high."

Victor looked bemused for a second. Then his brow cleared.

"I guess I forgot to say," he said. "When the shot was fired, Miranda was kneeling on the ground."

There was a sharp pressure on Kate's ribs, as if someone had sat on her chest. It took her a moment to realize it was because she had stopped breathing. She inhaled a lungful of the chalky, red-scented tennis court air, then another.

That day walking out of Victor's house . . . crowing to Louise that Theo was innocent, that he couldn't have done it . . . it had all been wrong. All of it. Her self-satisfied smirk. Thinking she was such a great investigator. Her softening toward Theo. Trusting him. All of it wrong, wrong, wrong. And the worst part was, if she had just let slip to Victor what she was thinking, or if she had somehow known what to ask him to get that vital piece of information, she could have avoided the entire mess. All this time, she thought she had figured out something no one else had figured out. But she had been pursuing a fact that wasn't a fact. A phantom.

"I still don't know how he would have gotten the blood off him," Victor said, "or how he could have lied so easily. That's why I say it's an instinct. Not an answer."

"B-but—" She heard a voice, it was her own voice, stuttering, stumbling, rumbling. "But why would he do it?"

Meaning Theo. Not that she thought he had done it. Killed Miranda. Did she think that? She didn't know. Again she had that sick, winded feeling, like all the unknowns were flooding her system.

"You must have thought he had a motive," she insisted.

Victor glanced over her shoulder at Frank, then lowered his voice. "My theory was jealousy."

She didn't follow. "Jealousy over what?"

This time, the pity on his face was unmistakable.

"Miranda was pregnant," he said. "Three months along. She and Jake were going to have another child."

MIRANDA

SERIES 2, Personal papers

BOX 9, Diary (1982–1993)

OCTOBER 14 1993

I was supposed to be at the Guggenheim today for my retrospective.

I dreamed of this moment when I was younger, back when my ambition was a pure and glittering thing. Hard as a diamond, impossible to cut.

I thought I would glide into the room and bow to the applause and revel in the knowledge that I've made it, really made it. That I am seen. That I am known.

But that was a dream. For a week I've woken up dizzy and drained. Yesterday almost threw up twice. I forget to do the dishes. I keep thinking the lights are dimming. I can spend hours staring at a slide, lost in the absolute blackness of a silhouette, or the sharp afterglow the light box leaves on the insides of my eyes.

This is the true Miranda Brand.

An ulcer of a person, an acid wound.

No one would want to toast to that. Not to the huge balloon of me. Oozing and sliming. They would eye me and laugh.

They would say, *Women like you always end up like this.*

OCTOBER 24 1993

I cannot have this child.

    I cannot have this child.

    I know it like I know the shape of a sunburst in the lens. Like I know the dial beneath my fingers. The cowlick on my own son's head. The developer on my hands, eating the skin away.

For two months, the creature has been growing inside me, without me knowing.

There is nowhere to go from here.

    I try to see paths out, but they all dead-end. They all end dead. Abortions require cars, friends, time, healing, secrets. Jake will find out. Jake will know. And if I have the child, I will spend the rest of my days in white walls. Jake will find me. Jake will make me. More shocks. More treatments. More publicity. More howls on the street. More names to be called. More failures. More pain. He will consent.

OCTOBER 27 1993

Lately when I wake up, I think: If only I could live forever in this moment between sleep and understanding. The golden light catching the hairs on my arms, the sheets warm against my body. My limbs heavy and happy, unwittingly fertile.

    Paused in that gap before the fruit ripens. Before its flesh swells, and the skin bursts.

    An exit from numbness. A feeling of the future.

OCTOBER 30 1993

Still no inspiration.

If I'm realistic with myself I think my next great masterpiece will be my death. I don't know how it will happen but I have a vision of it. Me spread out, like a collage.

Theo came home from school today crying. Not just crying: hysterical. He said everyone else had gotten to go to the lighthouse today, but he didn't get to go because he didn't have the permission slip.

You didn't sign it? Jake asked me.

I guess not. I guess I forgot.

Theo stopped crying for a minute.

Then he said, sounding forty years older: You never listen to me. You never do anything you're supposed to. I wish you would die. I would shoot you dead with Dad's gun.

I gave Jake a look. Dad doesn't have a gun, I said.

He does. I've seen it. It's in his studio.

You shouldn't be in my studio, Jake said. And you shouldn't say those things to your mother. It's not nice.

I mean it, Theo said. I would do it. I would shoot her to die.

26.

KATE

Kate knew the main strip of Callinas like the back of her hand. The low peaks of the converted houses, the webs of weeds that spidered through the cracks in the asphalt, the fleece-wrapped residents walking their chocolate labs on monogrammed leashes. She walked down Balboa and saw the clumps of greenery and rocks on the crystal shop porch; the sparkling new handicapped sign on a parking spot, belying the town's curated appearance of neglect; the clapboard façade of the bed-and-breakfast, with its overpriced restaurant downstairs and its little rooms for rent tucked in the gables above.

She had seen it all a hundred times before, but as she left the tennis courts, wandering toward the town center like a robot returning to her docking station, everything came as a surprise. It was as if a veil had blocked her vision for weeks, papering over the irrelevant portions of her surroundings with nondimensional semblances, like a skyscraper whose scaffolding has been printed with an image of the building underneath. Now the veil was rent in two, the scaffolding came down, and she saw the town the way she had seen it the first time, when she had no idea what each part would come to mean to her.

Eventually she arrived at Wingwater. She wanted the beach to be empty, but it was warm out, and the waves were pocked with surfers, the sand strewn with blankets and chip bags and dropped toys.

How long ago had she and Theo gone surfing? One week? Two? Time scattered when she tried to hold it. She remembered the pinch of the wet-suit, the shuddering trees, and the way they lay in the car afterward, her head tucked up against the door handle, her fingers toying with the unlock button.

Someone called out her name, and her head jerked up. But it was just one of Louise's friends. Kate waved back, shielding the sun from her eyes with her other hand, and then turned and walked in the opposite direction, toward the rocky end of the beach. She waded through the heavy dry sand up to a collection of rocks that was halfway between a cliff and a dune. It was not private, exactly, but far enough away that anyone would have to trudge across a wide swath of sand to approach. Defensible area, they would call it in the wildfire brochures. She chose a flattish rock and sat down. Her heart pounded against her rib cage like a prisoner begging to be let out.

Two gulls swooped low over her head and glided out to sea. They slowed down until Kate thought they might drop right out of the sky, and then suddenly one of them leaned forward and dove, streaking through the air like a comet, entering the water with a splash. Ten seconds, twenty, and then the gull resurfaced, empty-mouthed, its beak bent permanently into a sullen frown. No fish.

Was this view what Miranda had seen her first day in Callinas: the silver plane of the water, the blue swing of the sky, the miraculous beyond? Maybe she had tripped out of the car and run barefoot down the white slope, over the rocky tide line and the wet brown frills of sand where clams had tunneled down. Maybe she had plunged in, deeper and deeper, swinging her arms as the water fought back against her, until at last she could dip her head into that cold Pacific sea. Christening herself. Being reborn. She wouldn't have realized until it was too late that the riptide had got hold of her and was pulling her under.

The wind picked up. Kate watched the gulls dive again and again, and at last one caught a wiggling silver fish, bearing it aloft for a moment before tipping it backward into its mouth and swallowing it whole. But by the time this happened, there had been so many failed attempts that one success alone wasn't enough. The gulls accumulated kills the way a child looks for new shooting stars in the night, thinking, this one will give me my wish. This one. This one. This one.

When Kate entered the Brand house later that day, the walls pressed in around her. Wooden like a coffin. The foyer's familiar hand-looped rug, even more faded and matted than when she had arrived at the Brand house that first day. Of course, she hadn't noticed it that first morning, because she had entered through the backyard. That memory sent a cold jolt up her spine. *That's where she died.* If he had killed her, he would know.

Theo came pounding down the stairs, nearly skidding down the last step, his expression panicked.

"There you are," he said.

"What? What's wrong?"

"What do you mean, what's wrong? It's eleven thirty."

"It is?" That meant she had left the tennis court almost two hours ago. She wasn't sure where she had been in the interim. Maybe walking.

Theo gave her a strange look. "Yes."

Kate averted her eyes and took her tote bag off her shoulder, hung it up on the coatrack. She hadn't been prepared for the rush of seeing him: his long frame, the tattoo, the pale eyes. It all affected her like a line of expensive coke, a reaction that, now that she thought about it, couldn't be healthy, couldn't be advisable.

"I've been texting you," Theo said.

"Didn't come through." The truth was that she hadn't looked at her phone.

"Where have you been?"

"Around. Slept in."

Sentence fragments were all she could manage. It was too hard to talk around the lump in her throat. She wished Theo would leave the room, just for a minute. She just needed to get herself together, recalibrate. She couldn't do that while he was here. Maybe it had been a bad idea to come up here after all—certainly she wasn't going to get any work done today—but at some point while wandering—*yes*, she had definitely been walking, walking around town—she had found herself on the trail. Led there by routine. *When you don't know what to do, go to work.*

"I went down the path an hour or so ago," he said. "I was worried you had fallen. Hit your head or something."

"What, you need to know where I am at all times?" she snapped.

Theo recoiled. Then his face smoothed over in that way it did when he didn't want to look annoyed.

"No, of course I don't," he said. "But I was worried about you."

His tone was faintly accusatory.

Kate chewed her lip. She was acting wrong, she saw that, although she didn't know how to undo it or go backward. She didn't know how to stop her mind from finding all the possible interpretations for his words. Like how *worried about you* could mean *afraid for you* or *afraid of what you might do*. Care or control.

"I'm sorry," she said. "I'm just really tired."

She stepped into his arms and pressed her nose into his chest just long enough to remember the familiar grain of that same old shirt and the smell of his skin beneath. She wondered how many repetitions it took to ground such sensory details permanently in your memory. She'd like to stop one repetition short. Just enough that she would be able to forget him someday, if she needed to.

They wound up having sex. There was something off about it, something ragged, less mutual. At the crucial moment, Kate caught Theo's eyes, those familiar eyes, and she had the feeling of slipping sideways through mirrors and reflections, tumbling backward into another body, looking at another man, and it made her fierce and somehow angry. She wove her fingers through his hair and gripped his head tightly, as if she were trying to crush his skull with her bare hands, and she made him look at her until his eyes became green blurs, algae beneath the water's surface, a jungle's light, and only then did she close her own eyes, and her mind struck out into the hot red of her eyelids, the pleasure a billowing sail on a windy day. Her throat parched; the sun burning her skin.

While Theo worked upstairs in the early afternoon, Kate rooted through the folder of Miranda's medical records again, searching for any sign of the pregnancy, but there was nothing there. No blood tests, no ob-gyn appointment confirmations, nothing.

Kate put the folder back and ran her fingers over the newly labeled boxes until she found *Series 4, Household documents, Box 21, Receipts*. The box was almost full and mostly unorganized. She hadn't read the receipts carefully the first time around; she hadn't expected she would need to. After forty-five minutes, though, she found it: a receipt from the same Mill Valley pharmacy Kate had gone to when she didn't want anyone in Callinas to find out about her medications. The receipt was dated October 23, 1993, and it listed two pregnancy tests, paid for in cash.

"Heading to get the kids," Theo called out from the foyer.

Kate glanced up. "Okay! See you soon!"

The front door closed behind him, and Kate was alone again in the house.

Ever since Theo had painted over the drawings in the stairwell, Kate had worried that she might open the darkroom door and discover that the entire place had been emptied out, the equipment donated to Goodwill, those last remaining photographs gone forever. Every time she found the darkroom as she had left it, she was relieved. Today was no different. When she flicked the switch and saw the red safelight glint pinkly off the machines' pebbled finish, her shoulders relaxed. It was all here.

She turned off the light again. With the velvet curtain draped closed behind her, the darkness was total, unbreakable. She circled the central table by memory, moving slowly, feeling her way, letting her fingers drift over the table's edge, the familiar contours of the jugs and bottles. The taut drying line, the unfinished edges of the wooden clips holding the photos of Theo and Miranda in place.

When she had finished this circuit, she sat on the floor next to the sinks. Then sitting up seemed too hard, and she lay down and stared up at the invisible ceiling.

Something would show itself to her. *Miranda* would show herself to her. She hoped. Bold, cruel, brilliant Miranda, Miranda who had loved and hated, Miranda whom Kate loved and hated. True, she had never met her, but Kate still felt—as she lay on the cold, dusty floor—that she knew Miranda better than anyone had ever known her, because she had been forced to imagine her, because she had had to fill in the gaps. It had created an intimacy between them. An identity.

The darkroom could destroy all the external parts of her. Illuminate the inside and dissolve her skin. It could make the broken pieces look good again. It could wash her clean into a syncopated shadow. A negative of herself. The bad would be the good would be the bad.

So consider it, Kate, she told herself. Consider it here, at the heart of it. Let yourself think:

Theo killed Miranda.

That didn't undo everything that had happened between them. It didn't undo his kindness, the things he had suffered, how hard he had worked to repair his life. It could even have *shaped* it, shaped him. Encountering that worst part of yourself, you might spend the rest of your life doing penance, being good, hoping to undo that initial mistake.

Age eleven, holding a gun, finger shaking on the trigger, neglected, desperate to change something, used to video games . . .

Maybe there was a seed of violence at the beginning of everyone's story. Blood shed somewhere along the way, whether you remembered it or not.

could have hurt someone, Frank had said about his BB gun. At that age, kids were so irresponsible. They could make so many mistakes.

But how much of an accident could it be, to shoot your mother at close range while she was on her knees?

You would have to make her kneel in the first place.

You would have to bring the muzzle to her head.

Nestle it into her dark hair. Right near her center part, where the skin shone through.

And pull the trigger.

K ate?"
Kate jolted upright, hitting her head on the edge of the table. The pain kaleidoscoped into thousands of shimmering pieces, and she stifled a moan and lay back down. She wiggled her phone out of her pocket and checked the display—4:21. *Fuck.* What had she been doing? She could have sworn she just lay down five minutes ago.

"Hello?" Theo called. He was somewhere in the studio. She wasn't sure where; the sound was muffled by the heavy velvet curtains at the door.

Again: "Hello?"

Closer this time. *Fuck.*

She didn't move. Barely even breathed.

The door opened, and the drapes whooshed backward into the vacuum of air. Theo came through and flicked on the safelight, and there was a split second after the scene was doused in red light when Kate saw Theo not see her. One last second of him not knowing. Then he looked down and saw her still lying on the floor.

She had so often imagined Theo discovering her mid-search that the moment felt like something she had already lived. Her dreams had been filled with this moment, she realized now, as the memories surfaced all at once. In her dreams, the room was tinted gray and she was holding up some indistinguishable but important object. Then Theo came in and said *What are you doing in here* and the words exploded into a cloud of lilies and shredded documents that rained down around her like confetti, and she tried to get up so she could clean it up, but her limbs were chained to the floor. Someone was watching from the corner, but when Kate tried to turn her head to look, the person kept dodging away, so that all she saw was a flare of black cloth.

The reality felt like a performance of the dream where everyone had missed their cue. Parts had slipped away. There was no other person in the corner. No confetti. Kate was not locked to the floor. Theoretically, she could move if she wanted. But she couldn't seem to make her body work. Bile made her mouth slick and sour.

"Kate," Theo said. "What are you doing in here?"

"Hi. Hi." She struggled to sit up, leaned against the leg of the table for support, and said—with all the nonchalance of a high schooler who had just been caught in her parents' liquor cabinet—"Just looking around."

There was a beat.

"Don't worry," she said. "I didn't drink any dangerous chemicals."

The joke didn't land. Or she didn't think it did. It was hard to tell. The ruddy darkness fuzzed his features like Vaseline on a lens. Only hours ago, she had been close enough to see each pore on his face. She pushed herself to her feet, trying to ignore the swift spike of sadness between her ribs, more particular than any dreamed sensation had ever been.

"I asked you not to come up here," he said. "Remember?"

A condescending edge to the question that she didn't like. She remembered that morning: *I was worried about you.*

"I just wanted to look around," she said.

"Kate." He closed his eyes, passed his hands over his face. "Please stop lying to me."

There was something off about his reaction. It took her a moment to put her finger on it. When she did, it thrummed like a swollen vein.

"You aren't surprised," she said slowly.

He brought his hands down. Shook his head.

"No," he said. "I knew weeks ago that you were coming up here. That you were going through the whole house."

Now, through the jellied light, she saw that his expression was resigned. And angry. Not the kind of anger she had expected, but something slower and darker. Embers in an ignored fireplace.

Her mind sloshed around, trying to find purchase.

"H-how'd you know?" she asked.

The look he gave her said, *How do you think?*

"I found some strands of blond hair on the floor in my bedroom. Before you were ever in there with me," he clarified. "So the next day I set up a camera in there, and I saw you come in and read the diary."

Kate opened her mouth. Closed it. Opened it again. "A camera?"

"A friend owns a company that manufactures tiny baby monitor cameras." Theo pressed his thumb and forefinger together, the width of a lima bean. "She had sent me a prototype back when Oscar was born, and I brought it up here in case . . ." He trailed off.

In case he needed to spy on her.

The sour taste in her mouth intensified. She imagined the camera recording them having sex, a little red light beeping as she writhed and moaned. A grainy capture of her somewhere, sliding down Theo's body. Almost like Miranda's photographs of Kid.

"And you've had the camera on this whole time?" she asked.

"No. I took it down when we started . . . when things changed."

"But you didn't tell me you had found out."

He arched an eyebrow. "I don't really think you have the moral high ground here. This is my house."

His tone—chilly and condescending, just like it had been on that first day—got under her skin.

"If you want to set up cameras, set up cameras," she snapped. "But you were so worried about the *power dynamics* of us fucking. And you didn't think it was an issue not to tell me you had been filming me?"

"I wasn't *filming* you," Theo said. "Not the way you're making it sound. I wanted to know what you were doing in my house when I wasn't here, that's all."

"So you deleted all the tapes? You don't have *any* of those recordings stored anywhere on your hard drive?"

Theo was silent for a moment.

"You're changing the subject," he said. "You went all over my fucking house. You read my private stuff. You came up here, even after I asked you—*as your boss*—not to."

"I thought you didn't think of me as an employee," she said.

"You lied to me."

"You *let* me lie to you!" she cried out.

In no moment of anticipating this crisis had she ever expected that she would be the one to feel betrayed. But she did. All the energy she had spent keeping this secret from him, and the whole time, he had known. She tried to remember if he had ever let on that he knew, or tried to lead her into lying. Maybe he had relished the manipulation.

"I just want to know why you were doing it." Theo swept his arm around, gesturing at the darkroom. "What are you looking for?"

"I told you. I want to know what happened to your mother."

"Why does it matter so much to you?"

"Why *doesn't* it matter to you? She was your mother, and you don't give a shit about how she died!"

"Of course I do!"

"You know people say you did it?"

"Of course I know," Theo bit out. "Trust me. If you've heard it, it's been said to my face, probably in front of my kids."

"Well?"

"Well what?"

"Did you?"

He looked incredulous. "You're *asking* me that?"

He came forward into the safelight's dim wash. She clasped her hands together. She would have thought her palms would be sweaty, but they were perfectly dry, cold and terrified.

"There's a reason the rumors started," Kate said. "I don't . . . Theo, maybe I don't even *care*. You were so young. There are so many things that can happen. I know you didn't have a happy childhood. And I know about the baby."

"What baby?"

Kate stared at him. "Your parents' baby."

"I don't know what the fuck you're talking about," Theo said. "But if you need an answer—if you're really fucking asking me this—then no, Kate, I didn't *shoot my mother* when I was *eleven years old*."

Kate pushed back her shoulders. "Someone did. It doesn't add up. There were inconsistencies in the case. The police ended the investigation because they had a scandal, and I think she's being ignored, Theo, and I need to know the truth, I don't know how to explain it, but I *need* to—"

"The truth," Theo interrupted, "is that she killed herself."

"You don't *know* that."

"Yes, I do."

"How?"

He looked straight at her. "Because I saw her do it," he said.

MIRANDA

SERIES 2, Personal papers
BOX 9, Diary (1982–1993)

NOVEMBER 10 1993

Without me the grocery store is still open. People still move through the aisles pinching tomatoes, cradling pears. Without me the post office is still open and sells stamps with hand-drawn birds on them and corrects zip codes. Without me there are still roads and people to drive on them. The beach is still there and the waves hitting the shore over and over and over again. The redwoods are still outside, growing by millimeters. Without me the world hums at its usual pitch. I remember when all I wanted was to make my mark. Now I see there are so many marks that you can't see one for the other. It's all part of the texture.

Without me the light is still there. The shadows are still there. The camera is still there.

Sometimes it feels like I have been missing my whole life.

NOVEMBER 12 1993

I believe in pain and I believe in art.

I believed they could create each other.

But this pain creates nothing. It does not emanate. It only absorbs.

NOVEMBER 14 1993

I used to be so afraid of dying. There was so much I wanted to finish. I imagined all my ambition and talent exiting my body with that final breath. There were times I wanted to die, and that image saved me. The idea that without my body as its stove, that fire would burn out, curl up and out like a wisp of smoke.

But picture the wisp: how it might dance in the wind. It might be more beautiful than anything I ever dreamed.

27.

KATE

Kate shook her head in instinctive denial. Theo went over to the sink and wrapped his hands around the edges, bracing himself against its heft.

"You want to know what happened?" he asked, his back to her. "I'll tell you. It was a Friday. I woke up early. I had to finish a science project. I had done it all myself. Other kids got their parents to help. Mine were busy. They were home all the time, but they were busy. I got dressed, brushed my teeth. Went to the kitchen to make breakfast. I made myself breakfast most of the time. Sometimes my mom set out some cereal or a bag of bagels, sometimes not. I remember the kitchen was so quiet. No sounds even coming from overhead. Usually I could hear one of my parents bumping around at that hour, but not that day. I had an hour to finish the project before school. I was pouring myself a bowl of Cap'n Crunch. That's how well I remember that day. I know what cereal I was eating. I know because I can't stand the smell of it anymore, even the texture . . . I was pouring it into the bowl when I felt . . . *something*. A zip up my back. I looked out the back window and I saw it. Her.

"She was standing in my dad's raincoat down at the bottom of the yard, right before the trees start. She was staring out at the woods. Staring at nothing. I thought about opening the door and calling out to say hi, but I didn't, because if she was in the middle of working I wasn't supposed to disturb her. And sometimes it was hard to tell if she was working. I watched her, wondering what she was doing, and then she knelt down. Like she was praying. I had never seen her pray before but I had seen pictures of church on TV. Then she took something out of the coat pocket . . . I thought it was one of her little Leicas. I don't know when I realized it was a gun.

"I saw her put it up to her head but I still didn't understand. Then I sort of understood, like the way you see lightning before you hear the thunder, and I wanted to move toward her but my feet were stuck. And all of the sudden she went kind of stiff, and then her hand moved, and there was a loud noise. I still wake up to that noise. It goes off in my head over and over. It'll go away for weeks or months, but it always comes back. It's my alarm clock. The sound of the shot. How her body snapped to the side, and she fell.

"My feet came unstuck. I dropped my bowl and ran outside. The grass was wet. It's always wet that time of the morning. I hadn't put on a coat, it was cold. I was running . . . She . . . I couldn't see her head for a minute, it was in the grass. Then I realized it was because she didn't have a head. Half of it was pulp. I could see her brain through the hole. Everything was blood, black, red. I grabbed her. I don't know why. I knew she was dead. I was only eleven but I knew right away she was dead. Still, I grabbed her arms and I shook her. Nothing happened. Just more blood, coming out of her neck, what was left of her head, so much blood . . .

"I ran back inside and upstairs to my parents' room. Part of me thought she would be there. I wanted her to comfort me, tell me it was all going to be okay. She wasn't there. It was just my dad, who woke up when I came in. I pointed to the window and he went to look outside. When he turned back to me, his face had gone white. Then he said, 'What's on your shirt?'

"I looked down. My shirt was red and brown down the middle. He came over to me and I thought he was going to hug me but he didn't. He just stared at my shirt, and at me, and then he said, 'This is what we're going to do.'

"I was so shocked. I did what he told me. He made me go back out to her and wipe down the gun with my shirt. He stood by the door . . . watching me do it . . . I tried not to look at her, but I couldn't help it. I saw it again. Then we went to the bathroom and he washed the blood off my face and my hands. Then he washed his own. The soap smelled like roses. That smell still makes me sick, too. He made me take off my clothes and take them upstairs to her darkroom and put them down inside one of the big jugs of fixer so he could deal with them later. Then he told me to come downstairs and shower, and put on new clothes, and then I was supposed to call 911 and say I had just found my mother dead.

"I told him, 'But when I saw her she wasn't dead.' And he said, 'I know, but it's important to pretend. You have to pretend, Theo.' Because he thought I had done it. He thought he was helping me cover it up."

At last, Theo turned around. His face was wet. The way the red light reflected off his tears made it look like his cheeks were striped with fire.

"It ruined me, what he did that day," he said. "He never let me talk about it. He never brought it up again. So I've just carried it with me, my whole life. The thing I saw. The things I did. I never told anyone."

Kate's mind was rushing and rushing, unable to compute, unspooling and respooling like a fishing reel, all her conclusions collapsing around her.

"You must have told Rachel," she said, her voice rusty.

"No. Just you."

His gaze was bleak. Kate pressed her lips together so they wouldn't wobble. It should have been a gift, him telling her all this, and even through the haze of her fixation, she saw that she had dirtied the exchange.

"Maybe I should have called the police," Theo said. "But I didn't know how. My dad was an awful person. You don't even know the half of it. I haven't told you. He was terrible to me. He was terrible to my mother. He hit her, he undermined her, he yelled at me. He made us think we were crazy. He broke us down. Him lying that day was the one thing he ever did for me out of love. I couldn't . . . even when I hated him, I couldn't dishonor that. I couldn't refuse the only thing he had ever given me.

"And now . . . now that I have the kids . . ." He shook his head. "I just keep hoping everyone will forget about it. If I came forward, the journalists would pump it all up again. I would have to explain to the kids about all this stuff they're too young to get. I want to protect them. I want them to have all the things I never had. All the innocence. Why should I expose them to all that ugliness, if the end result just confirms what most people already assume? So I've kept quiet."

Kate made a quiet, involuntary noise.

"So I understand why I never told anyone," he went on. "What I don't understand is why did I do it? Clean up the way he wanted me to? Why didn't I just call the police right away?"

It took her a moment to realize that Theo's question wasn't rhetorical. He had been asking himself this question all his life and had never found an explanation that satisfied him. And she knew then, from the lost expression on his face, that Miranda had taken a part of him away with her that November morning, across the breach, into the wild unknown.

"You were in shock," she said. "And you were eleven, and you were used to following your dad's orders."

Theo shrugged. Seemingly exhausted by his disclosures, he walked over to the clothesline where the photos of him as a child were hanging. He studied them, his expression imperturbable, then went over to the rack and pulled out the one of him and Miranda laughing.

Without looking up, he said, "What did you mean earlier? About the baby?"

Kate was confused. "You didn't know?"

"Know what?"

She hesitated.

"She was pregnant when she died," she said.

A small tremor of surprise passed through his shoulders, then vanished, as if his body was too exhausted to react. Silence pressed at the room's walls, changing the air pressure until Kate's ears felt like they were about to pop.

"The police said she was only a few months along," she said, to fill the space. Then, desperate to prove all her work hadn't been in vain, she added, "I found a receipt for two pregnancy tests."

He nodded vaguely. He wouldn't look up from the photo. He was watching it like it was a film, moving before him.

"I should have known," he murmured.

"She probably wasn't showing."

"No, I mean . . . if I had finished the diary. If I had read it when I first got it. She must talk about it in there. I would have known." He slid the photo back into the tray. Like it mattered that he put it right back where it had been.

Kate shook her head to clear it. "What do you mean, when you first got it? I assumed you found it up here when you were putting stuff in the dining room."

"My mom's friend Lynn gave it to me when I graduated college. It was all sealed up. My mom had sent it to her to give to me . . . it was postmarked the day before she died. I guess she didn't want my dad to find it." His mouth turned up at the side, a little sardonically. "So her dying wish was that I get it, and I still never read it. I did try. A couple times. And I thought maybe up here, it might turn out to be . . . easier. But I never made it past the first few entries."

Reading those first entries, the ones right before Nangussett, had been hard enough for Kate. Reading them as a son must have been impossible, especially a son plagued by guilt. Yet she was still a little surprised that he had put it down, not only because she herself had been so absorbed by the little book, but also because she couldn't imagine Theo failing at anything. She had to work to wrap her mind around the idea.

"I guess it's all a moot point now," he said, caustically.

The sudden return of his bitterness made her uneasy. "You can still read it. It's not too late."

"If you give it back to me," he said. "I figured you had already sold it."

"What are you talking about?"

"Kate. Come on."

"No, really. I don't know what you're talking about." She stared at him blankly. "You're the one who moved the diary."

They stared at each other for a moment.

Then the truth dawned on Kate.

"Jemima," she said.

MIRANDA

SERIES 2, Personal papers

BOX 9, Diary (1982–1993)

NOVEMBER 13 1993

I took Theo outside today and arranged him by the side of the house for photos. Against those gray shingles that Jake painted when we moved in here, and I thought, He is painting a shell on, he is building us a carapace, he is making us safe.

Theo will be alone after this.

    He'll prefer it that way.

    His whole life, I have been strung up like a puppet. I have been held back.

When I developed the photos, I took such care. Even so, one has a stain at the bottom, a chemical reaction. It looks like the shadow of a man.

NOVEMBER 14 1993

I keep thinking about all the moments when I should have known who Jake really was.

    The one that replays in my head is this. Beers at a bar, I don't remember the name. Windows papered over. My mouth like ash. Pussy still sore where he had fucked me an hour earlier. We were a couple months into dating. We had already started talking about marriage. I asked him about his last girlfriend. He said she was crazy.

Crazy how? I asked.

You know. Crazy.

There are a lot of types, I said.

He hesitated. His eyes flicked to my face and then away again, to some sweaty guy playing a video game at the back of the bar. The guy was twisting the controls really hard, like he was strangling them. There was a stripe of sweat down his back.

Come on, I said. Tell me.

Jake sighed.

He said: We dated for six months. We fought a few times. She loved arguing. We broke up. Then a couple weeks after, I ran into her while we were out. We went back to her place and had sex. The next morning I woke up at her house and I said goodbye and left. The next thing I know, she was accusing me of rape. Seriously. Just like that. Actually, she never said it to my face. Which is how you know it's a lie. And she never even called the police. She just told some other people, some of our mutual friends, and they told me, because they knew she was lying. The truth was she had started dating someone new, and he found out about us, and she didn't want to admit she had cheated on him. So she said I had raped her. Get-out-of-jail-free card. It's made it hard for me to trust women. Not you, though. You're different. You know that, right?

How ironic. Me making all these pictures about how women see and know so much. Me not dating artists because Richard had plagiarized my work. Me saying men are the problem, it's a structural problem. Meanwhile I thought I had found someone who was immune.

I think I believed him just because he said I was different. Men do that. They separate us from the pack. And we are grateful, because the pack is a dangerous place to be.

That girl. I think about her so often. I dream about her. In my dream, she wakes up drunk and uncertain. She sees Jake next to her and her body tenses. She thought she had escaped. Now she feels it, though. The scraped flesh. The wet truth. She will have to live with that truth for the rest of her life. She rolls over onto the side of her bed and vomits onto the floor. A neat yellow oval.

She wipes her mouth and looks up. She has my face.

I no longer wonder what happened to her that night. I do wonder what happened after. I wonder if I have ever met her. In some ways I think she knows me better than anyone else. I wonder if she's seen my work, BRAND on the placard, and what she thought of it. I wonder where she is now.

I wonder what my life would have been like if I had heard Jake tell that story and had walked away.

NOVEMBER 15 1993

Tomorrow I will rise.

The air will be crisp. Frosted. Sweet with the sea. I know every needle on these trees, every whorl on their trunks. I know how the salt air will make my eyes water.

Already my heart is issuing its last beats. Tap tap tap. You can barely hear it inside the house. Out there it will be so loud. It will be the only sound in the silence.

Then a fox will rustle. Orange fur in the leaves. It will fix me with its keen eyes and then it will run away. It will live.

The gun will hurt in my hand. And it will also feel like silk. The barrel against my temple like a bobby pin pulled too tight.

I want my last thought to be of my photos. I want all of them to speed together in a collage, little licked shapes, the toys and the bloodied women and the portraits, Bottle Girls and *Threshold* and Inside Me and Capillaries, and my hands split open, my knee bubbling blood. I want to exit the world thinking about what I brought into it.

Will the recoil hurt? How soon can I get beyond pain?

I'll fall. The puppet strings cut. Unused blood slipping into the soil.

A heart unpossessed.

A person turned body.

In the distance, the blue dawn topping the trees like a crown.

28.

KATE

That same old cartoon jingle floated up the stairs from the living room, sweet enough to shrivel the wilted rosebuds on the wallpaper. Kate ran down the second-floor hallway, Theo hot on her heels. Freed from the stasis of the darkroom, her heart had started to race again, clawing and tripping against her rib cage as they hurried to the kids' room.

The reusable grocery bag of books was more or less where it had been the last time Kate set foot in the room, although Jemima had evidently shifted some items around for her library gambit. There were Post-It notes and markers around the bed, and several books had been stacked face-forward, as if they were on display. Kate glanced at Theo and got a quick nod in return, so she sat down on the bed and began rooting through the bag.

Almost as soon as she had begun, a shriek came from the doorway.

"Put those down!" Jemima screamed, her face turning purple. "They're mine!"

She rushed at Kate, but Theo grabbed her around the waist and held her back.

Kate pulled everything out of the bag. A children's nature magazine. A few books she recognized from the library presentation the other day. A Jehovah's Witness pamphlet that Jemima must have found on the street.

Then—there it was. The blue leather notebook. Slim and soft-backed, it had blended right in with the early readers.

When Kate opened the book, she discovered that Miranda's faded handwriting was now covered over with marker drawings: a green heart here, a yellow star. JEMIMA in big capital letters. The grandchild overtaking the grandmother.

She held it up wordlessly to show Theo.

"Careful!" Jemima was full-on sobbing now. "That one is special!"

Theo looked down at his daughter. "Did you take that out of my nightstand?"

"No!" she wailed. "Oscar did!"

There was a small gasp from across the room. All three looked up: Oscar had come in without them noticing. When they turned to him, his lower lip wobbled.

"Jemima made me," he said, before bursting into tears himself.

Theo lifted his eyes to the ceiling.

"Jesus Christ," he said, and he set aside the final revelations of one of the country's most celebrated photographers in favor of the more menial task of parenting.

It took twenty minutes to get the kids settled, chastise them for stealing, reassure Jemima that they weren't going to take any other books, convince Oscar that no one was going to give him up for adoption because of his part in the debacle, and get them settled with a game of Go Fish at the kitchen table. Kate played only a supporting role, naturally, and as she dealt the cards and helped Oscar up onto the chair, a lump grew in her throat. The adrenaline of the past hour—or was it days?—began to dissipate, replaced by a guilt that wrenched her insides around like a plumber tightening a pipe.

At last, the kids were asking each other for matching numbers (Oscar uncertainly, Jemima sullenly), and Theo gave Kate a little nod. They went into the foyer. On the way, they passed the console table where Theo had dropped the diary earlier, out of Jemima's reach. Kate wished he had put it somewhere else. The sight of it made her worried and guilty and, to her shame, so curious she thought she might drool.

"So," Theo said, his tone businesslike, authoritative, only then he didn't finish the sentence.

"I guess I'm fired." Kate tried to make her voice light. "Anyway. The finding aid is mostly done. I can write you an email telling you the last couple things to flesh out. There's a box of newspaper clippings still to sort—it shouldn't take long." Then, worried it sounded like she was assigning him work, she added quickly, "I mean, I can come back and finish that if you want me to."

Theo hesitated.

"Do you want to?" he asked. His tone inscrutable.

She tried to imagine it. He would stay upstairs. He might greet her cordially. He certainly wouldn't leave the door unlocked for her anymore. They would avoid each other. They would orbit around each other like opposing moons. The idea of spending even an hour like that made Kate feel sick.

"I'm not sure it's such a good idea," she said.

"I was thinking I would take the kids back home this weekend anyway," Theo said. "Their school year starts soon. We have stuff to buy. Binders. Notebooks." He waved his hand. "Stickers and things."

Yes, of course. Their normal lives.

She realized suddenly how little she and Theo really knew about each other. They knew the big secrets, but not the many smaller unconscious things, the habits of mind, the instinctive reactions, the daily defining elements of life. Did they tip well? Did they stop to pet dogs in the street? Did they remember their friends' birthdays automatically or did they wait for the Facebook reminder? Anything about how they interacted with the world outside this house had been sealed off, fed through filters, cleaned by narration. It was a silent pact they had made, somewhere along the way.

"I don't know if you're going back to New York," Theo said.

Kate almost laughed. "Me either," she said.

They looked at each other for a moment. She felt like someone had reached an ice cream scoop into her chest and removed all her organs. Her new normal state, she guessed. It was impossible to imagine regrowing the innards, refilling the scooped space.

"You should read the diary," she blurted out. "I mean, I understand why you haven't. But you should make yourself do it. If she wanted you to."

Theo folded his arms across his chest and studied her for a minute.

Then he gave a slow, small nod. Not a nod of agreement, but a nod like he had been thinking something over and had finally come to a decision. She noticed a paper cut on one of his hands, where it gripped his sweater. The white crescents of his cuticles, the broad flat nails. She remembered him spreading her apart earlier that day, and she flushed.

"I'll go," she said, opening the door into the quivering green afternoon.

She was on the threshold, one foot on the wide front step, when he said, "Kate?"

She turned back. "Yeah?"

"The NDA you signed? You know it still holds."

Nothing less than she deserved. Still, for a split second she hated him a little for saying it aloud. For pretending this was just the end of a business transaction. For acting like their relationship could be reduced to a few lines on a contract. *Will not disclose, divulge, or communicate any Confidential Information.* As if everything he had said to her, everything he had shared, he had done not out of some abstract sense of trust, but because he knew that she was legally bound to keep his secrets. But what about her? Her secrets had no protection.

How carefully she had orchestrated her own annihilation. How methodically she had gone about falling in love while also ensuring that he would never love her back.

"I know," she said, before she closed the door to the Brand house for the final time.

MIRANDA

SERIES 1, Correspondence

BOX 1, Personal correspondence

FOLDER: Toby-Jarrett, Lynn (incl. 12 photocopies of letters from MB, from LTJ private collection)

November 15 1993

Dear Lynn,

    I know we haven't spoken in a long time. I know I hurt you, and even worse neglected you over the years. Maybe that letter Candace sent me about you being out of the country was a lie, was just you, desperate to get rid of me. I wouldn't blame you.

    I figure by the time you get this package, you'll have heard the news. I'm counting on the shock prompting you to open this letter and doing what I ask you to do.

    You have been so much to me. A best friend, a soulmate, a help. Sometimes I think I was never as happy as those days in college when we would hang our arms around each other's necks and breathe in the dense city autumn, the promise of love before winter. Our futures like ripe, soft fruits.

    All my later joys are corrupted. Splashed and stained by what came after. That early happiness, our happiness, that stayed safe. It is intact and shining in my mind.

That's why I am entrusting you with this package. Keep the top part wrapped and give it to Theo, whenever you think you can be sure Jake won't get it. I won't go into it all now. It doesn't really matter anymore. But someday Theo might have questions and I think maybe what is inside will help him understand.

You can open the bottom package—it's for you. It's a print of The Threshold, *one of the last ones left from the first run.*

    You don't know this, but I originally made the photo for you. Because we were both this woman once. We both stepped over, although we had different things waiting for us on the other side.

    If you don't want to keep it, I understand. You should be able to sell it for a lot of money. Prices will skyrocket after the news hits. Artists are the only people who are more valuable dead.

    M

29.

KATE

The following week, Kate was driving Louise back from the East Bay when Louise reached under her arm and flipped the turn signal for her. "Take this exit," she said.

Kate obeyed. She had gotten accustomed to the flipping-the-turn-signal thing this week. Now that she was unemployed, her aunt had roped her into the daily gauntlet of retiree activities. Pilates, farmer's market, picking up a prescription, an unnecessary trip to a Home Depot almost an hour away. They drove all around Marin, from the oyster shacks north of Point Reyes Station to the tranquil glitter of Tiburon and the humble gray of Muir Beach. They visited a friend of Louise's who lived high in the hills near Mount Tam and they did chaturangas every morning at the local yoga studio and bought coffees from the Mill Valley espresso bar. Today they had been at a volunteer trash pickup in Berkeley, the only two people there who weren't doing court-ordered community service.

Kate neither liked nor disliked these activities. The morning after the fight with Theo, she had woken up exhausted, unable to do much more than shuffle to the bathroom and back again. It felt like someone had drained her blood in the middle of the night and replaced it with lead. Louise's whirlwind of activities didn't make a dent in the fog. Kate just plodded along dutifully after her. Louise made Kate her personal chauffeur, perhaps in an effort to get her to be more active. It turned out that in the throes of depression, Kate was a better driver than ever before: she slowed at yellows, never accelerated to merge, didn't get impatient with traffic.

"Where are we going?" Kate asked.

"There's an In-N-Out. You have to try it."

"I thought you were starting a new diet."

Louise sniffed. "They use only fresh ingredients, Kate."

The inside was packed with kids and balloons: apparently someone was turning whatever age was best celebrated with an endless high-pitched scream. They placed their order and took the burgers to the car, where they unwrapped their food in near silence.

The parking lot faced the highway. Rush hour was ending, and the cars slipped past faster and faster, flicking their headlights on against the incoming dusk. There was a glow in the distance, on the ridge of a hill: a small wildfire, striping smoke up into the night.

Louise wiped her fingers on a napkin and glanced over.

"Kate," she said.

That was when Kate realized that Louise had planned the entire day around this conversation. She had perfectly executed all the steps. Lull Kate into complacency with fries and special sauce, then go in for the kill. Maybe even the trash pickup had been part of it. Kate *had* thought it was odd that Louise wanted to drive an hour and a half to pick up trash when there were perfectly good piles of beer cans and single-serve salad containers on Wingwater.

"You're right," she interrupted before Louise could continue. "In-N-Out really is the best."

"I'm worried about you," Louise said.

That phrase again. Kate was so tired of being worried about, in all its senses. Feared, feared for. She wanted to bring something else into the universe. She had tried to, with Miranda, but look how that had backfired. She wanted to say *You shouldn't worry about me*, but obviously that would be a lie. Instead, she took a huge bite of her burger and chewed industriously, preventing her from talking.

"You've been manic, haven't you?" Louise asked, her tone practical, almost medical. "Frank told me about what happened on the tennis courts with Victor. Not that we hadn't noticed before. The pressured speech, the not sleeping . . . This obsession with Miranda . . . which I encouraged, I know. I just didn't think you would take it so far. I mean, Katie, did you really think you would find out anything the police department didn't?"

But I did find something, Kate thought. With a flash of bitterness, she recalled Theo's reminder about the NDA. But the legal threat wasn't what prevented her from telling Louise. There were the kids to think about. If Theo thought keeping his parents' secrets would protect Jemima and Oscar somehow, then Kate wasn't going to go against that. Besides, she couldn't bear the thought of reliving the whole argument in the darkroom. What she had believed.

She swallowed her food. "No," she said quietly. "Not really."

"And you've been different the past few days, too." Louise took a deep breath. "I called your mom. She wants you to come home."

Kate leaned her forehead against the window. She felt tears coming up in her throat, but they stopped there, as if even crying would require too much energy.

"Louise, I can't," she said. "I'd be right back where I started. It would mean this whole summer . . . it would mean I hadn't done anything."

"No, it wouldn't," Louise said with surprising vehemence. "You did a lot. You did that whole project. No matter how it ended—you still accomplished it."

Kate closed her eyes and shielded her mouth with one hand. Her chest was getting hot and tight, like she was having a heart attack.

She had been in California barely two months, and already the entire geography of her life had quaked and shuddered, rearranged itself into lean new valleys whose emptinesses she had yet to learn.

"I know I need help," she said through her fingers. "I can do that. I'll start medication again. I'll find a new psychiatrist. But I just can't . . . I can't go back, Louise. It has to be different this time."

Louise was quiet for a minute, thinking.

"Okay," she said. "So you stay with us."

Kate shook her head. "No, I can't do that to you. I know I haven't been an easy guest."

"You stay with us," Louise repeated more firmly, "but only if you get help. Only if you work on it."

Kate knew what this meant. Therapy, appointments, medication, conversations . . . all of it expensive, all of it probing at this hard hot thing inside her. The thought threatened to overwhelm her. She stared out the headlights sifting by, blurry and flat against the peony sky. Everyone inching back home.

"Okay," she said at last. "Thank you. Yes."

"Good." Louise gave a single, decisive nod. "We'll call your parents when we get home. Now let's go."

She fished the keys out of the center console and handed them to Kate, who took them with a wet laugh.

"And remember, Katie," Louise said as Kate turned the key in the ignition. "If you were easy, I wouldn't love you so much."

MIRANDA

SERIES 2, Personal papers

BOX 9, Diary (1982–1993)

NOVEMBER 15 1993

Theo, in my own way, I love you.

    You were worth the slow death.

    You will be worth the fast one, too.

30.

KATE

SIX MONTHS LATER

When one of Kate's four roommates brought the embossed envelope up to her little garret room in the house in Potrero Hill, Kate assumed it was Natasha and Angela's wedding invitation and slit it open without checking the return address. Inside was a heavy silk card:

> **THE MIRANDA BRAND PAPERS**
> A Semi-Private Auction Event
> March 9, 2018

Behind the card was a handwritten note from Hal asking if Kate would call him back to discuss her attendance. Kate wasn't thrilled about the prospect of talking to him again, but she did as he asked.

"I know there are certain possible buyers who would be very interested in having you there," Hal said. "There will be a cocktail hour after the actual sale, and you can talk to them about your experience working with the collection, your sense of Miranda. We're trying to translate any residual interest in the papers into the artwork, because we'll keep selling that off as well, though of course in much smaller batches, as we don't want to oversaturate the market." He added, in a tone of great dignity, "I should say that for someone with so little experience, you did a marvelous job handling the prints."

"Thank you," Kate said, rolling her eyes. "But I'm not sure I can make it."

Hal paused. "I'm not the only one who wants you to attend," he said. "Theo's the one who added you to the list."

Wrong of her heart, after all this time, to give a little thump. She and Theo hadn't spoken since the summer. Her final paychecks had been deposited into her account on schedule. Recently, she had been getting the agreed-upon bonuses as Hal started to sell off the prints. Sometimes she caught herself studying the transaction record as if it were a coded message from Theo, a bizarre expression of vestigial affection, and she had to remind herself that the payments were contractually obligated and most likely executed by some overworked assistant at his company. This invitation was the first actual proof that Theo even remembered her existence.

"I'll see what I can do," Kate said.

With no obvious seasons to guide her ("we *have* seasons," Frank would protest when she said this, "they're just more subtle"), Kate had tracked the fall and winter in other units. Three months with Frank and Louise. Hours spent finding a new psychiatrist, dealing with the insurance paperwork, starting new medication, talking to a therapist, then another therapist, then the same one again, three times a week for eight weeks. Menial work. Devastating and boring in equal measure. The same drive to the same office to answer the same questions and cry into the same tissue box before handing over her credit card for the same co-pay. Some days she would have what the therapist called a "breakthrough," teasing out some pattern of behavior that Kate had never noticed before—but these breakthroughs seemed to vanish instantly from Kate's conscious memory, only to reappear days later when she was in the middle of washing her hair. At a certain point, she began to feel ludicrous, rehashing the events of a life built around creating opportunities to rehash it, and she was relieved when the therapist said she thought they could cut back to once a week, which would let Kate move into the city and look for a job.

So, new units: Two weeks looking for an apartment. Dwindling digits in her bank account, refreshed by her summer earnings, then decimated by the new apartment's security deposit. An excruciating eight more weeks of job-searching, which finally culminated in a position as a copywriter at a small advertising firm.

She liked the new job, even though the CEO was four years younger than her and called every meeting a "summit." The work was fun enough and challenging enough, almost all of her coworkers were female or nonbinary, and Kate found herself, to her surprise, feeling excited about the idea of moving up, a sentiment she thought the Leonard situation had drilled out of her.

She liked the new house, too, with its thrice-Craigslisted furniture and spiky air plants. Two of her roommates, long-time SF residents, introduced her to the city. Before the job started, she rode trolleys through Pacific Heights and ate pupusas in the Mission and walked to the ruins of the Sutro Baths. She learned the inconsistencies of the BART, the best coffee shops with free Wi-Fi, and how to plan her jogs so that they ended by running downhill with a view over the bay. After work began, she reactivated her Instagram and used her commute to reconnect with the New York friends with whom she'd lost touch. There was a blizzard on the East Coast. The government was a disaster. A video of a tiger cub cuddling a mouse went viral. There was a new embezzlement scandal at a rival paper, and many people had forgotten about Leonard Webb.

If sometimes at night she had difficulty falling asleep, if the bed seemed to yawn around her and the darkness felt flat and cold, it did not mean she had made a mistake. It did not mean she was unhappy.

After her Sunday therapy sessions, she usually tried to go up to Callinas for dinner. The town seemed smaller and more harmless now that she no longer lived there. Louise often invited other people over for dinner— Roberta and Wendy, Nikhil and Sabrina, Esme—and the conversations were easy, and usually Miranda-free. The Brand house had been sold several months ago for an absurd amount, and a YouTube executive had moved in with his family and was now talking about gutting the entire building. He wanted to add a second well. He wanted to install a boat launch point on

Wingwater and a sign by the lagoon announcing you had arrived in Callinas. He had caused such a stir over zoning that people seemed to have forgotten that the house had ever belonged to Jake and Miranda at all. They
no longer called it "the Brand house," but instead "The Command Center,"
which was the name written on the ostentatious sign that the new owner
had installed down on Dunlop, right over the property line.

Tonight's dinner was just Kate and Frank and Louise, but Louise had
outdone herself as usual, serving up a heap of paella in a ceramic bowl the
size of a small coffee table. Pink shrimp and black-purple mussels glinting
against the saffron rice, chunks of chorizo throughout. A good Sauvignon
Blanc that tasted like lemon and butter.

When they had finished eating, Kate told them about the invitation to
the auction. They both said she should definitely go.

"It's weird, though," Kate said. "I don't even know how Hal found my
address."

Louise shrugged. "He must have gotten it from Theo."

The sound of his name still made her jump. "How would Theo have my
new address?"

"Well, I gave it to him when he asked for it."

Kate dropped her fork. "What? When did he do that?"

"He emailed me a few weeks ago," Louise said. "Olive, down! Good
Lord. You are *such* a naughty dog."

"And you didn't tell me?"

"I thought I did."

"You told me someone called to say I had been selected as a keynote
speaker at an embassy if I would just transfer five thousand dollars to an
offshore bank account," Kate said. "Is that what you're thinking of?"

"A valuable investment in your future," Louise said placidly, "just like
going to this auction. It's a networking opportunity."

"Number one, I already have a job. Number two, last time I saw Theo, I
accused him of killing his mother."

"Nothing he hadn't heard before," Louise replied, unperturbed.

Six months since Kate had seen Theo. Longer than she had known him.

Longer than she had spent in Callinas. She had learned—*again*—how to operate feeling like a piece of herself was missing. How to forge ahead. How to live without resolution. Seeing him again, peeling herself open again, would undo all this autumn's work.

Frank chewed thoughtfully. "That's nice about the embassy. But I wouldn't transfer any money to an account you don't recognize."

"Oh, Frank," Louise said. "Go find your iPad."

The auction was in a vast, high-ceilinged room with movable white walls. Lines of folding chairs were set up facing a podium. On the right wall was a series of stalls with computers and phone lines, where auction house representatives sat coolly, waiting for electronic bids. Invitations and credentials had been carefully checked at the door; buyers had to be pre-approved just to set foot in the auction hall.

The atmosphere was tense and businesslike. Kate had worn a cocktail dress and was now regretting it. Everyone else was in suits or woolen work dresses, or else jeans. Hal, who greeted her with his usual practiced enthusiasm and then quickly moved on, was wearing a navy blazer and green bowtie. A table was laid out with a hundred glasses of Möet & Chandon, but no one was drinking. The bartender had focused his eyes in the middle distance and was smiling blindly around, hoping someone would put him out of his misery. Kate felt sorry for him and took a glass.

The auctioneer tapped his gavel to bring people to order—auctions seemed a lot like jury duty—and everyone found a seat. Kate was headed for one near the front, but at the last minute she saw Theo sit down in that area and she panicked, scurrying into a middle seat several rows back.

The director was a slim, mousy man in a tweed suit. He gave a nice speech about Miranda and handed out an inventory based on Kate's finding aid. He talked about how the photographs would be sold separately by Hal and another dealer—a young British woman. Apparently this woman had once sold a museum a pile of dirt for $250,000. Now the dirt sat in the museum's central gallery and people came from all over the country to marvel at it. The whole audience applauded at her name.

"Before we get started," the director said, "Miranda's son, Theo, has a few words to say about exactly what is in this collection."

Theo stood and walked up to the podium. Kate realized suddenly that she only had Hal's word for it that Theo wanted her there. Hal could be toying with her, trying to get back at her for that tense visit to his gallery. Horrified, she slunk lower in her seat.

Theo was wearing a jacket, but also his same old dark jeans. The familiarity of them was a personal affront. After shaking the director's hand, he unfolded a piece of paper and put it on the podium. He shifted his weight and cleared his throat.

"What's being auctioned here today are my mother's and father's papers," he said. "Mostly my mother's, because she kept everything. My father was more organized."

There were titters in the audience, like this was a joke. Theo looked uncomfortable. Kate had forgotten he didn't like public speaking. His eyes scanned the rows, then dropped back down to his paper.

"My father was more organized," he repeated. "He was also violent, cruel, and abusive. And there is no doubt in my mind that he drove my mother to suicide."

The giggles stopped abruptly. Theo didn't look up from his paper. His face had begun to flush deeply, and Kate's stomach dropped.

"There are many reasons why I haven't spoken about this until now," he said. "I told myself it was out of concern for my children. But the real reason, I think, was that I was concerned about my mother. About what sharing this information might do to her legacy. As far as I know, my mother never wanted to be judged by anything other than her artwork, and I think everyone will agree with me that her artwork more than stands on its own. But over the past year, I've realized that the more I tried to hide the truth of what my mother experienced, both in Nangussett Psychiatric Hospital and in our home in Callinas, the more I was helping create a version of my mother that never really existed.

"So although I had originally expected to auction off a censored selection of her papers, I have decided to sell the entirety of what she produced. The only thing missing from the collection is the diary she kept from the time I was born until the day she died. And the only reason I'm excluding that is because next year, I will be releasing a transcript of the diary as a book, whose proceeds will go to charities for domestic violence and suicide prevention."

Kate's breath wheezed out like someone had punched her in the stomach.

"I don't know if the new information will stoke the curiosity about my mother or eliminate it," Theo continued. "Maybe reading it, you'll decide I made the wrong choice, and I should have kept it all private. But so many people have written about my mother. So many people have formed hypotheses and made assumptions and interpreted her. It only seemed fair that she should get a chance to tell her side of things. In the spirit of letting her talk, I will not be giving any further interviews or comments on this subject. I would ask you all to respect my family's privacy and the sensitivity of the issue at hand." He exhaled and looked up from his paper, folding it up again. "Finally, I'd just like to thank the archivist who organized this collection, Kate Aitken. Without her, the collection would not have been nearly as complete."

His eyes met hers across the rows. She realized with a jolt that he had known where she was the entire time.

Then he stepped down from the podium and sat down again. The auction began. Twenty minutes later, the collection had been sold to Columbia University for $3.8 million.

Afterward came the hors d'oeuvres. Tiny salmon blinis and overfried samosas. The bartender began to look less panicked. Kate positioned herself at the edge of the room, beside a tall and rickety table, and tried to look like her heels were not twisting her feet into cornucopias of pain. She didn't know anyone except Hal and Theo, but she guessed she should be ready in case someone figured out who she was and asked her a question. What would an expert look like? she wondered, and she pasted a vaguely bored expression on her face.

"Champagne?"

It was Theo. She was so surprised, she almost elbowed him in the stomach.

"Hi," she said. Her voice was garbled, like her tongue had swelled up from an allergic reaction.

"Hi," he said.

He looked healthy. His hair was a little shorter. He had a messenger bag over one shoulder. He gestured again with the champagne, and she took it and drank it without tasting it.

"Congratulations," she said.

"Thanks," he said.

"And thanks for inviting me."

"Thanks for coming."

Kate adjusted her tiny plastic plate with its tiny uneaten blinis. "How are the kids?"

"Great. Really good."

"Good."

They stood there together, unhappily. Kate began to fret with the edge of the plastic plate between her fingers. It was too much. The past months without him collapsed freshly onto her shoulders. It was all with her now, condensed into his body, his dear body, the chest she had kissed and scratched and slept on, the long legs, the rise of his throat. The smoke of the fireworks. His voice low in the night. The waves pushing over her, her heart in her mouth, the salt of him and the salt of the sea. Now the awkwardness, the uncertainty. They sounded like two automatons reciting programmed greetings.

"Theo . . ." she said, but what she meant was *I can't do this*.

The wall behind him burst into color: a slideshow of Miranda's photos.

She could do better than this, Kate told herself, and she looked Theo square in the eye and opened her mouth.

He beat her to it. "I owe you an apology," he said. "The way I acted this summer. You were right that I was manipulating you. I didn't think of it that way at the time, but it's true, that's what it was."

"Oh," she said, thrown. "I was going to apologize to *you*."

"Thanks. Apology accepted."

She stared at him, then stamped her foot in frustration. "It doesn't work like that. You have to think about it."

"I have been. But I can think about it more if you want. In the meantime, I have something for you."

He took a padded envelope out of his messenger bag and handed it to Kate. She was so dazed that she took it automatically and looked inside.

A slim blue book.

She looked back up at him, blinking. "Is this . . ."

"It's a facsimile. Kind of a more image-based version of what's coming out next year. I'm keeping the original for Oscar and Jem. But I wanted you to have the chance to read the end before everyone else does. I know what it meant to you."

Her eyes started to feel hot. On the screen, the Capillaries photograph, the man and the woman in the diner.

"Theo . . ." This time it meant something different, something like: *I'm sorry I hurt you. I'm sorry I'm broken. I tried to fix myself. I don't know if it worked. I might still love you, if I know you. If we know each other at all.*

"I didn't come here for the diary," she said instead. "I came here for you."

His eyes crinkled at the corners. She forgot that her feet were hurting.

"Can we talk somewhere more private?" he asked.

"Like where?"

He gestured at a partition in the movable wall. Through the gap, Kate glimpsed what looked like a storage area for a mishmash of Greek sculptures and eighteenth-century furniture. She glanced around the room to see if anyone was watching.

"I don't think we're supposed to go back there," she said.

He raised his eyebrows like, *Really?* When she heard the irony of what she had said, she smiled, too.

On the edge of a cliff now. A fragment of earth piercing a dark sea. The tide going out, imprisoning fishes, dirtying the sand. All around the world, people were jumping off, scissoring their legs against the air until they were small flecks far below, as small as a baby tooth in the palm of a hand, a sunspot in film. Kate's toes gripped the wet rocks. Her eyes watched the distant storm. It was stupid to jump. Smarter to stay safe up here, to know what was coming, to control it. But her legs wanted the taste of water. Her heart missed the thrashing joy.

Threshold flashed up on the screen. The indecision. The crossing over. There was sea enough to catch her.

"Okay," Kate said, and together they slipped through the gap.

ACKNOWLEDGMENTS

My deepest thanks to so many brilliant minds:

My agent, Alexandra Machinist, an absolute champion who helped me dream bigger than I thought possible, then made those dreams a reality. Everyone else at ICM, especially Ruth Landry, Hillary Jacobson, Sophie Baker, Felicity Blunt, and Josie Freedman, for their dogged advocacy.

My editor, Daphne Durham, who believed in this project so strongly and edited it with such care and kindness. I cannot imagine a better person to bring this book into the world, and I am grateful every day that it wound up in your capable hands. Lydia Zoells, who I think may be an actual angel brought to earth.

The electric, fantastically wonderful team at MCD and FSG, especially Chloe Texier-Rose, Naomi Huffman, Sarita Varma, Lottchen Shivers, Jeff Seroy, Daniel Del Valle, Pauline Post, Jackson Howard, Sara Birmingham, and Sean McDonald. Everyone else at Macmillan whose hands have touched this book beyond my ken: copy editors and proofreaders (thank you for catching so many embarrassing mistakes), the sales and marketing teams, permissions, fulfillment, and more. A flush-left, spot-glossed thank-you to everyone in the art, design, and production departments, especially Alex Merto, Gretchen Achilles, Nancy Elgin, and Rodrigo Corral, for making this book so beautiful, inside and out.

Catherine Down, first reader, astrological powerhouse—I would have given up on this book a long time ago without you. Bree Barton, my longtime comrade in this publishing circus. The beloved friends who, in addition to improving my life in innumerable ways, read and commented on various early drafts, most of which were really, really bad: Cordelia Loots-Gollin, Elizabeth Della Zazzera, Aku Ammah-Tagoe, Sarah Matherly, Anjie Zheng, Helena Smith, Amary Wiggin,

Siobhán Jones, Annie Schatz, Katie Simon, Rob King, and Cody Delistraty. And Emma Teitelman and Jack Dwiggins for their at-the-buzzer archival assists.

Plus the many other dear friends who also held me up along the way, especially Batia, Noam, Dani, Craig, Clare, Eleni, Alex, Grace, Marie, Cat, Claire, Kate, Stephanie, Ariel, Tasha, Morgan, SaraEllen, Honora, Chris, Gad's, my Penn English friends, the whole Paris crowd, and my Uni High friends, who continue to inspire me always. The women of Yurt Feelings (Anjie, Seguin, Joan, Emily, Alexa, and Aileen), the only people who could make me smile at an "89 unread messages" notification.

My writing community, especially Emma Copley Eisenberg, Hilary Leichter, and my gorgeous debut squad, including Mary South, Rachel Monroe, and Peter Kispert—thank you for making me feel less alone. Barrelhouse Writer Camp. The Susan Sontag estate. All the other authors and book people who helped me in ways big and small: getting to connect with you has been one of the most special parts of this whole process. I am particularly grateful to the lovely, luminous writers who took the time to read and blurb this book.

My dissertation chair, Jed Esty, and my other mentors at the University of Pennsylvania, especially Paul Saint-Amour and Josephine Park, for their unfailing support of this crazy fiction thing as well as my academic work. I owe you so much. The rest of the Penn English Department, Kelly Writers House, and the Andrea Mitchell Center for the Study of Democracy. David St. John and everyone in the University of Southern California English Department and the USC Society of Fellows in the Humanities—it is a privilege to work with you. And thank you to the many educators who have shaped my writing and intellectual growth.

My family, especially my brother, Christopher, and my sister, Laura, and Carol and Peter Derrico. The Castillo family. The Mahieus, for their boundless generosity. Jay and Alicia Scribner.

My little Los Angeles nest: Wilkie, my sweet, perfect angel, for teaching me to be brave. Max, you potato-shaped heartthrob, for "helping" me write. An immense, tearful thank-you to David Castillo. You are amazing. I don't know how I would have gotten through this process without you. I am so profoundly lucky to have you in my life.

Finally, my parents, Steve Sligar and Mary Schuler, who have made everything possible for me, over and over again. I love you. Thank you from the bottom of my heart.

A NOTE ABOUT THE AUTHOR

Sara Sligar is an author and academic based in Los Angeles, where she teaches English and creative writing as a postdoctoral fellow at the University of Southern California. She holds a Ph.D. in English from the University of Pennsylvania and a master's in history from the University of Cambridge. Her writing has been published in *McSweeney's*, *Quartz*, *The Hairpin*, and other outlets. *Take Me Apart* is her first novel.